I0633585

THE APACHE KID: ARMY APACHE SCOUT

also by
W. MICHAEL FARMER

The Iliad of Geronimo: A Song of Blood and Fire
The Odyssey of Geronimo: Twenty-Three Years a Prisoner of War
Trini! Come!: Geronimo's Captivity of Trinidad Verdín

Chato's Chiricahua Apache Legacy
Desperate Warrior: Days of War, Days of Peace
Proud Outcast: Days of War, Days of Peace

The Life and Times of Yellow Boy, Mescalero Apache
Killer of Witches
Blood of the Devil
The Last Warrior

Legends of the Desert
Mariana's Knight: The Revenge of Henry Fountain
Knight's Odyssey: The Return of Henry Fountain
Knight of the Tiger: The Betrayals of Henry Fountain
Blood-Soaked Earth: The Trial of Oliver Lee

The Vanishing Trilogy
Hombrecito's War
Hombrecito's Search
Tiger, Tiger Burning Bright: The Betrayals of Pancho Villa
Conspiracy: The Trial of Oliver Lee and James Gilliand

Nonfiction
Geronimo: Twenty-Three Years as a Prisoner of War
Apacheria: True Stories of Apache Culture 1860-1920

THE APACHE KID: ARMY APACHE SCOUT

THE APACHE KID CHRONICLES
VOLUME ONE

W. MICHAEL FARMER

WILL ROGERS MEDALLION-WINNING AUTHOR OF *DESPERATE WARRIOR*

HAT CREEK

HAT CREEK

An Imprint of Roan & Weatherford Publishing Associates, LLC
Bentonville, Arkansas
www.roanweatherford.com

Copyright © 2025 by W. Michael Farmer

We are a strong supporter of copyright. Copyright represents creativity, diversity, and free speech, and provides the very foundation from which culture is built. We appreciate you buying the authorized edition of this book and for complying with applicable copyright laws by not reproducing, scanning, or distributing any part of it in any form without permission. Thank you for supporting our writers and allowing us to continue publishing their books.

This work is the product of human creativity and effort, crafted without the use of generative artificial intelligence in its writing or storytelling. While AI is a valuable tool in many creative fields, we are committed to publishing works by humans about the human experience. Without any limitations on the author or Roan & Weatherford Publishing Associates' exclusive copyright, any use of this publication to train generative artificial intelligence is expressly prohibited.

Library of Congress Cataloging-in-Publication Data
Names: Farmer, Michael W,, author.
Title: Army Apache Scout/W. Michael Farmer | The Apache Kid Chronicles #1
Description: First Edition | Bentonville: Hat Creek, 2025.
Identifiers: LCCN: 2025935498 | ISBN: 979-8-89299-026-4 (hardcover)
ISBN: 979-8-89299-027-1 (trade paperback) |ISBN: 979-8-89299-028-8 (eBook)
Subjects: BISAC: FICTION/Indigenous/Historical |
FICTION/Native American | FICTION/Historical/General
LC record available at: https://lccn.loc.gov/2025935498

Hat Creek trade paperback edition December, 2025

Jacket & Interior Design by Casey W. Cowan
Jacket Art by C. Michael Dudash, *1880 Fort Apache Scout*
Editing by Rachel Santino

This book is a work of historical fiction. Apart from the well-known actual people, events, and locales that figure in the narrative, all names, characters, places, and incidents are the product of the author's imagination or are used fictitiously. Any resemblance to current events or locales, or to living persons, is entirely coincidental.

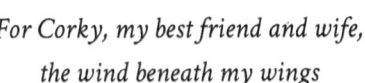

For Corky, my best friend and wife,
the wind beneath my wings

ACKNOWLEDGMENTS

THERE HAVE BEEN friends and professionals who have supported me in this work, and to whom I owe a special debt of gratitude for their help and many kindnesses.

This project would not have been possible without the historical research and notes provided by Phyllis Morreale de la Garza for her biography of Apache Kid and to whom I'm indebted for insight, facts, and copies of references to long dormant work from people who personally knew Kid and in their later years wrote stories about his life. Her comments on the draft manuscript were invaluable. Phyllis made a major contribution to this work, and I salute her efforts.

Lynda Sánchez has written historical essays to answer questions about events where Apache Kid is a major figure and about his life among the Sierra Madre Apache. Her contributions to an understanding of Kid's complex life through her essays has provided guidance through often conflicting historical records. For her support in this work, I'm grateful.

Audra Gerber provided her usual excellent editorial support, which contributed to this manuscript's clarity, and I thank her for her beautifully done job.

The patience, encouragement, and support of my wife Carolyn through long days of research and writing made this work possible.

The references listed in Additional Reading that I found particularly helpful were those by Phyllis de la Garza, Lynda Sánchez, John Paul Hartman, Clare V. McKanna, Jr., Dan L. Thrapp, Helge Ingstad, Edwin R. Sweeney, and Angie Debo.

TABLE OF CONTENTS

CHARACTERS

HISTORICAL

APACHE & RARÁMURI

- **Binday:** *Apache scout who killed Mauricio Corredor.*
- **Cha-deisa:** *Yavapai chief.*
- **Chato:** *Geronimo's* segundo *(number 2), leader of Chiricahua peace fraction, first sergeant of Apache Scouts for Lieutenant Britton Davis*
- **Chihuahua:** *leader of a band of Chokonen Chiricahua Apache. Highly respected warrior.*
- **Chiquito, capitan:** *chief of Pinal Apache and band of Toga-de-chuz.*
- **Chita:** *daughter of Hashke Bahnzin and wife of Apache Kid.*
- **Chuntz:** *Yavapai chief.*
- **Cochinay:** *Yavapai chief*
- **Corredor, Mauricio:** *major in Mexican Military. A Rarámuri (Tarahumara) Indian who was a great hero in Sonora and Chihuahua. Corredor claimed to have killed Victorio at Tres Castillos. He was leader of the Tarahumara paramilitary attacking Captain Crawford in Mexico, January 1886.*
- **Dutchy:** *trusted Chiricahua Apache scout. Crawford's striker (an orderly) on last mission into Mexico..*
- **Fatty:** *a lead Chiricahua scout.*
- **Geronimo:** *Bedonkohe Chiricahua Apache Shaman and war leader.*

- **Gon-zizzie:** *brother of Rip and murderer of Toga-de-chuz*
- **Hashke Bahnzin:** *(Anger Stands Beside Him) chief of Aravaipa Apache also known as Eskiminzin.*
- **Juh:** *Nednhi Chiricahua Apache Chief and Shaman.*
- **Kaytennae:** *young Chihenne warrior and Nana's segundo who Crawford later sent to Alcatraz.*
- **Loco:** *peace leader of Chihenne Apache.*
- **Lozen:** *sister of Victorio, highly respected warrior, messenger for Geronimo.*
- **Na-ti-o-tish:** *leader of renegades who fought army after the death of the Dreamer.*
- **Naiche:** *youngest son of Cochise. Became chief of Chokonen Chiricahua Apache after elder brother, Taza, died.*
- **Nantaje:** *scout who led Crook to the cave of Chuntz and Delshay in the Salt River Canyon.*
- **Nneez ishkiin:** *(Tall Boy) later known as Gonshayee who replaced Toga-de-chuz as a chief in Capitan Chiquito's band.*
- **Noche:** *Chihenne Apache scout who took over from Chato when he went back to farming after a six-month tour chasing Chiricahua in Mexico. He advised General Miles how to find Geronimo-Naiche camps in Mexico..*
- **Noch-ay-del-klinne:** *Apache name of the "Dreamer," a shaman who started the Apache ghost dance with claims he could raise the great chiefs and bring back the game when the White Eyes left.*
- **Nolgee:** *Nednhi Apache chief.*
- **Poinsenay:** *mature Chokonen Apache warrior who believed Taza was too young to be chief.*
- **Rip:** *brother of Gon-zizzie who murdered Toga-de-chuz.*
- **Skinya:** *mature Chokonen Apache warrior who believed Taza was too young to be chief.*
- **Taza:** *elder son of Cochise. Became chief of Chokonen Chiricahua Apache after death of Cochise..*
- **Tlodilhil:** *(Black Rope) White Mountain Apache army scout, clan leader, and friend of Kid.*
- **Toga-de-chuz:** father of Apache Kid, a chief in the band of *Capitan* Chiquito.
- **Tzoe:** *Chiricahua Apache scout who guided the Crook expedition into Mexico to the Apache camps at Bugatseka.*

- **Ulzana:** *brother of Chihuahua and his segundo.*
- **Victorio:** *great war chief of Chihenne Apache.*

SCOUTS WITH KID WHEN HE KILLED RIP

- **As-ki-say-la-ha:** *Kid's youngest brother in the scouts at San Carlos who help him go after Rip.*
- **Bachoandoth:** *Kid's friend in scouts who help him go after Rip.*
- **Margey:** *Kid's younger brother in the scouts at San Carlos who help him go after Rip.*
- **Nahconquisay:** *Kid's friend in scouts who help him go after Rip.*

.

HISTORICAL BLUE COATS & WHITE EYES

- **Beauford, Clay:** *lieutenant U.S. Army stationed at San Carlos, later chief of tribal police for John Clum.*
- **Blocksom, Augustus P.:** *lieutenant U.S. Army, commander of Company C of the Apache scouts.*
- **Chaffee, Adna R.:** *captain U.S. Army, agent at San Carlos.*
- **Clum, John:** *San Carlos Reservation agent. Only man to capture Geronimo.*
- **Concepcion:** *trusted interpreter for U.S. Army at San Carlos.*
- **Crawford, Emmet:** *captain U.S. Army, agent at San Carlos when Geronimo returned in 1884. Joint commander with Captain Wirt Davis under General Crook during Geronimo's last breakout.*
- **Davis, Wirt:** *captain U.S. Army, joint commander with Captain Crawford under General Crook during Geronimo's last breakout.*
- **Davis, Britton:** *lieutenant U.S. Army, commander of Chiricahua, 1883 – 1885, chief of scouts for Captain Crawford in Mexico.*
- **Diaz:** *interpreter for Captain Pierce who on his own told Kid and the men with him that they would be sent to Florida or Alcatraz.*
- **Elliott, Charles P:** *lieutenant U.S. Army, leader of a cavalry troop chasing Kid et al on the run after Sieber was shot.*
- **Grijalva, Hermenegildo:** *(also known as Hermenegildo) Apache trusted interpreter for U.S. Army*
- **Horn, Tom:** *packer supporting U.S. Army expeditions in 1883 and chief of scouts under Captain Lawton in 1885/1886.*
- **Whitman, Royal:** *lieutenant U.S. Army, 1871 commander of Camp Grant.*

- **Maus, Marion P.:** *lieutenant U.S. Army, second in command under Captain Crawford in 1886.*
- **Morgan, George H:** *lieutenant U.S. Army, commander of scout company at Fort Whipple.*
- **Pierce, Francis C.:** *captain U.S. Army, agent at San Carlos.*
- **Shipp, William E.:** *lieutenant U.S. Army, commander of scout company under Captain Crawford*
- **Sieber, Al:** *General Crook's chief of scouts.*
- **Sigsbee:** *rancher in the Tonto Basin.*
- **Stevens, Jimmie.:** *lieutenant U.S. Army, commander of scout company under Captain Crawford.*
- **Sweeney, Martin:** *retired Army cavalry sergeant and administrative assistant to John Clum.*

FICTIONAL CHARACTERS

- **Bil gozhóó:** *(He is Happy) fictional boy who started race between Gonshayee and Kid*
- **Gar:** *ranch owner.*
- **José:** *messenger from Kid while on the run to Captain Pierce.*
- **Kitsizil Ligai:** *(His White Hair) instructor of boys guarding Aravaipa herd in Galiuro Mountains.*
- **Old Juan:** *Aravaipa elder.*
- **Singing Tree:** *Apache Scout under Sieber.*
- **Zenogolache:** *(the Crazy One) fictional boyhood friend of Kid.*

APACHE WORDS
and PHRASES

- *Ch'a'olgheed:* he runs away
- *Ch'ik'eh doleel:* all right; let it be so
- *Dínyaa:* you go
- *Di-yen:* medicine woman or man
- *Doo dat'éé da:* it's okay; it doesn't matter
- *Enjuh:* good
- *Haheh:* a young girl's puberty ceremony
- *Idiits'ag:* I hear you
- *Nakai-yes:* Mexicans
- *Nakai-yi:* Mexican
- *Nant'an:* leader
- *Nant'an Lpah:* Gray leader, the Apache name for General George Crook.
- *Nawode nánigheed:* run fast
- *Nish'ii':* I see you
- *Pesh-klitso:* yellow iron (gold)
- *Rarámuri:* the name the Tarahumara call their People
- *Tipi:* a portable tent made of skins, cloth, or canvas on a frame of poles
- *Tobaho:* Tobacco
- *Tohono O'odham:* the name Papagos call their People
- *Tsach:* cradleboard
- *Tulepai:* (Lit. Gray water) Corn beer, also known as *tizwin*
- *Wickiup:* dome-shaped lodge with a frame covered in matting or brush
- *Ussen:* The Apache god of creation and life

Reckoning of Time & Seasons

- *Harvest:* used in the context of time, means a year
- *Handwidth (against the sky):* about an hour
- *Season of Little Eagles:* early spring
- *Season of Many Leaves:* late spring, early summer
- *Season of Large Leaves:* midsummer
- *Season of Large Fruit:* late summer, early fall
- *Season of Earth is Reddish Brown:* late fall
- *Season of Ghost Face:* lifeless winter
- *Sun:* used in the context of time, means a day
- *Time of shortest shadows:* noon

Spanish

- *Acequias:* irrigation trenches
- *Adios:* Goodbye
- *Amigo:* friend *(male)*
- *Arroyo:* a small steep-sided waterway with a flat floor and usually dry except during heavy rain
- *Bueno:* good
- *Bosque:* brush and trees lining a waterway
- *Capitán:* Captain
- *Casa:* house
- *Comprende:* Do you understand?
- *Comprendo:* I understand.
- *El Tigre:* jaguar
- *Espinosa del Diablo:* the devil's backbone
- *Llano: open grassy plain, dry prairie*
- *Mañana: "Tomorrow" or "morning" (depending on context)*
- *Muy bien: very good*
- *Playa:* the flat sandy, salty, or mud-caked flat floor of a desert basin usually covered by shallow water during or after prolonged heavy rain
- *Reata:* a rope made of rawhide
- *Rancheria:* small, rural settlement
- *Rio:* river
- *Segundo:* second in command
- *Teniente:* lieutenant
- *Vomito:* vomit or puke

INTRODUCTION

APACHE KID WAS one of the most feared and mysterious outlaws in the Southwest at the end of the nineteenth and beginning of the twentieth century. After over ten years of robbery, killing, and kidnapping women on both sides of the United States-Mexico border, Kid disappeared into northern Mexico accused of more crimes than he could possibly have committed.

Historians disagree on his true Apache name, and the Apache who know won't say. Historical literature has given him four or five different names, some of which might be the same name but spelled differently. I have chosen to use a name appearing for his younger years, Ohyessonna, which means "hears something in the night." For Kid's later years (Volume 2), I use a name for which he is commonly known, Has-kay-bay-nay-ntayl, and means "brave and tall and will come to a mysterious end." In his boyhood and young-man years, Ohyessonna worked many different jobs for merchants, tradesmen, and miners in the booming mining town of Globe, Arizona. Those he worked for found their tongues didn't do well with the Apache language and not pronouncing his name very well, just called him "Kid" and later, to distinguish him from other kids, "Apache Kid." The name stuck, and Kid was the name the army used for him on his enlistment papers during the six-month tours of duty he signed for in his early twenties.

As a young man, Kid was gifted with phenomenal eyesight, athleticism, and charisma that made him a natural leader, and he was known as a phenomenal marksman with a rifle. Kid might have been a chief among the Aravaipa Apache, but he turned down the offer to be chief from elders of his band after his father, who was a chief, was murdered. He was a hard worker in Globe, Arizona, and a first-class horse wrangler and sometime-cowboy for ranches surrounding the San Carlos Reservation. He became friends with an Anglo named Redmond, who had a butcher shop business in Globe. He hired Kid to herd cattle to his holding corrals and helped him learn to speak good English.

Kid became close friends with Al Sieber, General Crook's well-known chief of scouts; Clay Beauford, former army officer and chief of San Carlos Reservation Tribal Police; and Martin Sweeney, a retired cavalry sergeant who worked as administrative assistant under San Carlos Agent John Clum. Sieber, Beauford, and Sweeney taught Kid much about the army. In a series of six-month tours of duty, using knowledge about the army that he learned from their mentorships and his natural abilities, Kid quickly became a first sergeant of army scouts and a trusted leader of scouts in battle maneuvers against Western Apache and Chiricahua renegades.

A time came when Kid had to choose between his native culture and army rules. He chose his native culture. That choice separated him from the army and ultimately drove him to become the outlaw for which he is most often remembered.

This is the first of two novels about *Apache Kid: The Apache Kid Chronicles, Volume One, Army Apache Scout.* Volume One tells stories, some historical and some imagined, that follow the dictum that the boy is the father of the man and suggest how his life as seen through that lens was shaped before the army court-martialed him. *The Apache Kid Chronicles, Volume Two, Vanished Outlaw,* covers the years beginning with his court-martial and the army and civilian injustices which drove him to become an outlaw. In the years of the two novels, Kid grew from a hardworking, precocious man-child to an admired first sergeant of scouts with a family who won acclaim for his courage and daring in army battles with renegade Apache, to a feared outlaw who roamed the border southwest until he mysteriously disappeared. His is a story filled with tragedy and pathos, deep friendships, and betrayals. It is a story of a gifted man suspended on a cross of two cultures.

W. Michael Farmer
Smithfield, Virginia
October 2023

PROLOGUE

NEAR THE JOINING OF THE RÍOS YAQUI AND AROS, SONORA MEXICO, 1935

I AM SASPULÍ Shulála (Star Heart), a daughter of the great warrior known to the White Eyes as Apache Kid. To his People, the Aravaipa Apache, my father's name in his young-man days was Ohyessonna (hears something in the night), and some people know him by that name even today. In his later years, an old *di-yen* (shaman) had a vision and gave Ohyessonna the name Has-kay-bay-nay-ntayl (brave and tall and will come to a mysterious end). He was the victim of White Eye and Blue Coat evil when they unjustly attacked him. In those suns he entered a time of darkness, hunted like a deadly outlaw by army scouts, White Eyes, and *Nakai-yi* (Mexican) army soldiers. My father left all those pursuing him behind when he disappeared into the Sierra Madre canyons and mountains of northern Mexico after two Mormon men claimed they killed his little daughter, his wife, and him. However, it was Has-kay-bay-nay-ntayl's brother and his family they killed.

Rarámuri and Apache are often blood enemies. *Rarámuri* men took my father prisoner as he looked for his White Mountain Apache wife and baby daughter stolen away by a small band of Chiricahua. He made peace with the men in the *Rarámuri* band after my mother, the daughter of Chief Silíami Iyótshi (Chief Gray Fox), decided she wanted my father for her husband, and he wanted her.

Ussen blessed them. Together they are a powerful pair. A Moon after their marriage, my father ran with nine men in our village in a challenge race of one hundred fifty miles against ten men from another village. He won that race, and the *Rarámuri*, to the man, accepted him as one of their own. They continue to admire and respect him as he does them.

My father knew he would endanger my grandfather's band if his enemies found him camped in the band's village and that his wife was a *Rarámuri* chief's daughter. They decided to live away from my grandfather's village but close enough to help when needed. *Rarámuri* men helped my father build a small stone *casa* near where the Río Bavispe joins the Río Aros and less than a hand on the horizon—about a White Eye hour—run to my grandfather's village. The land my father and mother chose for their rancho supports small gardens of vegetables and has fenced pasture for a few cattle, sheep, goats, and horses. Even after the house of stone was finished, my mother and father lived in my grandfather's village. She still carried me in her belly and wanted the help of her mother and sisters to deliver me. A few moons after I was born, my father's little family moved to the rancho and its stone house.

A brown robe came to the village of Lampazos—about twelve miles in a straight line from the *Rarámuri* band camp—where we went each harvest for supplies that we couldn't make or grow. Brown Robe said he had wanted to "preach the gospel," but his first mission was to teach the Lampazos children how to read, write, and do sums. He started a small school in Lampazos. I begged Father to let me go to Brown Robe's school after I saw all the wisdom and stories in things he called books with pictures and black water tracks that each carried. Father, after much thought, finally agreed to my attending Brown Robe's school. He told me not to talk much around the people at Lampazos. If they found out he was my father, there might be trouble.

At Brown Robe school, I learned to read and make "black water tracks on paper" as my father called writing. I read many Brown Robe books and wrote many stories about my dreams and life before school. Those books, like plants on fertile soil, grew those stories in my mind.

Soon after becoming a woman, my suns at the school were over. Father wanted me back home until I married, even though I wanted no one at Lampazos. I returned to the ranch as father said I should. When I wasn't weaving, gardening, or helping Mother prepare meals, I read books Brown Robe lent me and wrote the stories inside my head.

After I begged him for stories from his life, my father told them to my mother and me. Father told me when I was very young, "Never speak your true name to strangers. Protect yourself from the living and the dead, until *Ussen* protects you with your medicine, your Power." *Ussen* has given me my Power on the tip of this little writing stick, and it is in these stories my father told my mother and me of his life before he married my mother. I have told you my name. I have my Power. Now, I write Father's stories as he told them to me and heard them again as I wrote them and read them back to him asking if I spoke true. I wrote Apache Kid's, Ohyessonna's, and Has-kay-bay-nay-ntayl's stories in the evenings while I lived with my mother and father. It took many nights for me to write the journals you hold. They speak what he spoke. They tell the story of how the best army Apache scout at San Carlos became the most feared outlaw in southwest borderlands and then disappeared. Read them and learn the lessons *Ussen* teaches us.

THE APACHE KID: ARMY APACHE SCOUT

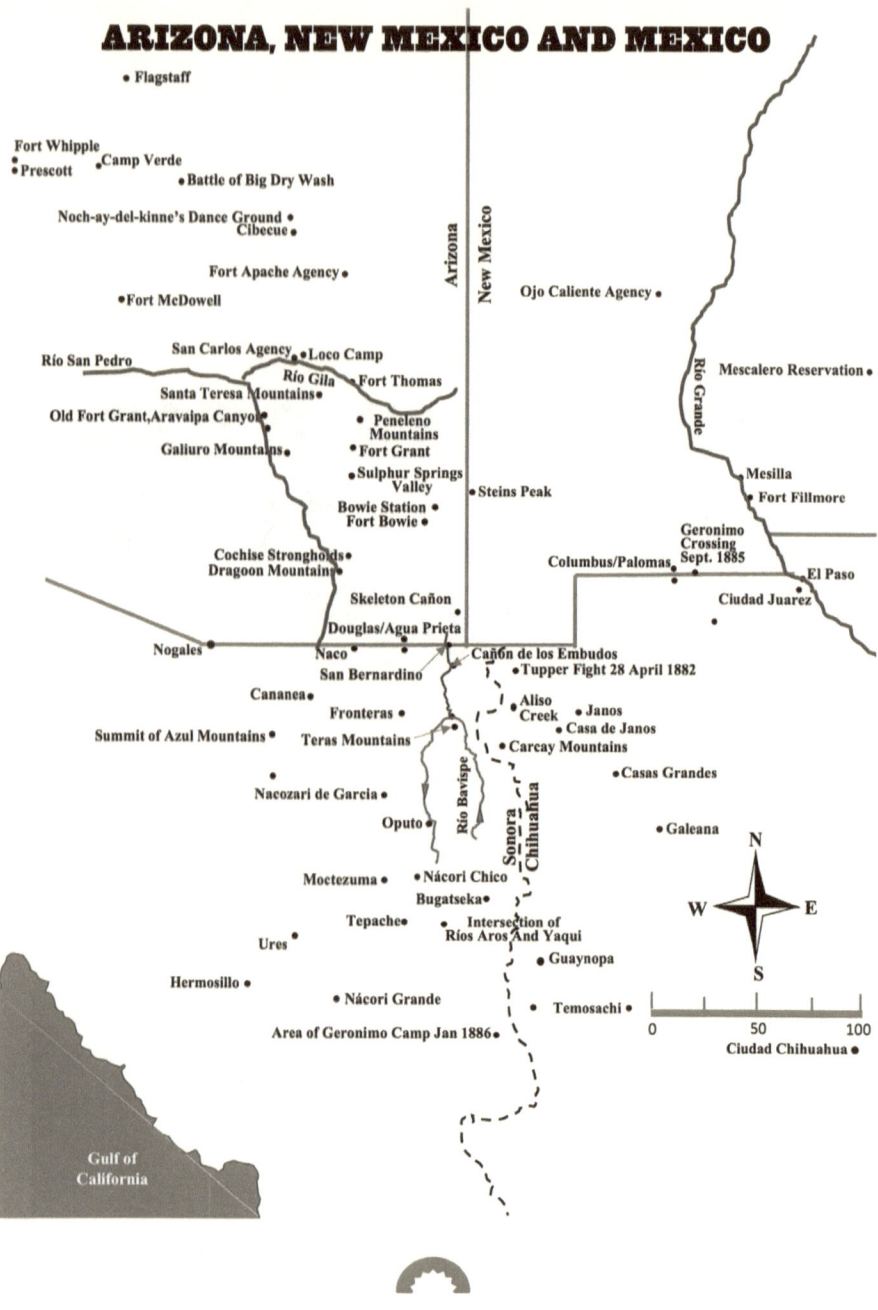

ARIZONA, NEW MEXICO AND MEXICO

• Flagstaff

Fort Whipple •
• Prescott • Camp Verde
           • Battle of Big Dry Wash

Noch-ay-del-kinne's Dance Ground •
           Cibecue •

Fort Apache Agency •   Ojo Caliente Agency •

• Fort McDowell

Río San Pedro   San Carlos Agency • Loco Camp   Mescalero Reservation •
                        • Río Gila • Fort Thomas
        Santa Teresa Mountains •
Old Fort Grant, Aravaipa Canyon •   • Peneleno
        Galiuro Mountains •   Mountains   Mesilla •
                           • Fort Grant   Fort Fillmore •
                    • Sulphur Springs
                        Valley   • Steins Peak
                    Bowie Station •   Geronimo
                    Fort Bowie •   Crossing
        Cochise Strongholds •   Sept. 1885
        Dragoon Mountains •   Columbus/Palomas •   • El Paso
                                                        Ciudad Juarez •
                        Skeleton Cañon
                        Douglas/Agua Prieta
Nogales •   Naco •   Cañón de los Embudos
                San Bernardino   • Tupper Fight 28 April 1882
        Cananea •   • Aliso
                    Fronteras •   Creek • Janos
Summit of Azul Mountains •   Teras Mountains   • Casa de Janos
                                        • Carcay Mountains
        Nacozari de Garcia •   • Casas Grandes
                    Oputo •
                                        • Galeana
                Moctezuma • • Nácori Chico
                        Bugatseka •
                    Tepache •   • Intersection of
        Ures •   Ríos Aros And Yaqui
                                        • Guaynopa
        Hermosillo •   • Nácori Grande
                    Area of Geronimo Camp Jan 1886 •   • Temosachi

Río San Pedro (label), Río Grande, Arizona, New Mexico, Río Bavíspe, Sonora, Chihuahua (map labels)

N
W — E
S

0   50   100
Ciudad Chihuahua •

Gulf of
California

Places in the Apache Kid Story 1871 – 1888. Modern locations have been provided for common reference.

ONE

DAY OF DARKNESS

ARAVAIPA CANYON, ARIZONA
MAY 1, 1871

EARLY ONE MORNING when I was eleven harvests, I sat up in my blankets shivering from fear in the cold canyon air. I saw only ghostlike wisps of fog in the moonlight rising off the slow-moving creek. Looking down Aravaipa Canyon, there was a low, yellowish-orange glow wavering against the darkness on the canyon walls and through the bosque trees. I heard the faraway echoes of the hissing snap of gunshots and terrified screams. I stretched across the space between our blankets and touched my father's arm. He sat up in a smooth, flowing motion as he cocked his rifle, glanced over at me, and whispered, "What is it, my son?"

"Father, look down the canyon and listen."

He looked down the dark march of trees along the creek in the canyon below us, and saw the low, faraway yellow glow that shouldn't be there. He cocked his head to one side, straining to hear what I thought was there.

"Hmmph. Hear faraway gunshots and women and children screaming. Maybe this noise and light come from our camp."

He glanced toward the trail lighted by a waxing gibbous moon nearly as bright as a full moon low in the southern sky and made the trail down to the creek easy to see.

"Roll up your blanket and grab your bow and arrows. We leave for home camp now. You're a good runner, but I doubt you can keep up with me. I get too far ahead? Follow the creek. See someone coming, don't show yourself unless you know who they are."

"I run fast, stay with you."

"*Ch'ik'eh doleel* (All right). Let's go."

We rushed to bundle our blankets and pull on our moccasins.

I glanced east back over my shoulder as I ran down the path to the creek. I saw a glow in the gray night sky behind the eastern mountains. Dawn was coming.

I was not yet big for my age, but I could run long distances as fast as the wind blowing down Aravaipa Canyon. There along the creek, I was slow to stay close to my father, Toga-de-chuz. It was a rough run, easy to slide down in the creek from slick moss or step on a big rock barely balanced—or a foot could land in the wrong place, forcing a fall with a broken bone. Somehow, in the moonlight and shadows along the creek, our run never threw us in the creek or broke our bones. Even though I fell three times I kept up with Father, who never looked back.

APPROACHING OUR TRIBAL camp, the creek grew wider and the yellowish-brown canyon sides disappeared into the *llano*. As we splashed along the creek edge, the smell of wood smoke filled with death and destruction filled our noses. The stink of the smoke was like the burning flesh of men Chief Hashke Bahnzin tortured as a warning to other tribes, Blue Coats, and Anglos that taking our land had great penalties. The smoke's smell made my stomach churn like I had eaten bad meat, and its stink hung in the still air waiting for the morning breeze. The fire making the glow we had seen from our camp now burned low in the smoking, black embers of once well-built *wickiups*. Our village *wickiups*, strung out along the creek, stood about six miles up the creek and began three miles from the Blue Coat's Camp Grant, where the creek ran into the Río San Pedro.

My father stopped without warning. He bent over, his hands on his knees, and moaned like a man in great pain. There were no village *wickiups* in the gray dawn light, only black outlines of where they once stood and smoke slowly drifting toward the Río San Pedro. Bodies smoldered in the *wickiups'* ashes, some with low, yellow smoky flames still burning. There were many women and children, but few men. The bodies were scattered across the village, their skulls crushed, some shot, others with arrows buried in their backs and chests, and the children had their throats cut. Some girls and young women, not burned, had their skulls crushed and their skirts thrown up over their heads or torn from their private places. Drying blood, black like the shadow of death, covered their inner thighs. The old men told stories around the council fires about what enemies did to Apache women. Even at my age then, I knew these women and girls had been raped.

I saw the bodies of boys I knew. I had raced them across the hills, learned to sling and dodge their accurately thrown stones, shot against their targets with arrows for accuracy, or tended livestock with them in pastures near the mouth of the creek. They were once my friends and competitors. Now they lay scattered across the campsite, skulls crushed, bodies pinned with arrows, some shot with a rifle or pistol. Some near their mothers running from the camp lay scalped with their scalped mothers and sisters. A feeling of helplessness overpowered me. I had a sense of rage that I had never known and I never satisfied it against those who did this.

I wanted to cry, but I didn't at first. A man doesn't cry. Then I saw the streams of water flowing from my father's eyes. I moaned as I squeezed my eyes shut before a flood broke from them like a dam on the creek giving way during the season of floods.

My father looked at markings on the arrows in the bodies. We found a broken war club, its polished wooden ball smeared with dried blood. I heard him growl, the anger a now-roaring fire burning in his belly. He mumbled, "These are weapons of the *Tohono O'odham*. We will find who did this. We will have our revenge. *Ussen* will guide our hands."

We saw mixed among the *Tohono O'odham* moccasin tracks in the camp, the tracks of *Nakai-yi* (Mexican) and White Eye boots. Now we were certain, *Nakai-yi* and White Eye criminals were among our Indian enemies helping them kill us.

We found the family of Aravaipa Chief Hashke Bahnzin, his women and children all dead and mutilated. But he and one of his little girls, the one I knew who was named Chita, were not among the dead. My father's chief, *Capitan Chiquito*, had taken most of his warriors on a raid two days before. We found two of his wives dead and mutilated.

Other men who had been hunting like my father and me in the hills around Aravaipa Canyon, began to appear and walked through the camp stunned, in shock, looking at the bodies of the dead women and children and praying they were not part of their family. They, too, wept, but with doubled fists some screamed from their guts in rage. One started running toward Camp Grant to tell *Teniente* Whitman, the officer in charge, what had happened and to ask what he would do about it.

On learning what had happened, Whitman offered a hundred American dollars to anyone who would go into the hills and explain to the Apache that his soldiers had nothing to do with the murder, rape, and scalping of the People, but no one would go.

I learned later that Whitman sent a Blue Coat *di-yen* (medicine man) with twenty helpers to gather and return with the wounded, but there were no survivors. The Blue Coat *di-yen* and the men with him solemnly dug graves for all those killed. My father and I watched all this from the canyon rim while we waited for my mother and the other women and children to return from finding and baking hearts of mescal for the feast Whitman wanted us to have. Now there would be no feast, only sorrow and grief for murdered loved ones.

THOSE WHO HAD been up in the hills gathering food for our feast learned what had happened to our People and village from those who had escaped the *Tohono O'odham* attack. They gathered around Hashke Bahnzin, who had walked down out of the hills on the south side of Aravaipa Canyon with Chita still in his arms. Women wailed their sorrow, the children sat quiet and still with their faces puzzled by what was happening, and the men sat, waiting, the light behind their eyes counting the ways of vengeance. My father and I sat with our family. We were part of *Capitan* Chiquito's band. I was happy to see my mother and my brother and sister younger than me, unharmed after the attack. They had food with them, the hearts of mescal they had cooked and dried, which kept us from hunger.

Capitan Chiquito returned with his men from a raid in the South. He met with Hashke Bahnzin and learned what had happened. *Capitan* Chiquito burned with anger and swore vengeance for his murdered People and two wives. Hashke Bahnzin and *Capitan* Chiquito decided to talk to Whitman before they did anything and rode down the creek to Camp Grant.

In council with the men after their talk with Whitman, Hashke Bahnzin and *Capitan* Chiquito said they told Whitman everything they knew. Whitman said that the *Nakai-yes* and *Tohono O'odham* would never come back, and even if they did, soldiers at Camp Grant would know about it first. He said he and the Aravaipa had always been on good terms and were friends and had gotten along well until this attack. He sent rations to those who survived and said they should come back and settle down along the creek again. Hashke Bahnzin and *Capitan* Chiquito spoke together for a while before telling Whitman they would return but would put our *wickiups* closer to Camp Grant so the soldiers would be near enough to protect us from attack if our enemies tried to attack us again.

I GATHERED LONG saplings from the bosque along the creek and helped my mother build our family *wickiup* in the new village closer to Camp Grant. This camp was right at the end of the water in the creek where it disappeared into the sand in the dry seasons. A moon passed and our lives were much as they were before the attack except for the people we had lost, and memories of the dead and our burned village that came often to our minds.

The peace that had returned to us disappeared when Hashke Bahnzin and a party of men went hunting up the canyon. A cavalry patrol from Camp Apache in the north came hunting deer in Aravaipa Canyon. The patrol leader was surprised to see a band of Apache—Hashke Bahnzin with his hunters—and the soldiers opened fire on the hunters, killing a warrior named Munaclee. When the Apache hunting party returned to Camp Grant, Hashke Bahnzin told soldier chief Whitman that the days of peace between the Blue Coats and Aravaipa were over and that he was leaving Camp Grant. My father told our family that Hashke Bahnzin said to Whitman, "We go now, back to the mountains, to avenge our dead."

TWO

INTO THE
GALIURO MOUNTAINS

WE QUIETLY LEFT our camp on Aravaipa Creek one night long before the dawn came. We ran and rode down Aravaipa Creek in the darkness of shadows from a fingernail moon and then across the foothills that carried us south of Camp Grant to the wagon road beside the Río San Pedro. I was told later by a Blue Coat friend that Whitman never knew we were gone until the middle of the next day. By that time, we had left the wagon road and headed east deep into the Galiuro Mountains, where *Capitan* Chiquito and Hashke Bahnzin camped in a long narrow canyon with springwater flowing in a small stream. From there they and their warriors raided the Americans and *Nakai-yes* to take revenge and treasure.

The women in the two bands picked the spots for their *wickiups*. Our *wickiups* hid under tall junipers near a big spring-fed natural water tank. The tank overflow made the small creek in our canyon, formed by steep walls from high ridges. Green grass grew along the creek's path, producing good grazing for our livestock.

My brother, sister, and I helped our mother set saplings in the ground to form a rough circle and then bend them over to weave and tie them together for her *wickiup* frame. We dug a place near the *wickiup* door for a cooking fire surrounded by stones from a nearby cliff. Our band hid its *wickiups* well. From the canyon rim, a scout couldn't see them. A scout from San Carlos was not likely to find it unless he already knew the only trail into our camp.

After my brother, sister, and I finished the *wickiup*, we gathered wood for Mother's fire while she sorted through her supplies to decide what she needed for future meals, but her first interest was for our evening meal. We had in hand little except dried mescal and ground acorn meal for making bread.

While we worked to erect the *wickiup* and dig the fire pit, my father met in council with *Capitan* Chiquito and Hashke Bahnzin and the other lead warriors. They decided where to go raiding for what their women had told them we needed in supplies besides ammunition—we always needed ammunition—plus where to put lookouts for the camp, and how to manage the livestock and food supplies.

MY MOTHER MADE a good meal with roasted venison that first night in the canyon. A warrior had taken a deer as we entered the canyon and given my father a haunch for our family. There were also steamed, dried sliced hearts of baked mescal, acorn bread, steamed yucca tips, and steamed, dried juniper berries. After we finished her meal, which we gobbled down like there would be none tomorrow, my father said he wanted to talk with me and told my brother and sister to go play with the other children as twilight fell into the darkness.

Our *wickiup* was near the water tank, and the tree peepers and frogs near the water were in full voice. The sounds of children laughing and playing were heard up and down the canyon under the piñon trees, and far up on the canyon rim, Wolf called his brothers. It was a peaceful time, soothing the agony of our memory of the *Nakai-yes*, White Eyes, and *Tohono O'odham* attacking and killing our sleeping people.

My father poured a cup of coffee and offered to pour me some. Feeling grown up that he wanted to talk with me privately, I took a cup, although when I tasted it the first time my mother offered it to me as a little boy, she laughed at the face I made at its bitterness. My father took a swallow of the hot black water, smacked his lips, and said, "Ummph. Coffee good." My mother nodded and smiled as she cleaned up after our meal. Finished with her chores, she crawled into the *wickiup* and sat by the door as was our custom to listen unseen to talk between "men."

Father said, "My son, these have been hard times for our People, but I'm proud that you act as a grown man. When the *Tohono O'odham* attacked our camp, you heard their war cries, shots, and the terror of our women and children before I did. You are alert in your sleep. Until you grow to another name, taken as a man, I give you a new name to remember *Ussen's* gift of hearing to you. I call you, Ohyessonna (hears something in the night)."

I bowed my head. "Father, you honor me."

"You are still a young boy, but you have done well supporting our family. You have much to learn, but as you become a man, I can see you will be a leader."

I looked in his face. "Then I will work hard to make you proud."

He took another swallow of the coffee, clenched his teeth at its heat, and said, "This I know, my son. Now we speak of important things that will keep all our People safe and proud.

"You know the *Tohono O'odham* carried away many of our young as their slaves. Among them were boys a little older than yourself who kept watch over the horses and mules, made sure they were watered when they needed it, and kept the hunting cats, bears, coyotes, and wolves driven away. They often brought the horses and mules to their riders when they needed them. Now many of those boys are gone. Gone to *Nakai-yi* slavery, everyone. We will try, but it's likely we will never get them back. We spoke of this in council. You are a little young, but we want you and three of the other boys about your age to guard the horses and mules during the day. At night, warriors will be on guard when the horses and mules are most likely stolen. What do you say? Will you do this for the People? It means no more games with the other boys."

My heart was thumping like a dance drum. It was a great honor to guard the People's horse and mule herd. It was the beginning of tribal work for me as I came to manhood.

"Yes, Father, I will do this for our People."

He smiled and said, *"Ch'ik'eh doleel.* You are still too young to handle a rifle or pistola. Take your sling and bow and arrows to fight off animals after our horses and mules. When you are ready, I show you how to use a rifle or pistola. Kitsizil Ligai (his hair white) will work with you and the other boys to teach you how best to herd and guard our horses and mules. Remember, to be good at herding the animals will take moons of hard work. It won't happen in a day."

Inside, I trembled with excitement. "I will work hard to learn well what Kitsizil Ligai teaches me, Father. I make you and Mother proud of me."

He smiled and nodded.

I barely slept that night. Soon I would do an older boy's work and make myself ready for manhood.

AFTER PRAYERS FACING *Ussen* in the rising sun and a morning meal, Father and I followed the little gurgling creek still in deep shadow down to a long stretch of meadow where sparkling night water covered the grass. The horses and mules grazed there. They had gathered near some brush on the far side of the meadow and watched us with ears raised as we walked into the brilliant light that made my eyes squint. We stopped and watched the herd a little while until they decided we had not come for them, and began to graze again while keeping an eye on us.

A whispery old man's voice spoke out of the shadows behind us. "They know you but not your purpose in coming to watch them. They watch you until they know what to expect." The unseen speaker made me jerk around in surprise and my smiling father turn in his direction.

An ancient old man—his long hair as white as tops of towering afternoon clouds in the Season of Large Leaves, reaching to the middle of his back—appeared as if out of the air. I hadn't seen him when we walked past him and into the sunlight. His face carried many wrinkles, canyons of old age. He wore a white breechcloth pulled inside canvas pants with legs that covered the tops of his tall shaft moccasins common to our People and a light green, long-sleeved pullover shirt the color of new mesquite leaves.

My father said, *"Nish'ii'* (I see you), Kitsizil Ligai, who guides our horse guards. I bring you my son, Ohyessonna, to learn the ways of horses and mules and to help you as you tell him."

The old man looked me over for a couple of breaths and said, *"Nish'ii',* Toga-de-chuz, great warrior of the Aravaipa, and his son Ohyessonna, who one day will be a great war leader and rider of horses." He saw the short little wrinkle of disbelief on my father's brow, but Kitsizil Ligai, nodding his head, said, "This thing I see in the night visions *Ussen* gives me. Your oldest son will make you proud, Toga-de-chuz. Come with me, Ohyessonna. There is much to do and much to learn."

He turned and walked toward the cliff on the western side of the canyon. I looked at my father, who nodded and made the all-is-well sign, swinging the flat of his hand in an arc parallel to the ground. I followed the old man through the wet morning grass toward the brown-and-white-streaked stone and shadows splotched on canyon cliffs. At the cliffs, he used hand- and footholds that had been cut in the cliffs many harvests ago and climbed up to a crevice, a wide shallow cave, that went back fifteen paces into the cliffs. It was my height tall with a smooth flat floor and about ten paces up off the canyon grass. Unless one knew it was there, a first glance said it was just another shadow on the cliffs. My father, his arms crossed, watched me climb to the crevice and join Kitsizil Ligai. Then he turned to walk back to my mother's *wickiup*.

It was cool in the crevice, where it was easy to see the horses grazing in the meadow. Kitsizil Ligai already had a couple of bladder skins filled with water, baskets of food, his blanket, and his rifle, a fine, new lever gun, lying with three boxes of cartridges on his blanket.

We sat and watched the horses while we waited for the other three boys to come. Kitsizil Ligai asked me about my skill with my boy's weapons and asked to see my bow made from mulberry wood. He ran his hands over the limbs sighted down its length and nodded.

"The man who made this bow knew what he was doing."

I grinned. "My father made the bow from mulberry wood. He says a bow with only one arc like mine is easier to carry than one with two arcs but can't be drawn as fast and isn't as powerful. My best arrows he also makes. I've used them to win many arrows from my friends in our shooting contests."

"Hmmph. Let me see one of his arrows." I pulled my best arrow from its quiver and handed it to him. Kitsizil Ligai sighted down its spine, looked at the feather placement, and rubbed the nocking between his thumb and forefinger. He lightly tapped the barbed point made from barrel iron on the fingers of his left hand. "It is a good arrow. Not all the warriors can make truly good arrows. Any stick can be used for a bow, but not many for an arrow." He looked out over the meadow below us. Near where we stood by the creek that morning was an old log, looking like it was brought there by a flood in the Season of Big Fruit.

"See that log in the grass close to where we stood earlier and talked with your father? Do you think you could hit it with your arrow from here?"

I looked at the log. For an arrow shot from my bow, it was within range. But it was a tricky shot. From up high like we were, the arrow would be falling most of the time, and normal aiming would carry it beyond the log. I looked at the leaves on the trees and saw there was no breeze. I had shot at targets from high above before and had learned where I had to aim to hit the log.

"Where on the log do you want the arrow?"

Kitsizil Ligai crossed his arms and grinned. "I like your confidence, Ohyessonna. See the place where the first big limb grew off the trunk? Put the arrow on the log just below that place."

I stared at the place until I was sure I understood where to aim to hit what he wanted. I nodded to him. "Do you want me to shoot now?"

"Shoot. I know it is a hard shot. You are too young and not skilled enough?"

I strung my bow and wrapped my wrist guard in place so the sinew string would not cut my arm. He gave me the arrow. Still no breeze moved the tree leaves. I looked and marked the place I needed to aim and laid the arrow across the bow and nock against the string. I put one finger above the arrow nock and two below, took a deep breath, and relaxed. I held the bow vertical and pulled the arrow back to my chin in full draw while my eyes and muscles guided the iron tip to the spot I had marked with my eyes to hit the log. There was a thummm from the string as I released the arrow. It sailed out into the bright sunlight, riding the still air, falling, falling toward the log. In the blink of an eye, it thunked into the log just below where the big limb began.

Kitsizil Ligai pulled his soldier glasses from their leather case, brought them to his eyes, and studied the log. Even without soldier glasses, I could see the arrow struck where I wanted to place it. A big smile filled his face. "You are already better with your bow than most warriors I have known. My night visions speak true. *Enjuh* (Good). You will be a leader of men, Ohyessonna."

THREE

HORSE GUARDS

SOON THE OTHER boys and their fathers walked out of the shadows at the edge of the meadow where my father and I had spoken with Kitsizil Ligai. They stopped near the log as they twisted and turned, stretching their necks as they looked around and down the canyon for Kitsizil Ligai. The oldest and biggest of the four boys saw my arrow and walked over to the log. He reached to pull it out of the log, when Kitsizil Ligai called, *"Nt'ah* (Wait)!" As he stood near the center of the crevice, his voice sounded like a roar from a giant, many times louder than it was. The boy reaching for the arrow jerked his hand back like a scorpion had stung him and looked around. All the men and their sons jerked around and looked up the cliffs and into the trees trying to see where the voice came from. None recognized that the crevice was more than a shadow on the cliffs.

Kitsizil Ligai smiled and shook his head. He called, "Wait where you are. I send Ohyessonna to guide you to me." Pointing to a rope tied off to a big boulder and hanging down the side of the cliff in the shadow of a crack in the rocks, he said, "That rope goes to the ground. Climb down and show your brothers where we are. The fathers don't need to come with the boys. Leave the arrow in the log. I'll let you pull it out before the long shadows come."

He watched me let myself down the rope to the ground. The rope had evenly spaced knots that made it easy to use. But it was not something we used or practiced with in our play. I felt a little awkward using it at first but soon used it with ease. Kitsizil Ligai yelled again, "You boys, follow Ohyessonna. You men, return to your camp. Tell your wives that their sons will return for their mothers' nighttime meals."

The men turned to go when they saw me coming toward them. The boys ran to meet me, the oldest with a scowl on his face. He told me later that he thought he should be the boy leader for Kitsizil Ligai because he was the biggest and oldest, but it looked like I had already taken that work. I showed them where to climb. We gathered in a semicircle around Kitsizil Ligai as he explained how and when we would watch the horses.

Then he said, "You boys are of an age where you should be good with your bows. I need to learn who among you are the best shots. When you came here with your fathers, you saw an arrow stuck in a log at the edge of the trees. String your bows and choose your best arrows. Show me how close you can come to the arrow in the log while you stand at the place I've marked at the edge of our crevice."

The biggest boy we called Nneez ishkiin (Tall Boy), and was later named Gonshayee, had already strung his bow and, taking an arrow, walked to the marked place from where I shot. The sun was high enough that the air was growing hot and reaching for the clouds, thirsty for their water, and creating breezes that rushed past us and made an arrow's path uncertain, but Nneez ishkiin didn't seem to notice. He turned to Kitsizil Ligai and said, "It is a long shot. The morning wind makes it unsure."

Kitsizil Ligai nodded. "Yes, I know. A good warrior should be able to fight and shoot whether the wind blows or not. Shoot your arrow. Let us see who is best."

Nneez ishkiin laid his arrow on his bow, looked down its spine, and drew it to full length, paused for the breeze to steady, and then released the string. We watched the arrow sail out into the bright sunlight and pick up speed as it fell toward the log and thumped into the ground about three paces from the log. Nneez ishkiin made a face, looked at me, frowned, and stepped back into the shadows.

The other two boys smaller than Nneez ishkiin and me took their turns. Their bows were not very strong, and their arrows fell far short of the log and off to one side.

Nneez ishkiin said, "Ohyessonna shot earlier than we did, when the air was still. He wouldn't be so lucky now."

Kitsizil Ligai looked at me. I accepted Nneez ishkiin's challenge. I tied on my wrist guard again slowly, deliberately, pulled another of my best arrows from my quiver, and walked to the edge of the crevice. I waited, my arrow on the bow, watching the breeze shake the trees. It wasn't steady but seemed to come and go. I picked a strong gust rolling down the canyon and waited for it to pass. As it started to die, I raised the bow, pointed the arrow to the place I had used before, and waited a little more. As soon as the breeze died to little or nothing, I took a good breath, pulled the arrow to full draw, and released it. We watched it sail falling straight and true in an arc that ended with a thump in the log not a forearm length from the first arrow. The jaws of two smaller boys dropped and Kitsizil Ligai smiled.

Nneez ishkiin was frowning and shaking his head. I said to him, "Take care *Ussen* doesn't fix that frown on your face for all your days." Kitsizil Ligai and the other two boys laughed. Nneez ishkiin raised his brows and nodded. I said, "A good bow shot waits for the right time whether the wind blows or not."

Kitsizil Ligai said, "I think Ohyessonna is our best bow shooter. He will be my *segundo* (number two) until someone better comes. Now I begin to train you how to handle herds of horses and mules. First you need to learn how to use a basic tool every horseman uses around his horses."

He went to the back of the crevice and returned with four coiled *reata*s, ropes of rawhide, one for each of us. My *reata*, like the others, was long and smooth, made from thin braided leather strings. When I ran my hands along its length, it made them feel like they held power, power enough to hold a big animal like a horse. Men in our band knew how to make a good *reata*, but it was long, time-consuming work. Our *reata*s, taken during raids in the land of the *Nakai-yes*, came from vaqueros. Our *reata* makers were young when *Nakai-yes* took them for slaves and taught them how to work rawhide into *reata*s and other horse gear. When our *reata* makers escaped, they brought their skills with them. *Reata*s were common among us but, as boys, we didn't feel a pull to use them as weapons like we did for bows, lances, slings, or war clubs.

Kitsizil Ligai had us take our bows and *reata*s and climb down the rope to the canyon floor. He found a shady place and showed us how to make a loop with our *reata*s, swing it, and throw the loop over a nearby boulder. When we could loop our boulders without missing, he had us increase the distance and practice throwing the loops again and again until we didn't miss. Then we would move to increase the distance again. He made us practice for two hands against the horizon with our *reata*s every day.

Long shadows falling on the east-side canyon cliffs from the disappearing sun began to appear. Kitsizil Ligai told us to collect our arrows before the light was gone and to coil our *reata*s to carry with us. He said he expected to see us at first light from the next sun and we should bring our bows, *reatas*, and a water jug or canteen. We left him to run down the brush-lined trail along the creek toward the good smells of our mothers' evening meals.

MY MOTHER HAD our morning meal ready, and I ate with her and Father just as birds in the brush began to call. When I finished and pulled my bow quiver and *reata* out of the *wickiup*, she handed me a water jug and a sack of trail food just as I began my run back up to the pasture. The sun, just above the canyon rim, shot long lances of light through the mists rolling through the trees on the western side, and flocks of bushtits scattered in the brush and trees were beginning their chorus. I came to the edge of the grazing grounds, the grass sparkling again with night water as light spread on the west-side canyon wall. The horses drank around a small pool in the creek. Some took a drink while others watched for enemies. I had been around horses since I was off the *tsach* (cradleboard) but had never noticed this drink-and-watch way of acting before. I was surprised when one of the warriors who had been keeping watch on the herd overnight suddenly appeared out of the shadows.

He said, "Nishi'ii', Ohyessonna. Tell Kitsizil Ligai the horses act as if Cougar is nearby, but we have not seen him. Keep close watch. This is a time of day he likes to hunt and has been studying the herd looking for weak ones while it was dark."

I made the all-is-good sign that I understood his words, and as the second warrior joined us from the east side of the canyon, they nodded acknowledgment of my arrival before running down the path under the trees to their family's *wickiups*. I turned back to the horses near the drinking pool and saw all had their heads up and their ears raised as they stared at a spot near the bottom of the east-side cliffs still in deep shadow. I slipped my quiver and bow case and *reata* over my head and onto my shoulder and made fast work pulling myself up the rope hanging out of the crevice I had used the day before.

Puffing like I had just made a fast run, I crawled into the crevice and stood to look where the horses stared. A cougar, not more than forty paces from the nearest horse and in the far cliff shadows, hugged the ground in deep grass, its tail slowly sweeping back and forth as it concentrated on its intended victim.

I took my bow from its case, strung it, and pulled three arrows from my quiver, two to hold and one to shoot. I laid the arrow on the bow. The morning air was still, not a leaf moving. I chose the targeting point for sighting the arrow tip relative to the target like I had yesterday. I saw the cougar creep forward two steps and stop and knew it was time to act if I had any chance of stopping it. I pulled the arrow to its full length, sighted its point, and released it with the string making its usual satisfying thumm. The arrow flashed in the sunlight and made its deadly arc for the ground. It plunged deep into the cougar, behind its left shoulder. Cougar jumped and screamed in rage as the horses stampeded toward my side of the canyon. I shot my second arrow, but the cougar had left my aim point and the arrow only struck the ground. Cougar, snarling its rage, wanted to run, but its left front leg wasn't having it. He headed for the horses now under me. I fit my third arrow in my bow and waited for my best shot as it came closer to the horses now huddled in a group, and a big roan stallion stood in front of them ready for battle. Cougar stopped to snarl at the stallion. That pause was all I needed for a good shot as I sent my arrow straight and true deep into the chest of the big cat. It took two more steps clawing at the arrow and collapsed in the grass never to rise again.

My cheeks puffed a sigh of relief as I climbed down the rope. The horses had already scattered to new grazing places on the canyon floor. I approached the cat pulling my knife, given to me by Toga-de-chuz when I was eight harvests. It was beautifully made with an antler-horn handle, a long blade that narrowed to a double-sided tip, which, under the tutelage of Toga-de-chuz, I had spent many hands against the sun making very sharp. I tensed, ready to strike with my blade and jump out of the way of its big claws tearing at me. But there were no claws slashing the air, for this cougar was no more.

I used my knife to open its throat so it would bleed out to save the meat.

"Ohyessonna, you have done a thing of great power early in a sun's rising. Toga-de-chuz, I, and all the People are very proud of your skill and courage."

I jerked around when I heard Kitsizil Ligai's voice. I had not seen him approach. "I only did the best I knew to do, Grandfather."

"It was far more than most boys your age can do. Truly, your courage will make you a leader of men. I'll get my horse. When the other boys come, they can stand watch while we carry the carcass to your mother. She knows how to dress the cat and cook the meat, and she will make you the best of quivers and a bow case out of the hide."

KITSIZIL LIGAI WAS right. Many of the People just wanted to touch me so they, too, might have my courage. Mother made me a quiver and bow case out of the hide and tail that even *Capitan* Chiquito, our great war chief, would have been proud of, and she often referred to me as her "great hunter" son when she spoke with other women. The boys who were to watch the livestock, even Nneez ishkiin, were deferential to my judgment.

Kitsizil Ligai trained us well in many herding skills. We had been around and on horses since we were off the *tsach*, but he taught us all kinds of riding tricks he had learned before he escaped the Comanches when he was a young man near our age. We learned to herd cattle from horseback and how to handle stubborn mules. All this training I knew we were lucky to get, but I often wondered where *Ussen* was leading me.

We changed canyon camps in the Galiuro Mountains four or five times during the next two harvests as Hashke Bahnzin and *Capitan* Chiquito fought the White Eyes and Blue Coats. The big chief Blue Coat had decided the only way to win against the Apache was to organize Apache to fight Apache. There was often enough bad medicine between the bands that allowed him to form a Blue Coat unit he called the "scouts" that helped him bring the other Apache to reservations designated for them. I wanted our People to stay wild and free, but I was impressed with the scouts and how they fought and worked together under the command of their Blue Coat chiefs.

Hashke Bahnzin and *Capitan* Chiquito agreed to stop fighting and raiding provided they returned to Aravaipa Creek. The Blue Coat chief agreed to this. We left the Galiuro Mountains and once more made our camps again on Aravaipa Creek. We were satisfied with our life in Aravaipa Canyon, but it didn't last.

FOUR

MARKSMAN

WHEN I WAS fourteen harvests, our chiefs decided to return to Aravaipa Canyon. This was in the harvest when they raided without much success in the Seasons of Large Leaves and Large Fruit. The warriors took some of their best horses to ride in the raids with Hashke Bahnzin and *Capitan* Chiquito. The horses and mules we guarded while the men were away made a ragged-looking herd, but Kitsizil Ligai taught us much about horses and how to handle herds using them. When we returned to Aravaipa Canyon, the other boys and I knew more about horses and mules and how to herd and handle them than most of the warriors in the camp.

Capitan Chiquito resisted returning to Camp Grant. He knew these were his last raiding days, but he wanted the White Eye agent to understand who he was dealing with. He was also very angry that Hashke Bahnzin had broken the peace with the White Eyes and Blue Coats, which made the times hard on all of us.

I and the other herd guards and women and children were allowed to sit quietly in the dark behind the warriors around the fire and listen to the councils *Capitan* Chiquito had with his leaders, among them my father. It was there that I heard the story of Hashke Bahnzin killing his friend, the White Eye rancher, Charles McKinney.

McKinney's small ranch bordered the Río San Pedro. Less than a moon of suns after Hashke Bahnzin left Aravaipa Canyon, he stopped to talk with McKinney about cattle best suited for the ranch he was planning to start. McKinney asked Hashke Bahnzin to have an evening meal with him and they'd have a long talk about cattle. Hashke Bahnzin dismounted and followed McKinney into his house after telling his men to wait.

The meal lasted two hands of the sun against the horizon. At last, Hashke Bahnzin and McKinney came out on the porch holding their coffee cups. They were laughing at a story Hashke Bahnzin was telling in that deep rumbling voice of his. But, after McKinney sat down in his porch rocker, Hashke Bahnzin drew his big Walker Colt revolver and shot him in the head. Standing there on the porch, Hashke Bahnzin looked at each warrior. They had all dropped their jaws in surprise. Hashke Bahnzin said, "Any warrior will kill an enemy, but it takes a strong man to kill a friend." He motioned his warriors to their horses, and they all rode away. They left McKinney slumped in his chair. His head was tilted to one side leaking blood that pooled on the floor under the big exit wound. I thought of that lesson often, and what it meant for me. I couldn't imagine killing a friend to prove myself strong.

NOT MANY SUNS after we arrived on Aravaipa Creek and camped where our People were massacred, my father sent my sister to find me and tell me that he waited for me in the family *wickiup*. I knew whatever he wanted to tell me must be important. He had never called me to our *wickiup* like this before, and when he saw me coming, he waved me into the *wickiup*'s cool darkness.

I sat down in front of him. No one else was in the *wickiup*. My mother, the children, and other women were looking for acorns, walnuts, and mesquite and paloverde pods up the canyon. Those nuts and pods, they ground to make good bread.

My father had something lying on his knees. It was long and wrapped in a red wool Navajo blanket covered with designs looking like small squares centered within larger squares. He reached into a vest pocket and pulled a beaded pouch of *tobaho* (tobacco) out, made a cigarette, lit it with a twig from Mother's fire, and smoked to the four directions. He gave it to me, and I smoked to the four directions before returning it to him. He threw the last bit in the fire and, looking directly at me, said, "My son, you have worked hard with your friends as horse guards. You have been their leader and destroyed cougars, wolves, and coyotes that would have taken our horses and mules for food. Your friends follow you with devotion. Watching you work, I saw your Power help you. You have the Power to be a chief, and I am proud of you."

He held the blanket-wrapped thing toward me and said, "I think it is time you had this."

My heart was pounding with expectation as he laid it in my hands. I thought I already knew what it was. Unfolding the blanket, I wasn't disappointed. Across my blanket-covered knees lay a new repeating rifle with a brass receiver. Its light coating of oil made it gleam in the light passing through the door and made it smell like the weapon I knew it was. It was a .44-40 caliber rifle made by a man the White Eyes called Winchester. Our People, like the Mescalero and Jicarilla to the east, called the rifles with the brass receivers "Yellow Boys." Some of our warriors had rifles like this. Others had a different kind of rifle made by a man called Henry. Both rifles had loop levers behind the trigger guard. Moving the levers cycled new cartridges into their firing chambers. Two boxes of cartridges were also with it. I opened one of the boxes and glanced at the rows of shiny brass shells with gray lead tips.

I ran my fingers over this beautiful thing made of steel, wood, and brass and said, "My father honors me, and I'm very proud of this fine rifle."

My father grinned and nodded. *"Enjuh!* Tomorrow, I show you how to shoot and where I hide my ammunition. It's your choice as to how accurate and powerful you are with this new weapon. You still have much growing to do. I ask that you don't take the rifle out for the next two or three harvests unless I'm with you."

"Father, I will not make you sorry you have given me this rifle."

He crossed his arms and nodded. "I know, my son." Then he showed me how to load the cartridges through a trapdoor in the brass receiver and, warning me to keep my finger off the trigger, had me work the lever to load and then eject each cartridge. He taught me to count the number of cartridges I had loaded, and then count the number I had ejected after shooting a load. If I shot fewer than I loaded, I was to work the lever to claim all the cartridges that went into the rifle plus work the lever once more to ensure that the firing chamber was empty and that no more cartridges were in the rifle.

THE NEXT MORNING, my father and I took my new rifle and a box of cartridges and ran up Aravaipa Canyon following a trail along the creek bosque. We looked for a wide place where he could show me how to shoot without my shots endangering others. He came to a canyon with rough white walls with layers of dark brown, I never learned its name, that ran into Aravaipa Canyon. It was over a hundred paces wide a short run from where it connected to Aravaipa Canyon. My father decided this was a good place for me to learn to shoot. On the east bank, he found a sandy spot that was bush-free and had a little bench waist high. He stuck two sticks upright and crossed and tied them together at the top to make a target like I had used to practice on when I was learning how to use a sling. If I shot and missed the sticks, the origin of the spray of sand from the bank behind them would show where I had missed the cross sticks.

He had me sit down in the sand and showed me how to support the rifle with my elbows on my knees when I pointed the rifle barrel at the crossed sticks. He showed me what a sight picture was with the little blade at the end of the barrel appearing to stand in the middle of the little notched metal piece on the barrel near the receiver. He told me to put the sight picture on the target, to take a deep breath and let half of it out to steady the sight picture on the target, and then to squeeze rather than jerk the trigger to fire. He asked if I understood all this, and I nodded that I did. He told me to load ten cartridges and not to forget to count as I loaded. I loaded ten. He told me to hold out my hand, where he dropped two balls of wax and said, "Roll them around with your fingers and fit them in your ears to make the noise less when you fire. Otherwise, you'll have a hard time hearing for a while after you shoot. A *di-yen* has blessed them and says his Power will keep our hearing good even when our hair is gray." I did as he told me. After I nodded that I was ready, he said, "Aim and shoot while I watch."

I did exactly as he told me. He was right, the sight picture didn't wiggle as much when I let half my breath out. I squeezed the trigger and the rifle roared and jumped against my shoulder. It wasn't painful, but I knew if I shot many times, my shoulder would be sore and I'd have a good bruise. The smoke from the cartridge was easy to see through, but the explosion of sand the bullet raised behind the target hid the crossed sticks for a short time. After the dust was gone, we saw that the crossed sticks had disappeared.

My father said, "Ho! My son, you will be deadly with a rifle when you are a man. Keep your finger off the trigger and I'll set up more crossed sticks." He set them up and returned to stand behind me. "Shoot again." I levered a new cartridge into place and went through the little ceremony he taught me to hit the crossed sticks. Once more, he went and planted two sticks. When he returned, he said, "Come." I followed him to the far bank of the canyon and found a place to sit and shoot. It was at least four times the distance from where I shot the first two times.

"Can you see the target?"

"Yes, Father. It's much smaller."

"*Enjuh.* I can barely see it. Try to hit it from this distance."

I sighted on the point where the sticks seemed to cross. I was ready to shoot when Father said, *"Nt'ah."* He reached down and flipped up a piece of metal where the notch site was mounted. The flipped-up piece looked like a ladder with one step that could slide up and down, and the step had a notch in the middle. There was a series of markings up the sides, and Father pulled the ladder step up a little to a mark labeled 2. He explained that the farther we shot, the more a bullet fell below where we aimed. The trick to hitting things at longer ranges was to tilt the rifle barrel up a little so the bullet traveled in an arc like an arrow to hit the target as it fell. The ladder sight helped the shooter do this. It made the shooter tilt the rifle up to put the sight picture on the target for the distance. He didn't have to think about it but once to set the ladder height for the range he shot. Father set the ladder step to the 2-shaped mark on the side of the ladder and nodded. The notch didn't look much higher than the original one I used before. I shot again using the ladder notch. I hit the crossed sticks a little high but destroyed the target just the same.

My father stared at the target across the canyon and shook his head. "Truly, my son, *Ussen* blessed you with great talent in the use of a rifle. The way the other boys already follow you, you will be a powerful chief one day."

I shrugged my shoulders as if to say "Who knows?" and then said, "Father, you honor me with your words. You have taught me much. I hope, one day, I will honor you with the life I live."

He smiled. "Of that honor, I have no doubt."

Cartridges cost much of the thing the White Eyes used in trades, what they called "money," and were often hard to find in the right size—what the White Eyes called "caliber"—during raids. My father let me shoot all ten of the cartridges I had loaded in the rifle, each one at a longer range down the canyon. I fired the last cartridge for the ladder notch set to the mark "5"—five hundred paces.

FIVE

THE RACE

FATHER PROUDLY TOLD his best friends what I had done with my new rifle, and word spread like a dry-time wildfire through *Capitan* Chiquito's camp. Many said that I was a natural-born deadly shot and one day might be a chief. My belief in myself grew from the gossip, but I never believed I'd be chief. My friends said nothing about the talk in every *wickiup*. They waited for me to tell them in my own way. I could tell they had more respect for me than they had earlier when we played and trained.

A moon after the winds of gossip about my rifle shooting blew through *Capitan* Chiquito's camp, we boys were up the canyon shooting targets with our bows and arrows. During a game we used to win each other's arrows, Gonshayee, the tall boy—then named Nneez ishkiin—with whom I had learned to guard horses, said to me loud enough for all to hear, "If my father gave me a rifle, I'd be a better shot than you'd ever be."

I knew Nneez ishkiin was angry because I had won two good arrows from him in our shooting contests that morning. I should have kept my silence, but couldn't resist an answer. "Ho, brother. If Coyote hadn't stopped to make dirt, he would have caught Rabbit. Only *Ussen* knows the future."

Gonshayee's face grew dark like the clouds in a coming storm. He was mad enough that his hand reached for the knife in its sheath at his back. I didn't move, kept my eyes fixed on his face, and waited until I knew for sure what he was going to do. His shoulders relaxed and his hand paused at the knife's handle and went no farther before returning his fingers to the arrow nocked against his bow string.

I still don't know what made me challenge him to a race. I said within the hearing of all those around us, "You're a head taller than me. Your legs are longer. If we race, you could leave me in the dust and all would see how superior you are."

Gonshayee grinned. His white teeth, brilliant in the bright sunlight, glowed against his dark skin. "I've seen you run. I know I'm faster and stronger than you. I always beat the other boys who race me. I rarely see you beat the boys you run against." He scowled as a thought filled his mind. "Why do you want to race me when I will beat you?"

I looked at the ground to hide the grin trying to force itself onto my face. "It's always good to know a leader's strengths and limits. The harvests are not many before some of us go on raids or to war. I want to know who to follow. I want to know your strengths and limits. I want to know how much stronger you are than me."

I wasn't lying. I did want to know all those things. I also knew I was much faster than him and would lead rather than follow. Again, came his toothy, all-knowing grin. "Then I teach you my strength in a race. How far and where we race? You choose."

I crossed my arms and thought. I knew I could beat Gonshayee in any race. I wanted the race to be hard enough that he would never burden us again with his claims of superiority over me or anyone else.

"There is the wagon road the Blue Coats used to haul their wood before they left. It runs from where we stand now along the side of the canyon and ends where the creek turns east and then southeast near where the big canyons off the hills connect to our canyon. That wagon road is smooth and has some good climbs and downhill distances that will test our strength.

"I say, next sun, let us begin where the wagon road ends in the heat of the day at the time of no shadows and finish here. We can leave our knives stuck in the post when we go to the starting place. Whoever first reclaims his knife stuck in this post wins. Any others who want to run with us, come too. We soon see who can endure and is as strong as Gonshayee."

There was general mumbling among the other boys before four or five more said they would race too.

I said, "We can trot up to the starting place after leaving our knives in the post, rest a little while, shoot an arrow high, and start the race when it hits ground. One who is not racing can bring his bow and shoot the arrow." I pointed at one of the younger boys and said, "Bil gozhóó (He is Happy), will you shoot your bow for us to begin?" He smiled and nodded.

Gonshayee nodded and said, *"Ch'ik'eh doleel* (Let it be so)." All the other boys said the same thing.

We resumed our contest for collecting good arrows. I took another from Gonshayee before we ended our game.

BY THE TIME I returned to my mother's *wickiup* for our evening meal, the news of a race primarily between Gonshayee and me was already flying through the *wickiups* up and down the creek and betting had begun. Most bets seemed to favor Gonshayee. As we ate mesquite bread, roast venison, and wild potatoes, the chorus of frogs and insects sang to us by my mother's fire, the creek burbling nearby. It was very peaceful. As we ate, my father asked me about the race plans and why I had challenged Gonshayee. He listened, occasionally saying, "Hmmph," or nodding as I talked. When I finished my story, he rubbed his hands on his moccasin shafts and nodded.

"Hmmmph. I don't know where you get your wisdom, my son, but what you did with Gonshayee today is something an experienced and wise chief would have done. You changed his attention from your rifle shooting to a contest that can show him better than you, but I doubt he will do this. Race well tomorrow. Many bets will change hands. I think most of the bettors against you will lose. Soon we see. Rest well."

I smiled and shrugged my shoulders. "I will try, Father. I hope you lose nothing valuable."

DAYLIGHT WAS COMING. Brilliant gold light behind the eastern mountains turned the northeastern walls of the mountains and canyons defining Aravaipa Canyon a warm yellow while the southeastern-side canyons and foothills remained in shadows. I crawled out of my blankets, visited the brush for personal business, and took my mother's axe with me to make wood for her fire.

When I returned with an armload of firewood, she had already brought the fire to life with leftover wood and brush from her supper fire. She had made coffee and poured me a cup out of the old, blackened pot into my blue speckled cup to help drive away the morning chill. We sipped the hot black water and listened to the chorus of bushtits flitting through the brush looking for seeds, berries, and slow-moving insects.

My mother was a beautiful, hardworking woman. *Ussen* had blessed my father, Toga-de-chuz, and me when he chose my mother for us. I had heard the stories of how he had bested a powerful warrior, Rip, in courting her. Both men badly wanted her and Toga-de-chuz mocked and teased Rip because my mother didn't choose him. I was glad my father had won her. I didn't like Rip, or the rest of his family, and I could have wound up being just like them. But I didn't think it was smart to deliberately make an enemy like Toga-de-chuz had with Rip. A man goes through life accidentally making too many enemies. He doesn't need to make one deliberately.

This day, Mother had steamed dried mescal slices and mesquite bread to eat with honey for our morning meal. She knew these foods would keep me strong on the wagon road run. As we ate, feasting on her fine meal, I thought about my race strategy. The road was downhill most of the way but had two climbs that were about thirty paces high straight up, the first hill shortly after we started and the second about the middle of the race. Both climbs were about the same height. I decided to push Gonshayee when the road first climbed to make him waste his strength and then let him get some distance in front on the downward side of the first climb but run like the wind on the downward side of the second climb all the way to the post holding our knives. I hoped I hadn't misjudged his speed and endurance. I knew I was faster, but how much strength he would have left after those two climbs to chase me to the post, I didn't know.

Our meal finished, I tied my breechcloth around my crotch so it fully supported me and wouldn't get in the way of my stride. My parents watched me, and as I made ready to leave, my mother said, "I know you will do well, my son. We'll be watching for you. *Dínyaa* (You go)! *Nawode nánigheed* (Run fast)!"

I smiled and nodded at her. "This I do for you, my mother."

ALL THE BOYS in the race showed up at the knife post at about the same time and took turns finding where they wanted to leave their knives stuck in the post. I jammed my knife within a hand length of the top of the post when Gonshayee came up. He grinned and nodded at us as he stepped back after stabbing his long blade into the very top of the post. I smiled at him and said, "Why don't we use the creek path and save our strength for the race?" He shrugged his shoulders and motioned for me to lead on.

Our trot along the path through the creek bosque was cool and pleasant. The hard part was holding back so we didn't have a race on the path along the creek. We reached the place where the wagon road ended about a hand on the horizon before the time of shortest shadows and found places in the shade to rest. The boy to shoot the arrow that would start us was already there, having ridden his pony on the wagon road.

Near the time the shadows shortened to their least length, the boy with the bow stepped out into the middle of the wagon turnaround, strung his bow, and laid a long arrow's nock on the string. He called to us. "Come, brothers! It is time to run! Stand in a shoulder-to-shoulder line behind me and begin your race when this arrow strikes the ground in front of us." We stood in a line behind him about an arm's length apart. The canyon was wide there with the creek on the southeast side to our left and our line of sight looking down the flat road into the high southern wall of white stone that curved to the north blocking any further view of the road. The boy with the bow pulled the arrow back, aimed for the sky, tilting it a little south, and released it with its sinew string singing thumm as he stepped behind us to move out of our way. The arrow disappeared into the blue, and then the sunlight had it on its way down. We were all tensed and ready to run when the arrow's long shaft struck the ground with a quiver and a thunking sound. We all charged forward down the road. The race was on.

Gonshayee sprinted a long bow shot—a hundred paces—to the front of us all. I had to get closer if I wanted to push him on the first climb. By the time the canyon began to narrow as it curved toward the northwest, I had closed the distance to about half what it was and thought that was enough for pushing him on the first long climb. The other boys were now far behind us. The air was cool and pleasant and made our running easy.

As the wagon road began to climb, I closed the distance between us until he was only two or three bow lengths in front and struggling. I pushed him all the way to the top of the climb and then eased back to give him a little more running lead on the way down. The downside of the climb was about the same length as what we ran from the start to the beginning of the first hill climb. When we started the next little climb, I closed the distance again, getting closer than I was before. I pushed him to run even harder that time. As we topped the hill, he looked back showing me his teeth in a grimace and then shot downhill again, putting separation between us. I looked down at the creek in the bottom of the canyon and saw groups of men sitting on their ponies scattered along the creek using soldier glasses to watch us.

I let Gonshayee run. I could tell he was tiring. I still felt strong. We ran holding the same-distance separation until we came to the second big climb. The climb was about the same height as the first one but stayed high for two or three times the distance of the first one and wound around many more curves. He must have seen me coming and pushed hard to get far ahead of me. I let him go. After we passed this hill, there were no more climbs of any significance and I could tell from the last time we were close together, his strength was leaving him. I still felt strong and could push hard to catch and pass him when I wanted.

I lost sight of Gonshayee in the winding curves of the road across the top of the bare sandy hills showing only an occasional cactus or twisted mesquite. The road made a tight turn, tracking the opposite sides of an *arroyo* after it crossed the road. I looked down the road on the far side of the *arroyo* before it disappeared around a curve, but I didn't see any sign of Gonshayee. I decided I had to catch him now before he got too far ahead of me.

I took three long strides when, out of the corner of my vision, I saw him charge me from his hiding place behind a big green bush. He was running hard toward my path. Before I could react, he was on me, his head down like a bull and his shoulder hammering my side and pushing me off the edge of the road to roll down the steep *arroyo* bank with big rough stones exposed and cactus growing between them. He kept his balance and stayed on the road. He shouted back to me as he headed down the hill, "Ho! Catch me now, if you can, rifle man!"

The dirt where I landed had a scattering of small sharp rocks in the sand, scattered cactus, and bushes, and dropped five rifle lengths before there was a ledge with another longer drop down into the *arroyo*. I was lucky. I didn't crash into any big stones, and no bones were broken. In the rolling tumble, I threw my feet wide and slowed down enough to grab the second bush down and hold on. I pulled myself to my knees and then into a crouch that let me churn and dig in the sand around the rocks up to the road. I brushed the dirt off, some formed in lumps of mud after mixing with my body water and pulled some long cactus needles off my right thigh. Boiling with anger, I wanted to charge after him but kept my wits and decided the best revenge would be his embarrassment by beating him to the knife post by a good margin. I saw two groups of men down by the creek, who had been watching us. They turned their ponies back toward the village as I began to run.

The sun was hot and strength draining as I gathered speed and felt the burn from all the little sharp rock cuts that covered my body. I felt scattered spots on my upper body carrying cactus needles. By the time I reached the hill bottom and was on the straight, flat stretch of road running to a curve around a hill, I saw Gonshayee pass out of sight.

I was surprised to see him and decided his strength must be leaving him in a hurry. A piece of rope was lying by the side of the road. Blue Coats used this road often and must have lost it when hauling supplies to woodcutters down the canyon. It was a bow length long and had been lying there a while but wasn't falling apart. I realized I could use it and swooped it up as I ran.

Anger gave fire to my strength as I clenched my teeth, and I charged down the trail. No more hills to climb, we were following the trail that was going downhill toward the fields at the bottom of the canyon. I was gaining on him fast. He looked back over his shoulder and saw me. His eyes grew large. He tried to run faster but his legs moved like they were strapped with bags of rocks. I approached within a hundred, then fifty, and soon twenty paces of him. The knife post was not yet in sight. I flicked my wrist, and the piece of rope made a popping sound as Gonshayee stumbled forward trying to yell through a throat parched dry and croaking, "Come... on.... Come... on.... Catch... me... if you... can... rifle... man."

I caught up with him and lightly flicked his shoulders with the rope like I was driving a cow to slaughter. He groaned each time the rope touched his back, but I left no red marks. I saw the knife post in the distance, flicked his shoulders once more, and then ran past him. He came to a stop and bent over to suck more air into his lungs.

Soon I was at the knife post. I looked back the way I came and saw Gonshayee, a small bright figure in the falling sunlight, slowly moving toward the post. I jerked my knife from the post. Bil gozhóó who shot the arrow to start us and several men were nearby watching me. I had won the race and needed a drink of water and a bath from the creek.

SIX

TOGA-DE-CHUZ CHOOSES
SAN CARLOS

AFTER I BATHED in the soothing water of the slow-moving creek, I sat on a boulder nearby to dry in the warm afternoon sun. I looked at the cuts and bruises all over my body where I had landed and rolled after Gonshayee pushed me off the edge of the road. I watched him slowly walk up to the knife post with the other boys, little dark figures in the distance, and pull his knife. Those who had seen me pull my knife watched him too. There would be no disputing who pulled his knife first. It had been a good race, and I was glad I had challenged big-mouthed Gonshayee. I thought, *This race ought to teach him to keep his thoughts to himself unless he was ready to, as the White Eyes say, put up or shut up.*

With the excitement of the race and pursuing Gonshayee gone, I soon realized I was sore in places I hadn't expected as I walked to my mother's *wickiup*. A fine pinto pony with a saddle and bridle worked in silver stood nibbling grass and brush near the back of her *wickiup*. I wondered who was visiting my father riding such a fine pony. When I rounded the *wickiup* to my mother's cooking fire, only my father and mother were there. Father was enjoying a smoke and coffee, and she was on her knees grinding mesquite pods in a metate. They both smiled when they saw me. He motioned for me to sit to his left, a place of honor, and offered a cup of coffee, but I shook my head.

Father said, "You won that race in good style. I'm very proud of you, and I know your mother is too. What happened that you were driving your opponent to run faster by flicking him with a piece of rope, and you looked like you had been rolling in the dirt?"

I told him what had happened with Gonshayee pushing me down the *arroyo* bank and then my climbing back to the road and finding the piece of rope. I told how I had planned to whip him with it, even leave scars, but I decided that shaming him without the whipping was better.

He stuck his lower lip out and nodded before saying, "Again you show me that you are wise beyond your years, Ohyessonna. If you had whipped him, everyone would have said you were within your rights, but you would have made an enemy for life until you had to kill him. A little shame goes a long way toward making things right, and he knows it. You may even be friends one day if you accept him."

My mother looked up from her work grinning and said, "My son is a man soon. My heart swells with pride for him."

I smiled at her and said to Father, "Whose pony is that mounted with the fine saddle and bridle and grazing behind the *wickiup*?"

"You won the race. I made the bet. The pony, saddle, and bridle are yours. The man I won it from won it on a monte game bet with a Chiricahua riding with Juh. Those Chiricahua steal good things and are usually better card players than the man who lost it. Always be careful around those Chiricahua. They'll take anything. You might come home without your breechcloth."

I laughed and slapped my knee. *"Muchas gracias, padre.* I'm very honored with this fine gift. What did you bet to win him?"

"My long rifle that shoots today and kills tomorrow."

"That was a big risk you took. I know you love that rifle."

He shook his head. "I never doubted you wouldn't lose. Now, listen closely. I have news of my own. *Capitan* Chiquito and Hashke Bahnzin say they will join *Nant'an Lpah* to hunt the Yavapai chiefs Chuntz, Cochinay, and Cha-deisa in the Season of Earth Is Reddish Brown. This I will not do. Our little band will leave in the night before the next sun and go to the canyon in the Galiuro Mountains, where you learned to work with the horses and mules. I think *Capitan* Chiquito and Hashke Bahnzin use bad judgment to fight against other tribes. I think they make mistakes if they help the Blue Coats fight them, but I believe they may do this. It is best we leave *Capitan* Chiquito's leadership for a while."

"I understand, Father. I think you are very wise to do this. We don't need to make more enemies by siding with the Blue Coats against our own People. The pony and saddle make my heart proud. I'll be ready to ride tonight."

He took a swallow of coffee and, grinning, said, *"Ch'ik'eh doleel."*

THAT NIGHT, TOGA-de-chuz led his little band to the canyon in the Galiuro Mountains that *Capitan* Chiquito had used when we first left the Aravaipa Canyon two harvests earlier. Two other boys and I looked after the horses and mules while the men hunted. For a moon, we had plenty to eat, and nothing, neither men nor wild animals, disturbed our horse and mule herd or us. It was a time of peace with life lived as it should be. But then, Beauford, the big Blue Coat, came with his scouts and changed our lives forever.

I had just started the last watch one sun before it fell into the western mountains after we had camped in the canyon over a moon. The mules started braying, and the horses nervously gathered in two or three groups and stared down the canyon, their ears raised in curiosity. Father let me carry my rifle to use guarding the herd. I practiced with it often and had learned how to hold it steady without supporting my elbows. I pointed it toward the tree line, pulled the hammer back, and waited. I could see dim, dark figures of men running across pools of yellow light. The tweeting calls from flocks of bushtits that often filled brush and trees were silent. Then into the bright light lying over the meadow like a carpet fringed with shadows, where the horses and mules grazed, a big, lone Blue Coat rode out of the tree line with his hat pulled over his eyes and his great long knife, the White Eyes called "sword," in a metal sheath jangling from his side. He hadn't ridden more than four or five horse lengths out of the shadows before I saw a long line of scouts stretched out across the canyon behind him. I glanced up at the canyon rim on both sides and saw scouts watching everything with soldier glasses. The big Blue Coat saw me, and that I had lowered my rifle. He rode slowly toward me, the top half of his face still in his hat's shadow and a big growth of hair under his nose. Pistol and rifle holsters hung from separate sides of his saddle, and his horse, a big black gelding with a white blaze on his face, seventeen hands high, carried him with ease. He was the most impressive Blue Coat I had ever seen, including those who came to General Howard's meeting at Camp Grant in the Season of Many Leaves earlier in the harvest. *This is a man I should study. He can teach me much about White Eyes and how they do things, things I need to know and understand.*

The Blue Coat stopped his great horse right in front of me and said, *"Habla español?"*

I made the small sign of my thumb and forefinger not quite touching, *"Un poco."* The Blue Coat turned in his saddle and motioned forward a man with a big black mustache and disheveled hair sticking out around the edges of his hat crown. I recognized him as Hermenegildo Grijalva. He could speak both Spanish and Apache well and was at General Howard's conference as an interpreter a harvest ago. We had become friends, he talking to me to pass time while he waited between meetings at the conference, I to learn all I could about what was going on at the conference and how it might affect me and my People.

He said to me in Apache, "Ho, Ohyessonna. Moons have passed since we speak as friends. This Blue Coat wants to speak with your father. If we wait, will you go and ask him to meet the Blue Coat here?"

I nodded. "Soon I return." As I ran down the path through the bosque along the little creek to where our *wickiups* stood, I heard the big Blue Coat give a command and, glancing back through the trees, saw him dismount and his scouts squat in the grass and hold their rifles upright with their butts on the ground—a sign of peaceful intentions.

I RAN TO my mother's *wickiup*, but my parents weren't there. I ran on up the path and found Father in council with his men. A man was speaking, but when Father saw me, breathing hard, he held up his hand, palm out, to stop the speaker and motioned for me to come forward. I went to his side and said in a soft voice, "A big Blue Coat comes with many scouts. Some sit in the field of horses. Others are on the canyon rim. Hermenegildo Grijalva is with him. The Blue Coat says he wants to talk with you—I think now."

Father puckered his lips. "Tell the Blue Coat soon I come."

As I left the council, I heard Father say, "Brothers! My son says a Blue Coat comes with many scouts and asks that I come to speak with him at the edge of the horse field. I ask that you come with me so that you know his true words."

I ran down the path and didn't hear the council end, but I was certain Father, and his men, would come soon. At the edge of the horse field, I found the Blue Coat and Grijalva smoking and talking. I paused. Grijalva motioned me over to them, his brows raised in question. I told him that soon my father comes. He nodded and spoke to the big Blue Coat in the Mexican tongue saying that soon the boy's father comes. The Blue Coat mumbled something I didn't understand and spread a red-and-black Navajo blanket with beautiful designs in the short brown grass where he and my father could sit.

True to his word, Father came with his men, all unarmed, to speak with the Blue Coat. Grijalva, who had known my father a long time passing, moved to meet him, each making the all-is-well sign as they spoke with smiles and nods like old friends. Grijalva soon asked the Blue Coat, whom he called *Teniente* (Lieutenant) Beauford to come meet a great chief of the Aravaipa, Toga-de-chuz.

They each made the all-is-well sign by waving their palms parallel to the ground. They said nothing as they eyed each other like two Mexican roosters making ready to fight. Then the Blue Coat smiling, said something in the Mexican tongue, which my father spoke well, and motioned for my father to sit with him on the blanket. The *teniente* made a cigarette. He lit it with a White Eye fire stick called a "match." He smoked to the four directions and gave it to my father, who smoked and returned it to the *teniente*.

This was serious business.

The Blue Coat spoke a short time before motioning toward his scouts squatting behind him with their rifles butted. He then looked to the scouts on the canyon rim, where all we could see were dark outlines of their heads and shoulders looking out from boulders. The Blue Coat motioned in the general direction of our village and then back over the mountains to Aravaipa Canyon. My father raised his brows a couple of times but said nothing as *Teniente* Beauford continued speaking.

When *Teniente* Beauford finished speaking, he crossed his arms and nodded at my father to speak. The men sitting behind Father had faces that showed no smiles, but they showed no anger either. Toga-de-chuz said something to *Teniente* Beauford, who thought a little and then nodded he agreed. They went back and forth like this until long shadows from the western ridge on one side of the canyon began to darken where the horses grazed.

At last, my father drew in a deep breath, stood, and said loud enough for all the People to hear, "*Teniente* Beauford says we must go to the San Carlos Reservation. His great chief far away to the east demands it. The *teniente* has agreed to how and where we can live on the reservation."

Teniente had told him they could put their *wickiups* anyplace not already occupied on San Carlos. If we didn't camp close to the agency, we must still come to the agency to get our rations once every seven suns. There were other rules besides these, but none sounded so bad that we couldn't live with them.

"I, Toga-de-chuz, am ready to leave this canyon and move to San Carlos to keep peace with the White Eyes. To leave now is a better way to live than to fight our way out of this canyon or any other. The big chiefs, *Capitan* Chiquito and Hashke Bahnzin, are expected to return soon and will gobble up the best places to camp if we don't already claim them. We will move first light of the next sun. I have said all I will say."

There was silence across the crowd of our People. Then first one man and then another stood and said, *"Enjuh.* Next sun, we go."

SEVEN

TENIENTE BEAUFORD

SHAFTS OF LIGHT were streaming through the mountains, painting the treetops with shades of gold, when *Teniente* Beauford led my father's People out of our canyon and across the hills and ridges to San Carlos. The San Carlos Agency adobe *casas* sat on a big gravelly bench where the Río San Carlos disappeared into the Río Gila flowing west.

The land on the bench was ugly, mostly brown sand, dust, and gravel around the agency buildings. There was a scattering of trees in the bosque along the río, and downstream along the Gila, we could see eight canyons with washes that emptied into the río. The land at the top of the canyons was flat and mostly covered with thirsty creosote twigs, cactus, and other rough brush. Snakes were everywhere. Beauford warned us to watch where we stepped. No-see-ums close to the river were biting, leaving blood spots everywhere on exposed skin. We came in the very hot Season of Big Leaves. After I became a scout and worked a while supporting *Teniente* Davis at Fort Apache for Captain Crawford, I heard Davis call San Carlos "forty acres of hell." After I learned what the White Eyes meant by "hell" and "acres," his name for San Carlos Reservation fit it well.

Beauford led us to the adobe building he called "the agency" and introduced my father to the White Eye chief of San Carlos. I don't remember the agency chief's name, but he and Father talked a long time while our band waited in the shadow of the agency building. Even in the shade, the air around us felt like we were sitting in a sweat lodge. After it was clear Toga-de-chuz would be a while talking with Beauford and the reservation chief, my friend *Zenogolache* (the Crazy One) and I decided we'd use our slings to see who could throw rocks the greatest distance down the Río Gila or who could make a flat rock skip on the water the most times. It was fun to see our stones hopping as if they were alive across the gray-green water. *Zenogolache* won about the same number of throws both for distance and number of skips along the río's surface as I did.

When I saw Father and the reservation chief come back to the patiently waiting people, we raced back to the crowd. The chief and Father had agreed that we would camp in the second canyon down the Gila from the agency until the men had a chance to look for a place where they could grow crops and keep their horses, mules, and cattle safe. Ration day was every seven days. Anyone who held the brass pins with letters and numbers identifying who the bearer was and how many were in a family could pick up rations for a family.

There was still enough daylight left for us to move to the second canyon and begin making *wickiups*. Beauford led us there all the while talking to Father about how the Blue Coats liked to see things done. When we arrived at the second canyon, the women picked the spots for their *wickiups* but first made fire pits to cook the night meal for their families while their children gathered wood for the fire. After I brought in my load of wood, I stood near Father and Beauford, listening to them talk as Beauford told Father that he believed the Great Father had plans to put most of the Apache together on one reservation. Father shook his head and said that could never be. There were too many Apache who were enemies of other Apache. Bringing them together in one place would mean constant war.

Beauford nodded and said, "I know. We're going to listen and watch the different bands very closely." He saw me watching and, holding out his hand, curled his fingers toward me as a sign for me to join them.

He said to Father, "May I speak with your son?"

Father grinned and nodded.

Beauford said, "When I first came to your father's canyon, I saw you guarding the horses with a rifle. How well can you shoot?"

"*Muy bien,* I think."

Beauford looked around the canyon and decided twilight was getting so dark that it would be dangerous for me to shoot targets.

He said, "It's getting too dark for us to see what we're doing if we're going to use a gun. If I come tomorrow before the time of shortest shadows, then you can show me how well you shoot?"

"*Sí. Mañana,* you come. I shoot."

He stuck out his hand, and I gave it two good pumps like I had seen Father do with the Blue Coats, and he pumped my arm. "See ya tomorrow, then, before the time of shortest shadows. *Adios.*"

I nodded. *"Adios."*

MY FATHER'S FAMILY slept around my mother's fire that night. As dawn came creeping and the stars started disappearing above the eastern mountains, birds in the brush along the wash sang loudly, welcoming the coming light from behind the mountains. I left my blanket to sing my morning prayer and do my personal morning business. I returned for my mother's axe and gathered her enough brush for her morning fire. Then I went looking for saplings along the Gila that could be used for her *wickiup.* I cut eight or nine good, long straight cottonwoods before dragging them back to her fire, where she and Father drank their coffee as the day grew brighter.

My father raised a cup to me, and my mother grinned when they saw me coming with an armload of saplings in the golden light of a growing morning. He said, "Ho, Ohyessonna, I see you have the good beginnings for your mother's *wickiup.* Have a little coffee before you go out again and she makes ready the morning meal."

I laid my collection of saplings to one side and took the cup of steaming hot coffee my mother offered me from her fire-blackened pot. A tiny sip convinced me to wait a little while for it to cool. She smiled and nodded. "My son is wise to let that boiling black water cool a little. Are there enough saplings by the río to make all a good *wickiup?*"

"I think there are enough for every family to easily make one. Father, I have a question."

He slurped his coffee and said, "Speak. I will answer."

"Why do you think the Blue Coat Beauford wants to see me shoot?"

Father shrugged his shoulders. "I don't know. We see soon. My guess is he wants to know who to recruit for the scouts when they are old enough. You are a born leader, Ohyessonna. I'm sure he sees that. I think he has a job for you that we don't know about. Soon you shoot good. Then we know."

We watched families eat their morning meal and their young people go for *wickiup* saplings as the bright morning light made long shadows toward the west. I gathered another armload of saplings while my little brother and sister helped Mother make our lodge and then went to the Gila for a wash and swim before helping Mother put up the *wickiup*. The sun was halfway to the time of no shadows when Beauford rode up to our fire.

He dismounted from his big horse and spoke to my father, and I heard him ask if it was a good time for me to shoot. Father motioned me over to them and asked if I was ready to show *Teniente* Beauford how well I shot. I nodded and went to get my rifle and some cartridges out of our supplies. When I returned, he said, "Let's go over the next canyon downstream. No one else is camping there yet."

We followed the path through the bosque along the Gila. The no-see-ums were out in force. We were waving them away when he turned into the next canyon down the río from ours and walked up its wash. The canyon sides were sandy and not too steep, and in fertile places junipers had taken root on its sides. About a long shot from my father's shoot-today-kill-tomorrow rifle—about three hundred paces—the canyon branched. One part continued as the main canyon, while the new canyon looked like it didn't go very far. Here Beauford stopped, picked up three stones about the size of a man's head, and put them about head high in the sand on the west side of the main canyon. The closest stone was about fifty paces, then another about seventy-five paces, and the last one about a hundred paces away. When he returned, he pulled a long stick of brown, rolled *tobaho* from inside his coat pocket and, using a firestick from another pocket, lit it with a flick of his thumbnail against one end. He sucked on the glowing *tobaho* until smoke filled the air and the no-see-ums seemed to leave. The smoke burned my eyes and had a nasty smell, but I said nothing.

"Damned bugs, they'll drive anything crazy when they swarm! Ohyessonna, you see where I put a rock about fifty paces away, and one at seventy-five, but the one at a hundred paces is hard to see. In fact, I'm not even sure I see it, so don't worry about it, just shoot the other two."

"I see the stone at a hundred paces. Can I shoot it too?"

He pulled out his soldier glasses and held them up to his eyes. "All right, I can see where I walked to the spot where I put the rock on the sand. If you can see it without these glasses, you've got mighty good eyes. Go ahead. Load up and show me what you can do."

Father, smiling, reached in his vest pocket and pulled out three cartridges for me to load. I pushed the cartridges into the loading gate on the side of the rifle and levered a cartridge into the barrel. The rifle felt good in my hands, like a good tool that I hadn't used in a long time.

"Shall I shoot the one at longest range?"

"Let me use my glasses. I think I have enough field of view to see the sand spray if you miss." He held his soldier glasses to his eyes while puffing on his *tobaho*. "Go ahead and take your best shot at the hundred-yard rock."

I had practiced many times at this distance with Father coaching me, and the distance didn't bother me at all. I took a deep breath sighted on the rock, let half my air go, and squeezed the trigger as I had been taught. Instead of a little geyser of sand, the rock exploded, creating a small dust cloud and sending fragments of stone everywhere.

The long stick of his rolled *tobaho* swung precariously from the gaping lips of *Teniente* Beauford's mouth. He grabbed the *tobaho* and said one word, "Gawd!" He was silent for a couple of breaths before he said, "Son, can you do that again?"

"No, *Teniente*. I cannot."

"Why?"

"No stone left."

"Hmmph, so I see. Let your father hold your rifle and run up there and put two stones the same size as last time and an arm length apart."

I handed my rifle to my father and ran up the wash to where my target had been. I found and pulled two stones the size of a man's head out of the brown sand and gravel and placed them like I thought the *teniente* wanted them. He was watching me with his soldier glasses, and when he saw me look his way, he motioned for me to come back.

When I returned, Father gave me my rifle back and the *teniente* said, "Shoot them as fast as you can."

"What if I miss?"

"It's all right if you do. I want to see how accurate and fast you are. *Comprende?*"

"*Si, comprendo.*"

"Shoot when you're ready."

I levered a cartridge into its firing place and sighted down the barrel, released half a breath, and fired. The stone didn't break like the other one but went tumbling through the air like someone had picked it up and tossed it. I paid no attention to it as I sighted on the second stone and fired. The second stone didn't break either but showed a clearly visible scrape across its top as it tumbled across the sand and down the bank.

Teniente Beauford grinned and shook his head at me, saying, "Great shooting, Ohyessonna. Really fine shooting."

He turned to my father. "Before I speak with Ohyessonna, I want to ask if you would be willing to let the boy help me with my duties on the reservation? If he worked with me until he was eighteen or nineteen harvests, he could join the army as a scout. I think he'd be sergeant, a chief, in the scouts in no time at all. I wouldn't take him off the reservation, and he could sleep in your lodge as long as he was at my quarters by dawn. There could be times when I have to travel off the reservation for a moon or two. Then he's free to roam as he pleases over the reservation. What do you think?"

My father crossed his arms and stared at the ground a long stride in front of him as he thought about the *teniente's* offer. He paced around on the big slab of rock, where we stood for a while, and then said, "Ohyessonna is much more than a boy. He is ready to be a warrior's novitiate if we were still raiding or at war. He has shown much talent and wisdom in leading others. I think he always tries to do the right thing. I'm not afraid for him to work for you and learn White Eye ways. It's his choice to make."

Teniente nodded, smiling. He turned toward me, but before he could open his mouth, I said, "*Sí, Teniente*, I help."

EIGHT

GLOBE

AS WE WALKED back to my mother's *wickiup,* my father was constantly swinging one hand or the other to drive away the no-see-ums who were trying to land on every small piece of exposed skin. I began to understand why *Teniente* Beauford kept his shirt buttoned up as high as it would go. Even so, he, too, was waving away the no-see-ums as we walked fast for the smoky fire my mother had burning with low sputtering flames as she worked on a basket.

Her smoke kept the no-see-ums at bay, and she offered us coffee from her pot always sitting on or near the fire.

We all took a little coffee, and although we were near the hottest time of the day, the hot brew still lifted our mood.

Teniente Beauford raised his cup and nodded at my father and me. He said, "We are agreed, then, that Ohyessonna can be my helper as long as he wants?"

I looked at Father and nodded, and he gave the all-is-well sign for *Teniente* Beauford, who grinned and said, "I'm very glad we can do this. I've needed a helper for a long time, especially one who can shoot. Have you given any more thought to where you want to live on the reservation?"

Father nodded as he fanned some smoke around his face. "I want to live where there are no no-see-ums, and I want to live away from those who are enemies."

Teniente Beauford, his cup halfway to his mouth, grinned, showing big white teeth hanging behind the big pile of hair under his nose. He took a slurp of his coffee and said, "So does every other chief we bring to San Carlos. There may be places to grow crops here, but they will be close to a river or creek where there are no-see-ums if the water flows too slow. Let's get our horses and I can show you places that might work. You can look for more tomorrow or the next day."

My father stuck out his lower lip in determination, nodded at the *teniente*, and said, "We go now. Come, Ohyessonna. Let us find a good place for my village."

I FELT PROUD to be riding by my father and *Teniente* Beauford as we rode to the agency and then up the Río San Carlos, sometimes on a trail by the río and sometimes up on the flat land above its banks forming canyons that led into the río. After a hand above the horizon, we saw several pieces of land that could yield crops but in my father's eyes were too close to the río and the no-see-ums. We came to a place called Peridot Mesa, which was covered with blooming desert plant life that gave much beauty to the land, and there were several places where crops of corn or small grain might be grown. If we lived on the other side of the fields away from the río, the no-see-ums wouldn't be as bad.

Father said, "This is a good place. Still, I want to see where else we might live."

Teniente Beauford made a half smile, half playful frown. "These are the best places for growing your crops. We can go on up the río because there are other canyons and bluff tops where you might want to live and grow your crops, but they're all close to places where the no-see-ums grow big and mean. The only other places that I know of are off to the northwest near Bucket Mountain and a little mining camp. There is land for pasture there but little else. You'd get your water from a spring or well, and you'd have to ride twenty miles in one direction to the agency for your rations."

My father frowned, crossed his arms, and turned, looking around the countryside. "Hmmph. For this day, put my village here. I still want to see this place you call 'little mining camp.' Maybe you have scout who will show Ohyessonna and me the way there?"

Teniente Beauford took a little box filled with small thin skins he called "papers" that were all attached together on one side—he called it his "little black book"—and a small stick with a black point he called "pencil" from his coat pocket. He kissed the pencil tip and then made tracks in the little black book, which he said meant that most of Peridot Mesa was ours. It was much land and covered with blooming weeds and gourds. It was fertile enough to grow our crops.

When he finished making tracks in his little black book, he put it in his pocket and said to Father, "This mesa is now assigned to you and your People for growing your crops. I send a man at dawn to go with you to the little mining camp. If you see something there that you'd rather have than this spot, then I'll make it yours to work. I want Ohyessonna to learn his way around the reservation, so I ask that he goes with you. Then the next day, he comes to my quarters and begins his work for me. Is this good for you?"

My father nodded. *"Ch'ik'eh doleel.* We ride with your scout at the rising of the next sun to this little mining camp."

Beauford made the all-is-well sign, and we rode back to my father's village. *Teniente* Beauford left us at his quarters at the agency and said he would expect me early during sunrise sun after next. I made the all-is-well sign, and we rode to the back side of our canyon, where we had roped off a corral for our horses. Father handed over his pony to me and went to Mother's fire. I unsaddled and brushed our horses down with handfuls of dried grass before I carried our saddles and my rifle to my mother's *wickiup*, where she had a venison stew cooking that made my stomach growl at its great smell. She sat talking with Father, and her eyes brightened when she saw me. She looked at my father and said, "Are my men ready to eat?"

He grinned. "Bring us food, woman. We're hungry."

The sun had fallen behind the mountains, painting the clouds in soft, dappled oranges, reds, and purples. It was a beautiful evening as we watched the sun set and heard children laughing and playing close to the río. My little brother and sister appeared as if by magic as soon as Mother began spooning her stew into Father's gourd. They knew respect demanded that Father and I be served first, and they sat down to patiently wait.

THE SUN GLOWED in a great golden arc hiding behind the mountains to the east, giving the mists rising off the Río Gila a warm yellow glow. The birds in the brush near the top of our canyon's mesa had been chirping and eagerly gathering in crowds flying from one bush to another. I sat with my father at my mother's fire after my father and I had prayed to *Ussen* and bathed in sage smoke. She poured us her strong coffee mixed with ground piñon nuts.

The birds suddenly stopped their chatter and a quiet, expectant stillness surrounded us. I faintly heard a horse moving down the canyon trail through the mists. Then rider and horse appeared as though I was seeing a ghost. It was a buckskin pony ridden by a young San Carlos warrior dressed in a shirt, long pants, a vest, and a hat with a big brim—clothes like White Eyes wore. I liked his clothes. I wished I had some like them. He stopped at the edge of our camp to talk to a woman working by her fire on her morning meal. She eyed him suspiciously at first but seemed to relax when I heard him say something about Toga-de-chuz. She pointed him toward us.

The young warrior dismounted and, leading his pony, walked toward my mother's fire. My father stood with arms crossed and watched him come. The young man stopped a respectable distance from our fire circle and made the all-is-well sign. My father made the same sign. The young man said, "I am Tlodilhil (Black Rope). My friend *Teniente* Beauford asks that I show Toga-de-chuz and his son a good way to the place where the White Eyes have a camp and scratch in the dirt like badgers looking for *pesh lickoyee y klitso* (white and yellow iron, specifically silver and gold)."

My father pointing at himself and then me said, "I am Toga-de-chuz, and he is my son Ohyessonna. Come, join us for morning coffee and food before we ride." Tlodilhil smiled and nodded as Father motioned for him to sit to his left. I stayed where I was as Mother brought our guest a cup with white dots scattered over its blue surface and poured him coffee.

As we waited on my mother's morning meal, my father and Tlodilhil talked. Father asked him questions about the land and about his background. Tlodilhil told us he grew up on the western side of Fort Apache in the area around Cedar Creek. His uncles taught him woodcraft, desert survival, and how to hunt the large animals like black-tailed deer, elk, and bear. He said he had yet to face a bear but had taken deer and elk.

Coffee finished, Mother gave us gourds filled with steamed, baked heart of mescal, juniper berries, and a thick piece of mesquite bread. Then she and my younger brother and sister joined us. Tlodilhil was a serious, even-tempered young man. I could tell he wasn't more than two or three harvests older than me. Father and I liked him, and over the next two or three harvests, we became the best of friends.

After we finished our meal, Father and I walked up the canyon to get our ponies while Tlodilhil waited for us with his buckskin by the trail up to the canyon mesa top. Soon, we rode up out of the canyon and Tlodilhil led us on a narrow trail winding through the mesquite, cholla, prickly pear, graythorn, and many other plants with which I was familiar. I wiggled around in my saddle to see where they were relative to our canyon and to ensure I knew how to find the good patch of graythorn I saw, knowing that my mother would want to pick the berries when they were ripe and I wanted to eat them.

Our trail pointed toward a big, gray stand-alone mountain in the distance, and Tlodilhil set a steady pace in its direction. We passed an open gate made from newly cut wood. Tlodilhil said it marked the new edge of the San Carlos Reservation. Before now, its place had been much farther up the wagon road toward Globe. The White Eyes moved back the edge of the reservation after they found silver and then gold. They didn't want any dispute over land holding gold. The agency chiefs had agreed to the boundary change without checking with the people whose land it was. It was desert, but it didn't seem right to me or my father to take our reservation land without first asking the People.

We came to a wagon road after three hands on the horizon. Deep dust in the ruts showed its heavy use. I asked Tlodilhil about this and he said it was the main wagon road from some of the other little mining camps into the mining camp named Globe. It was fast becoming a town filled with all kinds of trading posts, White Eyes, *Nakai-yes*, and places to buy whiskey.

We began passing White Eye *casas* that, as we approached the camp, were built closer and closer together, and White Eyes passing us on the road gave us looks that said we shouldn't be there. Tlodilhil saw those looks and soon turned off the road to ride up into the foothills to the north. We crossed a couple of shallow canyons and, climbing out of the second one, rode to the top of one of the next-higher hills and looked west into a wide canyon where the wagon road we had followed passed through. It was like looking at an anthill.

Men in miners' clothes crowded the main street, while others dressed more like storekeepers passed among them. Men in the stores came out rolling barrels of supplies to wagons parked nearby. There was a line of men waiting to go into a building that I learned later was called the Assay, Claims, and Records Office. Women—in long dresses with hats of cloth on their heads and followed by small children—talked to other women or stared in windows of the trading posts standing shoulder to shoulder along the road. Other women walked without children, their dresses in many shiny colors and hats with great bows on the front or in arrangements of fancy feathers and flowers. Near the end of the street, in the backs of trading posts, were places where men and women with narrow slanted eyes rubbed big buckets of clothes against boards with rippling metal surfaces, which my father said made them clean. I didn't understand this. Our women beat cloth with stones in a creek to make them clean. On the other side of the road as it left the town was a corral that held several head of cattle behind a big building where the White Eyes kept their horses and mules out of the sun. My father said they called the building a "barn" when I pointed at it. I had never seen such crowds coming and going except when we had a great feast. It was exciting to watch what was happening on the wagon road, and I wanted to come soon to wander around alone.

NINE

HELPING *TENIENTE* BEAUFORD

WE RODE UP to my mother's fire just as the setting sun painted the western sky in many shades of orange, yellow, red, and purple, and the frogs along the Gila's bank were tuning up. We invited Tlodilhil to join us for Mother's evening meal, but he told us there were chores to do for the *teniente* before he slept and thanked us much for offering him so much. He said he would ride again with us someday soon, swung up into his saddle, and rode toward the agency. Neither my father nor I had any doubt that Tlodilhil would stop by *Teniente's* lodge and tell him what he thought of us. I hoped Tlodilhil gave the *teniente* a good report on us, and after watching the two of us ride together and occasionally talk about the reservation, Father believed it would be a good report.

The next morning, just as dawn was driving away the eastern stars, I squatted next to *Teniente's* door, shivering a little in the cold desert air, and waited for him to come out. Soon his door creaked open and his big dark outline in front of yellow light from a kerosene lamp filled the doorway. He saw me and grinned. "Oh? Are you here?"

"*Sí*, here, *Teniente*."

"I'm headed for some personal business out back in the little house. Go on in and make a fire in the stove and put some coffee on. I'll be back shortly. Then we can decide on our breakfast." He disappeared in the shadows toward the back of the house while I made a fire in the stove where orange coals still glowed. I made the coffee in a big, speckled iron pot like I had seen Mother do many times as I grew to manhood.

Teniente soon returned and smiled when he saw me squatting by the stove door and heard the coffeepot bubbling. He put on and buttoned up his shirt, stuffed the bottom in the top of his pants, and brought his suspenders up over his shoulders and straightened and smoothed their wrinkles until they appeared to blend into his shirt, doing a perfect job for a well-dressed cavalry officer. I watched him closely. I secretly hoped I could wear some fancy clothes after I was old enough to join the scouts and he would show me what to do and how to choose good clothes.

"Are you warm enough squatting by that stove, Ohyessonna? You think the coffee is ready?"

"I'm warm enough, *Teniente*. The pot has been bubbling. Water is black. It's ready."

The *teniente* sat down at a table where he had papers with many black tracks. He pointed to a shelf behind me where metal cups were stacked. "Pour me half a cup and let me see how it tastes."

I poured him half a cup and watched as he blew the steam off the coffee and took a sip. His face immediately wrinkled in a frown. "Damn! That's hot, but good. How did you learn how to make good coffee?"

I shrugged my shoulders. "I watch Mother many times. She always makes good coffee. Always strong. Father likes strong coffee."

"You're a very observant kid. You might live a long time in this land of your fathers. My guess is you're wondering why I'm here in your land in the first place."

I was surprised he said this, and I was curious. "Why you here, *Teniente*? Why all the Blue Coats here?"

He took a swallow of coffee and smiled on one side of his face.

"It's a long story, you won't understand now, but when you're older you'll know what I mean. In my younger days, I fought the Blue Coats for my father's land, but they won the war, so I joined the Blue Coats, and they sent me out here."

He nose pointed to the cups on the shelf behind me. "Take one of the cups on that shelf. It'll be yours while you're my helper. Make the fire and coffee every day like you did this morning and I'll be happy."

He watched me get a cup, pour the coffee, and frown like he did because it was hot. He laughed and nodded.

He took a slurp and smacked his lips. "It's hot, ain't it? Now where was I? Oh yeah. I got here about two moons after the Fort Grant massacre and just before *Nant'an Lpah* arrived in Tucson. I was in the Fifth Cavalry and we chased Eskiminzin, *Capitan* Chiquito, and many others all over the country. Then the

Great Father in the East, President Grant, sent a man who didn't know anything about fightin', Vincent Colyer—come to think of it, he didn't know much about Apache either—to choose land for reservations as much to protect your People as mine, and I admit he tried to be fair. He's the one that made a little reservation for your People around Aravaipa Canyon.

"The next year, *Nant'an Lpah* had his soldiers organized to go after the Apache, but General Howard appeared at Camp Grant on a mission from the Great Father, and that made *Nant'an Lpah* put his plans on hold again. Howard held a peace meeting at Camp Grant to explain what the Great Father wanted. After the talks, where some bitter enemies agreed to keep the peace, Howard said the Great Father wanted to give them a place with plenty of water, and that place was where the Río San Carlos ran into the Río Gila and there would be enough land for your People and the White Mountains. Eskiminzin and *Capitan* Chiquito thought that might work, but before they moved their People from Aravaipa Canyon, they decided to serve as scouts for *Nant'an Lpah* to learn if he was worthy of their trust."

Teniente Beauford smiled and leaned forward in his chair, carefully holding his coffee.

"That's what made your father want to stay away from those two. He didn't see Apache killing other Apache for the Blue Coats as any way for an Aravaipa treating other Apache unless they were enemies. You may know this already, but your papa was ready to separate your band from *Capitan* Chiquito's over this, and it wasn't long before he took you and his People and ran for the Galiuro Mountains.

"Major Randall, who was the big chief for San Carlos, had orders from the Great Father to bring all the Aravaipa to San Carlos, and he was sending out cavalry troops to find the scattered ones. I had gotten good enough at rounding up the scattered bands that the major let me pick my own scouts and go where they led me. In your papa's case, this meant straight to the Galiuro Mountains. And it wasn't long before they picked up your trail and found you. You know the rest of the story since then."

I nodded I understood. I liked the way *Teniente* Beauford explained all the threads that pulled us to San Carlos.

He leaned back in his chair and said, "*Nant'an Lpah* was after the Yavapai chiefs Chuntz and Delshay. His scouts and cavalry found and destroyed the winter *rancheria* of Chuntz, but Chuntz lost none of his People and they had disappeared. A woman had seen the Blue Coats coming and sounded the alarm.

One of the scouts, Nantaje, said that he knew of a cave in the Salt River Canyon that could hold many Yavapai and he would lead them to it as soon as he could find what the White Eyes called the Dog Star.

"The soldiers and scouts found the cave entrance a thousand feet off the floor of the canyon in the early morning light of the day we White Eyes call 'twenty-seven December.' Studying the cave, it was part of a cliff overhang, forty feet deep and about a hundred feet wide. It didn't appear possible to challenge those inside the cave."

I had heard Father talk about the great cave of the Yavapai and how they believed it couldn't be breeched. In Father's opinion, the Yavapai were right. But they were wrong.

Teniente Beauford sat thinking for a little while as I stared at him before he said, "They were asked twice to surrender, but they were so sure of their position they replied with answers like, 'We're not fools, Blue Coats. You'll never get in here. Go away.' After the fightin' started, the scouts shot volleys of bullets into the roof of the cave that ricocheted into the people below. Before long, there wasn't any return fire. Some soldiers charged the cave from the wall of rocks in front of the cave opening. They were ready to carry the fight to the Yavapai, but few were alive—seventy-six were dead, thirty-five of them women and children dead or wounded. They say you could hear babies crying and there were moans from bodies protected by those who had fallen, but that was all."

In my mind, visions of all those people killed and wounded and piled together on the floor of a cave grew like sunlight on a close mountain, and I felt like my stomach wanted to throw away all I had eaten the night before. To murder people like that just wasn't right. It must have been the reason the Blue Coats used scouts to do their dirty work. *If I'm ever a scout, I won't kill people like that.*

Teniente Beauford took another swallow of coffee, smacked his lips, and said, "Damn. That's good."

He thought for a time, staring out his window at the brightening day. "Officer friends who were there have told me *Capitan* Chiquito showed great bravery and leadership all during the fight. They say that *Nant'an Lpah* was so impressed with his bravery and fighting skill that he's asked the Great Father to give him the Congressional Medal of Honor, the Americans' highest award for bravery in war. And you know what? They'll give it to him."

Capitan Chiquito and Hashke Bahnzin went back to their *rancherias* in Aravaipa Canyon and talked about leaving the canyon for San Carlos. When my father learned this, he decided it was time for his little band to move to Peridot Mesa and avoid any arguments with *Capitan* Chiquito and Hashke Bahnzin, or so it seemed, over land use and who should camp where.

Teniente Beauford set down his cup with a thump that jarred me out of my reverie over what my father might do when *Capitan* Chiquito and Hashke Bahnzin decided to leave Aravaipa Canyon for San Carlos. He said, "So let's get to work. I want you to understand that you won't be paid by the army like a regular striker. I'll pay you out of my pocket because you'll not only help me but mostly be doing chores a striker wouldn't do, like delivering messages for me or listening to what's being said on the reservation or who is making or heading for trouble."

"That sounds like being a spy, *Teniente*. I won't be a spy."

He slowly shook his head. "No, I don't think so. If you were a spy, you wouldn't want people to know you were listening. Whatever you hear, you listen like you normally do, and that's it. But if you think it will affect the reservation, then you must tell me what you heard for the good of your People. *Comprende, amigo?*"

I nodded. *"Sí, comprendo."*

"*Bueno.* I know there are a lot of things you're not yet skillful at, but you'll learn. Your capability with a rifle will be a big help if one of the bands goes renegade and breaks out attacking anyone in its path. One of the things you need to learn well is the tongue of the White Eyes. Your Spanish as we sit here and talk is good enough, but if you want to lead scouts, you need to understand your commander's words and thoughts. That means you need to speak 'English,' which is the White Eye tongue, and I'll teach it to you. It'll be hard to learn and master like a lot of things you need to learn. Just don't give up when you make a mistake. Think of your mistakes as opportunities to learn more about something you want to know. You'll be fine. Now, let's go to the shed, for my saddle and bridle, and I'll show you how I want you to saddle my big horse."

I smiled. At last, there was real work to do for the *Teniente*.

Over the next eight moons, I didn't do that much for the *teniente*. The agent Clum had him busy on long rides chasing renegades or helping him talk to army officers about how best to bring in renegades and their punishment.

One sun *Teniente* told me he was gone too much or too busy chasing renegades for me to stay around and to look for other work. I told him I was proud to know the lessons he had taught me and that I would find work in Globe.

When I told *Teniente* this he smiled and said, *"Enjuh."*

TEN

RUSTLERS

WHEN I WAS sixteen, I worked as part of what the White Eyes called "the fall roundup." I had been driving Cross S Ranch cattle out of the canyons near Bucket Mountain and heading them toward the big herd for counting, sorting, and branding. Jimmy Gibson, an old cowboy who mostly worked cattle and whom I helped sometimes when I wasn't breaking horses, came loping up to me just as I had a small herd started out of the canyon. He moved out of the way and stopped so the cattle and the dust they raised would pass while he rolled and lit a cigarette as I came down the canyon.

As I approached, he blew his smoke up into the still, slowly clearing air and grinned. "Howdy, Kid. Boss Man sent me over to tell you he's sold ten steers to Redmond."

I had done some herding work for Redmond, a butcher in Globe, and we were friends. Redmond paid me good wages for me driving cattle and sheep to his slaughter holding pens. *Teniente* Beauford and then Redmond had been teaching me to speak the White Eye tongue. I could now understand most of what was being said even if I didn't yet do well speaking in the White Eye tongue. Beauford was no longer a Blue Coat. Now he was San Carlos Reservation Agent John Clum's chief of tribal police, but he still paid me well to run errands for him.

"Boss Man already has 'em picked out, and they're in that canyon we use for a holdin' pen about a mile from here toward Globe. Boss has already been paid his money for the animals and wants you to take the steers to Redmond, who asked that you bring 'em 'cause he's a-wantin' to talk to you."

I nodded and gave Jimmy the two-finger hand wave off the edge of my hat like I had seen White Eyes often do.

THE BIG GREEN tumbleweeds growing beside the canyon trail saved my life. I was driving the cattle out of the holding pen canyon when my pony stumbled and slumped to its knees. I heard the distant crack and echo of a long-range rifle shot while I was already diving from my saddle to land on my chest, raising a cloud of trail dust. I rolled between two of the tumbleweeds and turned so I could see down the trail where the cattle went. As the dust cleared, a cowboy, one I had never seen before, came riding a light tan mustang. Reins in one hand, his rifle in the other cocked and ready, butt resting on his hip, he came trotting up the canyon toward my fallen pony. He stopped twenty-five paces from my pony, stood in his stirrups, and looked over the area around me. I was lucky. The dust, churned up by my pony's fall, hid the trail I made when I had crawled behind the tumbleweeds and made it hard to see up the trail where I hid. The cowboy started walking his horse toward my dead pony, my rifle in its scabbard and other gear in plain sight. My hand closed on my knife handle in the sheath stuffed behind me on my belt. I heard a distant yell, "Come on. We got to get these steers down to Gar's holdin' place. They's a buyer waitin', and we're supposed to deliver tomorra."

The cowboy settled into his saddle, turned his pony with a side jerk on the reins, and disappeared in a plume of dust down the trail I had been following. I listened until I heard no cows or men and then pushed between the tumbleweeds to get back to my pony. I had to struggle to get my best saddle, bridle, and rifle free, and then hide them in the brush where I could find them again.

I pulled my rifle from its scabbard and ran up the canyon's side. On the canyon ridge, my soldier glasses would let me see where these cowhands were taking the cattle I was supposed to deliver to Redmond. I found a good place to sit, comfortable and well hidden, in some stunted junipers. I watched where they were taking my stolen cattle with soldier glasses Beauford had given me. I wondered where they were taking my cattle.

It was the time of no shadows in the Season of Large Fruit. Even sitting in the shade, water poured from my body as though I was in a sweat lodge, and thirst began to grow in the back of my mouth. I watched two cowboys herd the cattle into a low spot behind a hill next to the road. The cattle were all but invisible from that location. After making a rope corral to keep them from wandering out of the low spot, the cowboys made a little smokeless fire, unsaddled their horses, and waited for beans and coffee to cook. I knew the path to take from studying the land down to the hill and where the cattle grazed. They would never see me when I went after the cattle.

The run down to the low place was an easy one. I kept my body conditioned with good hard runs every sun. As my father often said, "A warrior has to keep his strength and wind even if he works for the White Eyes."

Running, I tried to remember where I had heard of this boss, "Gar," before and tried to reason why he would want to risk being branded a thief for stealing the few steers I was herding. *Teniente* Beauford had said a rancher named Gar sold the reservation cattle for ration distribution. So, Gar was stealing and using other ranchers' cattle to sell to the Apache. He could always claim Apache were at fault for bungled deals if he was caught. Clever man, Gar.

My mind began to race. I counted the days left until the next ration release. There were three. That meant Gar planned on keeping the cattle for a sun before driving them down to the agency. If the Cross S Ranch wasn't supplying cattle this next ration day, then how would the agency explain the buying of cattle with mixed brands. They couldn't unless the agency chief said the cattle were acceptable. Clum was the agency chief, and he always spoke with a straight tongue. Then I realized Clum had taken Hashke Bahnzin and the chief of the Chokonen Chiricahua—Cochise's eldest son, Taza—and eighteen others he picked to ride the iron wagon east to show the Great Father and other White Eyes "what Apache were really like." Clum and our People were supposed to be gone for two moons. That gave Gar plenty of time to try out different stories on the man Clum left in charge to get money for differently branded cattle and never deliver his own. If I had anything to do with it, Redmond would get his cattle and the Apache their rations from the true seller.

I WATCHED THE cowboy camp all that afternoon and evening and in the bright glow of the moon rise from behind mountains. They talked and laughed and enjoyed their meal of coffee and beans and bacon they cooked hanging on sticks they angled over their fire. How the White Eyes could eat nasty pig meat I never understood.

One of the cowboys pulled a whiskey bottle from a saddlebag, twisted the stopper out, and took a long pull before he handed it to the next man. The bottle went around the circle, with two of the men refusing to drink. I saw later that they were sentries for the first part of the evening. The bottle came back empty to the man who had shared it and with a curse he hurled it far into the brush. Soon the two who drank were sprawled in their blankets snoring and the two sentries were on either side of the rope corral. I could have slipped into their camp and killed them all, but I knew that if I did, the White Eyes would make all the People suffer. Instead, I found a long, dried yucca stalk and put a sharp point on it before carrying it with me to their camp.

I waited until the moon was approaching the top of its arc, eased up to each sentry sitting near the rope corral, both fighting to stay awake, and cracked them on their heads just hard enough with a rock to ensure they slept a while. Then I went into their camp and made sure those who slept stayed asleep.

I took their horses first, led them to the road, and sent them trotting toward Peridot. I cut the corral ropes and, gently poking the cattle with the sharp point on the yucca stalk, drove them to the road before prodding them in the direction of Globe. When I was out of range of the cowboys hearing even a steer bawling, I picked up the pace by poking the cattle harder to make them trot. Some tried to wander off into the brush by the road, but I was faster. They soon learned to stay on or close to the road as I hurried them along. I had to chase two or three out of mesquite-filled *arroyo*s that were determined to get away from me. The mesquite thorns tore my shirt and pants and made my scratched arms and face look like I had been in a fight with Cougar. I didn't care about the shirt, pants, and scratches all over my body. At least I'd gotten back the cattle owed to Redmond.

As the growing sunlight hid the stars in the east, I had the steers headed down the big trail in Globe that passed by Redmond's corral. I ducked down a space between buildings and ran to Redmond's corral. I was lucky he had no stock in the corral, allowing me to open its big gate into the street as my steers approached and wave their leader into the corral with the others following.

I walked over to the watering trough, pulled off my ragged shirt, and washed the dirt from my body. Drying off, I jumped a little when I heard Redmond's familiar voice behind me.

"What's happened to you, boy? Looks like you've been in a fight with a wildcat."

I looked over my arms and belly as I turned toward Redmond and grinned. "Yes, look that way. Gar ranch cowboys take cattle you buy. I get them back and bring them to you. Chased three, out of *arroyo*s filled with mesquite. Mesquite thorns attack, but I still get all ten here. You ask Boss Man for me to bring. Say you want to talk. I here. We talk?"

Redmond was a strong man with big muscles in his arms and a smile that never left his face. He said, "Coffee's on the stove. Come on and have a cup with me and I'll find you a shirt. Kinda chilly out here. Then I'll take you to breakfast in the little café up the street and we'll talk. How's that?"

I grinned and nodded. *"Ch'ik'eh doleel."*

WE WENT TO Libby's Café just up the street from Redmond's meat shop. He bought me a big steak meal that included beans, bread, and coffee. Everything was on the big heavy bowl-like thing made from baked clay the White Eyes like to eat from, which they call "plate."

I was full from the meal at Libby's Café, getting sleepy, and thinking about asking Redmond to let me sleep for a while in his hayloft. He pulled out his cigarette fixings and offered them to me, but I shook my head. Redmond rolled his *tobaho* in a thin paper, lit it with a match, took a deep draw, and blew the smoke toward the ceiling.

"Speak, Redmond. I listen."

Redmond smiled. "I was just thinking about you here in the last moon. Your People say you're a great shot—I believe your People but I've never seen you shoot. You're good at herding the stock, and you just proved it again this morning getting my steers away from Gar's cowboys and then on foot driving them to my corral. You're known as one of the best horse wranglers around. You often help Beauford with his tribal police chief duties. For one so young, you show a lot of capability. What do you think you'll do when you reach a man's age?"

I hadn't thought about it much so just shrugged my shoulders at Redmond's question. "Not know. Whatever is there for me to do, I do."

Redmond nodded. "I thought so. You ever think about being a scout for the army?"

"Father say he no kill other Apache if no enemy. Father speak good words. I no scout for army."

"Yes, your father is a wise man. But he said 'no kill' unless an Apache is your enemy. The way the army uses scouts, you can agree to be a scout while the army fights your enemy and then choose not to be a scout."

This sounded like a good way to fight enemies. "Hmmph. Light behind your eyes. Why you tell me this?"

"There's a man I know who is chief of scouts for General Crook. He's coming down to Globe from Camp Verde for supplies today or tomorrow and is always on the lookout for men who would make good scouts. I think he'd want you in the scouts. He's been fighting the Tontos for General Crook. I'd like for you to meet him. It'll get you some work in a harvest or two. What do you think?"

I thought about it as I rubbed my face to feel where I needed to use my tweezers to pull a hair.

"What name this scout chief?"

"Al Sieber."

ELEVEN

AL SIEBER

I WAS TAKING a swallow of hot coffee and started choking when Redmond told me the man coming to Globe was Al Sieber. Sieber was known everywhere in Apacheria as a White Eye warrior no Apache wanted to face in battle or go man-to-man in a fight. He was deadly with his rifle and his big bowie knife.

Redmond grinned when he saw my face. "I know Sieber has a reputation for being a hard man, but you have nothing to fear from him or his scouts. You're livin' peacefully at San Carlos, helpin' White Eyes on their ranches, and making your own farms. You've got a lot of light behind your eyes. I think Al Sieber could teach you a thing or two."

"Hmmph. That is so. I speak to Sieber. First want sleep in your hayloft. You let me sleep there?"

"Of course. Sleep in my quarters if you want." I shook my head. The lodges of the White Eyes made me nervous. But I didn't know why. "I know you've been without sleep for the past two or three days. Go on over to the hayloft and get some sleep. *Adios, mi amigo.* I'll get you when Sieber comes."

"You good *amigo*, Redmond. I go now. *Adios.*"

IT WAS DARK. I could hear the distant screams of women and children and the occasional pop and echo of rifle fire. Father sat up in his blankets, staring off into the darkness and trying to decide where the sounds came from. Then another voice came out of the darkness. "Kid! Kid! Are you awake? Come on down. Mister Sieber wants to meet you."

My eyes snapped open. A blade of light made by a crack between two of the barn's siding planks sliced into the hayloft where I slept. Dust off the hay floating through the blade of light looked like flakes of *pesh klitso*. The blade of light tilt showed the time was halfway between the time of shortest shadows and darkness. I heard the low rumble of men speaking to each other. I shook the sleep mists from my mind, rolled to my feet, and yelled to Redmond, "I come."

I brushed the straw off my clothes and out of my hair. Grabbing my rifle, I climbed down from the hayloft. I saw the outlines of two men standing in the glare of the open barn door and walked toward them. Redmond grinned and motioned toward the other man. "Kid, this is the man I was telling you about. Al Sieber. Al, meet Kid."

Sieber was a little taller than most White Eyes. He wore a hat with a short crown and wide brim, and he carried a big revolver in a holster on a cartridge belt strapped around his waist. There was a big, ugly bush of black hair under his nose, and he had hard eyes, black like polished obsidian, that missed nothing in their unassuming stare. Al Sieber was well dressed. I liked men who dressed in nice clothes like Beauford. He grinned and stuck out his hand, and we gave each other a couple of good pumps.

"I'm always happy to meet young men who have light behind their eyes and will one day lead their People. I can see Kid has a claim on both accounts."

Sieber's words were too smooth for me. I just nodded.

"I think he'll make a good scout, but scouts need to be able to shoot with some speed and accuracy. Most Apache can shoot. Redmond, you told me Kid is a great marksman. I'd like to see a little demonstration of his marksmanship."

Redmond nodded and pointed toward a place on the far side of a holding corral fence a short distance from the barn corral. The far side of the holding corral fence looked like it fronted the entrance to a deep *arroyo*. "If you shoot at targets down that *arroyo*, you ought to have a range of about three hundred yards. That long enough for ya?"

Sieber took a long draw off his cigarette and, blowing the smoke out his nose, nodded. I hadn't paid much attention to it before, but Redmond had fixed up the *arroyo* into a shooting range when he wasn't slaughtering stock and making meat for his butcher shop. We walked across the big holding corral to the place Redmond indicated. Redmond had cleared the brush on both sides of the *arroyo* and positioned little mounds of dirt in a straight line down the *arroyo* middle. They were about fifty paces apart. The White Eyes called the mounds of dirt "berms," the first good rainstorm certain to wash them away. On top of each berm stood a target--a can or an empty whiskey bottle.

Redmond nodded down the *arroyo*. "I've already put some bottles out for targets. They're about fifty paces apart. You can just barely see the glint off the one at three hundred yards. Which one would you like Kid to use for a target, Al?"

Sieber leaned against the corral fence post and stared down the *arroyo* at the little berms. He scratched the whiskers on his cheeks and made a face as though deep in thought. "I can barely see that last bottle in this light. Why don't you just shoot the most distant one you think you can hit. That '73 Winchester you're carrying would have to shoot like the bullet was following a rainbow to hit anything at three hundred yards. I don't think that would be a fair test of your shootin' ability. Go ahead and take a shot."

I wasn't sure what Sieber was talking about when he mentioned bullets and rainbows, but I was sure I could hit the most distant bottle. I flipped up the ladder sight and set the notch piece for three hundred yards. Sieber watched me with one raised eyebrow that said I was going to make a fool of myself. Redmond had a little smile. He'd heard enough stories about my shooting from others that he believed he knew what I could do.

I levered a round into my rifle's chamber, sighted at the distant glint and, at half breath, squeezed off a shot. There was a short delay, and then the bottle at three hundred yards exploded into many shattered pieces. Sieber's jaw dropped. He looked at me and then back where the bottle was and shook his head. "Kid, that was one great shot. Can you do that for the bottles at one and two hundred yards?"

I nodded, set the ladder notch to two hundred yards, levered a new round and, taking aim, shattered that bottle. I flipped the ladder sight down since the rifle was accurate without it at one hundred yards, levered another round into the firing chamber, and quickly blew that bottle into many sparkling pieces of glass.

Sieber looked at me and grinned. "You don't miss, do you? What's your longest shot?"

I grinned back at him. "I no miss. Use Father's buffalo gun. Shoot deer on edge of clearing in Galiuro Mountains canyon. Father say best shot he ever see with his buffalo gun."

Sieber laughed. "I expect that it was. You must have exceptional eyesight. Did you use a telescopic sight on the rifle?"

"Hmmph, I see far. Nothing on rifle. What is telescopic sight?"

Sieber smiled and shook his head. Redmond said, "It's a big eye like those used in soldier glasses and another little eye attached to the ends of a long brass tube. That combination makes things easier to see and hit at a long range. Your People call this big eye in a tube a 'Shináá Cho.'"

I stared at the ground for a short time, thinking about what Redmond had just told me. "Yes, I can understand why a Shináá Cho would be big medicine on or off a rifle."

Sieber studied me with a critical eye like a man looking over a horse before he buys it. Shadows began settling over the land. Soon darkness would be on us. He crossed his arms and looked first at Redmond and then at me. "I think Kid here has the brains and skills to be a first-class scout, even a sergeant of scouts, but he looks a little young to me. How many harvests are you, Kid?"

"Not sure. I think sixteen or seventeen."

"Have you been a novitiate on a raid with the warriors?"

"No. No go with warriors. *Capitan* Chiquito and Hashke Bahnzin come to San Carlos before my time to go. Days of raiding and war no more on San Carlos Reservation."

"I think you're too young to be a scout now. We can work something out in a harvest or two. I'd sure like to see you in the scouts. I think you have a promising future. Thanks for bringing this young man to my attention, Redmond. Be seeing both of you sometime in the future about his career as a scout."

Redmond nodded and gave Sieber a two-finger salute off his hat, and I did the same. I still didn't know what the two-finger salute was supposed to represent.

IN THE GROWING darkness, Al Sieber disappeared up the street where White Eyes bought whiskey by the glassful. Those places didn't allow Apache inside. Redmond told me he would send a paper with tracks to my boss man about why I was late returning and that I had stood proud for the Cross S and driven the cattle owed him without losing any after Gar tried to steal them. I stayed that night with Redmond and, early next morning after bread and coffee, left to rejoin the fall roundup.

I first returned to the canyon where I had left my saddle, bridle, and other things. I saddled a pony in the remuda and rode back to the big herd where I knew I would find Boss Man at the place the White Eyes called "chuck wagon camp." He looked angry and ready to tell me I worked no more for the Cross S, but I handed him the paper with tracks Redmond made, and after he read the tracks, he grinned. He said there were more cattle in the canyons where I had been before, and I should return to that job. While I was gone, he and some of the boys were going over to have a little talk with señor Gar and his boys. By this time, I knew, when a White Eye said he planned to have a little talk with someone, it usually meant a fight was coming. I was happy he couldn't take me because I was on a pass from San Carlos. I wanted no part of White Eye arguments or fights that might follow.

I spent another ten suns finding and driving cattle out of the canyons that were part of the big herd. After cattle separation by owner, branding and other work completed what the White Eyes called fall roundup. Boss Man paid me and said he wouldn't need me until next Season of Little Eagles—he called it "spring." A new roundup for cows and calves born in the Ghost Face started then. I told him I'd be back. I was glad to do what I wanted during what was left of the Season of Earth Is Reddish Brown and Ghost Face.

My mother and father were glad to see me return to her *wickiup*. But after three days of mostly playing hoop and pole, I was restless. I sat thinking about what to do, when my friend Jimmie Stevens, whose father was a White Eye and mother a White Mountain, came looking for me. Jimmie was a good friend. He had worked with me to learn the White Eye tongue, and with the help of Redmond and Beauford, I had learned to speak the White Eye tongue good.

Sitting by my mother's fire, its flames and shadows painting his face, Jimmie had an evening meal with us and answered Father's questions about what was happening around his father's ranch. After we ate, he said he wanted to get some venison for his mother and asked if I was interested in going deer hunting with him in Aravaipa Creek Canyon. He had heard that black-tailed deer were especially plentiful there. I looked at my father. He smiled and nodded. The wave of his hand said "go."

TWELVE

HASHKE BAHNZIN'S DAUGHTER

AS THE SUN drove the stars into hiding, Jimmie and I saddled our ponies and picked out two mules from Father's livestock to pack the meat we would take and the supplies we carried. We tied our ponies and mules near my mother's *wickiup* and ate the bread and drank the coffee she gave us before we rode over to the trading post to get things we needed before leaving for a hunt that might last several suns.

THE COLD EARLY mornings made it feel good to stand close to the heat from the big potbellied stove in the middle of the room at the trading post. The men had a cup of coffee while warming their backs. They told stories about discovering farming tricks and hunting and fighting adventures they had in the old days. Their women looked at cooking pots, axes, and felt the cloth they could use in making shirts and dresses. They needed and wanted a plethora of supplies now that they were settled on the reservation and didn't have to leave them running from enemies.

My ammunition reserve was getting low. I needed to buy more cartridges after the usual shooting contests with the roundup cowboys and the shooting demonstration for Al Sieber. Jimmie wanted an axe, a cast-iron skillet, several well-made *reata*s, and vegetables for our cooking pot. While he waited for the clerk to gather his order, I studied the new rifles the sutler had acquired.

Particularly interesting were the new trapdoor Remington carbines like the scouts used that shot the big .45-70 cartridges.

The front door creaked open and closed. I turned to see Hashke Bahnzin walk in nodding and smiling to everyone. One of his wives and a beautiful girl, who must have been their daughter, followed him. Her hair was loose and fell to the middle of her back, her skin was lighter than mine, her nose thin and well formed between almond-shaped eyes, and her lips reminded me of the White Eye symbol for a heart. I didn't recognize her. Then, in a flash of memory, I recalled the little girl Hashke Bahnzin had saved the night of the Camp Grant attack. She was a pretty child, now fast growing into a beautiful woman, but there had not yet been a womanhood ceremony for her. Even though agewise she was still a girl, she acted like a grown woman. I wanted to know her. Someday after her womanhood ceremony, she might want me for her own. If we became friends soon, I could be at the head of her line of suiters. I wondered how I could meet her.

While his wife and daughter went to look over bolts of cloth, Hashke Bahnzin nodded to and spoke with every man around the stove. One of them got him a cup and poured some coffee that he accepted with a grin and said something funny to the men, who all laughed. He saw me looking at the new rifles and walked over to the counter where I stood.

As he approached, he said, "Ho, Ohyessonna. I learn of your skill and courage in stopping Gar's men from stealing Boss Man's cattle. How you do this?"

"Ho, Hashke Bahnzin. Boss Man sold cows to Redmond the White Eye meat maker at Globe and told me to drive them to his corral. The Gar men attacked me and killed my pony, but I was lucky to get away and find a hiding place where I watched them take the cattle to hold near the wagon road. When it was dark, I took the cattle back, drove off their ponies, and on foot drove the cattle to Redmond's corral. *Ussen* was with me."

"Yes, I think your Power was with you." He saw me glance toward his fine daughter and grinned. "I think there is much more to this story than you tell me now. You come to my *wickiup* and tell me all during an evening meal prepared by my woman and our young daughter? Although she is still a girl, she learns to cook for and serve great warriors, she will be a fine wife someday."

Very little escaped Hashke Bahnzin's sharp eyes. It was my turn to smile. "I will be much honored to eat at your fire and tell my story. My friend Jimmie Stevens and I now gather supplies for a deer hunt in Aravaipa Canyon. When we return, I visit your fire?"

I glanced at his daughter, who was looking through a stack of blankets nearby. She had her ear turned toward us, and I saw enough of her face to see her smile. I was happy to see that smile showing that she favored me. It was hard to keep my mind on what Hashke Bahnzin was saying.

"Yes, I hear there are many blacktails this year. It'll be good to take some before Ghost Face. Why don't you come eat at our fire in ten suns. I doubt your hunt will need to last longer than five suns."

"*Enjuh.* I will be at your fire in ten suns with the stories of how I beat Gar's men and our hunt." I could tell Hashke Bahnzin's daughter was still smiling when he nodded, took a big swallow of coffee, and said, *"Ch'ik'eh doleel."* He nodded at me and walked back over to the coffeepot and the men around the stove.

JIMMIE AND I loaded our supplies on a mule. I checked to be sure I had the pass Beauford had given me to be off the reservation, and we headed for Aravaipa Canyon. It took us most of the day to get to old Fort Grant riding cross-country following canyon and ridge trails that led toward Aravaipa Canyon Creek and then to Río San Pedro. There was still plenty of water in the creek as we followed it upstream until we came to *Capitan* Chiquito's old camp where so many of our People had died. We followed the bosque up the creek past the big grave of many killed in the massacre.

The shadows were long and the night air was growing cold when we stopped to camp at what the White Eyes called a mile of distance from the massacre site. We unloaded the horses and mules, and while Jimmie dug a deep pit for the fire, I led our horses and mules to a grassy place near the creek, let them drink all they wanted, rubbed them down with handfuls of grass, and left them hobbled to graze as they pleased. I carried bridles to the fire where Jimmie had a bubbling pot of stew working and coffee bubbling in an old pot that he carried with him. He already had his bedroll spread out next to the fire and my things stacked nearby. I laid out my bedroll as the stars filled the black velvet above us and poured myself some coffee. It was a routine we had followed when we had hunted and roamed all over San Carlos and Fort Apache in earlier harvests.

It was peaceful sitting under the cottonwood and sycamore trees, watching the stewpot bubble, and listening to the slow burble of the creek below us. Jimmie stirred his stew, poured more coffee in his cup, and offered me some, but I shook my head, and he sat back on his blanket to stare at his fire.

"Hashke Bahnzin must be interested in you as a son-in-law for that good-looking girl of his after he invited you to come to a meal his wife and daughter would fix."

I smiled. "I was just thinking today that I would like to know more about her. She's a fine-looking young woman even if Hashke Bahnzin says she has not yet had her womanhood ceremony. I guess Hashke Bahnzin being chief and not one to put up with foolishness makes the men think twice before asking him to court her."

Jimmie put a couple of gourds on the ground side by side and, taking the stewpot by its handles, poured some stew into the two gourds before returning the pot back to a flat stone next to the fire. He gave me a spoon and motioned for me to take a gourd.

He had taught me to eat like a White Eye with a spoon, the way his father had taught him. I thought it was a better way to eat than with our fingers like most of the People did. I knew that was the way soldiers ate, and after talking to Al Sieber, that was the way I wanted to eat too. Jimmie always made good stew. He had brought a piece of beef with him for this trip and had bought vegetables and chile peppers at the trading post that morning to make the stew. The pot he fixed tonight would last us through most of the hunt.

Jimmie took a bite of his stew and nodded. "As my father says, 'Good, mighty good.' When do you think you'll be ready to take a wife?"

"Not for a long while. I want to be able to support her and give her children when she wants them."

"How you do that?"

"Join the scouts. I have already talked to Sieber about it. He has seen me shoot and said I would be a good scout for the army. They pay scouts the same as a regular trooper, give you guns and ammunition, and you must make your mark to serve three to six moons at a time, and you only serve when you want. Maybe I join for three months sometime next harvest. Of course, you worry about some fool putting a bullet in you, but every warrior must do that. It is part of living."

Jimmie nodded. "Sounds like you've been thinking a lot about scouting. Why?"

I thought for a moment, tapping my spoon against my gourd and watching the fire's shadows ripple across Jimmie's face. "Times are changing. Having to live on a reservation, I will never get to be a warrior and go on raids like my father unless I became a renegade but then the scouts would chase me into the ground."

Staring into the fire, I shook my head. "I will never be a renegade. But I can still act like a warrior, still do good things for my People as a scout. Make a good life for my family, and still free to do what I want unless my Blue Coat chief says do only his way."

We finished Jimmie's serving of stew, and while he cleaned up around the fire, I went to check on the horses and mules. They seemed a little nervous and kept looking up the creek. I stood still, listening and sniffing the breeze that came down the canyon. Nothing. If coyotes or wolves were creeping around, our smell and the fire would keep them at a respectful distance and the horses and mules were strong and could defend themselves.

THE NIGHT WAS peaceful, the only sounds coming from the creek burbling, frogs in chorus, and little animals scrambling in the leaves and dry grass. We were up before dawn, had more stew, and loaded the horses and mules to head up the creek. We waited for the sun to run the long shadows off before we moved. I led the way since I knew the trail well from my childhood days. I had decided that the best place to camp while we hunted was at the beginning of the wagon road just above us where I had raced Gonshayee four harvests ago. When we finished our hunt loaded down with venison, we planned to take the wagon road out, a much easier way for the mules than trying to follow the creek path.

We looked for deer signs along the way and saw many signs but no deer. Halfway to the start of the wagon road, we came to a bench that came from the north wall that narrowed the creek bed and made the water run faster as it passed the bench. An old cottonwood tree, long dead, most of the branches gone and its big roots sticking out like twisted broken fingers, had swept downstream and beached on the bench. I noticed it because something had torn much of its bark off. There were torn places about a rifle long in one place on the trunk near the roots. Those places gleamed like white, new wood in the sun.

Jimmie took one look at it and said softly, "Big cat."

THIRTEEN

EL TIGRE

JIMMIE WAS RIGHT. It looked like a big cat had been sharpening its claws on the old cottonwood trunk. I slid off my pony to look for tracks. The ground was soft. I expected to find good sets of tracks as I studied the thin grass and leaves on the ground near the trunk and the ripped-up wood from the claw sharpening. I wasn't disappointed. About two long paces from the trunk, I found a good set of tracks, made like the cat had stood there while studying the trunk. The deep impressions made by its hind feet showed it jumped from that spot onto the trunk where it did its claw sharpening. I motioned for Jimmie to come see the tracks. When he approached, I kneeled and spread my fingers to cover one of the front paw prints, and the prints were larger than the hand span I could generate. I had hunted cougar and followed their tracks before, but I had never found tracks this big.

Jimmie shook his head. "These tracks not from Cougar. Too big."

"What do you think made them?"

"I see these in Mexico three or four harvests ago when *mi padre* takes me hunting in Sierra Madre near Río Bavispe on west side of *El Tigre* Mountains. These are tracks of *El Tigre*. *El Tigre* big and strong. Makes no sound when it moves. No afraid of men. Kill what it wants when it wants. Hunt this canyon because many deer here. This is mucho far north for *El Tigre*."

"Do you think he'll leave us alone while we hunt? Otherwise, we'll have to hunt and kill it first."

Jimmie shrugged his shoulders and looked up and down the creek. "Who knows what it might do at any time. We must watch for it and hope that it doesn't decide to come after us."

I nodded and pointed my rifle upstream. "We go."

ON THE WAY to the start of the wagon road, we found many deer tracks. I didn't remember so many tracks this time of year when my People lived in this canyon. Despite the many tracks, we saw no deer by the time we reached the starting place of the wagon road. The beginning of the wagon road was on a big bare place near the intersection of a narrow canyon that fed Aravaipa Canyon from the north where the big canyon turning east made a big arc that became a southwest canyon for the creek. A series of hills formed big *arroyos* from the creases of the hill intersections on the west sidewall of Aravaipa Canyon. One hill intersecting another on the west side of the canyon formed large *arroyos* that fed the creek when it rained. On the east side, the hills were higher and wider, and the *arroyos* fewer. Across the creek from where the wagon road began was a bench between fifty and eighty paces wide and filled with tall trees. The bench ran southwest two long rifle shots—about five hundred yards—until the creek bed hooked southeast, where it turned into a small rapids flow and then, at the bottom of the falling water, formed a deep pool before continuing southwest.

Jimmie and I rode around the bench and creek area for two hands on the horizon and could find no place we thought would protect us and our horses and mules from *El Tigre*. We decided to make our camp on the bench in a small clearing with tall trees on opposite sides. Each tree had a limb three or four rifle lengths above the ground and was big enough to support our weight. Our plan depended on the livestock warning us when *El Tigre* was nearby. As soon as we heard the mules or horses warning of danger, we would climb a tree and watch for *El Tigre* when he came after a horse or mule. When we saw him, that would be his end. For the venison we took and prepared, we would haul it high up in the two trees until we were ready to leave.

We made a fire pit near the middle of the clearing and spread our blankets by our saddles nearby. I rubbed down the horses and mules and hobbled them so they could graze on the thin grass but not wander much while Jimmie worked at the fire. The sun was just a glow behind the western mountains and the canyon filled with shadows on the west side but sent enough light to see ground features on the east side. Jimmie had heated the stew and mesquite bread and served it up in our gourds. After a long day looking for paw prints and deer tracks and thinking of a plan to protect ourselves from *El Tigre*, the hot stew and bread was a feast we would long remember.

THERE WAS STILL enough stew for a morning meal before we hunted. Using a *reata* swung over a high limb, Jimmie hauled the stewpot up into a nearby tree. He brought out the coffeepot to make coffee to go with our morning meal and hauled our supplies high up in another tree. I took the axe and chopped a good pile of wood and brush that would make a big fire and should be slow to burn down. We rinsed and washed our gourds in the creek and washed the sweat of the day from our faces. I felt good despite the tinge of worry about the big cat.

We checked our rifles in case we needed them in the night and to ensure that they were in good shape for the hunt tomorrow. The creek sang its song as it burbled over its big stones. Bats swooped and dove after insects. Moths fluttered about the fire, and a bird squawked as it sailed up the creek. A sense of peace settled on us.

I said, "How many deer do you think we should take before we return to San Carlos?"

Jimmie lifted his brows and shrugged. "I'd say no more than four. It'll take us at least two days to butcher and save the meat and salt down the hides so our family's women can make them into fine leather. Too bad we're not married to good women. We could have brought our wives with us to work on the meat and hides while we hunted."

WE TALKED A while longer about how important women were to their men and ranching on the reservation as the sun's glow faded into the blackness of the night sky. If we had not had the fire light, it would have been darker than the inside of a cave. The only light in the night sky was the great white river of stars that glowed in a great arc rising out of the notch on the horizon formed by the canyon walls. As the fire burned down to big, glowing orange and red-and-black embers, we wrapped in our blankets with our rifles loaded and knives handy, hoping we could get some much-needed sleep.

I was at the edge of floating off to sleep when, from the top of the hills north of where the canyon turned east, a deep and throaty coughing-like roar echoed down the canyon like a string of coughs. "Uh, uh, uh, uh," and then lower, "uh, uh, uh." I felt the hair on the back of my neck stand out and goose bumps cover my arms. I wanted to run to a safe place, but there was no place to go. I heard Jimmie lever a round into his rifle, and I did the same. The mules began to bray. Something bad was coming. I rolled to my knees, threw more wood on the fire, grabbed a stick, wrapped my bandana around one end and held it in the fire until it was in flames, and used it like a torch so I could see the horses and mules. I laid my rifle on my blanket and told Jimmie to cover me while I went to bring the horses and mules closer to the fire. I didn't have to go far before I found them standing shoulder to shoulder in a line facing the stream. I raised my torch to give enough light to see the opposite bank of the creek.

I had to clench my teeth to keep from throwing down my makeshift torch and running. On the far bank not more than thirty paces away was the biggest cat I had ever seen. Muscles rippled everywhere on his legs and shoulders and massive chest. His fur covered with big, dark rosette spots with orange spots in the middle had the light-orange color of good White Eye whiskey. The orange color faded into white on his underbelly, where black spots and black stripes had collected. He was bigger than any cougar I had ever seen. It wasn't much taller than a big cougar, just a lot more of him. His eyes were like red circles of glass reflecting the torch light as his tail swung slowly back and forth like a stick used on a dried hide to keep time at dances. He ignored me, leaned down, and lapped the cold, clear creek water. Finished, he stood and stared at each of us, taking our measure, before giving a couple of low "uh, uh, uh" coughs and then wheeling to bound off into the darkness. My mouth was dry, and my knees felt like water as I turned to lead the animals back to the fire where Jimmie waited with his back to the fire and his rifle butted up against his shoulder, ready to save us all.

I tied the horses' and mules' halter lines to a *reata* I stretched and tied between two trees close to the fire. I sat down next to the fire and took a couple of long swallows from the canteen Jimmie tossed me before tossing it back to him.

"What do you think, Ohyessonna? Should we stay or get out of here at first light? If we stay, *El Tigre* will surely come after us after we make meat."

Without thinking, I let my gut feelings lead me and shook my head. "No cat runs me off. We have as much right to hunt here as he does. Leave if you want. But I'm staying even if it comes down to just me and him fighting it out."

Jimmie grinned. "You won't be alone to fight it out with that cat, *mi amigo.*

I'm staying too. We have two mules. One ought to be enough to carry the meat and hide of *El Tigre*."

The fire was burning down again. I nodded, said, *"Enjuh,"* and lay back on my blanket, my hand on the lever of my rifle.

WE WERE UP before the sun brought much light to the west side of the big canyon across the creek from where we camped. There were no more roars that night from *El Tigre*, and after eating the rest of the stew while the rising sun lighted the canyon, we were ready to hunt and decided to try the bosques on the north and south sides of the canyon soon after it turned east. Jimmie chose the north-side bosque, and I took the south side. There were many more blacktails in the bosques on both sides than I had guessed. Within two hands of the sun above the horizon, we had each taken a fat doe and returned to camp. We tied a crosspiece between the two trees where we had the *reata* line stretched to tie the horses and mules to after we had faced *El Tigre*. We hung each doe from the crosspiece to do the skinning and meat butchering. We laid out the meat cuts we took to dry then salted and wrapped the skins for future work by women much more skilled in skin tanning than either Jimmie or me.

As the shadows grew long on the northwestern hill sides of the canyon, Jimmie washed in the creek and started a fire to cook us a fine meal of mesquite bread, steamed mescal, yucca tips, venison on skewers roasting over the fire, and White Eye potatoes baking in the outer edge of the fire's coals, and coffee. It didn't take him long to cook it all either. The smell from the roasting meat dripping in the fire made our bellies roar from hunger and sigh from satisfaction when we ate it with Jimmie's other good things.

After we ate and enjoyed our coffee, we cleaned up around the fire, and Jimmie added a handful of weeds he had collected that burned slowly with enough smoke to cover up the smell of the drying meat and what was left of the carcasses. In the middle of the afternoon, I chopped a big pile of wood and brush for our fire. Later, I carried the offal from both carcasses up the big *arroyo* coming into the creek from the northeast and spread it out. I hoped *El Tigre* would find it and leave us alone in our camp. I also washed both our ponies in the creek to get the blood smell from the deer off them. To keep it away from prowling animals, we wrapped the drying meat in pieces of canvas and hauled it up to the crossbar we had used to butcher the carcasses, and we decided to take turns being a camp sentry to guard our animals and meat since either might draw all kinds of predators, including *El Tigre*.

THE STARS SAID it was two hands before dawn. A half-moon casting cold white light down the canyon was falling in the southwest. Mists were rising off the burbling creek, their little clouds that looked to me like wanderers from the Happy Place. Jimmie had kept watch until the moon started down toward the southwest from the top of its arc when he shook me awake for my turn at sentry. Now he slept wrapped in his blanket and breathing with soft puffing breath.

We had climbed to a small flat place up an *arroyo* a little south of our campfire, where we could see most of our camp and spread our blankets for naps. Nothing happened while Jimmie watched. Staring into the mists rising off the deep pools in the creek and then drifting down the canyon, I began to think we had wasted half a night's sleep watching for nothing. I noticed the low noise from the flowing water sounded different, like little splashes made by something crossing the creek.

I stared toward the creek where I thought the sounds began. Slow and deliberate, *El Tigre* stepped out of the mists in the creek and jumped up the low bank near where we had our fire. I thought, You're not going to take our hard-earned meat. You'll die if you try. I toed Jimmie awake. When he sat up, I put the edge of my fingers to my lips for silence and nose pointed toward *El Tigre*, who stood looking over our camp. Jimmie nodded and reached for his rifle.

El Tigre studied the trees and crossbar where we had hung the deer carcasses and where we put the meat we were trying to save. Watching him stand there, head tilted back looking at the crossbar, I had no doubt he was deciding the best way to get the meat we had labored long and hard over. It was time to put an end to our fear and his tyranny. We had to kill him when we took our shots. Neither of us wanted to hunt an outraged, wounded killer waiting for us in the thick brush below. I leaned over to whisper in Jimmie's ear. "We need to fire at the same time. You aim for his chest. I'll aim for his head. Shoot when I say fire." Jimmie nodded.

Moonlight fell on *El Tigre*, making him a perfect target. I put my rifle sight in the center of his head. I heard Jimmie whisper "Ready." I said, "Fire," but *El Tigre* started lowering his body to make ready for a jump. My bullet grazed his head between his ears and his eyes, leaving a black stripe of blood. I was aiming for an eye. Jimmie's bullet hit him somewhere in the upper part of his thick, muscular neck. It whirled and dropped to the ground where it lay, reflex moves making its paws tear at the air, and then it was still.

Jimmie and I stared at each other and shook our heads. We headed down the *arroyo* to look over the big cat, proud that we had taken such a ferocious animal. We were out of sight of our camp a little while as we worked our way through the trees and brush from the *arroyo* where we had hidden to the cleared area where our fire and the crossbar butchering rig stood. As we approached where *El Tigre* lay, my stomach suddenly felt like I had eaten some bad meat. *El Tigre* was gone. A blood trail led into a dark hole through the brush from where *El Tigre* fell. We heard his low grunts—uh, uh, uh, uh—deep in the brush.

Jimmie said, "He ought to die pretty soon. Let's take the meat we have and get out of here."

I shook my head. "As soon as it's good light, I'm going to follow his blood trail and finish him off. If he dies in a sun or two, it'll be in agony. If he lives, he'll be the death of many innocent people. I can't let that happen to anyone."

Jimmie nodded. "You're right. Stories of your courage will last around the council fires for many harvests. Rest and I'll make some coffee."

Two or three times before daylight, we heard "uh, uh, uh" coming from the nearby brush. We watched with eyes straining against the disappearing darkness. Jimmie's coffee was good and strong and helped me grow more alert. When the coming sunlight spilled over the canyon walls, I loaded my rifle, made sure I had my knife in its sheath stuck in my belt behind me and, raising my hands, said my morning prayer to *Ussen*.

The hole into the brush where *El Tigre* and I crawled was still dark from all the shadows, but I had enough light to tell where I was headed. My arms and knees were soon bleeding from the thorns and sharp rocks I had to crawl over following *El Tigre's* blood trail toward the canyon wall. After crawling a while, I saw a large bright spot in the brush not far ahead. I figured the brush was thin there, and when I pulled myself toward it, I saw *El Tigre* lying in the middle of the bright spot, calmly waiting for me. When he saw me, he snarled, showing his long saber-like teeth, and gave his "uh, uh, uh." It was his challenge—only one of us would leave alive. As he strained hard to rise, I pulled back the hammer on my rifle to full cock even as I wanted to break out of this tunnel of thorns and shadowed light and run, but I knew I couldn't. My heart was thumping like a big drum. I could feel it in my ears. I was breathing like I was running fast. Steady, steady, don't be a fool or a coward. I took a deep breath and slowly let it out. My hands were sweating but steady as I brought the rifle up and made a shot picture on his head as he reached forward to pull himself toward me. I squeezed the trigger and my rifle roared, leaving my ears ringing and me hard of hearing. The shot hit him between his eyes. It was a good death, one worthy of a great warrior.

FOURTEEN

CHITA

JIMMIE AND I decided that meat from two deer and the big *El Tigre* was about all we wanted to handle before returning to San Carlos. We were careful skinning *El Tigre*, as its hide would make a beautiful quiver and bow case fit for a chief. We finished drying and smoking all the meat, scraped and salted *El Tigre*'s hide, and loaded our mules with the meat and hides. We made it back to San Carlos in two suns and in time to have an evening meal with my mother, father, and the crowd of my younger brothers and sisters, who stared at us as though we were chiefs. They begged us for stories about our hunt in Aravaipa Canyon, and we told them.

Father, very happy we had taken *El Tigre* before it came north to San Carlos, said he had heard stories of such animals but had never seen one. We spread out *El Tigre*'s hide by the flickering red-and-orange flames of my mother's fire. My family stared at it in disbelief. I asked my mother if she could make a bow case and quiver out of it. She slowly nodded and said, "I'm happy to do this for you, my son, but what of Jimmie and his share?"

"Jimmie and I have talked. He says that since I went into the brush after *El Tigre* alone, I alone should have its hide and meat. I said he should have at least half the meat, and he agreed to take it."

My mother smiled. *"Enjuh.* I hear camp gossip saying that, in two suns, you will join Hashke Bahnzin at his fire for a meal prepared by his wife and woman child, Chita. Does the gossip speak true? Do you have any interest in the chief's daughter even though she is not yet a woman?"

I, too, smiled. "Gossip speaks from too many mouths. Hashke Bahnzin's daughter is a sweet girl who knows when to be silent, has a bright smile, knows how to speak with adults to ask serious questions, and works hard with her mother. I want to know her better, and from eyes she used to watch me at the sutler store, I think she wants to plant a seed in my mind that I would want her after her womanhood ceremony. Hashke Bahnzin invited me to come to his wife's fire, where she and her daughter would fix us a fine evening meal. I would never say no to such an invitation. I want to see her in her best clothes, eat a meal she helps prepare, and let Hashke Bahnzin size me up for a possible son-in-law."

Everyone around my mother's fire was looking at me and smiling. They all knew this was a new test for me. Perhaps when it was over, I would be first in line to court a chief's daughter. My mother's eyes twinkled with delight. She said, "I'll work on the *El Tigre* skin and make Hashke Bahnzin a fine bow case and quiver if you like. But it will take a moon or two before it's ready. Will this please Ohyessonna?"

"Yes, Mother, it would please me very much."

"*Ch'ik'eh doleel.*"

JIMMIE LEFT EARLY the next morning hoping to get to his father's ranch on Eagle Creek before dark with his share of the meat. I knew he was anxious to see the fine pony his father had promised to find him. We promised to get together again after spring roundup, which was five or six moons away. I hated to tell my friend *adios*, but we both had work we needed to finish and people to see.

In the evening of the second day after Jimmie and I returned from Aravaipa Canyon, I followed the path to Hashke Bahnzin's big *wickiup* for an evening meal made for us by his wife and young daughter. I dressed in my best White Eye clothes, which they called a "three-piece suit." I liked the look and feel of these suits and had used some of the money I made wrangling horses and herding cattle to buy one. I didn't yet have enough money to buy one of the little machines to wear in a vest pocket that followed the sun's path with numbers and was much more accurate than guessing the number of hands above the horizon we normally used. But I expected that, with another warm season or two, I would make enough money to buy one and, as the White Eyes said, "Be on time."

As I approached the *wickiup* of Hashke Bahnzin, I saw him sitting near the fire, watching his wife and daughter in their feast clothes busy with pots of good things and working to grill the beef that dripped grease into the fire and filled the air with a smell that made every mouth in the village grow wet with hunger. Hashke Bahnzin's woman said something to him and nose pointed in my direction. Wearing his big-brimmed White Eye hat, he turned, saw me and, smiling, waved for me to come to the fire and take a seat to his left, a place of honor.

"It is good for my eyes to see the young warrior Ohyessonna. You want my woman to pour you coffee she mixes with ground piñon nuts? Very good. She tells me soon we eat."

I smiled and nodded. "Yes, Hashke Bahnzin, piñon-nut coffee fills my mouth with very good flavor."

His daughter poured the black water from the coffeepot resting on a stone in the fire circle into a *Nakai-yi* clay cup. She handed it to me with a smile showing teeth whiter than a long-dry playa. The smoke from the cooking fire rose slowly high in the still air before bending over and flowing parallel to the ground like a high black río in the direction of the Gila.

After I took two swallows of the hot coffee, Hashke Bahnzin said, "Ohyessonna, there are many words on the village breezes about the successful hunt you and Jimmie Stevens had in Aravaipa Canyon. Tell us of your hunt."

Although his wife and daughter were busy around the fire, I was glad to see that they kept their ears turned toward me while I told the story of the hunt and of the *El Tigre* we had taken in addition to two black-tailed does. When I got to the part about crawling through the hole in the brush the wounded *El Tigre* took, the girl and her mother stopped to listen, their fingers covering their open mouths to hide their excitement. Hashke Bahnzin was smiling and nodding through most of the story. He knew exactly the fear and excitement Jimmie Stevens and I felt in dueling with *El Tigre* and how lucky we were to bring him in with ourselves unscathed by his mighty claws and jaws. I finished, and Hashke Bahnzin shook a fist and said, *"Enjuh.* You young men did very well for yourselves."

His wife signaled she was ready with the night's meal and Hashke Bahnzin gave a little wave of his hand that she should serve it. His daughter brought me a gourd filled with a very nice piece of roasted meat, slices of steamed dried mescal, mesquite and acorn bread, potatoes, and green chiles. Every part of the meal was perfectly done, and after wiping our hands on our moccasins, we were given bowls of mixed dried juniper berries, walnuts, and acorns we finished with another cup of piñon-nut coffee.

The women were quick to finish up around the fire, and when I had eaten all I wanted of the dried berries and nuts, Hashke Bahnzin flipped his right hand toward me and said, "Now tell us what happened with the Gar rancho cowboys. I'm anxious to learn how one lone Aravaipa Apache took back his cows from four cowboys who stole them. Speak. I will listen."

I knew the wind carried much gossip about me and the Gar cowboys. I was careful to tell all the details, including why Redmond had asked that I bring the steers he had purchased from my boss man, and my shooting demonstration for chief of scouts, Al Sieber. Hashke Bahnzin listened, smiling with bowed head and nodding in agreement when I made decisions that worked out well. His wife laughed at my tricks against the cowboys, and his daughter's sparkling eyes never left me.

When I finished my story, Hashke Bahnzin shook his fist in the air and they were all saying, *"Enjuh, Enjuh."* He said, "Let us smoke, Ohyessonna. I have a thing of importance to discuss with you after my women leave us." This talk was unexpected, and I wondered what the chief had in mind.

His wife and daughter nodded, rose, and disappeared behind the blanket covering the door of their *wickiup*. I knew they would be listening on the other side of the door blanket. From his vest pocket, Hashke Bahnzin pulled a White Eye sack of *tobaho* and papers to make a cigarette. He lit the cigarette with a flip of his thumbnail against a red-head match, smoked to the four directions, and handed it to me, and I also smoked before handing it back to him to finish and toss the last bit in the fire. The stars were out, brilliant points of white light glowing on a black sky of velvet. They were scattered on both sides of a stream of stars looking like a milk river rolling over shallow water shoals. Night birds called and squawked all along the río.

Hashke Bahnzin listened to the night for a little while and then turned so I could see his face lighted by the flickering yellow-and-blue flames in the fire pit. "Seven or eight harvests ago, we were living peacefully in our villages when, one night, the *Tohono O'odham*, goaded on by White Eyes and *Nakai-yes*, attacked us in our sleep when most of the men were off on a hunt. You know the story well because you and your father heard the screams and yells of women and children being slaughtered from your camp up the creek and came running, but it was too late to do anything. I was sleeping in the camp with my family when I heard the attackers' war whoops and women screaming. I jumped up to see what was happening, but when I pulled the door blanket back, I was hit by a glancing blow by a war club that stunned me and knocked me off my feet. Where I fell, I covered my little daughter. The raiders never saw her. I was stunned for a short time but managed to stand, see two of my wives had been killed, pick up my little daughter, and run to a hiding place along the creek while the murderers shot bullets into ones they had already killed. My little daughter never made a sound, never endangered us as any child might with cries of fright. She is special, Ohyessonna. That child is the one who helped her mother tonight. Her name, if you don't already know, is Nahthledeztelth, whom we fondly call Chita."

I nodded I understood his words. Where, I wondered, is he going with this?

"Chita thinks you are a great warrior, bound to be a chief someday. So do I."

"Only coming suns and moons will tell, Hashke Bahnzin. I only do the best I can with what I'm given."

He nodded. "I agree. This is true of every man and woman. For some more than others, *Ussen* has given Power—supernatural power. I think *Ussen* has given you the Power you need to be a great chief. This is my proposal. I promise to give you Chita for a wife after her womanhood ceremony. I will not require a great bride gift for her and will consider no offers from others. She will be yours if she still smiles on you. What do you think of my offer?"

I was astonished. I liked little Chita, but she wasn't even a woman yet. Women could be much different than the girls they were. I had heard of fathers mutually agreeing that their children would marry when it was appropriate, but the agreement was between the fathers, while the children were young and had no say-so in the arrangement. Now I had the offer to marry a chief's daughter after her womanhood ceremony. I had planned to just study her from a distance and learn about her until she was ready to marry. Dare I let this opportunity get away?

"Hashke Bahnzin, you need to understand that I plan to work with the Blue Coats as a scout in the next harvest or two. Does this make you want to withdraw your offer?"

"No. *Capitan* Chiquito and I were scouts for the Blue Coats at the Río Salt cave fight. We were doing the right thing then, and I believe you'll do the right thing, too, when it comes to your People."

I felt at peace with his answer. "Hashke Bahnzin, your offer is a great honor. Yet I ask that you let me think on it and ask *Ussen* for wisdom before I give you my answer. I will not keep you or Chita waiting a long time. Before my answer, I would talk with her in your sight. I want to know her well. If she speaks with me as I think she will, I will give you my answer and later come to your lodge with a bride gift."

Hashke Bahnzin grinned and made the peace sign, waving the palm of his hand parallel to the ground, and said, *"Ch'ik'eh doleel."*

FIFTEEN

AL SIEBER RETURNS

SITTING BY MY mother's fire drinking coffee with my father, I told him what had happened at Hashke Bahnzin's lodge and what he had offered me. Father's grin stretched all the way across his face, and his raised brows left deep canyons of wrinkles in his forehead after he heard my story. "Ho! Ohyessonna, Hashke Bahnzin recognizes that one day you'll be a great chief." Father held up two fingers. "The two major things a chief must have are first courage and second a heart for his People. You have both. He wants you in his family. Don't make him wait long for your answer."

I shook my head. "I treat all chiefs with respect, Father."

"From what I've seen, his daughter will be a fine woman, the pride of any chief." After hearing my father, I had no doubt that I would tell Hashke Bahnzin I accepted his proposal to promise me Chita for a wife after her womanhood ceremony.

Cold Ghost Face winds blew from the west and north, keeping the People in their *wickiups*. Sitting in the orange-and-yellow glow of their fires, the women made baskets and things for babies. These they sold at the sutler's store. The men cleaned rifles and dried blood from arrows, replaced the arrows' feathers when needed, made new arrows and bows and toys for their children, and gambled and lounged around the big potbellied stove at the sutler's store, where they told stories of revenge taken and battles fought.

I had three or four meals with Hashke Bahnzin and his wife and daughter. We talked of many things. I sensed he was always probing my mind to learn how I thought and what I would do in battles or in domestic trials where I might want to beat my wife. After these meals, he and his wife casually moved toward the back side of their *wickiup* to leave Chita and me alone to speak softly in the firelight and learn more about each other. The more I talked with Chita, the more I liked her and valued her wisdom and growing beauty as the winds battered and shook the canvas- and hide-covered *wickiup*. She wasn't shy, saying she hoped she would be the wife of a chief someday and planned to give him good advice and many children. I always left the *wickiup* of Hashke Bahnzin happy after I visited with him, and more importantly with Chita.

NEAR THE END of the first moon of Ghost Face with its cold and knife-sharp winds, a rider brought me word that Redmond wanted to see me and asked that I come to Globe in the next few suns to talk with him. The next sun, the winds were still and the sun bright and warm. I headed for Globe and, after stabling my pony, found Redmond before the time of shortest shadows. He was trimming a carcass hung from a ceiling beam in his butcher shop. He nodded and grinned when he saw me as I came through his door and motioned me in. "Ho, Kid. No wind, bright sun, a good day to ride and for friends to speak."

I gave him the soldier's hand wave, which the Blue Coats called a "salute." "Yes, Redmond, we friends. You call for me?"

"Come on in and let's sit by the stove a spell where you can warm up after a long ride in that breeze. Have some coffee."

Redmond kept his place cooler than the other places that sold things. It helped keep the meat fresh and the stink of drying blood down. He kept a small stove over in a corner of his shop to provide a little heat and keep the coffeepot hot. I took a cup off his shelf, poured some coffee—Redmond's coffee was always strong and good—and found a chair with a woven cane seat nearby. He slipped off his blood-splattered apron, hung it on a nail in the rough wood wall behind the counter, and poured his coffee before sitting down next to me.

We talked a while about what was happening with John Clum, the new agent on the reservation, the many miners coming to hunt their fortunes in Globe, how his business prospered, and the rumors of how I was courting Hashke Bahnzin's daughter when she wasn't even a woman yet. We had a good laugh about that one. I didn't care what the rumors were and didn't want to say that, in this case, they were close to the truth.

"Redmond, why you say come see you?"

He made a face showing disgust. "I hate to ask it, but I need your help. Most of the ranchers that sell me their cattle, usually at a good price, are shorthanded. Their cowboys are leaving to do some prospecting or maybe work in the mines in and around Globe. The ranchers need every cowboy they can hire. The ranchers will drive the stock I've bought to my corrals but want extra money on the price of their cattle for delivery. That's okay, we've worked things that way for the past few years. This year, there is little money for anybody, and the ranchers are asking outrageous prices to drive a few cattle to Globe. They're charging by the head. I can't afford the cattle at their delivery price, and even if I could, I don't have the buyers I need to pay for expensive meat.

"I'm hoping that you'll agree to drive the cattle I'm buying into Globe for me for a top hand's wage rather than charging me by the cow. I'll give your family and your girl's family an extra supply of meat. And I'll give you a place to live with me in the back of the store if you're no longer fearful of living in a White Eye *casa*. What do you say? Is it a deal?"

I didn't have to think long before I gave the all-is-good sign, waving my palm parallel to the floor. "I can sleep in barn, but I stay. I herd the cattle for you."

Redmond grinned from ear to ear. "Come on, let's get some dinner at the café down the street and decide what to do next."

THAT GHOST FACE, I was often out in the cold and wind all sun driving small herds of cattle to Redmond's corrals. By sunset, I wished I was by Mother's fire listening to stories or making toys for my brothers and sisters, but Redmond was my friend and he paid good money for what I was doing, and at night he continued the job he and Jimmie Stevens had started the previous year teaching me the White Eye tongue. By the time of Little Eagles, I wouldn't hesitate to speak to anyone using the White Eye tongue and had no doubt what a White Eye said to me.

One sun in the Season of Little Eagles, no cows were ready for driving to Redmond's corrals. I sat by the stove drinking coffee and watching riders pass by in the dusty street. Suddenly a White Eye appeared at the hitching post in front of Redmond's butcher shop and dismounted. He looked familiar. It didn't take me long to realize Al Sieber was tying off his big horse and checking his gear before stepping up on the boardwalk to the door. I walked in the back, where

Redmond was working on a side of beef, and said, "Looks like Sieber is back in Globe and headed this way."

Redmond made a little frown and shrugged his shoulders. "I wonder what he's up to. Things have been quiet up north since January. I haven't heard of any raids around the reservation lately, have you?"

I shook my head and turned back to my seat by the stove. It wasn't long before Sieber came inside. When he saw me, he grinned and said in a loud voice, "Well if it ain't Kid. You've grown since I last saw you. Where's ol' Redmond?"

Redmond came through the door wiping his hands on a cloth he called a "towel." "Hey, Sieber, when did they let you out of jail?" They laughed and walked over to the stove for coffee and sat in chairs next to mine as the sun cast shadows of window rectangles on the walls and floor, and dust drifting through the sunlight was sparkling *pesh klitso*. They swapped gossip and tales about what they had been doing. Redmond often turned to me to verify what he said was true or to add to it. When they finished swapping gossip, Sieber looked at me and grinned. "Kid, I'm headed to San Carlos Agency to see ol' Marty Sweeney. You want to ride with me? You impressed me with your shooting demonstration last fall. I'm sure Marty would want to see it too. No doubt Beauford told him what a shot you are. They might want you in the tribal police. I want you in the scouts when you're old enough—it won't take long to make you sergeant. We always need men like you. You won't be old enough to join the scouts until next fall. Now, I can use you as my civilian striker. What do you say? There's lots to learn about the Blue Coats before becoming a scout."

"What is striker?"

Sieber scratched his rough whiskers and said, "A striker helps an officer with his chores when the officer needs to be doing other more important things."

"Hmmph. Sounds like woman's work. What chores?"

Redmond laughed a little, the sunlight reflecting off his cup, and said, "Kid's a lot smarter than you think he is, Al."

Sieber grinned and nodded. "I'm glad he's got a good head on him." He turned to me and said, "Well, chores can be anything from running errands like getting the mail to delivering messages to helping keep track of which company is supposed to be doing something, to even cleaning weapons to saddling and loading animals to setting up a tent and cooking when we're on the trail."

"Hmmph. Sounds like slave work, too, but I ride with you and learn what scouts do when Redmond say I can go."

Redmond nodded and said, "He works for me full time now, Al, but if he wants to learn from you, he can go. I have enough cattle penned up here that I can get through another month without a new delivery. I think by then the cattlemen will want to be selling off part of their herds and their costs won't be so high. I'll keep him on the payroll if you'll let him come when I need him."

Sieber nodded at Redmond and then looked at me. "Is what Redmond says good for you, Kid?"

"Good for me, Sieber."

Sieber grinned and stroked his fuzzy chin again. "Looks like we got us a hand, Redmond. Let's go get some dinner at that café you like up the street and I'll talk about some of the work Kid and I are likely to see. Then I'm going to visit a saloon most of the evening before I retire for the night for a long night's rest. I'll come by this place about sunup to join up with you. Is that good for you, Kid?"

"Good for me, Sieber."

REDMOND PULLED ON a jacket and locked up his doors, and we headed up the street to his favorite café. Al told us things had been quiet through the Seasons of Large Leaves and Large Fruit last harvest and he had spent most of his time in saloons in Prescott or hunting around Fort Whipple and Camp Verde. Many of his scouts had finished their promised number of suns in the army required by "touch the pen" contracts—since most of the scouts couldn't read or write, they just touched the pen of the officer making the black-water tracks representing their names to their enlistment papers. He was going to have to recruit several to keep the scouts ready when trouble broke out, and he said, "I have no doubt that it will." He asked what I had been doing besides driving Redmond's cattle to his pens from the ranches, but I told him little. There were no exciting stories I wanted to tell.

We finished our meal and walked outside. Sieber said as he lit his pipe, "See you at sunrise, Kid. See you my next time through, Redmond."

Redmond smiled and nodded. "Stay out of crooked card games, Al. See you next time through."

Al stalked away, and we watched him cross the road and head up the street for one of the better saloons.

SIXTEEN

MARTIN SWEENEY

SIEBER SET A good steady pace and didn't stop until we were at San Carlos two hands before the time of shortest shadows. He wanted to talk with Martin Sweeney, and he also wanted Sweeney to see me shoot, but I didn't know why. Sieber and I rode over to the agency where a Blue Coat sergeant, whom I recognized from my days with Beauford as Sweeney, was teaching tribal policemen drill commands. I couldn't tell the difference between tribal policemen and scouts except for the men who commanded them.

Sieber guided his pony over to one side of a big rock on a brush-free sandy patch of ground. The agent, John Clum, called it his "parade grounds." Sieber relaxed and, staying mounted, watched the drill, and I joined him. Sweeney saw us and waved but kept up the drill. I had never seen drills before. I wondered if Sieber visited Sweeney to learn tribal police training. I knew Sieber was also looking for policemen good enough to join the army as scouts.

Sweeney's commands were loud and crisp. There was never any doubt of the command.

"Fall *in!*"

The men were standing around relaxed, laughing, and talking. On command, they suddenly formed straight rows of ten men each. They each wore a Blue Coat jacket, their boots shined to give reflections like black mirrors.

"Ten-*hut!*"

They all snapped to standing straight with shoulders back and chest out.

"Dress right—*dress!*"

The men straightened their lines and, within a line, stood an arm's length from the next man.

"Present *arms!*"

Every policeman had a rifle, which they held vertically in front of them, each holding his weapon in the same places along the barrel and behind the trigger guard.

"Right shoulder *arms!*"

Using the same motions, every man laid the barrel of his rifle on his right shoulder and held the weapon's butt with his right hand held at his side.

Sweeney gave a series of these kinds of commands, which the men standing in a rectangular block of five rows performed perfectly. I watched in disbelief. How the Blue Coats made the group of men do the same thing from a single short command was beyond my understanding. But I could imagine the power such commands could give a chief in a battle. I wanted to learn these commands. I wanted to be a chief who knew how to give those commands. If I joined the scouts knowing these commands, the Blue Coats would make me a chief. I needed to watch much more as Martin Sweeney taught those commands.

WE WATCHED SWEENEY drill the policemen for about a hand. Then he dismissed his policemen and rode over to talk with Sieber. I hadn't paid much attention to Sweeney during days when I helped Beauford. I was usually working in Globe or on a ranch. I wasn't around much to help and didn't see Sweeney that often. Now that I studied his face, I saw he had a nose that had been broken and battle scars around his eyes, and red hair streaked with gray stuck out from under his hat. I could tell from the way he handled his horse that he must have been in the cavalry before he left to serve as Clum's number two.

Sweeney gave a little nod to Sieber but was studying me as he said, "Mister Sieber, I ain't seen you in long time. What do you think of my boys drilling? Normally, old Beauford, who's chief of police, works 'em out in drills, but he had to leave with Clum for a little while."

Sieber said, "Them boys looked well trained to me, Sweeney. You fellers is doing a good job with them. When you gonna send 'em to me for the scouts?"

"You ain't seeing none from this side of the fence until the agent, whoever it is, decides he don't need 'em no more. I 'spect that's gonna be a while."

Sieber nodded and said, "I thought so, but you know how shaky things is between the army and BIA. You never know who's gonna control San Carlos. I admit, ol' Clum is more than holding his own. I hear Juh and Geronimo, who escaped Clum, your policemen, and some cavalry when he moved the Chokonen here, are still roamin' and raidin'. If you need any help runnin' 'em down, just let my commander at Fort Apache know and we'll be happy to come." Sieber pulled cigarette fixings out of his vest pocket and held it up for Sweeney to see, and he nodded, caught the bag with *tobaho* and papers tossed to him, and made himself a cigarette. They smoked but never offered me the makings for one. I didn't care. Let the White Eyes smoke to nothing. I smoked for important business talks.

They had smoked about half their cigarettes when Sweeney said, "Looks like you're collectin' Apache. Is this kid a prisoner or a recruit?"

Sieber looked across his shoulder at me and grinned. "No, he ain't neither, but I intend to use him for my striker here pretty soon. I wanted you to see how good he is with a rifle. Why, he could hold his own in a shootin' match with me. You might want to use him for a while with your policemen before he starts workin' for me."

Sweeney made a show of looking me up and down before he said, "Why, he's still a kid. Ain't changed much since he was servin' as Beauford's helper, and for what I don't know. I've seen him workin' around the agency and Beauford told me he does good shooting with a rifle. I don't need or want to be no papa for Apache kids."

Sieber said, "I'm tellin' ya. This one can shoot. You ought to check him out."

I said nothing.

Sweeney grinned. "You found a child prodigy, eh, Sieber? Let's go ask my striker to fix us some dinner. After we eat, then I'll watch what the kid can do, but I don't expect much out of him. He's too young." That last comment made Sieber grin, but he said nothing.

SWEENEY'S STRIKER WAS an old gray-headed man from Hashke Bahnzin's band. He knew how to cook like the best of women, and he served up big white plates filled with vegetables and cuts of meat and hot coffee. He raised his brows and dropped his jaw, surprised to see me. He said my name and nodded when Sweeney introduced us. I remembered him from the time before the Camp Grant massacre, but he had disappeared for a long time afterward. I had no idea what had happened to him and was too polite to pry. Sieber wasn't shy with his questions. We soon learned the old man had hidden in the mountains until he saw Hashke Bahnzin's band come to San Carlos and set up their *wickiups*. He needed something to do after his wife died, and Sweeney had given him a paying job. He was glad to be back with the warriors again, even if it was as a servant for Sweeney.

We finished our time-of-shortest-shadows meal with coffee and a handful of dried berries. When the coffeepot sounded rattled like there was little coffee left, Sweeney told Sieber to tell me to go get my rifle. Sieber shook his head and said, "Tell him yourself. He understands the White Eye tongue and speaks it good."

Sweeney made a face of disbelief and said, "Go get your rifle, young man. I'd like to see you shoot."

I said, "Yes, sir. It is in a holster on my pony. I meet you outside with it."

Sweeney frowned in disbelief. "That'll be fine, son. Sieber, what in hell have you been teaching this kid?" Sieber just laughed.

I pulled my rifle from its saddle holster, put some cartridges in my vest pocket, and met them as they came out the door. We walked downriver until we came to a canyon with a trail that led to the flat land on top. Sweeney turned into the canyon but walked past the trail leading to the top and followed high walls coming together near the end of the canyon. About a hundred yards from the entrance of the canyon, Sweeney told Sieber and me to wait while he went forward and made a stack of flat rocks at several places before he came to the end of the canyon, where he made a big stack of flat rocks and then walked back to us.

He said, "Think you can hit those piles of rocks I put up there, Kid?"

I shrugged. "I'll try."

"Okay, then go for them."

I pushed cartridges into my rifle, levered one into the firing chamber, and put the balls of wax I used in my ears. I said to Sweeney as Sieber watched with a smile, "You point me to your rock piles, and I'll shoot."

Sweeney frowned, the wrinkles deep across his forehead. "You sound like you want this to be some kind of speed test, when all I want to know is how accurate you are with your rifle."

"Hmmph. You point. I shoot."

Sweeney nodded and immediately pointed toward his furthermost stack of rocks. I expected he would do that and was already swinging my rifle in the direction he pointed. I didn't sight on his target more than a two count— thousand one, thousand two—before I fired. Rocks from the top of his pile went spinning and tumbling in a cloud of dust, and the shot's echo sounded like thunder bouncing between the canyon walls. Surprise filled Sweeney's face, and Sieber laughed out loud and slapped his backside. Sweeney pointed to the intermediate rock piles he had created up and down the canyon. They also were short work with my fine rifle.

Sweeney shook his head and stared down the canyon, "Sieber, what did I just see?"

"You saw some of the best shootin' in this here part of the country. I plan to sign him into the scouts in a year or so, or he could be a policeman here. Either way, he can make a real contribution to how we guide and manage San Carlos people and in bringing renegades to justice. I think he'll be a much better soldier if someone like you trains him, rather than those wild bull sergeants I have at Fort Apache. What do you think?"

Sweeney scratched his chin and smiled. "Just how many of these wonder children do you have?"

"Just this one."

They both looked me up and down and nodded.

Sieber said, "Okay, Kid, what do you think? What do you want to do?"

I scratched my chin like I had seen Sieber do when he was thinking, though I didn't have to think a long time on that one, and said, "I stay here, learn from Sweeney. Fight renegades with you."

Sieber grinned and said, "*Enjuh.* I think that's the best training I can give you before you enter the army. You need to stay on this end of the reservation, where you can learn from Sweeney every day."

"My father and family move to Peridot. I sleep there while I work and learn from Sweeney and chief of tribal police, Beauford."

Sweeney said, "I think I already have a job for you, Kid. Every ration day, we get cattle to provide meat for the People and the tribal police are supposed to kill them. Tribal women and old men are supposed to do the butchering. The police are usually busy with other duties and take most of a day to shoot the cattle. I'm thinking with you doing the shooting, we'll save a lot of time. The People ought to get their beef ration a lot quicker. What do you say?"

"Hmmph. I try. Good target practice."

As we walked out of the canyon, I followed Sieber and Sweeney and listened as they talked about what was next in the government's concentration plans to force most of the Apache onto one reservation. If this happened, they knew, and I did too, bad times were coming.

IT WAS AN easy walk back to Sweeney's lodge at the agency. As we approached his quarters, he turned and said, "Come on and I'll show you where you'll be killing beef on ration days." We kept walking and soon came to a circular corral made with adobe bricks. It was about shoulder high so the cattle couldn't see out and the Apache couldn't see in.

Sweeney said, "The way meat allotment works is, before every ration day, the ranch where we're buying the cattle drives 'em across the river, where we weigh them and then drive 'em over to this corral."

Sieber said, "This is where those cowboys who stole the cattle you were driving to Redmond were planning to take them. Weren't so long ago that the ranchers would take their poorest stock, make 'em go without water for a couple days before they drove 'em to the river, where they'd let them drink all they wanted. At the next stop where the agency weighed 'em, they were extra heavy because of all that water they'd drunk, so the government was paying for a lot of water. We put a stop to that business right quick. That's why they wanted Redmond's cattle so bad. They were fat for real, not just water fat."

Sweeney crossed his arms. "Sieber's right. The tribal policemen now watch the cattle. They make sure there's not more cheatin' goin' on. Your job is to kill the cattle so selected women and old men can butcher the carcasses for the family meat ration. You should be here about two hands after sunrise and see me before you start shootin' to make sure people are out of the way. You follow what we've told you?"

"Yes. I follow. Where I find you on ration day?"

"You know the building where the People show their brass identification tags and get everything but meat?"

I nodded.

"That's where I'll be."

"Can I walk on top of the adobe wall and look things over?"

Sweeney nodded. I handed my rifle to Sieber to hold while I found a toehold in the adobe bricks to give me a boost up. It wasn't hard to mount the top of the wall, which was about two hand spans wide. The view from the top of the wall looking down into the corral told me I would have to move around on the wall top to get a good line of sight on my targets. I knew from my days with my father's family in the Galiuro Mountains that the best place to shoot cattle was the center of the spiral circle of hair on their faces—one shot did it every time.

I tried a slow run on the top of the corral wall and didn't think I'd have any trouble. I jumped to the ground. As Sieber handed me my rifle, I asked Sweeney when he wanted me to start. He said, "The next ration day is in four days. I'll look for you then."

I made the peace sign by waving my hand parallel to the ground. "I be there."

SEVENTEEN

BLUE COAT SCOUT NOVITIATE

SIEBER LIKED WHAT he had seen me do for Sweeney and was happy that Sweeney agreed to give me scout training as long as I'd accept it. He decided to return to Globe that day and visit with Redmond before the saloons generated some card games where he might take advantage of a miner and win his claim. He told us he planned to take life easy in Prescott when he left Globe, and that if he wasn't in Prescott, he'd go to Fort Whipple. He gave us the peace sign after he mounted his pony and jogged down the trail toward Globe.

In the days that followed, I slept with my father's family at Peridot when Clum allowed Hashke Bahnzin and *Capitan* Chiquito to move their People there in order to have enough land to plant crops that would support their People. My father had moved to Globe and then back to Peridot after he and *Capitan* Chiquito had come to an understanding over their previous dispute about scouts killing other Apache for the Blue Coats.

Living on the reservation made it hard to impossible for young men to become novitiates supporting warriors on raids. In the days before reservation life, after doing well on four raids, which meant doing camp work, not getting lost, and anticipating what the warrior would need in the heat of action, they might be asked to join the warriors as a warrior on their next raid. I thought about this as I learned Blue Coat scout craft from Sweeney. It seemed to me that this was like my novitiate with *Capitan* Chiquito and his warriors except I was showing my skills and learning the way of a Blue Coat scout. I wondered if my People would accept me as a warrior if I became a Blue Coat scout. I hoped that they would.

Every morning before sunrise, I left the camp at Peridot and rode down to the agency and waited in the cool, sweet desert air for Sweeney to open his door.

When Sweeney started my training, he taught me to cook his breakfast, which usually included cooking bacon and eggs along with a slice of bread some woman made for Clum. The hardest part of that training was forcing myself to handle bacon and eggs. Pork and eggs are nasty foods, which *Ussen* told us not to eat. The White Eyes didn't know this and ate it every morning. The bacon frying in the big iron skillet on Sweeney's stove smelled good, but I couldn't bring myself to eat it.

After breakfast, Sweeney taught me the drill commands and what they were telling me to do. From the time we are off the *tsach*, Apache are trained to have good memories because most of our People can't make or read the black-water tracks on paper like the White Eyes. We had to have a good memory to keep track of the things the White Eyes kept track of with black-water tracks on paper. We had to remember everything from the shapes of mountain ranges against the horizon to family relationships that allowed us to marry without committing incest, to instructions for warriors spoken by a distant chief.

Sweeney was impressed that he only had to go through the names of the drill commands once and I remembered them, but he had trained many Apache, and it was rare that a man's memory failed him. Sweeney gave me a rifle like the soldiers used. It was a single-shot Springfield trapdoor carbine that used the big .45-70 army cartridge. It had a much longer range than my rifle and carried a harder punch. Since I wasn't yet a policeman or a scout, he kept the rifle at his quarters but let me use it whenever I wanted. The day he gave the carbine to me, after the day's drill and eating at the time of no shadows, he gave me a loaded cartridge belt to carry with my rifle and we walked back to the canyon where I had shot for him and Sieber before.

We stopped at the entrance to the canyon. He looked down the canyon with his soldier glasses, and where the canyon ended, he saw a big boulder about the height of a man. He handed me the glasses. "Do you see the big boulder at the end of the canyon that's about the height of a man next to the west wall?"

"I see boulder." In fact, I could see the boulder very well without soldier glasses.

"I know this is your first experience with big-caliber army ammunition and that trapdoor carbine, but I'd like to see what you can do now using it."

He watched me work the trapdoor, load a cartridge, and adjust the sights for three hundred long paces—he taught me to call a long pace a "yard"—which was what he thought the range was to the boulder. He had already checked the sights to ensure they pointed where the rifle shot. Sweeney promised to show me how to check and adjust the sights another sun.

"If you can see the boulder, take a shot and try to hit it in the middle. I'll use my soldier glasses and tell you if you hit and where. Go ahead and shoot."

The carbine was a little lighter than my rifle, but it wasn't hard to hold it steady. I could barely see some kind of streak down the face of the boulder. I aimed at the middle of the boulder and tried to find the streak but had to guess where it was in the sight notch. I squeezed the trigger and felt the carbine jerk hard against my shoulder when it fired. The report echoed against the canyon walls and made my ears ring. A light breeze carried the smoke away as Sweeney studied the boulder with his soldier glasses and muttered "Damn!" under his breath.

He lowered his glasses and slowly shook his head. "What were you aiming for, Kid?"

"I wanted to hit near center of the boulder. I thought I saw some kind of black streak down its face and tried to hit it. Did I miss?"

Sweeney laughed. "Kid, you don't miss. I don't think even Al Sieber could have made that shot. There's a lot to teach you about being a scout or policeman, but good shootin' ain't one of them. When Beauford and Clum get back from their little jaunt over to new Camp Grant, I want you to meet Clum so he understands the shooter you are, and I'm certain he'll encourage you to join his policemen. Go on now and see how close you can come to that first mark with the rest of these shells."

He laid four shells in my hand. I pulled my wax ear stoppers out of my vest pocket and fixed my ears. When Sweeney saw me do it, he pulled his ear stoppers out of his chest pocket and pushed them in his ears before nodding for me to continue. The next four shots landed within a hand span of each other.

Again Sweeney nodded. "You did that shooting with no coaching from me. Kid, you're worth keeping around just for personal protection. I'd say you're the best shot on the reservation. It's getting late. Let's get on back to quarters and I'll have the old man whip us up some grub. Pay attention to him. He can show you a thing or two more about how he cooks while I have my evening toddy."

"You show me much today, Sweeney. Happy I work for you."

CLUM AND BEAUFORD returned to San Carlos within a moon after I had shot the carbine for Sweeney. While we waited for their return, I did many little jobs for Sweeney. In addition to the carbine, he gave me an army-issue Colt revolver with a belt and holster and showed me how to load and shoot it while standing and from a galloping pony. His policemen also carried Colts, and he let me sit in on his lessons about when and where to use a short gun.

When Beauford returned, he took back the training of Clum's policemen, and Sweeney returned to his work as Clum's number two. Suns later, he had me come to Clum's workroom after he told Clum what a natural shot I was. Clum seemed anxious to meet me.

Sweeney led me to Clum's door. "Mister Clum, this is Ohyessonna, the young man I was telling you about."

Clum stood up from behind a table covered with stacks of paper with many black tracks and stuck out his hand. I understood he intended showing his friendliness pumping my hand in a ceremony the White Eyes called "shaking hands." He motioned toward two chairs in front of his table and said, "Ohyessonna, my *segundo*, Mister Sweeney here, had told me many good things about you. He says with the light behind your eyes and your natural shooting ability, you would make a fine San Carlos policeman. Is that something you want to do?"

Clum wasn't as tall as me. He had lost much of the hair on top of his head but had a big bush of hair under his nose. I could tell that, for an agent, he was very young. He didn't look more than three harvests older than me. I sat down in one of chairs and he took the other.

I knew Clum didn't get along well with the Blue Coat chiefs. I was careful with my answer. "Hmmph. Policeman or army scout. I watch Sweeney teach policemen. One sun I be policeman. Next sun I be scout. Some other sun an army scout."

Clum grinned and nodded. "With Sweeney teaching you, I think that's likely. Isn't your father Toga-de-chuz? Did he teach you to shoot?"

"Hmmph. Father, Toga-de-chuz. He give rifle and show how to use. When I have cartridges, I shoot targets often. I good shot from shooting many targets."

"Yes, sir, practice is what it takes. As long as you don't start with bad form, practice gives good results. Isn't your family in *Capitan* Chiquito's band? I've recruited both him and Skimmy to serve with the tribal police when I go down to the Chiricahua reservation to bring Taza and his People back here."

He saw me frown when he used the word "Skimmy" and said, "That's the name I gave Hashke Bahnzin when I first visited him in the new Camp Grant jail on my way here when I was assigned the agency for San Carlos. I think the army has his name as Eskiminzin."

"Good words are said of you for treating Hashke Bahnzin and many others good. Other agents take from us and force us to live where we don't want and where there is little or no food and bad water, so we go hungry."

Clum stuck out his chest and nodded when he heard my words. "I want to treat your People right. I'm proud to hear there are good words said of me, especially from someone young who has ridden the reservation and worked for White Eyes who own ranches."

He scratched his chin and rolled the ends of the pile of hair under his nose into curved points as he studied my face, staring to the point of rudeness.

"This isn't known yet by many outside this room, so I ask you not to speak of it anywhere for a while. The big chiefs in the East have told me to move Taza's people to San Carlos. They want to keep most reservation Apache all on one reservation and let the White Eyes use the land the Apache don't need. That way, they save money in not needing as many people to oversee the reservation and there are many more people to work the abandoned reservation."

I thought, *All to the good for stealing back the land White Eyes gave us in the first place.*

"Mister Sweeney has told me you're known as a fine rider and horse wrangler by the ranchers around the reservation. I know you worked for Clay Beauford as a striker for a while and delivered his messages. I'm going to need someone who can carry messages for me to the nearest telegraph station while we talk with Taza and his brother Naiche about moving their People to San Carlos. Are you interested in riding with us to the Chiricahua reservation and acting as my message carrier? I could pay you like you were an army private. What do you say?"

My mind raced with thoughts like a flood roaring down an *arroyo*. I wanted to go on this trip with the San Carlos policemen. I wanted to see how Clum treated other Apache. I wanted to go even if I had to ask. There was much to learn. Now, Clum wanted me to go. Surely, *Ussen* must be with me.

I nodded. "This I do. When we go?"

Clum smiled. *"Enjuh!* We'll leave in about a moon. Mister Beauford or Sweeney will tell you when we leave and what to take with you after I firm up our plans. I'm glad you agreed to ride with us."

He stood and stuck out his hand, showing me our talk was over. I took his hand, gave it two good pumps, and said, "My pony fast. Beauford says we go. I see you."

Clum, grinning, nodded as I followed Sweeney out the door.

EIGHTEEN

CHIRICAHUA RESERVATION

ABOUT THE MIDDLE of the moon the White Eyes called "May," Beauford assembled fifty-four Apache police near Clum's place at the intersection of the Ríos San Carlos and Gila. Beauford made sure that each of his policemen was properly armed with carbines and revolvers, carried two bandoliers filled with cartridges, and stored their tents and blankets in the supply wagon.

Early the next sun, Beauford led us out of the agency on the trail west of Mount Turnbull through canyons and over ridges that we followed to old Camp Grant and camped for the night. This trail seemed far out of the way to get to the Chiricahua reservation, and I asked Beauford why we used it. He smiled and said, "This is the easiest way to get to Tucson. Clum is waiting there for General Kautz. He's bringing over three hundred cavalry troopers and a hundred scouts from Fort Whipple to guard the east and west borders of the reservation against Chokonen trying to slip away. He wants to convince Taza that much blood will flow if his Chiricahua don't move to San Carlos. Kautz also sent five companies of cavalry to Fort Bowie if they're needed for quick support when the Chiricahua began moving to San Carlos."

We rode into Tucson as the sun was painting the clouds to the west a bright orange and deep purple. The brightness of the day was fast fading to twilight as it spread quietly over the surrounding desert. We dismounted in the rapidly cooling evening and loosened cinches on our horses while we waited outside of town for Clum to send us word on what we should do.

A rider wearing a blue coat with three yellow stripes on the sleeve soon appeared out of the falling night. He rode up to Beauford and told him Clum said that we were to put up our tents and eat, that several more suns might pass before General Kautz with his cavalry appeared, and that a wagon carrying wood for fires was coming. Beauford nodded he understood, and soon tents began appearing in the desert outside of Tucson like mushrooms on a shadowed cliff after a good female rain, one with plenty of water but not a thunder and lightning arrow downpour. After I set up the tents for Beauford and me, he asked that I help the cook make supper. I agreed to help without complaining. After all, that's what novitiates did when they supported warriors.

Three suns passed while Clum's policemen waited in the desert. Beauford kept his police busy doing drills and other training tricks in which I couldn't take part—I wasn't yet a soldier or policeman—but I watched to make sure I didn't miss any part of the maneuvers or their commands.

On the third day, Clum came and asked his policemen if they would put on a war dance in the square for the people of Tucson. The policemen didn't hesitate to agree to do the dance that night. It was a good dance, and the Mexicans and White Eyes watched with eyes wide, and their jaws dropped as the men shouted and jumped with wild yells while they circled the square. Hermenegildo Grijalva, Clum's interpreter, told the crowd what was supposed to be happening as the dance went on. When it was finished, there was much shouting of approval. The crowd followed the strange custom the White Eyes had of clapping their hands when they publicly approved of something or a performance.

Five suns filled with rumors, gossip, and training passed before we learned that Clum and General Kautz were going to lead us back to Fort Bowie. Beauford was surprised. He told me that he had expected to go to the Chiricahua Reservation Agency run by Tom Jeffords and, if need be, force the Chiricahua to move to San Carlos. The rumor was that Jeffords had spoken to Taza and his brother Naiche, who were close to refusing to move their People to San Carlos. Jeffords reminded the brothers of the promise they made to their dying father to live in peace with the White Eyes if possible, and that he, Jeffords, had promised Cochise to hold them to their promise. After a long evening of talk, the brothers told Jeffords they would move to San Carlos even as they bitterly opposed the move.

I learned later from Beauford that there were three separate groups on the reservation. Taza led one group that included about three hundred people. Chiva led another group of about twenty-five. This group believed that a much older man like Skinya or Poinsenay should be chief rather than Taza, who they thought was too young and inexperienced. The night before we arrived at

Fort Bowie, Skinya and Poinsenay tried to force the issue. This led to a closeup firefight in Bonito Canyon between Skinya, Poinsenay, and ten of their men against a group led by Taza. Naiche shot Skinya in the head and killed him. Taza wounded Poinsenay, and his group killed six of their men. That ended objections to Taza's leadership of the Chokonen Chiricahua. The third group, which numbered about two hundred, were Nednhi led by Juh, Nolgee, and Geronimo. Cochise had given the Nednhi a section of the reservation with its southern border defined by the border with Mexico. This meant that when the Nednhi wanted to raid in Mexico, they could come and go as they pleased, which they often did.

CLUM WITH HIS scouts and General Kautz with his soldiers rode into Fort Bowie about two hands before the time of shortest shadows. Jeffords met Clum and Kautz with Taza and about two hundred of his People and Juh, Nolgee, and Geronimo, who had agreed to come in with Taza to talk with Clum and Kautz about the Nednhi moving to San Carlos. Clum handed Jeffords a message he had from the talking wire. Jeffords read it, raised his brows, shrugged his shoulders, and, smiling, gave it back to Clum and rode his pony over to the sutler's store, where he dismounted at the hitching post and went inside. I learned later that the talking wire message said Clum was then in charge of Chiricahua reservation Apache. Taza and his leaders agreed to meet with Clum and General Kautz the next sun.

Taza, Naiche, Chihuahua, Cathla, and Nahilzay met with Clum and General Kautz. I was at the meeting room door because Beauford wanted someone who could run messages to the talking wire and other commanders and act to protect the two White Eye leaders if trouble broke out. After the usual introductions and comments about the weather, the leaders smoked a cigarette and got down to serious business.

Clum spoke first and told the Apache that he was very happy Taza had decided to move to San Carlos and that, as agent, he would do everything he could to ensure they were satisfied and well fed, and that their rations from blankets to beef were what they ought to be.

Taza said something like, "I would like to remain on the present reservation where my ancestors lived and died. I am in no way to blame for the current raids and acts of war, things you call 'outrages,' and I have ridden with your cavalry, sent out to make the world smooth again against the outlaws who were responsible for those outrages. At last, Naiche and I and our People have killed those who were in the outbreaks that killed many *Nakai-yes* and White Eyes.

"I have always kept the treaty made by my father with General Howard, and I always will. But if it is your wish that we should go to San Carlos, then we will go. You have treated me and my People well, and I will never forget that. My father's last words were for us to always live in peace with the White Eyes. We here will always live in peace with you. If we should, by some misfortune, all be killed off or die but one, the last one will never forget what you have done for us and will be your friend."

Clum's face was serious and appreciative as he nodded at Taza's words. All the White Eyes and Blue Coats in the meeting appeared to feel the same way in the stillness left by Taza's words.

Clum said, "I hear you. We are all grateful for your words. You have asked before that you don't live close to your enemies, the White Mountains, the Aravaipa, and Yavapai. The place the White Eyes call Camp Goodwin is far removed from these people and upstream from the agency on the Río Gila. This will be your place to keep. There you will be able to work the land and support yourselves with what the earth gives you from your labor."

Taza shook his head. "Apache men know nothing of planting and harvesting. This is women's work. This, men will not do. But we will hunt and find mescal, and our sons will help dig pits for our women to cook the mescal and other plants they prepare this way."

I saw Clum glance at General Kautz when Taza mentioned hunting. I wondered if they planned to disarm the Chiricahua, but nothing else was said at the meeting about that.

Clum told the Chiricahua about the rations they would get and that if they cut grass, they could sell it to the army to make money. He spoke of the chance that some of the Chiricahua men might become policemen and that all the Chiricahua must obey the police. Those arrested for serious crimes would face a system of laws applied by judges and juries made up of their own People.

The meeting lasted until the time of shortest shadows. Taza said his People would return to the reservation to get their things and leave for San Carlos in two or three suns. Juh, Nolgee, and Geronimo asked for a separate council and asked to come in the next day. Clum agreed and the meetings for that sun ended.

THE NEXT MORNING, the Nednhi met with Clum and General Kautz and the same men who helped them the sun before. First they smoked and Geronimo prayed to *Ussen* that all spoke with straight tongues. Clum spoke first and talked much about how San Carlos gave the Apache more opportunities than other reservations and that Nednhi needed to have their share. Juh, Nolgee, and Geronimo listened carefully with arms crossed, watching Clum's face as he spoke. When Clum finished, Geronimo and Juh had a private talk. When they finished, Geronimo spoke. Juh stuttered badly when he was nervous, and to avoid confusion over what he said, he had asked Geronimo to speak for him. Geronimo looked across the table at Clum and said, "Hmmph. We go to San Carlos. Return to our camp and gather our People. We ask twenty suns to do this."

Clum raised his brows in question and disbelief when Geronimo asked for twenty suns to get the Nednhi together and return. "Four suns are all I can wait before we return to San Carlos."

Geronimo frowned and spoke close to Juh's ear. After Juh nodded, Geronimo lifted his chin and said, "We gather our People and return in four suns."

Clum smiled. *"Ch'ik'eh doleel.* We will wait here at Fort Bowie and expect to see you in four suns."

Geronimo, Juh, and Nolgee left the room, went straight for their horses, and were soon riding out of Fort Bowie.

Beauford came to me and said, "Clum thinks Juh may not return when Geronimo said they would. He's sending two of his policemen to follow them out of sight and watch what they do at their camp. I want you to go with them. If it appears they're not keepin' their promise and running off someplace else, I want you to race back here and tell me. *Comprende?"*

I nodded and ran to get my pony and join the policemen following the three Nednhi. They thought at first that I might be a Nednhi spy trailing them, but they accepted my explanation that Beauford had sent me to join them as a fast messenger to bring him what they learned from watching the Nednhi.

The policemen all knew where the Nednhi village was and rode a different trail to get ahead of Juh, Nolgee, and Geronimo. They found a place up in the cliffs near the village, where, with their soldier glasses, they could watch what was going on. I was glad I had brought my soldier glasses Sieber had given me. I watched with them.

The three Nednhi arrived in the village a little before dark and the People gathered around them. Juh spoke to the crowd, waving his right arm in the direction of Fort Bowie and his left in the direction of Mexico. The crowd yell of

"Enjuh" before it broke up, along with the women hurrying to pack their things, the men catching their horses, and the boys catching and killing their dogs to maintain silence when they moved, told us the Nednhi were headed for Mexico, not Fort Bowie.

One of the policemen turned to me and nodded. "You go now. Tell Chief Beauford, the Nednhi run for the land of the *Nakai-yes.* They take less than a sun to cross the border. The Blue Coats not fast enough to catch 'em. We watch and return when we see which trail they take."

I nodded I understood and ran for my pony. I hated to ride at night. It was dangerous, but Beauford needed to know what the Nednhi were doing.

I MADE IT back to Beauford early the next morning and told him the Nednhi ran for Mexico. He shook his head and said, "I thought they would do that. If I saddled every policeman here and went after them, we'd never catch up with them before they crossed the border."

He looked at me while he scratched his chin whiskers. "Boy, you ain't slept in two days, and ain't had anything to eat except trail food. Go get something to eat and then get some rest. Now that we don't have to wait for Juh and his bunch, we can leave for San Carlos as soon as Taza gets his People back here in a day or two."

When Beauford told Clum that the Nednhi had slipped away to Mexico and there was no chance of catching them, Clum shook his head and said, "My money says we'll get those liars when their time is up. We'll make 'em pay."

I was surprised a year later when Clum and Beauford headed for Ojo Caliente expecting to arrest Geronimo and bring him and the great Chihenne chief Victorio and his People to the San Carlos Reservation.

NINETEEN

THE CHIRICAHUA
COME TO SAN CARLOS

FOR TWO WEEKS, the Chokonen Chiricahua peacefully moved up the wagon road toward San Carlos. Children played along the way, the women walked at an easy pace, and the army helped carry their family belongings in wagons. The Chokonen men rode their ponies and drove their livestock, mostly ponies and mules. At the end of the day, army cooks had a supper ready for the tired Apache, who were thankful the army was looking after them. I was impressed by the ease the army moved large numbers of people, fed them, and protected them. There was much to learn from the Blue Coat soldiers.

When we reached San Carlos, Clum sent Taza and his People up the Río Gila to the place once known as Camp Goodwin. This location would keep them out of the way of my People, and there were good places near the río where the women could plant their gardens, and up a little higher was good grass for the livestock.

Beauford told me at the agency he was proud of the way I had acted in bringing the Chokonen to San Carlos. He said he thought that, in a year or two, I'd be ready to join the army scouts or his tribal police force and that I clearly demonstrated I was officer material and didn't need any more training before I joined either service. His praise for my work made me throw out my chest with pride and grin from ear to ear. He suggested I return to work on a ranch so I could make some money, and that if I was needed, my father would know where to find me.

I thanked Beauford for taking me on this trip and made the hand wave from my brow the Blue Coats called a "salute" as I left.

THAT SAME SUN, I rode up the wagon road along sparkling, singing Río San Carlos to my father's lodge at Peridot. *Capitan* Chiquito and Hashke Bahnzin, who had been scouts traveling with Clum to the Chiricahua reservation, were also returning to their families in the village at Peridot.

We weren't out of sight of the agency before *Capitan* Chiquito said, "You not scout?" I shook my head. "Why you go with Clum to bring Chiricahua to San Carlos?"

Hashke Bahnzin, who leaned toward my side in his saddle to better hear my answer, was also interested in the question. I said, "One sun, I want to be a warrior. Now is no way for novitiates to learn from our warriors while helping them on four raids. I think the only way for us to do this is to serve as novitiates to scouts and serve as scouts.

"Al Sieber saw me shoot and says he wants me to join the army scouts when I'm a little older. Sieber introduced me to Agent Clum's *segundo*, Martin Sweeney, who also saw me shoot. Sweeney wants me to become a tribal policeman and has spent time training me in the things that policemen and scouts need to do well. They believed the Chiricahua under Naiche would come peacefully, and as you saw, they did come even if they didn't want to. I've been serving as a striker and messenger for Sweeney. He thought I should go with Clum and help the old man who's his striker, and with Clum's fast messages. Clum agreed. I consider it my first novitiate. Beauford told me a couple of hands ago that I did very well and the training I was getting riding with the scouts would make me a sure candidate for early promotion in the scouts or policemen."

Capitan Chiquito nodded. *"Enjuh.* You are doing good work for the People. This kind of work will help the boys who want to be warriors do a novitiate. I want to speak with you more about this."

Hashke Bahnzin's face filled with a big grin. "Ohyessonna has his eye on Chita for a wife. I save her for him. She wants him for a husband but won't wait until she's old and gray. I know he should come soon for a meal she prepares, eh, Ohyessonna?"

I grinned and nodded. Yes, I want Chita, but she must be patient or she might be a very young widow with no one to support her and maybe our child.

MY MOTHER MADE an extra-special meal that night to celebrate my return, and I was filled to bursting from eating too much. After our meal, my father and I smoked. We had a long talk about when I join the scouts. He thought I should follow Beauford's advice and find a job for a time. I could wrangle horses or herd cattle on a nearby ranch. He said I could live with them while I worked there. When I asked her about it, my mother looked pleased, smiled, and nodded her approval. I decided that before I rode over to the Circle S Ranch to ask for a wrangler's job, I'd go visit my old friend Redmond in Globe. He always had enough work to keep me busy.

I WAS ON the road between Peridot and Globe before the next sun rose in brilliant *pesh klitso* blazed over the eastern mountains casting long shadows in the desert from the mesquite, manzanita, and flagpole-tall yucca. The new light made the night water on all the plants sparkle like little shiny stones White Eye and *Nakai-yi* women sometimes wore. I rode into Globe the usual time Redmond liked to eat his morning meal in the little café near his butcher shop.

I tied my pony to the hitching rack while grackles whistled and called as they looked for food in the street and in horse apples scattered by riders passing by. I walked into the café. It was clean and neat, filled with the smells of cooking meat and baked bread that made my stomach growl wanting food. The café's curtains on the windows were pulled back and tied to let the early sun stream in with its bright yellow light. It was about half full, and I knew most of the men eating there. Some saw me and waved a welcome, and I waved back when I saw them.

Redmond sat at his usual table drinking his morning coffee. When he saw me come through the door, he jumped to his feet and, waving me over to his table, yelled, "Yo! Kid! Welcome back! Have some breakfast while we talk about old times." I nodded at him and grinned, pulled out a chair at his table, and sat down. He waved the waitress over and said, "Give this young man anything he wants for breakfast and put it on my bill."

I ordered steak, beans, fry bread, and coffee. After many harvests watching White Eyes eat, it was still hard for me to understand why Redmond, like so many other White Eyes, ate nasty food—eggs and pork of different kinds—for their morning meal. Eating it was worse than the grackles eating grain they found picking through the horse apples in the street, but I was learning to ignore the food they ate.

Redmond, leaning toward me and resting on his elbows, said, "Did Clum convince Cochise's sons to bring their People to San Carlos? I heard he came back with a crowd of Chiricahua."

"He did, but the Nednhi living on the reservation slipped away into the land of the *Nakai-yes* after Geronimo said they'd join the others and go to San Carlos." I told him all that happened on that trip to move the Chokonen, and that it had, except for the Nednhi slipping away, gone well.

Redmond grinned. "I bet they ain't gonna stay there long after they're attacked by the clouds of no-see-ums. It'll be downright awful to live there."

Our meals arrived and I told him about my training adventures while we ate. He told me that mining had picked up in Globe and he couldn't keep enough meat in to satisfy demand. I knew what his next question was going to be.

"How 'bout herdin' for me again? I'll pay you top hand wages, and you can sleep at my place and eat in cafés as you please like you did before."

I grinned. It was better than the deal I had hoped to get. "That sounds good, but I go over to the agency on the sun White Eyes call 'Saturday.' I shoot cattle they want to slaughter for rations. No take long. I tell Sweeney I do it. I no lie."

Redmond crossed his arms and leaned back in his chair. "I know you don't lie. Never knowed you to do that. Shore, you'n have Saturday off. I know you'll have more cattle in them pens than I'n handle in two or three days anyway. I've had so much business I had to hire a man to help me butcher."

I grinned and nodded. "When I start? Next sun I shoot cattle."

"Why don't you bring your stuff over the next sun after you shoot and get comfortable in your old room and start work the sun after that one?"

"Hmmph. This I do."

I FELL INTO a routine of herding Redmond's cattle he bought from local ranchers and shooting beef for slaughter at the agency for Sweeney. I saw Sweeney every slaughter day and he told me the reservation news. After a moon following my new routine, Sweeney told me Clum was going back East to see the big chiefs in charge of the reservations and he was taking about twenty Apache with him, including *Capitan* Chiquito, Hashke Bahnzin, and Taza and their wives. He wanted to put on shows for White Eye groups to show them what real Apache were like and not the bad way the newspapers showed them.

Sweeney was grinning when he said, "By the way, Clum plans to pick up a wife while he's on the way. I think that's why he's goin' in the first place."

I laughed. "That's a good reason to go. When they leave? How long they gone?"

"They'll leave in three days––before the next time you're back. He thinks they'll be gone three or four moons depending on how successful their performances are."

SWEENEY AS CLUM'S *segundo* took good care of business at San Carlos while Clum was gone. All the People got their rations on time and in the amounts that they were promised, until deliveries that Sweeney had been promised by government contractors were late arriving and he had to reduce rations to half what was promised for a while. He and the agent, Ezra Hoag, appointed for the Chiricahua subagency, let the Chiricahua and White Mountains leave their villages and camp in the Santa Teresa Mountains to hunt and find and cook mescal and gather acorns and other good things to compensate for the slow ration deliveries.

Taza had left Naiche in charge of the Chokonen, and they went about their business hunting, and the women planting their gardens, even making a batch of *tulapai* or two, but their drunks never got out of hand. Sweeney was able to recruit some of their men to become tribal policemen and had training sessions with them and others he recruited.

Hermenegildo Grijalva and Cathla returned to San Carlos near the end of the season Earth Is Reddish Brown with the sad news that Taza had died in the Great Father's town far to the East. Naiche was angry and believed Clum had used witchcraft to poison his brother. Many of the Chiricahua believed this too.

Sweeney told me that Clum returned early in the Ghost Face with his new woman and immediately went with Hashke Bahnzin and others who had been on the trip to tell Naiche his sorrow that Taza had died. Naiche's anger against Clum had not cooled, and he accused him face-to-face of using witchcraft to kill his brother. Hashke Bahnzin stepped in and told Naiche that was not true. Clum had brought in the best white *di-yens* with their medicine to help Taza. They had done everything good and proper for Taza, whose breath filled with gurgles and wheezes. He suffered from the disease the White Eyes called pneumonia.

No *di-yen*, Indian or White Eye, had a ceremony they tried that did any good before Taza rode the ghost pony. Hashke Bahnzin said Clum had a big funeral and burial for Taza attended by many great White Eye chiefs. Hashke Bahnzin's words comforted Naiche and cooled his anger toward Clum. Naiche even defended Clum later against others who claimed he had used poison to kill Taza.

THE SEASONS OF Ghost Face and of Little Eagles passed without conflict at San Carlos. The demand for Redmond's beef in Globe was high and kept him and all his men, me included, busy. I came to know every used trail across and around San Carlos and Fort Apache Reservations and a good distance west of Globe after driving small herds of cattle to their corrals and slaughter at Redmond's place.

One sun late in the Season of Little Eagles, I stopped at the agency on my way to a ranch east of and bordering on the reservation. I watched Sweeney and Beauford drilling and training a large group of policemen while another large group watched from the edge of the drill field. I had not seen such large groups doing these drills and wondered, given the peaceful air now on the reservation, why so many policemen drilled. My curiosity held me there until I could ask one of them why so many policemen.

They finished their drills and dismissed the men. Sweeney saw me, grinned, and came jogging over.

"Ho, Kid! If you want some excitement, time to become a policeman."

"Why you train and drill so many, Sweeney?"

"We're gonna need 'em. About ten suns ago, Clum got orders to take his policemen and go over to Ojo Caliente Reservation in New Mexico and arrest some Apache character the locals call Geronimo. He's been hiding out there and raiding the Pimas and others for a couple of moons. Clum's supposed to bring him and his leaders back here and turn 'em over to the Tucson sheriff, who'll see they get hung good and proper. That'll be the end of most of the murder and raiding problems. He's also supposed to talk Victorio into bring the Chihenne here rather than for them to have their reservation at Ojo Caliente."

Maybe so, Sweeney, but Geronimo is a powerful di-yen, and Victorio is no fool.

TWENTY

VICTORIO LEAVES
SAN CARLOS

THE NEWS THAT Clum would soon return and cross the Río San Carlos in three days spread across the reservation like a Season of Big Leaves wildfire. People from all over the reservation showed up to watch him return with Victorio riding like a great chief and Geronimo in chains with his leaders riding in a wagon. Over a thousand from the reservation tribes gathered at the wagon road coming out of the Río San Carlos. First to splash across the river was Clum and Hermenegildo Grijalva leading a wagon carrying four shackled prisoners and about fifteen on foot, unshackled prisoners, followed by twenty-five of Clum's scouts. We learned later Clum had sent Beauford and seventy-five policemen to Tucson, where they were to go after Apache raiders. Then followed a long line of Chihenne women and children, who waded across, followed by Victorio riding a big black horse and surrounded by his Chihenne leaders, among them Loco and Nana with their warriors behind them. I had never seen Victorio before. His skin was dark, a big muscular, older man with a frown that never seemed to go away and often made his face a dark forest to fear by his enemies and a protective fort to friends. Behind Victorio's warriors followed the supply wagons and twelve cavalry troopers.

The Apache crowd was very quiet. The men stood with crossed arms and the women tall and straight with a light breeze stirring their hair. They all stared at the long line of people wading and splashing out of the río to stream past them. In addition to the prisoners, Clum brought a large crowd of Chihenne, which my People often fought. Some families in both tribes still had blood feuds with the others from many harvests ago. Clum would need a big police force—more men than he had now—to keep them in line.

I saw the prisoner wagon and prisoners following it go to the guardhouse, and I watched what happened there with my soldier glasses. Scouts pulled out men in the wagon bed and pushed them into the guardhouse still in their shackles. Clum jumped onto the bed of the wagon, raised his arms, and made a talk to the unshackled prisoners and then apparently let them go before he rode back to the agency building and spoke to Victorio with Grijalva interpreting. I watched Victorio slowly nod he understood. He rode back to his People and, in a voice loud enough for me to hear, said they would find a place to camp at the next sunrise when they went up the Río Gila. They would sleep the night next to the agency, and the agency would give them meals for that night and next sunrise. There were no sounds in the crowd except for horses snorting, the clink of harness chains, the shuffle of many feet on the sand, and the gurgle of two streams flowing together. It was strange to see so many of the People in one place and not hear the hum of women's voices and the playtime calls of children. Sitting on my pony and looking over the crowd watching the Chihenne pass, I wondered what this silence meant.

The next day as the sun was spreading early morning light on the agency, Victorio led his People about thirty miles up the misty, gurgling Gila along the wagon road on which they had come the day before. He came to a creek about four miles downstream from Fort Thomas and moved southwest down the creek. He established his camp about a mile down the creek from the wagon road. Fort Thomas was about four miles farther on from the creek.

GOSSIP ON THE reservation two moons later said Victorio and his leaders were not happy with their camp location. The soil would not support much plant growth. The water tasted bad, and cases of smallpox had appeared. Those lodges had to be separated from the other lodges. It wasn't long before there were several cases of "shaking sickness"—malaria—which no *di-yen*, Indian or White Eye, could cure, and the clothes and food rations the Chihenne expected to receive were less than what they received at Ojo Caliente. As the suns passed, Victorio's frown deepened. He raged against Clum and the scouts who had told him and the People lies about how good life was at San Carlos. But before Victorio could confront Clum and his lies, Clum quit as the reservation agent a moon after he returned during an argument with his big chiefs over how much he should be paid and how best to manage the Apache at San Carlos.

THE WHITE EYES called the second sun of the moon they named September "Sunday." The first sun of the September moon was ration day, and I had come to slaughter the ration cattle and to visit my father and his family at his lodge near the Peridot village. After the evening meal, we talked into the night about how the Aravaipa Apache could avoid war with the Chihenne led by Victorio. By the time the half-moon reached the top of its arc southwest, we said all we had to say and were ready for sleep.

I was falling into a dream when I heard the low rumble of running horses and felt the ground tremble as their hooves pounded the earth. My father grabbed his rifle and ran past the *wickiup* door blanket, and I was right behind him.

The low moonlight showed us our herd of horses and mules driven south by silent Chihenne warriors swinging knotted *reata* ropes on the rumps of our animals to make them run faster. My father and I threw our rifles to our shoulders to take shots at the Chihenne driving our livestock away, but it was too dark and the riders too far to waste bullets on shadows. My father ran to awaken *Capitan* Chiquito and Hashke Bahnzin and get the village men on the run after the Chihenne stealing our livestock.

I ran for the agency and the scout lodges in camps nearby. I hoped the Chihenne had not run off with scout horses too. They would be hard to catch if they were on horses and western Apache men were on foot. But I didn't care. I wanted my fine pony back. I ran hard and reached the agency in a little over a hand. The moon, falling into the southwest mountains, lighted the trail well for me. I ran to the building where Sweeney lived and, puffing hard, banged on his door. Sweeney had taken care of the reservation people after Clum left until the big chiefs could find an agent to replace him. The new agent, Lyman Hart, had come to replace Clum but had no time to learn how best to handle trouble like this.

Sweeney, a big cavalry pistol in his hand, cracked the door and looked out only to see me.

He said with a squint as though he didn't believe his eyes, "Kid! What are you doing here? What's going on?"

I was puffing like a demon iron wagon. "Victorio's... People, they... take our horses and mules... cross the río and head for camp of Victorio.... I think they... run toward Ash Flat and follow trail up Natanes Mountain cliffs to Eagle Creek."

"Why do you think they're going to Eagle Creek?"

"Trail east through mountains back to Ojo Caliente."

Sweeney stared at his feet, thinking, and then looked me in the eyes. "I need for you to go to your father's camp and tell *Capitan* Chiquito and Hashke Bahnzin what's happened and that they should send as many men as they can to run with us. I'll supply the warriors with ammunition. Now, I have to shake my scouts awake and send some telegrams. Hurry."

I ran down the path toward the Aravaipa village. I wasn't as fast as when I was first up and running for the agency, but I still made it in a little over a hand. The village was at a high boil when I ran in. Boys, who in the early morning light had left to watch the ponies and mules, came running back yelling that the horses and mules were gone. What to do?

I found Hashke Bahnzin talking with *Capitan* Chiquito and some of our best warriors. I gave them Sweeney's message and all talk about what to do next evaporated as though it was vapor in a just uncovered pot. Since the warriors had to run to catch up with the Chihenne, they didn't carry much to support themselves on the trail. They assumed that Lyman Hart would provide all they needed in the way of food and ammunition. In less than half a hand, the Aravaipa warriors were running down the trail beside the San Carlos Río to join the scouts.

By the time the warriors and I had reached the agency, I was feeling weary. I had run about twenty-four miles that morning without first eating, and there was another thirty just to get to Victorio's old camp. Sweeney was busy organizing supplies for the warriors. He saw me and motioned for me to join him.

After I sat down, he studied me for a moment and then called his striker, the old gray-headed man who cooked and ran errands for him. Sweeney told the old man to fix me something to eat. The old man grinned and nodded. He was helping Sweeney manage the scouts when I had first shown up and had known me a long time. He gave me a steak he had cooking on a stick over his fire, some mesquite bread, steamed mescal slices, wild potatoes, and coffee. I devoured everything he gave me and felt my strength returning.

Soon I was running with the warriors led by *Capitan* Chiquito and Hashke Bahnzin down the wagon road toward Victorio's campsite. Running with us were San Carlos tribal policemen led by Sweeney, who rode his horse. We ran past Naiche's campsite. Its People with concern written on their faces stood among their *wickiups* and in their gardens to watch us run past. I thought I saw Geronimo and his family at the edge of the village watching us.

When we reached the creek where Victorio had made his camp, soldiers from Camp Thomas had just ridden up. The lieutenant leading the troops talked with Sweeney, *Capitan* Chiquito, and Hashke Bahnzin. Scouts with the soldiers had already found the canyon trail the Chihenne took to climb up to Ash Flat to reach the Natanes cliffs trail to Eagle Creek.

WE RAN THE canyon trail up to Ash Flat and found water in a tank fed by a spring a short distance from the top of the canyon we followed. The Natanes cliffs trail leading to the top of the Natanes Mountains and the trail to Eagle Creek was about eight or nine miles away. While we rested by the water tank, I climbed a nearby hill and used my soldier glasses. I found Victorio's People resting and eating by a water tank fed by *arroyo* runoff about a mile and a half from the trail up the cliffs. They had our horses and mules grazing on a flat place between a low ridge and the junipers lining the *arroyo* that fed their water tank. It looked to me like they had mixed their horses and mules in with ours. The way they were relaxing, they must have thought we couldn't catch up with them that day and that when they got to the good trail along Eagle Creek and one or two trails branching off to the east, we'd never catch them.

I shared what I had seen with my soldier glasses with Sweeney. He nodded and grinned. He had already seen the same thing. To ensure the Chihenne wouldn't just run off as soon as we appeared, Sweeney had the cavalry scouts ride to the cliff trail to stop Victorio's People from using it.

While we ate from our sacks of warrior trail food, Sweeney, who knew I was a good horse wrangler, asked me and two other wranglers from Hashke Bahnzin's camp to take as many horses and mules from Victorio's herd as we could and drive them straight back to the agency. Without horses to carry their women and children, Sweeney believed Victorio would have to move at a much slower pace leading his People back to San Carlos.

As soon as we finished eating, the other horse wranglers and I ran, staying out of sight in the brush, for Victorio's camp. The sun was fast approaching the mountains to the west, making our shadows long and cooling the earth to make running much easier than if it had been in the time of no shadows. As we approached the camp, we heard gunfire. The scouts Sweeney had sent to stop Victorio from escaping up the cliff trail had already engaged the camp. There would be no escape that night. The other wranglers and I circled around the tank where Victorio's People had camped and found the horse and mule herd on the south side of the camp between the junipers lining the *arroyo* and a low ridge. It was a good place for the herd. Victorio had four mounted boys about the age of novitiates watching the horse and mule herd, two each on the east and west sides between tree line and low ridge. The other horse wranglers and I decided to split up. Each one of us would take a corner of the herd and take out the boy on that corner. When the herd watchers were out of the way, we would drive the herd east and then swing around toward the water tank where we had rested. We worked out who would take a corner and a coyote call that would tell the others their corner was ready to move.

I saw that the boy watching the east corner of the horse herd sat on a black pony with a white blaze face. *Ussen* blessed me. The pony the boy used was mine. I crept through the thin grass, crawling past low bushes, and was within five or six long paces of the boy when I tossed my *reata* loop over him. Jerking hard, I pulled him off my pony, making his hands fly open and drop his rifle to roll backward off my pony. I didn't want to kill him and used the barrel of my *pistola* to stun him with a good whack to his head. I dragged him to some boulders close to the low ridge where the horses wouldn't trample him if they ran in this direction. I picked up his rifle. It was a good one, but not as good as mine. I heard a coyote give two yips and then a long howl from the northwest corner of the herd. Yips and howls soon came from the other herd corners. I answered and soon we had the horse and mule herd thundering east and then slowly turning in a big arc toward the water tank where we had rested earlier. It sure felt good to be on the back of my pony instead of the bottoms of my feet.

As soon as Sweeney saw the horse herd moving, he engaged Victorio's camp from the southwest side. The rifle fire from both sides was intense. After Sweeney returned with the San Carlos warriors and Blue Coat horse soldiers, he had several wounded warriors but none killed.

When we got down to the wagon road at the bottom of the canyon leading to the Río Gila, we let the animals drink and rest while we rested too. We returned to San Carlos late that sun, and the owners of the horses and mules were glad to recover their animals they had believed were gone forever.

Sweeney, with his warriors, returned later that night. They believed that Victorio would decide without horses and mules that it was best to come back to San Carlos. They were wrong. When the Chihenne didn't appear the next sun, Sweeney led companies of scouts back to the Natanes cliffs expecting to have a battle with Victorio that would wipe out the Chihenne. When Sweeney's policemen and army scouts got to the Natanes cliffs, Victorio and his People were gone. They used an old Apache trick where they broke into small groups and headed in many directions for some distant meeting place. There were never enough scouts and trackers that could follow every trail, and the army soon gave up trying to track them.

I learned some good lessons in the work to catch Victorio and make the Chihenne return to San Carlos. Chief among these lessons was that among the White Eyes and Blue Coats were men who kept their word and their honor, but for many, their word and honor were just vapors that drifted away with the first good puff of wind. Learning which men knew the difference often meant life or death.

TWENTY-ONE

CHANGES AT
SAN CARLOS

WHEN THE WARRIORS and tribal policemen returned to the Natanes cliffs, Victorio and Nana with their warriors had disappeared into the mountains and later joined the other groups that had disappeared in many different directions but returned to Ojo Caliente. Loco led most of the small groups not with Victorio. When the Chihenne gathered back at Ojo Caliente, they begged the army to let them stay. Colonel Hatch told them that if they behaved—that is, they didn't raid and kill and they stayed on the reservation—he would talk to the big chiefs in the East and try to keep them at Ojo Caliente. They were able to stay at Ojo Caliente a harvest before the big chiefs far away in the East said they must return to San Carlos. Victorio and Nana and their warriors slipped away into the mountains, leaving Loco to lead one hundred fifteen women and children and twenty-five warriors back to San Carlos.

The new agent at San Carlos, Lyman Hart, gave Hashke Bahnzin and *Capitan* Chiquito what they had been asking for since they had moved their People to Peridot, where they had worked hard, with little success, trying to grow crops. Lyman Hart let them move to the southern edge of the reservation where they had their villages before. Hashke Bahnzin, with the help of his villagers nearby, established his farm on the Río San Pedro about six miles south of where his camp had been at old Fort Grant. *Capitan* Chiquito went up Aravaipa Creek back to his old camp at the place of the massacre. The chiefs and their People spent the Ghost Face season clearing brush and weeds that had taken over the fields after we left for San Carlos, and they made ready to plant in the Season of Little Eagles.

My father decided the best thing for his family and followers was to stay where they were and work the fields *Capitan* Chiquito and Hashke Bahnzin had worked or begun. Sweeney still wanted me to help with the slaughter of cattle, and I continued every seventh day jumping up on the corral adobe wall and putting a bullet in the foreheads of the cattle for rations as I ran past them.

When we returned with the horses and mules we had taken from Victorio, I didn't go back with others to the Natanes cliffs to fight and drive Victorio back to San Carlos. Instead, after resting a day with my father and his family, I rode over to Globe to learn if Redmond still wanted me to herd cattle for him. I had disappeared for seven or eight suns without telling him I'd be gone. This might have put him in a bad place as far as deliveries of beef for his customers.

A small herd of cattle stood in Redmond's corrals when I rode up the street to his butcher shop. The sun had started to touch the western mountains, and clouds were turning brilliant reds and yellows with long streaks of orange. I dismounted and tied my pony to the hitching rack after giving him a drink from a nearby water trough. I had to push hard to open the door when I walked into his butcher shop. Redmond was standing next to a heavy table trimming meat for steaks. When he heard the bell ring on the door announcing a customer, he looked up, saw me, grinned, and roared, "I'll be damned! Welcome back. Looks like ol' Victorio didn't shoot you after all. I was a-feared that he'd killed you."

I nodded. "Yes, chase Victorio. Take back horses and mules, his animals too. Now Chihenne walk or run on their own feet. Warriors and scouts return to Victorio camp to finish fight. Chihenne go many directions. I think Victorio go back to Ojo Caliente.

"Attacking Victorio, I leave you with no cattle. I still herd for you? You still want me?"

"Why, shore I still want you. Stay and work. I had enough beeves this here week to keep my customers happy. I had a couple of fellers ride over to Joe Martin's place and pick up some cattle he was offering for a good price. If you'n get up to the north border of the reservation tomorrow, Jose Torres is holdin' a few head for me that'll get me through next week. Gimme a little time to finish my work on this here meat and we'n have us some supper down to the café while you tell me about yore adventures."

"Hmmph. I stay. I wait." I sat down on the floor and leaned back against the wall. The butt of my rifle rested between my moccasins with the barrel on my shoulder as I watched Redmond work. I was glad to be back with him. He was teaching me much that ranged from speaking and understanding the White Eye tongue to expert use of a sharp knife for making cuts of meat to dressing in fine clothes. As the night began crawling through his windows, Redmond lit a White Eye oil lantern and soon finished his work.

THE FIRST HARVEST after Victorio escaped, near the end of the Season of Little Eagles, the Chiricahua leaders Geronimo and Juh left San Carlos, taking their People—mostly family members—with them to the land of the *Nakai-yes*, where Juh had Blue Mountain—Sierra Madre—strongholds. On their way, they left many villages and homes places of blood and fire. It was a trail of stepping-stones like a fiery-footed giant used to stride across the land of southern Arizona and New Mexico.

White Eye soldiers and their scouts tried to catch these Apache as they raced for the *Nakai-yi* border, but the Apache knew the land better than the White Eyes, and for ways to attack and ambush the soldiers, Geronimo had much light behind the slits of his narrow eyes. Stories came to San Carlos about the raids Geronimo and Juh made trying to force the *Nakai-yi* chiefs to agree to a peace treaty they had talked about for many harvests but never made their tracks on treaty paper mainly because the Chihuahuan wanted to do peaceful trade with the Apache, but the Sonoran military wanted to kill as many Apache as they could and enslave those who survived. With Juh and Geronimo free, the ground was dark and bloody in northern Chihuahua and Sonora.

I WORKED FOR Redmond through the next harvest and slept many nights in the back quarters of his store. White Eye money was in my pocket and fancy White Eye clothes on my body.

One ration day in the time of many leaves, the sun was hot and wind kept the dust stirred on the gathering place where women waited their turn to collect their family's rations. I finished killing the cattle ration and walked across the women's gathering place to get my pony tied out of the wind behind the building the White Eyes called "warehouse." Nearby, women sat wrapped in blankets.

I noticed one of the women sitting near my pony had her blanket pulled up to cover her head but her exposed young face showed smooth, darker-than-most skin, large brown eyes, hair as black as a moonless night, and full lips shaped like the White Eye symbol for a heart. She was beautiful to be so young. Her looks grabbed and held my attention. When she saw me staring at her, she smiled and nodded showing bright, white teeth. She sat close by an older woman who resembled her. They both looked familiar. She said, "Ho, Ohyessonna. *Nish'ii'*. Remember me?"

Quick like a flashing arrow from the thunder god, I realized she was the daughter of Hashke Bahnzin. She had claimed the beauty she was promised not so long ago as a young girl, and the curves of her body would have interested any man despite her youth.

I grinned and stepped over to face her. *"Nish'ii'*, Chita. You are no longer a nice-looking girl but a beautiful woman. I remember you very well from when I had a meal with Hashke Bahnzin that you and your mother made. He is a lucky man to have a beautiful daughter who can draw men to his lodge like bees to a fragrant flower. Do you like living on the Río San Pedro? Many flowers draw bees growing along the Río San Pedro."

She grinned. "I may be Hashke Bahnzin's flower, but he keeps the bees away. I think you are the only bee he wants around his flower. The land around our village is much better for growing crops than that at Peridot, and we women and our little helpers don't have to work as hard to get a good crop. What do you do besides shoot cattle? I know you must be doing more than that."

A puff of wind rattled the warehouse roof as a small dust cloud whipped through the agency. I shrugged and said, "I do many different things for the White Eyes. Deliver messages, break horses, herd cattle for the butcher Redmond who lives and works in Globe. Sometimes hunt with my White Eye friend Jimmie Stevens."

She frowned. "You take no time to look over or court women for yourself?"

It was all I could do to keep from smiling. "I court no women—yet. I wait for you. You will be a woman soon enough. I want a woman who works hard and well and can give me children. I think one day you be that woman."

She glanced at her mother and grinned, and then looked up at me and frowned. "Go away, Ohyessonna. You want to make me look like a clown fool." She waved her arm toward my pony. "Go on. Go away." I could tell she was trying hard not to laugh.

I turned to my pony and, looking over my shoulder as she pulled her blanket farther over her head, said, "Plenty quick I see you again, Chita. Look for me when the sun hides in the west." I swung into my saddle and said, "*Adios,* pretty woman."

Chita's mother was watching me and laughed as I rode off.

I thought as my pony headed to Peridot, Chita will be a fine woman. Hashke Bahnzin wants me to take her. I think I will when I start work as a scout or a policeman. On the wagon road to Globe, I had many thoughts and images about my life with Chita. It would be good to have such a woman.

TWENTY-TWO

SIEBER'S ASSISTANT

IN MY SEVENTEENTH harvest, the one White Eyes named 1877, in the Season of Large Fruit, Lyman Hart replaced John Clum as the agent at San Carlos and the reservation quieted down for a while. I continued to herd cattle for Redmond and improve my ability to speak the White Eye tongue and buy nice clothes in Globe. I liked to wear good clothes like pants, vests, and coats of same material, white shirts with high collars worn with neckerchiefs of bright patterns, and black boots with fancy stitching on high shafts.

That harvest, I made two trips to old Camp Grant to visit with Hashke Bahnzin, listen to his stories about how to hunt and farm, and cast an eye on Chita. She smiled when she saw me coming. Just being around her made me feel good and stirred my desire for her. When I was at my work herding cattle or riding to deliver messages, I thought of her often and what life would be like if she were my woman, especially when a blanket covered the door to our *wickiup*.

Late in the Season of Earth Is Reddish Brown in the harvest the White Eyes call "1879," Redmond and I were eating an evening meal at his favorite café. It was already dark outside, and oil lamps cast a warm yellow glow over the room. I sat with my back to the door and, as we ate, watched the movement of men and animals up and down the lighted street. I saw a man in the shadows ride past and disappear in the darkness down the street. The way he sat his horse looked familiar, but I didn't recognize him with his face in the shadows. Soon the café door opened, letting in a puff of wind before it slammed shut.

Redmond turned from looking out the window and grinned as he waved whoever came in over to our table. I cringed at his eating manners when he said loud enough for all in the café to hear, "Ain't seen you in many moons. Come join us." I wanted to turn and see who it was but didn't want to appear rude as thudding boots approached our table. When his shadow lay over the table, I looked up. Al Sieber. He pulled a chair over to our table and plopped down between Redmond and me.

He reached over and grabbed my shoulder, giving it a little squeeze. "I ain't seen you in a long time, Kid. Whatcha been up to?"

"Herd cattle for Redmond. Shoot cattle for Apache rations on Saturday. Go see Chita two times in a moon." Sieber frowned as if he didn't know who or what I was talking about. I said, "You know her, she daughter of Hashke Bahnzin."

"Oh yes. I remember now. Beautiful girl. I hear the soldiers have named her 'Beauty.' You want her for your woman? Kinda young, ain't she? If she ain't, with her looks, why ain't she already taken?"

I grinned and nodded. "Hmmph. Someday, in a harvest or two, her womanhood come. I take her. Hashke Bahnzin wants me in family, runs other men off that ask for her. She very young. No womanhood ceremony yet. *Ussen* makes her a woman, I take her."

Redmond grinned when Sieber said, "Well that's good to hear. Young virile man like you need to start makin' children with his woman. It occurs to me that while you wait on her, you ought to start using all the stuff Sweeney, Beauford, Redmond here, and me taught you on army scoutin'. With Victorio killin' and takin' ever thing in sight and burning out settlers, the army is lookin' for good scouts. You'd shore fill the bill."

I took a bite of steak and shook my head. Sieber frowned. "Well why the hell not? I left you with Sweeney to teach you how to be a first-class scout. It's time to saddle up with the scouts."

"Sweeney teaches me much. I novitiate and messenger with Blue Coats when Clum brings Chokonen to San Carlos. But still much to learn. I not warrior yet and want to leave army to visit my woman when I want to see her, not when scout sergeant says I go."

Sieber laughed as the man who brings food in the eating place walked up with a white piece of cloth the White Eyes call "apron" wrapped around his waist and hanging down below his knees but above his boot tops. He asked what Sieber wanted to eat and took an order for steak, beans, and coffee.

The food carrier left to get Sieber's meal. Sieber said, "Victorio is winning most every battle he's had with the army since he left Mescalero angry and has been burning ranches and haciendas and killin' travelers on both sides of the border. Settlers and the army ain't happy about it. They need all the help they can get. You oughta join up. You've growed a lot with Sweeney since I saw you last, but Sweeney's gone. You wouldn't need him now anyway. You're lookin' like a man, not a boy."

I shook my head. "I wait until I learn enough."

Redmond was frowning. "What're you tryin' to do here, Sieber? Steal away the best cattle herder in a hundred miles? Kid can leave anytime he wants, but he's a good man. I want to keep him if I can."

Sieber looked at Redmond and made a half smile on one side of his face. "Aw, come on, Red, I ain't holdin' a gun to the boy's head to join the scouts." Redmond made his own half smile just as the food carrier walked up with a big white plate covered with steak and beans and a cup of coffee for Sieber.

Sieber sniffed over the food, grinned, and cut a piece of steak, its fat still searing hot and running out on the plate, and popped it into his mouth and chewed with a look of delight. He took a swallow of coffee and, leaning forward to rest his elbows on the table, said, "I got me a idea here, boys. Been thinkin' on it since I first watched Kid shoot those targets outside yore corral, Redmond. I admit Kid is still a little light in the britches to be a full-time army scout, but what if he rode with me as my assistant and I taught him all the things Sweeney didn't because there wasn't any fighting in those days?"

Redmond and I looked at each other and frowned. "What is 'assistant,' Sieber?"

Sieber put down his fork and scratched his chin in thought. "Well... an assistant helps with everything I do. He carries my messages, cooks, hunts, takes care of my animals, helps me scout trails, and kills bad guys. All the time, he's learning what an army scout does to support his commander and how he's supposed to act around other scouts."

Redmond nodded. "That sounds about right," and it did to me too.

"And how would you pay your assistant, and how much?"

Sieber stroked his big fuzzy mustache with his thumb and forefinger in thought as Redmond and I watched him. "I'll pay him like he's a private in the army. That's about half a dollar a day. I'll pay him out of my own pocket till he hires on as a scout with the army. He'n go visit Hashke Bahnzin and Chita or his family when I take a break for cards and whiskey in Prescott. Wanna be my assistant, Kid?"

Redmond sat looking at his plate, slowly shaking his head. I sat staring at Sieber, my heart pounding with excitement. He was offering me a place in the big dance, a chance to see the Victorio war up close, a chance to see a scout leader in action. I saw Redmond shaking his head. He knew I'd want to go with Sieber and my leaving left him without a hand to herd the cattle he needed for his butcher business.

I looked Sieber in his eyes and said, "Redmond good man. Always treat me fair. Needs help. I stay and help."

Redmond held up his hands palms out in front of his chest and said, "Whoa, Kid. Sieber is offering you a chance few men your age, if any, have and he's being very generous about it. You left before and I got by. It'll be all right. There are lots of wranglers around I can use, but few with the skills and courage you, not yet a recognized warrior, already have. You go with Sieber. I'll find somebody else to herd cattle for me. You can always come back if things don't work out."

I made the all-is-good sign across the top of the table. Sieber and Redmond grinned and made the same sign. "Sieber, I your assistant. Where we go?"

Sieber, rubbing his chin, said, "I've got to go down to the agency first thing in the morning and meet the replacement for Hart. I understand he's Captain Chaffee with his assistant Lieutenant Cruse, and the first thing they want to do is to make things right for the theft Hart and his boys were doing to the rations the Apache were supposedly getting but weren't. You're still staying at Redmond's place?"

I nodded.

"You go back to Redmond's and get all your stuff together to pack over to my quarters at the agency, and I'll meet you at first light to ride over to the agency. While you take care of your stuff, I'll talk to Chaffee and Cruse and find out what they want to do first. Then we'll get 'er done."

I nodded and said, *"Enjuh.* We go."

SIEBER CAME AT first light and helped me mount my paniers on his packhorse, and we headed across the desert along the trail to Peridot and then down Río San Carlos to the agency. The air was cool and the light soft from the early morning sunrise that kissed the desert to a slow awakening. Sieber said little as we rode toward Peridot. I thought his head must hurt from drinking White Eye whiskey the night before. As we rode through Peridot, I looked through the morning mists surrounding my mother's *wickiup* and most of the shelters in my father's village. I caught a glimpse of my mother working over her fire for a morning meal and my father sitting nearby having his morning coffee while he talked to her father, my grandfather, who was still vigorous and whose *wickiup* was nearby theirs. It was hard to ride by without speaking, but I knew Sieber was right to go on and speak with his army chief first. If we had stopped, courtesy and custom demanded we stay and eat and visit for at least two hands. I'd see them in suns after I shot the cattle for rations.

We crossed the big flat in front of the place where women gathered to collect family rations and tied our horses in front of the agency. Sieber stepped up to the door and knocked. I had seen other White Eyes do this before and realized it was their custom like the one Apache followed by standing outside a door blanket and coughing or clearing your throat to announce you're there. Immediately from the inside, we heard "Come!" and Sieber opened the door to face a *teniente* with hair on his head and under his nose the color of *pesh klitso*. The *teniente* sat behind a desk next to the closed door of the agent's room. He grinned and stood up from his desk and, sticking out his hand, said, "Lieutenant Thomas Cruse." Sieber nodded, took *Teniente's* hand and gave it a couple of good pumps, and said, "Albert Sieber, chief of scouts for Lieutenant Blocksom and stationed at Camp Verde." He motioned toward me and said, "This here is my assistant, Ohyessonna, one of the best shots in the territory, and he knows what's going on with the Indians here at San Carlos." *Teniente* stuck out his hand and I gave it a couple of good pumps. "You look mighty young for a scout, but I understand Mister Sieber knows his men." I started to tell the *teniente* that I was no scout, but I saw a tiny shake from Sieber's head and kept my mouth closed.

The *teniente* said, "What can we do for you?"

"Lieutenant Blocksom sent us down here to help Captain Chaffee straighten out the corrupt ways of Hart and his cronies used to steal rations from the San Carlos Reservation Apache. Is Captain Chaffee available to talk?"

"Let me check."

Teniente knocked on the door, heard "Come," and went in the next room. There was a low rumble of voices, and then Captain Chaffee said in a loud voice, "Of course! Show them in."

The *teniente* swung the door wide open and motioned for us in to meet Captain Chaffee. After the usual introduction ceremony, Chaffee motioned us to chairs around a table made of rough-cut pine, and he and Sieber talked about how best to sort out what and how Hart and his cronies had been stealing from the Apache.

Chaffee said, "The account books show a third to a half of all rations distributed this past fall. I think Hart kept the difference and sold it in Tucson. He even sold tools sent to help the Apache dig irrigation ditches. It's incredible that they used butcher knives to dig irrigation ditches. This is outrageous treatment of the Apache, and I intend to stop it before they run off to help Victorio fight and a trickle of blood becomes a flood."

Sieber sat nodding and said, "Yes, sir. I think that's also the main concern of Lieutenant Blocksom. He thinks that, among other things, the local contractors supplying beef to the reservation are cheatin'. Somebody told him that them ranchers sold the reservation thin, waterlogged cattle.

"Clum stopped letting the ranchers starve their cattle for water two or three days before they crossed the river with them. They'd let 'em drink all they wanted when they crossed the river so the government paid for a lot of river water and little beef while the Apache starved. My assistant here helps with the slaughter of beef delivered for rations. He thinks the weight reported for the beef delivered to the reservation ain't right. I think the rig they use to weigh cattle before slaughter is jiggered. We need to check it sooner rather than later."

Chaffee frowned, crossed his arms, and leaned back in his chair. "No doubt we do, Mister Sieber. In fact, there's a contractor delivering some cattle today. When we finish here, can we look at the scale?"

Sieber grinned and said, "Why, shore we can, Captain."

Chaffee also talked about how to defend San Carlos against a Victorio attack and the strategy for defending the border when he might try to return. I thought the "strategy" was not good. Victorio knew many places to cross the border. I believed he and his men were good enough to cross in front of the White Eyes in the dark of night, and some even at the time of no shadows. It was better to protect people in their villages and when they were on wagon roads than watch every place Victorio might want to cross.

SIEBER AND CAPTAIN Chaffee talked for about two hands before we went to look at the scale used for weighing cattle that the San Carlos Reservation bought. It looked complicated, and I didn't understand how it worked. Sieber knew exactly how it worked. He looked it over while Captain Chaffee and I watched. Sieber walked around the platform where the cow stood during weighing. There were levers and balance weights and pulleys and ropes, and it was clear all had to work together correctly.

When Sieber left the platform, he was shaking his head. "Looks like Lieutenant Blocksom was right. This weighing machine has been jiggered to give more weight than what's true. You'll think you're buying a six-hundred-pound steer when it only weighs four hundred fifty pounds."

Chaffee's face turned red. It even made his red hair look lighter. The contractor who had been using the weighing machine to report the weight of his cattle squatted in the shade of the rations building, having a smoke and talking to a couple of cowboys. Chaffee motioned a White Eye private to come join us. The man came and gave the sign of recognition and respect, the wave edge of his hand brought close to his forehead. Chaffee made the same sign back and said to the man, "See that man in the shade of the rations building smoking a cigarette?"

The soldier nodded and said, "Yes, sir."

"Well get over there and tell him I want to see him—now."

The private didn't waste any time summoning the man, who ambled over to see what the redheaded captain wanted.

When the man joined us, Chaffee said, "You been using these scales to weigh your delivery today?"

The man nodded and said, "Yes, sir. I do. It's in my contract that I do that."

"Any idea where that contraption came from?"

"Yes, sir. Mister Clum wanted it built, and I built it."

"Do you know that the weight it yields is about thirty percent too high?"

The contractor grinned and nodded. "Yes, sir, I know it. Never told Clum that. He loved these Indians, but I built it so it's screwing them damned Apache out of rations them fools in Washington is tryin' to give 'em. I hope to hell they starve as far as I'm concerned."

I had been around White Eye soldiers most of my life and learned what cursing was, but I never heard such a string of curse words out of the mouth of one soldier, especially a big chief, a captain. The man they called "contractor" took a step back from the fire coming out of Chaffee's mouth and Chaffee advanced. The contractor wasn't grinning anymore. Sieber stood taking it all in with his arms crossed and clenching his jaws, trying not to laugh.

Chaffee finally calmed a little and said with a lowered voice still filled with fire, "Now, Mister Contractor, you get your cheating, good-for-nothing tail off this reservation before sundown and don't ever come back. If you're not gone by sundown or you do come back, I'll have you in front of a firing squad. Do I make myself clear, mister?"

Contractor swallowed and took another step back, nodding. "Yeah, yeah, real clear. Don't worry about me ever comin' back to this hellhole. I was just giving them damned Apache what they deserved."

Chaffee bared his teeth and snarled, "These Apache deserved every bit of what we promised 'em, and we're damned lucky they haven't broken out and killed people because you've stolen food out of their mouths. If they do break out, I hope they catch your tail and do what they do best when they roast your head over a hot fire. Now git."

I liked this chief. I'd be glad to scout for him when it was time for me to join the soldiers.

TWENTY-THREE

CAMP VERDE

TENIENTE BLOCKSOM WAS commander at Camp Verde with its dark-skinned soldiers and Apache scouts led by Sieber. Before I followed Sieber to Camp Verde as his assistant, he showed me on the map he carried folded up in his shirt pocket that Camp Verde was on the Río Verde about a hundred twenty miles northwest of the San Carlos Agency and about forty miles due east of the town of Prescott, where Sieber often went when, as he said, he needed to let off a little steam by playing cards and drinking whiskey. At one time, Camp Verde was close to the center of fighting between Western Apache and General Crook's scouts and cavalry. It had seen a lot of action as General Crook fought the Tonto War with Sieber leading many of the fights using scouts he had recruited.

After Sieber helped Captain Chaffee get the rationing-theft business straightened out, we loaded the packhorse and headed northwest toward Camp Verde. It was a hard trail climbing steep ridges and following dry and flowing streams in deep narrow canyons. The country had many more pine, juniper, and piñon trees than the land south of the Río Gila I was used to. The white cliffs and canyons of the northern Mogollon Rim were half a day's ride southeast from Camp Verde.

At Camp Verde, Sieber led me to his white-wall tent with a plank floor. I dropped my jaw staring at the rows of bright white canvas tents occupied by his scouts—the tribal police at San Carlos didn't have their own tents, and they wouldn't have put them up in nice, neat rows like these. Sieber laughed when he saw my look of astonishment as I scanned the rows of scout tents.

He said, "Kid, I'm gonna ease over to see the lieutenant and find out what's been going on while I've been helpin' Cap'n Chaffee. Unload the packhorse and put the stuff in the back of my tent. There're two cots in the tent. You can use the cot that doesn't have any blankets. If you'd rather have your own little tent like the scouts, I'm sure we can find you one before the sun goes down."

I said nothing, just made the all-is-well hand wave parallel to the ground. Sieber nodded and headed toward another group of wall tents a hundred yards away, saying over his shoulder, "I'll be back."

Unloading the packhorse, I lay the paniers on the floor at the back of the tent and then opened my panier and, pulling out my blanket, rolled it out on the cot free of blankets. I thought about leading the packhorse with its frame over to the corral that held army horses and let him go after I pulled the pack frame off. But Martin Sweeney had taught me that every action in the army is done in an approved way. I was sure there must be some unchanging custom that soldiers and scouts followed for returning the horses the army gave them to ride or carry pack loads. I decided it was better for me to just wait for Sieber to return.

It wasn't long before I saw Sieber, with his horse loping across the ground between the small scout tents and the ones with walls the leaders used. I stood as he approached, and he grinned. "Ain't no need to stand when I come along, Kid." Seeing the puzzled look on my face, he said, "It's a Blue Coat custom to stand when a big chief walks in a room. It's taken as a sign of respect." I nodded I understood. The Blue Coats have many strange customs I must learn.

Sieber said, "The lieutenant told me things have been quiet here except one of my better scouts sneaked off to a tizwin party some of his people was throwing over in a canyon thirty miles north of here. I warned him and I told him to leave that damned tizwin alone, but it didn't do any good. He went anyway, got drunk, got in a fight, and was cut up purty good. His people brought him back, and Doc sewed him up before he bled to death. Looks like he'll live, but now Gen'l Crook says he's got to stay in the calaboose for a moon 'cause he weren't supposed to drink any tizwin and he left camp without permission. Learn these lessons well, boy. Don't you go drinkin' at no tizwin party, and don't leave camp without permission. *Comprende?*"

I nodded. "*Sí, Sieber. Comprendo.*"

"Now we got to go arrest the ones who cut up our scout or every Apache who hears the tale will think he can attack us and we won't take revenge. I'll show you how to turn in our packhorse and where you can keep your pony.

Then we'll have a bite to eat, load up, and go get the fools who had the tizwin party and sliced up our man. You ready to go?"

"Hmmph. I go."

THE MOON'S COOL white light, extra bright on the white alkali, cast deep black shadows as we rode for the canyons and cliffs along Wet Beaver Creek. Sieber didn't need to follow a trail. His man recovering from being cut in all kinds of places and sweating through the white *di-yen's* healing power had told him where the *tizwin* party had been and where his people who had been there were camped.

We rode up Beaver Creek to a little White Eye village with badly built houses scattered along the trail that Sieber called Rimrock and then up Wet Beaver Creek until we came to a piece of flat land by the creek that grew long straight rows of beans and other vegetables with no weeds in sight anywhere, and beyond the cropland was a *rancheria* of *wickiups* under pines and piñons. We rode on up the creek bank that went around the *rancheria* until Sieber motioned me under some trees that screened us from the camp. The moon had already started its arc down into Mexico, half the night already gone. We watered our horses, loosened their cinches, and tied them where they could graze on grass screened by bushes nearer the creek.

Sieber and I sat on a shelf of white rock that stretched from the creek back into the trees.

He said, "Here's my plan, Kid. Before dawn, I'm gonna ride back down to that field of crops, wait until good light, and then ride on into the *rancheria* and ask for the man who cut up the scout during a tizwin drunk. When he finds out I've come for him, he's gonna do one of two things." He pointed up with his forefinger. "One, he'll surrender peaceably, or"—he held up his index finger beside the forefinger—"two, he'll run out of the *rancheria* up the creek where he thinks there are plenty of places to hide. I'd bet money he runs. After all, he is a Tonto."

I frowned. "Why you say that—being a Tonto, he'll run? Father say Tontos good fighters."

"Do you know what *tonto* means in Spanish?"

I shook my head.

Grinning, Sieber said, "It means 'fool.' If that fool runs, he'll be coming in your direction. Put him in your sights and stop him. You don't have to kill him if he stops with a wound in an arm or a leg, but if he keeps coming, you kill him and don't hesitate to do it. *Comprende?"*

"Sí, comprendo." I didn't want to wound or kill the man. But Sieber knew how to survive. I knew that, to survive, I had to do what he told me.

WE SAT ON the rock shelf wrapped in our blankets, waiting for the dawn. When the black night sky began to turn a gauzy gray, Sieber stood and tossed a pebble up high, and we could see it all the way to the top of its path. Not long before daylight, he folded and rolled his blanket, tied it on his saddle, tightened his cinches, let his horse drink at the creek, mounted and said nothing. He rode out of the trees and toward the village's crop field. Already, the sound of axes and hatchets bounced along the gurgling stream as women gathered their morning firewood.

The sun in a coat of *pesh klitso* appeared gleaming over white cliffs, lighting the trees along the creek and field. A low mumble from women talking around their fires, children playing, and men mumbling to each other and their wives rolled up the creek to my ears, and birds in the bosque along the creek started their morning songs. I waited, enjoying the coming of the day. Suddenly, the hum of voices from down the creek stopped. I knew Sieber must have appeared at the edge of the village. I waited. The sun rose a little higher, and then I heard a distant yell, *"Ch'a'olgheed!"* (He runs away.) I knew Sieber was telling me to be ready.

I picked a spot where the sun was casting a light shaft on a piece of path about a hundred yards away. I sat in the shadows where I was very hard to see, levered a round into my rifle's chamber and, sitting down with my elbows on my knees, sighted on the bright spot by the creek. It wasn't long before the bird chorus became silent and I saw a man through the bosque trees pounding up the path toward the bright spot I had picked to shoot into. He looked a little older than me and wore his hair straight and long.

When he was ten or twelve steps from the bright spot, I yelled, "Hold! Or I'll kill you!" He jerked his head up and stopped in two or three steps, pausing a moment. He looked up and down the path and, not seeing anyone, plunged toward the bright spot I had selected. I had no time to debate with myself the rightness of what I was doing. If I only wounded him, one day he'd be back for revenge. Kill now or be killed later. I put the sight picture from my rifle on the man's chest and squeezed the trigger. The rifle bucked in my hands and thundered in my ears. A bright-red dot appeared in the middle of his chest between his nipples, and from the exit wound, I saw a spray of blood and flesh. He staggered back as blood flowed from his mouth and nose, and he fell backward, his eyes wide, filled with surprise. I walked through the brush that had hidden me and, squatting by him, watched the light of life in his eyes slowly dim and vanish as his blood stained the ground under him. He was the first man I had killed up close and on my own. Somehow, this makes me more like Sieber. I felt sick and wanted to puke, but my stomach held what I had in it, and I was glad.

Soon Sieber came riding up the creek with his big army revolver drawn and half the men from the village following him. He stopped behind me. I saw the village men standing on both sides of the creek. They craned their necks to see the dead man and me, the killer. I heard the creak of leather as Sieber dismounted and, in a couple of steps was on a knee beside me.

"Whew! Great shot, Kid. This man was dead before he hit the ground. Guess you thought it was better to kill him than to wound and chase him."

I shook my head. "He was still alive but dying fast when I squatted here. I killed him because he deserved to die and I didn't want to be looking over my shoulder when he healed and came after me to take his revenge."

Sieber nodded. "Hmmph. You did the right thing, Kid. I wouldn't want him chasing me for revenge either. We'll leave him here for his family. They'll want to bury him so he gets to the Happy Place sooner rather than later. I'll speak with the chief about this one while you get your pony. I'll meet you on the south side of the village by the creek, and then we'll go."

I nodded and went to get my pony.

AFTER SIEBER AND I killed the one who cut up our scout, it was quiet through the Ghost Face and into the early days of the Season of Little Eagles. I hunted with Sieber and learned he was the best of shots—except for me.

Sieber learned that a new agent had come to San Carlos. His White Eye name was Tiffany. He treated the People well, except he, like so many other Bureau of Indian Affairs agents, began stealing Chiricahua rations to sell in Tucson, and his big chief removed him. Victorio was in a death struggle with Major Morrow. The commander at Camp Verde awaited orders by his big chief to use his soldiers and scouts to support Major Morrow. But Camp Verde soldiers and scouts ready to support Major Morrow never went to those battles. The Season of Many Leaves peacefully stepped into the Season of Large Fruit while I hunted and did small scouting duties for Sieber at Camp Verde. But those times didn't last long.

Victorio, while destroying everything in his path on both sides of the border, was showing his strength in battles with the Blue Coat soldiers and threatened to appear at San Carlos and even the score with White Mountain scouts who, with others, me included, had taken his horses near the trail up the Natanes cliffs. The soldier chief decided the best way to stop Victorio's raids on the American side of the border was to face him with horse soldiers who rode the border from south of Fort Cummings on the east side of the Florida Mountains to Fort Thomas on the Río Gila thirty miles southeast of the San Carlos Agency. Foot soldiers and companies of scouts guarded the trails across mountains, common passes, and nearby water holes.

I rode with Sieber when the great assembly of soldiers under the big soldier chief essentially formed a line of soldiers one hundred forty miles long and swept everything thirty miles north of the border into the land of the *Nakai-yes*. Of course, all this power and desire to fight Victorio was wasted. No one saw an Apache during the entire operation.

For months, Major Morrow led the fighting in several big battles, giving as good as he got from Victorio and sometimes more. In the Season of Large Fruit in the harvest the White Eyes called "1880," Victorio went into Chihuahua low on ammunition and tried to rest near three little mountains in Chihuahua called Tres Castillos while Nana with his Power looked for fresh supplies of ammunition.

The *Nakai-yi* colonel, Joaquin Terrazas, with his soldiers and Tarahumara Indios after claiming Apache scalps for a big reward, were not far behind Victorio when he stopped at Tres Castillos. Terrazas attacked Victorio's band when his scouts assured him the Apache had no place to run. Scouts later told me that Victorio's men only had three bullets each for their rifles. When they had no more bullets, Victorio and some of his leaders stabbed themselves in their hearts rather than suffer humiliation as prisoners before the *Nakai-yes* killed them. When I heard this, I was proud of Victorio's courage. I hoped that if that kind of time ever came for me, I could kill myself and wrap my memory in a blanket of honor.

TWENTY-FOUR

SIEBER'S STORY

IN THE SEASON of Many Leaves after Victorio killed himself, a pot of wild and worried expectations began to boil. A Cibecue Apache, Noch-ay-del-klinne, a frail *di-yen* many called "Dreamer," claimed that he could commune with the dead and that when the White Eyes went away, the great chiefs would return to lead their People and the rapidly disappearing game would return. He held dances to help him call the great chiefs back. People from across San Carlos began attending the dances and ecstasy filled them as they danced. Word of the Power in these dances swept across San Carlos like a roaring fire in dry desert brush. Soon great crowds gathered at Noch-ay-del-klinne's dancing place and received his blessing. They danced around a tall pole together in their ecstasy in a kind of wheel dance Noch-ay-del-klinne's Power had given him. As each one passed him, he blessed them with a dusting of hoddentin, the sacred golden pollen taken from cattail reeds, and his Power filling the crowds grew ever stronger.

Tiffany, the San Carlos agent, and the big army chief learned that the Apache were gathering in great groups to dance away the White Eyes. The White Eye and Blue Coat chiefs worried the dances were a prelude to a big Apache war. The commander at Camp Verde sent Sieber, and I went with him, to learn what was actually going on at the dances. Neither of us believed the dancing meant anything. The next morning, as the sun poured gold on the mountains and the birds were beginning to stir and sing, we saddled our horses in the cold morning air. Sieber went to find a Cibecue Apache scout he knew and trusted, and I went with him. He soon found the scout sitting in front of his tent at a little fire he shared with other scouts.

Sieber said, "Ho, Singing Tree, *Nish'ii'*."

Singing Tree nodded but continued to stare at his fire while taking a sip from his coffee cup. "Ho, Sieber. *Idiits'ag*. Coffee hot and good. You and the boy have some. Birds sing good this sunrise."

Sieber looked at me and I nodded. He took two cups from five or six off a big flat stone near the fire and filled them from an ancient, blackened and dented coffeepot sitting on a stone at the edge of the fire. I blew across the steaming black water before putting the cup to my lips. Sieber took a swallow without blowing across the top of the cup, but its heat didn't seem to bother him. He sat down by Singing Tree, put his cup down, reached in a vest pocket, and brought out cigarette fixings. He rolled one, lit it from a twig he pulled from a piece of firewood, smoked to the four directions, and handed it to Singing Tree, who smoked and then handed it to me. I was surprised since I wasn't a scout, and this was all Sieber's business. Sieber gave me a barely perceptible nod to smoke, and I smoked before I handed it back to him. He took another puff and then threw the last bit in the fire.

Singing Tree said, "What you want me to do, Sieber? You know I go anytime."

Sieber nodded. "Yes, sir, you're always ready to go and a fine scout. I like that mucho. This morning, I just need a little information. My big chiefs are worried Noch-ay-del-klinne's dances might start another war. I'm to go watch one of his dances and tell 'em what I think. I need to know where his dance ground is before my assistant and I go riding down there. Can you tell us?"

"Hmmph. I tell. Follow trail up Salt Creek two miles from big Cibecue camp. Dances there on big flat field by creek. You see big pole where his dances go 'round in big circles with spokes."

He looked at Sieber and grinned. "I know what you want, Sieber. West and east sides' ridges not too far away. Good places to hide and watch. Closest ridge on east side. You go. You see."

Sieber nodded and stood. "Singing Tree is a good scout. I remember you." He nodded to me and said, "We go. Return four or five suns depending on the dancing. *Adios*."

SIEBER KEPT UP a pace that covered much ground as he rode down the trail toward Globe. Not far from Globe, we had two more hands of riding before we lost the sun behind the mountains. He turned east, crossed the río, and took a rough trail I had missed seeing when we first followed the trail toward Camp Verde. The trail roughly paralleled the Salt Río but had fewer twists and turns. It crossed many ridges using high narrow trails with deep drop-offs. I had ridden many trails like these most of my life and they didn't bother me. Sieber seemed relaxed in the saddle, and the drop-offs didn't bother him either.

We were losing light when he found a place to camp. Although the high, narrow trails didn't seem to bother him, he wouldn't ride them in the dark. Our camp was in a shallow box canyon with high cliff walls close to the río, which let us hide the light from our little fire. I made coffee, and Sieber and I ate army trail rations.

Wrapped in our blankets, we watched the fire slowly die. High on the ridge forming one side of the canyon, we heard a wolf howl and, not long after, a deer bleat that didn't last long amid snarls and growls. I saw Sieber take out his pistola and check its loads. I took the hint and did the same thing. I even loaded one under the hammer. Watching Sieber relax, I said, "Sieber, I ask about your personal life?"

He nodded. "Speak. I answer."

"Where you come from, and why you made chief of scouts?"

He focused his attention on the fire for a while before answering. "I was born across the big water in the East, a place called Rhineland. My father died a harvest after I was born, but I had a strong mother and several brothers and sisters. My mother with my oldest brother, John, decided the best place for her and her children was in America, so she sold her farm, house, and anything else she couldn't put in a trunk. We sailed with my brother John across the big water to New York City and settled in the farm and woods country of Lancaster County, Pennsylvania. By the time I got used to hunting in the woods there, my older sister, Theresia, married a man named Oswald and my mother, sisters, and I moved to the big timber country of Minnesota. When I was two or three harvests younger than you, I drove teams of horses pullin' logs to a sawmill. I hunted there in the big timber, and that's where I learned to shoot, but the winters in Minnesota are mighty cold and most of the big game were gone by then."

Just speaking of the cold winters in the Minnesota place made Sieber pause and pull his blanket closer and hunch his shoulders like it was winter in Minnesota, but I wasn't that cold.

"I know you know about the big war where the White Eyes fought each other over the right to own dark-skin men as slaves. I sided with those who said slavery was wrong, but I was too young to join the army when that war started. About a harvest later, I was old enough and I joined up as soon as I could get my mother to sign papers that said she agreed I could join even if I was still a little young. Over the next harvest, I fought in some mighty bloody battles until the battle the White Eyes named Gettysburg. Got shot in my right leg and hit in the head with a piece of explodin' artillery shell. It took about five moons for me to heal, and then I was given duties like guarding prisoners until the war ended."

Sieber rolled another cigarette, lit it with a fire twig, took a puff, and gazed at the milk river of stars in the soft blackness above us. He made one side of his face grin.

"When the war ended, I left the army, went back home for a little while, and then decided I was gonna go west and make my fortune. I wound up north of here, worked some on building the railroad, until there was time for some silver prospectin', and I did that for a while. Never had any luck findin' much gold or silver and finally quit and went over the mountains to California lookin' for a life where I didn't have to work so hard for so little."

He hunched his shoulders again and took another puff from his cigarette before he flipped what was left of the *tobaho* in the fire.

"Didn't find no gold or silver in California. So I throwed in with some cowboys drivin' a herd of horses from California over to this here part of the country around Hardyville. Them horses was like gold here in Arizona. After shooting at Walapais for a while, I got over here to Prescott. Mighty pretty place, but I had very little money to trade for supplies. I worked around a corral for five dollars a day and built me up a little stash. I did many a job around Prescott, including working with some of the best White Eye scouts this country has ever seen. Then a feller named C. C. Bean hired me to run a ranch he owned up in the Williamson Valley. The ranch was about twenty miles northwest of Prescott, and they were having a heap of trouble with Indians raiding in that area. I was on that ranch for about a harvest and had me some tussles with the Indians raidin' in that area.

"I left Bean's ranch and joined a couple of fellers on their ranch on Walnut Creek farther west from Williamson Valley. I learned most of my scouting from those men. Their names were Dan O'Leary and George Thrasher. I tell you, them boys were killers. Dan, he's about the best scout I ever knowed when it come to Indians.

"When General Crook came to Tucson the next year, Dan got me work as a scout with him to start his work of bringin' the Apache to heel. I was always learning things from Crook when I worked with him. I saved ol' Crook from a disaster a time or two, and he learned I usually had good advice about Apache. I worked with the scouts and kept gettin' promoted until I was a chief of scouts for one of his regiments. That's pretty much my story, Kid. It's all I have to say."

"Hmmph. Sieber, you mighty warrior. Happy I follow you. Learn much."

"Thanks, Kid. I'll be asking you about yore history here purty soon. Let's get some rest. We got a hard ride in the morning."

TWENTY-FIVE

BEGINNING SERVICE
WITH THE SCOUTS

AS USUAL, SIEBER knew what he was talking about. We saddled up at dawn and crossed ridges without number until we saw the Cibecue village and used the ridges around it to the east to stay out of sight as we followed eastern ridges along Salt Creek to Noch-ay-del-klinne's place of dancing. We found the dance pole and surrounding field used for dancing and decided Singing Tree was right. The best place to watch the dancing was the east-side ridge, which faced the dancing place. We followed a rough trail to the top of the ridge, found a place on top where there was enough grass to keep our horses out of sight and satisfied grazing while they were hobbled, and gave us a clear view not over three hundred yards from the dancing pole and surrounding dance ground.

Sieber and I used our soldier glasses to study the ground around the pole. We saw piles of firewood and ashpits for fires placed on the corners of a large square where the grass was worn away. Using the pole as the center reference, a line from the pole to each corner fire pit pointed in a primary direction for north, south, east, and west.

We saw people getting ready for the dance by arranging wood in the ashpits and by carrying water to three of the four big water baskets near the north-corner fire pits. A woman on a horse appeared with water baskets on either side of her knees. She rode to the water baskets and poured what was in her baskets into the big empty water basket. I heard Sieber say to himself, "Hmmph, that there must be *tulapai*, but it ain't much for a big crowd."

On the east corner near the fire pit were drums and stiff hides to keep the rhythms for the dancers. Soon those working were joined by others, and the crowd, I counted, quickly grew to over a hundred. Outside the perimeter of the square, other women started fires and cooked, giving away food to the workers. As the daylight time grew short, people in their finest clothes started appearing and lines of horses moved up the trail from Cibecue carrying riders wrapped in their blankets. Seeing those blankets made me notice that the sun was beginning to hide and the light around us was getting cooler, especially down on Salt Creek. I told Sieber I was getting my blanket. He asked that I get his too. Soon we sat hidden under our blankets like two boulders on the little cliff below us.

As it got darker, more and more of the People appeared as they tied their horses to trees up and down the trail. The hum of voices from the crowd dimmed. Soon there was an eerie silence, one that I had never noticed before a dance. There was total darkness except for the stars. We waited. From the place of the dry hides came a light thump from the stiff hides in a low, steady thumpity-thump heart-like rhythm. The People seemed to sigh in anticipation and happiness. A torch flared near the east corner, revealing a clown dancer. The scene and heartbeat-like thumping of the stiff hides and drums made the hair on the back of my neck stand up. The clown advanced, whirling and dancing, to light the fires on each corner, the north corner being the last fire. A crown dancer appeared out of the circle of light from each fire. They danced near the center of the great circle, passing through the fire sites while the clown danced on the edge. Still no singing, only the powerful pounding sounds from the stiff hides.

The drumming on the hides stopped, and out of the silence, a high single voice sang from the dark beyond the eastern fire. Noch-ay-del-klinne walked into the eastern firelight, and the crown dancers led by the clown surrounded him. When their ring was complete, the clown and crown dancers melted away into the darkness. Pot drums began a deep thumping and the Noch-ay-del-klinne sang four songs facing each direction as he turned east to south and ended facing east.

The drums stopped, and holding his arms out, he began to speak of his vision and Power given by *Ussen*, saying he had been shown that if the White Eyes would leave the land, the great chiefs had told him they would rise from their graves and come to help the People reclaim the land over which they once freely roamed. The wild game the White Eyes had driven away would return, and our days would be like those of our grandfathers. To call the spirits, he had shown the People a new dance to follow with their feet, and they had to keep its rhythm in their hearts to help him call the great chiefs that they might help all the People.

Holding his arms out like wings, Noch-ay-del-klinne called all the People to come to him and dance as he had taught them to receive a blessing as he sprinkled golden pollen on them. All the drums and stiff hides began the rhythm for the dance. Out of the crowd gathered around the square made by the four fires streamed young and old who had already danced before the call to the spirits. The dancers first grouped in a circle around Noch-ay-del-klinne then as if by some unseen power naturally formed spokes facing toward him. At a change in the drumbeat, he began a new song. Those who were first to dance circled around him, the hub of a wheel, to receive their scattering of the sacred golden pollen. People new to Noch-ay-del-klinne's dance watched the dancers a while to learn the steps and rotational moves and then joined as spoke members.

We watched the dance for a hand. Then Sieber stood and motioned me back toward the horses. He caught his horse, tied it to juniper, and saddled it. When I saw what he was doing, I knew he was ready to leave. I saddled my pony and we rode south down the western ridges along Salt Creek, passed the big Cibecue village, and rode west until we were out of sight and hearing from the village and made our little camp. We ate our army trail rations in silence until Sieber said, "Well, Assistant, did you see anything that should concern the agent?"

I shook my head. "No, I saw nothing to worry Tiffany. The Dreamer urges no war, only prayer to *Ussen* and dancing to help them pray. Did you see anything?"

Sieber grinned. "Naw. That Dreamer is harmless, and he ain't talking war—yet."

An owl in a big pine near us called. I cringed. It told me death was coming.

SIEBER'S REPORT OF what we saw didn't change Tiffany's mind about Noch-ay-del-klinne and ordered the commander at Fort Apache to arrest him. When the officer showed up at the Dreamer's *rancheria* and arrested him, Noch-ay-del-klinne didn't resist, but his supporters were outraged and there was a fight on the trail back to Fort Apache. An exchange of gunfire killed the Dreamer. Some of his supporters then roamed the reservation and killed any White Eye they found. They even attacked Fort Apache for a while but eventually disappeared into the back country or went back to their villages disappointed that the Noch-ay-del-klinne didn't have the power they thought he had. The big chief Blue Coat sent in more soldiers to ensure the bands fought no more and to arrest the leaders who started the fighting. The Chiricahua leaders, Geronimo and Juh, believed the Blue Coats were after them for their raids in Mexico and at the first hint the soldiers were after them, convinced the other band leaders to run for the land of the *Nakai-yes* with them and all Chiricahua left the reservation leaving only Loco and his People behind. The Blue Coats chased them south across the border but didn't capture any and only managed to kill one or two during their escape.

Al Sieber brought his scouts to San Carlos to support the troopers chasing Chiricahua. The big chief general knew the Chiricahua would be raiding north from across the border. To stop them, he had his soldiers patrolling the border and scouts to protect army camp areas in case the Chiricahua slipped by the patrols. Sieber and his scouts returned to Camp Verde and patrolled the ground that the Chiricahua might raid if they got past Fort Apache.

I rode out with Sieber on every patrol and saw traces of Apache trails made by Chiricahua and others that most of his scouts missed. When he learned that I saw true trails and reported them, he spoke with me one night as we sat by our fire while on patrol in the Season of Earth Is Reddish Brown. Sieber made a cigarette, and we smoked to the four directions.

He said, "Kid, you been ridin' with me as my assistant now for more than two years. We've seen a lot of action together, and you been growin' into a fine man, totally trustworthy to follow orders, do the right thing if the orders are wrong, and report true what you see and what you think it means. With them Chiricahua breakin' out and getting to Mexico with few if any losses means that they'll be raidin' and makin' war north. The army is gonna need all the help it can get. From what I hear from talking to a captain or two, they're guessing the army will bring General Crook back from the Platte command since the plains tribes look like they're under control. We'll see. I think it'd be a good time for you to join the scouts. They're looking for people now. I'm guessing with as much trainin' and experience you've got, you'll be a sergeant in less than a harvest, and a first sergeant in less than two. There's gonna be lots of action comin'. What d'you say?"

I was proud of Sieber's praise. He was a powerful warrior who knew how to win in battles, and he was saying good things about me. I thought on his words while I stared at the fire remembering images of the days we had ridden together and how we had helped each other. If he said I was ready to be a scout, then I was ready. I didn't know about being a sergeant within a harvest. That was something the passing of suns would show.

"Sieber, you speak good of me. When sun comes, I touch the little spear commander dips in black water to make tracks on paper that say my name. I touch the little spear for six moons. What you think, Sieber?"

Sieber grinned and nodded.

TWENTY-SIX

THE CHASE AFTER LOCO

THE CHIRICAHUA WHO had left the reservation near the end of the moon the White Eyes named September and had escaped the Blue Coats with the loss of one or two warriors in over three hundred people, decided that Loco should join them so his People didn't have to "suffer" at San Carlos. They sent three men who knew Loco well three times to first suggest, then ask again, and finally tell him to join them or expect warriors from Juh's stronghold who would force him to leave.

Though scarred in his face, an eye sagging in the scar from his fight with a bear in his young-man days, but its vision still good, Loco was no man's fool. The first time the Chiricahua from Mexico spoke with him, he told them that he had promised the White Eyes he would stay on the reservation, and he was a man of his word. The second time, he told them he would not change his mind. The third time they returned with a threat, the men from Mexico said they would be back in forty days and Loco and his People must be ready to go. Loco told them not to return or there would be trouble. A woman living with Loco told the Blue Coats what was happening, and Sieber with ten scouts—I was one of the ten—and *Teniente* Blake scouted the Dragoon Mountains, one of the favorite Apache trails into and out of Mexico, for trail signs of the Chiricahua visiting Loco, but we found nothing.

The Chiricahua chiefs were not men of idle talk. We all knew they would do what they said. We waited. There was a dead calm like watching a storm cloud out on the edge of the world with heavy rain falling approaching across the *llano*. We saw it coming but didn't know when its fury would descend on us. Forty days passed and no Chiricahua from Mexico appeared.

General Willcox sent two troops of cavalry to the border, and Sieber and his scouts went with them. Willcox knew enough not to expect that his forces would intercept the Apache, but at least the troopers were nearby when something happened.

Near the end of the moon the White Eyes called "March," Sieber and his ten men scouted the Steins Peak Mountain ranges. The ranges run north to south near the line on a map that divides Arizona from New Mexico. We found trail signs of a large group of Chiricahua headed for San Carlos on the north end of the Las Animas Mountains. Sieber sent a hard-riding scout with a message for General Willcox on what he had found, but we were too late to stop the Chiricahua-forced breakout of Loco's People.

Four years later, Chato told me the story of how Geronimo forced Loco into Mexico. Chiricahua under Geronimo, Naiche, Chihuahua, and Chato nearing Loco's camp cut the telegraph wires into the San Carlos Agency. Chihuahua hated Stirling, the chief of the reservation police, for accidentally killing a child when the police tried to arrest her father for making *tulapai*, but gunfire was from both sides. Chihuahua lured Stirling toward Loco's village with three or four rifle shots, which for certain the agency heard. Hiding in the village, Chihuahua assassinated Stirling when he and two policemen appeared. Meanwhile Geronimo, Naiche, and Chato ensured Loco left leading his People.

Loco stood in front of his lodge, shaking his head no, as his People ran past him down to the river and then stopped to look for him. His wives surrounded him while they waited for his instructions on what to do. Out of the swirl of people herded out of the village, Chato appeared in front of Loco. He jammed the end of his rifle's barrel against Loco's chest and said through clenched teeth, "Lead your People or die." Loco saw the fury in Chato's eyes and knew he wasn't making an empty threat. –Loco threw up his hands in resignation and led his People out of San Carlos and down the wagon road toward Fort Thomas following Geronimo while Naiche and Chato rode leading the column defenders at the rear of the long line of running villagers. Before they reached Fort Thomas, they turned east toward the upper Gila and then curved south along the Steins Peak Mountains.

SIEBER TOLD ME, who was just barely a private, and his scout sergeants that the commander of southern Arizona, Major David Perry, had deployed soldiers in small groups at all the known water holes and trails into Mexico expecting that at least one of the groups would intercept Loco's People on the run toward Mexico and then gain help from other nearby groups. Sieber, acting as chief of scouts, led us to support Captains Rafferty and Tullius Tupper's groups who had their soldiers ready to ride at Fort Bowie and at San Simon Station.

Sieber sent his scouts out in groups of three to scout the surrounding countryside and ensure the people running from San Carlos didn't surprise us. Sieber sent me out with Massai and Rowdy. Massai, a warrior from Loco's People, might have been running with Loco's People if he hadn't joined the scouts during the last Ghost Face. He had a strong sense of direction and was a good tracker. Massai taught me how to track better than I believed possible, and he was a good friend. Rowdy was aggressive, always ready to fight the enemy, and we, too, became good friends. I enjoyed riding with those two when we rode the country for Sieber. I always learned something new from them that would help me in the future.

We had been with Tupper's and Rafferty's soldiers for two or three suns and had stopped for the evening when we saw a dust streamer pointing for us. I could tell the source of the dust was a hard-riding White Eye by the way he sat his pony and how the dust streamer hugged the ground. The rider, covered with dust, his pony wet with sweat and mud from the dust, charged into camp with at least six carbines ready to fill him full of holes as he shouted, "Where's yore cap'n? Where's yore cap'n?"

Captain Tupper, who had been in his tent, came out frowning at the commotion with his sleeves rolled up and the straps he used to hold his pants up hanging loose from the top of his pants. The rider looked like he was wearing dirty miners' pants and lace-up boots, and instead of a shirt, he wore what the White Eyes called "long johns." Tupper said, "I'm the commander here. What can I do for you?"

The rider bent over and put his hands on his knees, out of breath and blowing hard as though he had been running instead of riding like a witch was after him. Sieber walked up closer to hear what he had to say. "I'm... Charlie Wiedner from over to... Galeyville mining camp. Just come from... Fort Bowie and told Cap'n Rafferty... that the biggest damn bunch of 'paches I ever seen come within sight of us at the camp.... Musta been hunderds of 'em. Fool deputy sheriff tried to stop 'em from tearing up some tents we had and they killed him, but they kept on movin' south. Looks like they's headed down the San Simon Valley. We're mighty worried they might come back. They's so many we wouldn't have chance if they started shootin'. Cap'n Rafferty wanted me to tell you that he's ridin' for Galeyville. Can you come, too, and help protect us, Cap'n?"

Tupper turned toward his first sergeant, who was lounging with his troopers in the afternoon shade of a grove of mesquite with his men. "Sergeant Hawkins! Off and on! We're headin' for Galeyville as soon as we can saddle up. Send a couple of men back down the trail and tell the packtrain to meet us there."

First Sergeant Hawkins saluted and said, "We're movin', Cap'n. Be ready when you are." He rattled off some names I didn't understand and told them to head for the packtrain. I thought we were moving plenty quick for as many men as we had. With Sieber's ten scouts in the front of the column, we rode down the eastern side of the Chiricahua Mountains and then swung through a pass west into the canyon that gave the easiest access to Galeyville. There, we met Captain Rafferty and his column. Tupper and Rafferty had their men dismount and rest while they waited. Tupper and Rafferty had their soldier glasses out studying the San Simon Valley but saw nothing. They guessed the Chiricahua would cross the Peloncillo Mountains into New Mexico and pass near Cloverdale to reach the trail down the eastern side of the San Luis Mountains. The trail would carry them across the Chihuahuan *llano* to a trail leading to Juh's stronghold in the Sierra Madre. The captains had too much experience as Indian fighters to take their columns out across the southern end of the San Simon Valley in daylight where the Apache could see our dust streamers and know we were still in the chase.

As the sun fell behind the mountains, the packtrain still hadn't arrived, but a hand on the horizon of daylight was left. As the sunlight dimmed, Tupper and Rafferty, after talking with Sieber, decided to risk the Chiricahua seeing us in the low light and ordered the men to mount. Sieber sent out his best trackers and we were soon moving. That night, we went across the northern end of the Peloncillos and down the Animas Valley. The trackers easily found the broad Apache trail in the moonlight, which allowed us to follow it at alternating gallops and fast trots. When the sun came, we stopped north of Cloverdale and rested in the shade of manzanitas.

Rafferty and Tupper decided to leave the manzanitas with less than a hand of daylight left. We passed a border marker and followed the Chiricahua trail into New Mexico after crossing the Animas Valley and reached a high pass that led down into a *llano* valley. The packtrain caught up with us in the pass, and Tupper and Rafferty decided it was a good time to stop, rest, and eat.

I was resting with my friends, Massai, Rowdy, John Black Rope, and Mickey Free, when I heard Sieber speaking to Rafferty and Tupper. His voice carried well in the evening dusk and pitched a little higher than those of his scouts—it was easy to identify.

Sieber said, "Gentlemen, we're in Mexico in a pass through the Sierra San Luis Mountains. The pass trail leads down onto the Chihuahua llano. I got me an idee Loco and them Chiricahua is camped down close to the Sierra Enmedio, where there's good water this time of year. When we get down close to the llano, we can stop and rest, but I want to take three scouts and find their camp. We'll scope it out, then come back here and figure out how best to attack it. What do you think?"

Rafferty grinned and said, "We'll go down to the llano with you and then make a camp for gettin' some rest until you get back."

Tupper saluted and said, "You boys, go on down the trail. We'll be along before you and your Apache return."

Sieber returned Tupper's salute and walked over to the rocks where the scouts sat and told us his plan. "I'm going out as soon as we get down to the llano and see if I can find the Chiricahua camp. I'm takin' three scouts with me."

He rattled off names that included me, Massai, and another scout who had been with Sieber a long time. I felt proud Sieber chose me to help him learn about the Chiricahua camp if he was right about where he thought it was.

We were soon mounted and following Sieber down the moonlit trail bathed in soft white light and deep black shadows. All of us thought we'd be off tracking across the llano looking for the Chiricahua's camp in less than a hand, but it took us over two hands. The trail overgrown by manzanita and so filled with green growth we had to fight our way through. Captain Rafferty's men following us had it easier through the brush than we did because we broke trail for them. Down on the llano, the scouts not going with Sieber started making a camp but, at his direction, made only small, deep fire pits behind boulders against canyon ridges so the Chiricahua couldn't see their light.

Before making a trail along the east side of the Sierra Luis Mountains, Sieber stood in his stirrups and, using his soldier glasses, stared toward the short range of mountains standing by themselves two or three miles east of the Sierra Luis. Those little mountains were the Sierra Enmedio, and that's where Sieber had told me he expected to find Loco's Apache, finally stopping in Mexico for rest where they should be safe from the cavalry chasing them and could casually move toward the Sierra Madre, where Juh had his stronghold.

TWENTY-SEVEN

THE BATTLE AT
SIERRA DE ENMEDIO

SIEBER LED US into the mountain shadows formed from the moon's light on the rocky crags above us on the eastern side of the San Luis Mountains. By now we could all see the fire across the valley two miles away. It was bright—must have been a big one. With our soldier glasses, we could see dark outlines of Apache dancing and celebrating escaping San Carlos and having a safe journey into the land of the *Nakai-yes*. Sieber looked the camp over, studied where most of the people slept, and looked for places where they could take cover and defend themselves. He sent Massai closer to the camp to see the layout close up and to count warriors.

When Massai returned, he said he had counted one hundred fifteen warriors and that most of them had been drinking. They would have aching heads when the morning light came. The scout said he could smell mescal baking and he saw Geronimo, Chihuahua, Naiche, and Loco drinking and having a good time. I heard Sieber say under his breath, "I wonder if they'll have a good time when we're on 'em come daylight."

We quietly worked our way back to Tupper and Rafferty, and in the light of a low, yellow fire, Sieber told them what we had found. Tupper, Rafferty, and Sieber talked about how to attack the great defensive position of the Chiricahua and decided to use coyote stealth and surprise to take good offensive positions before the attack. Scouts were sent to occupy a rocky hill about four hundred yards from the center of the main camp. Tupper sent *Teniente* Touey with Tupper's command behind a rocky hill about four hundred yards from the northern end of the Sierra Enmedio to stop any Apache trying to escape in that direction. Tupper joined Rafferty's troopers and they appeared out of a low place about a thousand yards from Loco's camp, quietly walking their ponies toward the Chiricahua. We were all in position about an hour before dawn and waited for the light where we could see to shoot. Scout shots were the signal for Tupper and Rafferty to make their cavalry charge down the valley toward Loco's camp.

I was with the scouts sent to the rocky hill and had found good cover behind a big flat boulder that tilted backward, but its top was still about three feet off the ground and gave me good cover for shots of about four hundred yards around the fire. Some of the Chiricahua were still dancing and making an occasional whoop as the light slowly grew brighter.

I tried to rest leaning back against my cover boulder and stared into the sky at the big, beautiful milk river of stars sweeping over us. I wondered how it was that the Chiricahua, renegades all, had as much access to the beauty of the stars shining in the black velvet of the sky as we who were chasing them.

Off in the mountains to the east, there was a glimmer in the cold morning air of the sun's pesh-klitso glow, and the glow slowly grew brighter. I trembled inside. This was the first battle I had been in where I wanted to kill the enemy and he me. I looked at the scouts around me. It appeared that we all blew steam in the cold air and trembled with eagerness for the light to get bright enough to start the attack.

Our instructions were to wait until there was enough light for us to see targets in the camp. That first shot was the signal for Rafferty and Tupper leading the cavalry to charge the camp. Voices, women's voices, surprised us from just down the ridge slope below us. The sergeant in charge of us waved for us to be still and wait. I looked around the edge of my boulder and down the hill. I saw two young women with an older woman and a young man I learned later was Loco's grandson, now known as Dexter. There was enough light to see that they were approaching a cooking pit for mescal hearts. One of the young women left the others who were talking and laughing to check the baking mescal. Nearing the cooking pit, she picked up a yucca stalk to probe how close the baking was to being finished for the mescal hearts. She walked to the edge of the pit ready to use her yucca stalk, when a scout carbine roared, echoing across the little mountains. A dark red spot appeared on her shirt, and she fell face-first into the brush covering the top of the pit. *Why? Why did you do that, fool? Now every Chiricahua knows we're here and will see the cavalry charge too soon. They won't have a chance.*

The sergeant in charge of us must have understood the same thing and ordered us to lay down a covering fire across the camp. We loaded and fired our carbines and shot at likely targets in the camp as fast as we could. Sieber told me later that he estimated the scouts must have shot about eight hundred rounds into the camp in four minutes.

The Chiricahua ran to a little rock-covered hill about a thousand yards from where we were, some even returned our fire. I saw one who looked like Geronimo at the rocky hill using his arms and hands to give orders telling the warriors to hold their fire. I could see that one good round of fire from all those Apache rifles would wipe out all the mounted soldiers stretched out in a line to sweep through the camp. The thunder of their horses pounding the ground stirred up a great cloud of dust, and I felt the ground tremble. I watched with my stomach feeling as though I had eaten bad meat as the troopers drew closer and closer to the waiting Apache. Three hundred yards. Two hundred yards. Still no fire from the Chiricahua. One hundred yards and the Chiricahua guns roared.

I stared in disbelief. Not a single trooper was hit. The excited Chiricahua were higher than the troopers and their aims too high. They all shot over the troopers' heads, giving the troopers a chance to jump out of their saddles and stretch out in the dirt and sand to scramble backward for ground cover before the next volley came. The troopers started crawling backward using their elbows and staying low on their knees to push themselves along staying as close to the ground as possible. Two troopers were shot in the retreat, one killed and one badly wounded. When the troopers got back to their horses, Captain Tupper ordered *Teniente* Blake to make a fast sweep of the Chiricahua horses by riding between the Chiricahua and their herd. When I saw what was happening, I thought Blake and his troopers were never going to make it, but they did manage to drive off most of the Chiricahua horse herd, leaving Loco and the Chiricahua practically on foot.

As the sun, bringing bright morning light and a gauzy blue sky, floated higher, the rate of fire from both sides slowed. Each side saved ammunition and looked for targets where a bullet wasn't wasted.

In the middle of the morning, Loco stood up and shouted at the scouts. "Scouts! Why do you attack your brothers? We have done nothing to you. Don't betray us like this. Help us. Don't kill us."

Some of the scouts answered with insults. "Old fool! You can't get away from us. You should have stayed where you were safe. Now you betray your People. Soon you die!" On our ridge, most scouts answered with their rifles and Loco took cover with a minor leg wound.

A little later, an old woman stood up on top of the rock butte where the People had gone for cover. She called to her son Toclanny, who was a scout. "Toclanny, don't kill your mother's People. Help us. Help me. Come." A scout with a lucky shot from a thousand yards killed her. Toclanny was not with us. He and six other scouts were on duty in New Mexico.

I learned later that it was Chato who led three young men up in the rocks on the next ridge east of us and began sending a rain of bullets falling on us. Exposed as we were to their fire, and fire from the rocky hill where Geronimo was, we backed off our ridge in a hurry, sliding down the protected side getting scratched and cut by the brush and rocks we had to pass over. I don't think that attack killed anyone, but it was good we left our cover. All of us were counting the few cartridges we had left.

Tupper and Rafferty decided their soldiers and scouts were also so low on ammunition that we needed to retire back to our base camp and rearm from the packtrain at the end of the Espuela Mountains out of sight of the Chiricahua camp.

Back in camp, all the scouts refilled their bandoliers and pistol belt loads and ate a good meal the packers had provided. Sieber wandered among us asking each man how he was and if he needed anything. We all felt good about our day's work, and I was ready to go after the Chiricahua again with my scout friends. Tupper, Rafferty, and Sieber decided it was best to wait until morning before pursuing the Chiricahua further.

Early in the evening, we saw a big dust streamer headed for us and could hear the pounding of many hooves as they drew near. It was a big column, and it was led by Colonel Forsyth, who, upon arrival, immediately assumed command from Rafferty and Tupper and, with combined forces, made an army of nine companies of cavalry and three companies of scouts. Sieber told his scouts, "Boys, looks like we got us an army here of over five hundred men. If we catch the Chiricahua now, they'd best surrender or be wiped out."

Early the next day, Tupper and Rafferty led Forsyth and the column to the Apache camp. Scouts picked through what was left and burned the rest. Then we followed the Chiricahua trail south, expecting to catch them in a day or two if not sooner because most were on foot.

By the time the sun was falling into the western mountains, we had been tracking south beside a weak flow of water in a creek bed about a man deep and four or five man heights wide. In the distance down the fast-darkening valley, we saw smoke and the flickering glow of a small grass fire. Colonel Forsyth decided to camp for the night before following the trail early the next morning.

I didn't like this camping place. The smell of smoke and death was in the air. We heard many calls of wolves and coyotes that night.

We crossed the creek soon after we broke camp at dawn on our way, still following the creek, when a *Nakai-yi* soldier with much klitso braid on his uniform and a small column of soldiers following him approached us. They didn't look like they had hostile intentions, but all the soldiers and scouts had weapons ready. We stopped and waited as the *Nakai-yi* colonel rode up to Forsyth and said something I couldn't hear being back halfway down the length of the column and off to one side. Forsyth motioned for Mickey Free to come interpret.

I learned from Sieber that the *Nakai-yi* was Colonel Lorenzo Garcia, who some said was the best *Nakai-yi* military Indian fighter. He wanted to know why we were in his country. Forsyth explained that his column was chasing Apache who had fought at Sierra Enmedio two days earlier, and that he wanted to finish the fight. Garcia told Forsyth that he needed to leave. He had no business south of the border. Forsyth kept insisting he needed to finish the fight. Finally, Garcia told Forsyth that he had fought, routed, and scattered the Apache the day before and Forsyth had no more reason to be in Mexico. I'll never forget the look of surprise on Forsyth's face as his jaw dropped. He asked to see the battlefield and Garcia proudly led the way. As we moved down the creek, bodies of mostly women and children were lying scattered along the trail and farther along across the valley reaching toward the Espuela Mountains.

I had seen death before, but nothing on the scale I had seen in the past three days. There were over a hundred women and children, scattered over the llano, and their bodies had started to swell and stink. I counted ten warriors scattered among them, but I knew there must be more. The rest had gotten away. I felt like I needed to empty my stomach but refused to show weakness in front of the other scouts and Sieber. The looks on the faces of other scouts showed they felt the same way.

Garcia showed us the place between two *arroyos* that ran into the creek where the Apache had fought his men all day the day before. There were dead horses and soldiers scattered over the battlefield, but I saw no Apache. Garcia had lost three officers and nineteen soldiers killed, and three officers and thirteen soldiers wounded. There were seventy-eight Chiricahua bodies, mostly women and children, before we reached the *arroyo* from where the Apache fought. *Nakai-yi* soldiers were collecting the soldier bodies for burial but weren't burying any Chiricahua. The Mexicans had also captured thirty-three women and children, Loco's daughter among them. We tried to buy them back from Garcia's command, but the *Nakai-yes* wouldn't sell.

Both *arroyos* showed many signs of bloodstains. Even puddles of water in the Apache-side *arroyo* were still red. Garcia claimed the Apache had set the grass fire to escape through its smoke, but I wondered if he had tried to burn them out. He had no doctors or medicines for his wounded men and food was in short supply, his men on half rations. Forsyth ordered two surgeons to help the Mexican wounded and had the packers give Garcia enough supplies that would get him and his men back to Casas Grandes without starving.

The doctors finished their work on the Mexican soldiers. Our scouts and the commands of Tupper and Rafferty headed back to Arizona, while Forsyth rode on to New Mexico.

TWENTY-EIGHT

THE SECOND ENLISTMENT

SIEBER DECIDED HE and his scouts would refit and rearm at Fort Whipple, near the town of Prescott, where he liked to gamble and drink. I had learned much during the trip over the border to fight and catch Loco and the Chiricahua who had come up from Juh's camp to force Loco off the reservation. I think the most important lesson I learned was the value of organization for soldiers so they could fight as one when their leader so directed them. I decided the Chiricahua were fierce fighters and it would be a long time before they decided to surrender to the Blue Coats. And, most importantly, I had learned the value of friends in a battle. John Black Rope, Mickey Free, Rowdy, and Massai had become good friends after I enlisted and, in that battle, gave me help when I needed it. I knew they would be there in the future if they were still scouts. I followed officer commands. My friends and the Blue Coats said I was a good fighter and a leader.

We left the land of the *Nakai-yes* early in the moon the White Eyes call May. After the attacks the Chiricahua had suffered from the Blue Coats and the *Nakai-yes* under Garcia, Sieber thought it would be a long while before the Chiricahua tried to cross the border and raid again on the American side.

Sieber set a steady pace as he led his scouts toward Fort Whipple. It was a good ride. The sun was hot and bright, the mountains gray in the distance, desert plants like yucca, gourds, and ocotillo in full bloom filling the air with nice smells close to the plants. We were two suns reaching Fort Bowie and another six reaching Fort Whipple.

As we rode, I thought about what I wanted to do in the future. I wanted to see Chita even if I had to sit in her father's lodge with her mother watching us. Chita was fast becoming a fine-looking woman. My six-moon enlistment in the scouts would be up in about a moon. I wondered when Chita would be ready to marry. I asked myself if I wanted to farm and raise cattle. Did I want to continue as an army scout or a tribal policeman? Chita, of course, would support her husband in whatever I wanted, but I had learned she often had wise thoughts that she grew after listening to her father. What would she think I should do? All those thoughts and questions mixed with the perfume of the desert flowers made my brain feel like it was floating somewhere above my skull.

One night on the way between Fort Bowie and Fort Whipple, Sieber came to my fire and asked to speak privately with me over a cup of coffee. My scout brothers went over to other fires to visit. While I poured coffee for both of us, Sieber took papers and *tobaho* from a vest pocket and made a cigarette. He lit it with a splinter from the yellow-and-blue fire pit flames, and we smoked to the four directions.

The stars in the milk river sweeping over us seemed especially bright that night, and I could hear bats swooping through the cool night air collecting insects. Off toward the north, Wolf howled and then Coyote. It was a beautiful night, one that lives in my memory.

Sieber said, "Kid, I wanted to talk to you about what you plan to do when your six-month enlistment is up. Do you think you'll reenlist? Do you plan to be in the scouts a while? I expect the Chiricahua are gonna be runnin' wild after they heal up from that beatin' we gave 'em. I understand General Crook is gonna be comin' back to command Arizona Territory and maybe even New Mexico. I hope so, 'cause he knows what he's doin'.'"

I took a swallow of coffee and, staring at the fire, said, "I be scout. Wait for Hashke Bahnzin daughter, Chita, to have her womanhood ceremony. Then we marry. She already strong, wise woman I think of many times. Why you ask, Sieber?"

"I watched how you fought against the Chiricahua. You did just like I thought you would. Cool under fire and still a great shot. If you stay in the scouts, I want you to become a first sergeant."

I raised my brows in surprise and Sieber grinned.

"That's a step up from the time to become a first sergeant as we talked about earlier. You knew all the drill commands and how to do them when you joined. I never saw you make a drill mistake when you drilled after signing up. You know the rules and you're a natural leader. It'll mean extra pay if you're also a first sergeant. What do you say?"

I smiled. Sieber and I had talked about this before. Now that he had seen me in action, he had no doubts about wanting me as a sergeant leader. More money? I'd have better clothes like White Eye friends if I have more money. I could buy cattle, buy my woman nice things, and take good care of family.

"Yes, Sieber. I be first sergeant as we talk before when I your assistant."

"That's great to hear, Kid. I'll put in the paperwork when we get to Whipple. Take half a moon off before you sign up again. It's been a hard march these past six months."

"Hmmph. This I do, Sieber."

Off in the distance, I heard Coyote and thought of the saying "Coyote waits." I knew I had to be very careful with this new offer of responsibility.

I POLISHED THE leather of my empty bandoliers. None of the other scouts did, but I thought they looked good. I cleaned and oiled my carbine and pistol and its leather. Then I took care of my army saddle and other things the army gave me as a scout. The day came that my first enlistment was complete and went to see Sieber to touch the pen on ending my service and ask what to do with the equipment the army gave me.

I found Sieber at the tent of *Teniente* Frank West, and they invited me in to sit with them. They were discussing how to handle a White Mountain renegade named Na-ti-o-tish, who had developed followers after trying and failing to free the prophet Noch-ay-del-klinne.

Sieber said, "Lieutenant West, this is the young man I mentioned to you. His enlistment ends today, but I expect he'll sign for another six-month stretch here in two or three weeks after he visits his folks—his father, Toga-de-chuz, is a leader in *Capitan* Chiquito's band, and the young woman who's promised to him is a daughter of Eskiminzin. They're nice company, but he'll be back. I want him to be a first sergeant in the scouts when he returns."

The *teniente* was smoking a pipe with a carved bowl shaped like a White Eye with a beard. He nodded, his pipe clamped in his teeth, and leaned back in his chair to look me over. I kept my eyes on his face and saw no disfavor in his expression. He pulled his pipe and blew a puff of smoke up toward the top of his tent.

He said, "He looks a little young for a first sergeant, but you know how to pick 'em, Sieber. I'm sure Chaffee won't have any objection, and he's had good experience in that fight with Loco's boys down in Mexico."

Sieber grinned. "That's good. Thanks, Lieutenant. Excuse me for a little while and I'll get this man cleared out."

Teniente West gave Sieber a weak salute of understanding and nodded toward me. "Glad to meet you, Kid." I nodded and gave him a formal salute as we left the tent.

I followed Sieber over to his tent. He already had a paper ready for me to end my enlistment, and after I touched the pen, he signed it for me. I asked where I should leave the things I needed to return. He said to leave them with him, and he would see that I got them back when I reenlisted. I was glad that he kept my equipment and uniform because I had everything polished up and ready to use. In less than a hand, I had my pony headed east and then south toward Globe.

I STOPPED IN Globe for a short time to see my friend Redmond. He was busy in his shop and had two White Eye boys helping him. He grinned when he saw me at the door and motioned me in while taking off his apron. He washed his hands and forearms in a rinse bucket, dried with a ragged towel, and then poured our coffee. I told him about my adventures chasing Loco and fighting in the big Tupper battle across the border, and things I had learned as a scout.

He told me how his butcher business was making enough money that he now had a boy doing my old job and he was teaching another one how to slaughter animals and cut meat. We talked through two cups of coffee before I told him I had to leave to visit my family at San Carlos but said I'd stop by on the way back and have more time to visit. He grinned and said for me not to forget about him. I waved my flat hand parallel to the floor and promised I wouldn't forget.

Clum had allowed Hashke Bahnzin, *Capitan* Chiquito, and their People to establish their farms in the Aravaipa Canyon and Río San Pedro areas when their Ríos San Carlos and Gila farms didn't produce like Clum hoped. In less than three years, the People no longer needed rations from the reservation.

When the Chiricahua left San Carlos in the 1881 harvest, General Willcox created safety lines around San Carlos. He said the People had to stay inside the lines or be considered renegades subject to army attack. This forced the chiefs and their People out of their comfortable, productive farms and back to the miseries at San Carlos. They were angry. Why did they have to suffer because the Chiricahua left the reservation?

Willcox finally eliminated the safety lines, and the chiefs went back to their farms with their People. From Globe, I forded the Río Gila at the San Carlos agency and took the trail west of Mount Turnbull across the ridges and canyons to Aravaipa Creek to visit my mother and father and my brothers and sisters. They had stayed with *Capitan* Chiquito to farm and raise fruits and vegetables.

I APPEARED AT my mother's evening cooking fire the second sun after I left Redmond's place in Globe. My brothers were approaching manhood, and my sisters neared their womanhood ceremonies. They had just begun their evening meal of steamed yucca tips, acorn bread, and venison when Mother saw me and covered her mouth with her fingers to avoid yelling with delight. My father saw her and looked in my direction and made a big smile that seemed to stretch across his full cheeks to his ears. My brothers and sisters were laughing, shaking a fist like they had just won a big race. My father patted a place beside him to sit down while Mother got me a gourd filled with her good evening meal.

My father said, "Ho! Our son and brother returns from chasing Chiricahua into the land of the *Nakai-yes*. Sit, eat, tell us of your adventures."

I said, "My heart is full to see my mother and father and brothers and sisters. Let me eat and I'll tell my stories."

After eating, I told them of my adventures as a scout and they all carefully listened. My two oldest brothers asked many questions about being a scout and what Sieber was like as chief of scouts. I knew they must be interested in being scouts and thought they could be good ones. Father laughed when he said the youngest looked so much like me and loved fine clothes like I did that the army would want to hire him thinking he was me.

Father and I spoke of what was happening on the reservation and how things had quieted down now that the Chiricahua had left. He shook his head in disgust when I told him the rumor that General Crook was coming back and would get the Chiricahua back on the reservation or leave them dead in the land of the *Nakai-yes*. He said, "I hope they stay there. They're nothing but troublemakers." I nodded agreement but thought of the losses Loco had endured at the hands of Geronimo and the other chiefs and decided my father's sweeping statement about the Chiricahua didn't apply to all of them. I just knew I wanted to be with my brother scouts if Crook returned and went after them.

I spent two suns with my father's family talking with Father and Mother about their part of the farms along the creek and what they had endured when the Chiricahua had left the reservation. I spoke with my brothers and asked what they wanted to accomplish and my sisters if they had eyes for young men for marriage. My brothers spoke of nothing but being scouts, and my sisters mentioned some young men they hoped would want to court them after their womanhood ceremonies.

On my third day with my father's family, I left to ride six miles down the Río San Pedro to visit with Hashke Bahnzin and to see Chita. It was an easy, comfortable ride. My father told me what landmarks to look for to find Hashke Bahnzin's farm and village. When I rode up to his lodge, Chita was sorting through a basket of vegetables and didn't see or hear me coming. I stopped my pony, so she saw its shadow before her. She looked up in surprise, covered her mouth with her fingers for a moment as I grinned at her, and then was up and running, saying in a low throaty voice, "Ohyessonna, you come. I'm very happy." She held out her hands and I took them, gently squeezing them in my delight to see her. She had the curves and body of a grown woman, and I wanted her.

She called in a loud voice, "Father, Mother, come see who is here." The blanket over their lodge door flew up, and Hashke Bahnzin and her second mother—the mother who birthed her had been killed during the Camp Grant massacre—came out of their lodge, and upon their seeing me, big smiles filled their faces.

Hashke Bahnzin said, "Ho, the great warrior and scout returns to us. Our hearts are full. Chita's face shows much happiness. Let us sit in the shade of that big acorn nut tree yonder by the river and tell me of your life as a scout while my women fix us a meal that we all can share in the time of no shadows."

We walked over to sit in the shade of the big tree. It was cool there, and the stream at this place was slow and at least knee-deep. Hashke Bahnzin found a grassy spot to sit and motioned for me to join him. Birds were making noises against us, but the burbling river flowed smooth and steady and it was easy to hear each other.

Hashke Bahnzin told me how he and *Capitan* Chiquito were prospering on their farms on the San Pedro Río and Aravaipa Creek and how the Chiricahua leaving for Mexico had brought them hard times until General Willcox let them return to their farms. Nevertheless, his crops and fruit trees seemed to have recovered, and he was making money with his team and wagon hauling loads for the People with their farms. He said even the White Eyes were starting to ask his help and if they had the money, he would find the time.

The women brought a big flat basket with piles of acorn and mesquite bread and bowls of hackberry jam, dried juniper berries and elder berries, and prickly pear sweet tuna. Chita saw my eyes light up as she approached Hashke Bahnzin and me and laughed like a grown woman. Hashke Bahnzin invited his women to join us and waved to me to tell them stories of my six moons of adventures in the scouts. I told them my stories about chasing the Chiricahua into Mexico and the battle at Sierra Enmedio after the women joined us. I knew there was no love lost between Hashke Bahnzin and his People and the Chiricahua, but Hashke Bahnzin and his women listened to my story with their heads bowed looking at the food they took with their fingers.

When I finished my stories, Hashke Bahnzin looked at me with sad eyes and shook his head. He said, "There is little love lost between the Aravaipa and the Chiricahua, but I'm very sorry for what happened to them. I hope they'll come back soon and sleep in peace on the reservation." I nodded and made the sign of peace.

THAT NIGHT, CHITA and I went for our customary walk, this time down the wagon road running by the río, with her parents walking a discreet distance behind us so we could talk privately. I was glad her parents walked nearby. Chita's hair framed a beautiful face any woman would be proud of and walked with her man to serve as her husband. My desire for her grew each time I saw her, and she knew it.

She said in a low throaty whisper, "Do you still want me for your woman?"

I frowned and looked at her like she was crazy, and she giggled.

"Of course. You know I want you. My body yearns for yours, and my heart beats fast anytime you are near. Otherwise, I wouldn't ride all over the country looking for you. When do you think you'll be ready to marry?"

Her eyes found the trail in front of us. She shook her head. "I don't know. I can only ask *Ussen* that it is soon. Hashke Bahnzin and my mother are eager that you become their son-in-law but not as eager as me that you become my husband and give me many babies over our years together." Those were words I was happy to hear.

BEFORE I RODE back upriver to my father's lodge, I thanked Hashke Bahnzin and his women for the good meals and promised Chita I would come again when I could. She crossed her arms and, looking at the ground, said, "You come soon. My father will be glad to see you, and so will I."

I left my mother's lodge early in the darkness next morning when even the birds were not yet calling to each other. I told my brothers I would get them in the scouts when they were old enough, wished my sisters good luck in choosing a man when their womanhood came, and promised Toga-de-chuz and my mother I would return as soon as I could.

It was a long trail back to San Carlos in a day, but I wanted to see old friends before I returned to Fort Whipple and joined the army again. I was surprised when I crossed the Gila to see army tents in place around the agency. I soon learned that *Teniente* Frank West was there recruiting for Sieber and Captain Chaffee. Chief Na-ti-o-tish was raiding along the Mogollon Rim with about fifty warriors, and the army was planning to take him down. Sieber was to be chief of scouts for the expedition. Twenty-five scouts who had already touched the pen were planning to meet Sieber at Fort McDowell.

I found *Teniente* West and touched the pen for another six months of enlistment. I said nothing about being a first sergeant for Sieber after deciding he would have to make many tracks on paper for his chief if he truly wanted me to lead the other sergeants in his scouts. Veteran scouts drilled the new scouts and taught them basic army skills before we marched to Fort McDowell to join Sieber.

TWENTY-NINE

BATTLE AT BIG DRY WASH

THE NEW RECRUITS and returning scouts who had signed up again with *Teniente* West ran across the Superstition Mountains and the Ríos Salt and Verde to Fort McDowell, where we were to report to the chief of scouts, Al Sieber. A packtrain of supplies followed us, and we ran about forty miles a day. We could have covered more ground in a day, but the packtrain struggled to make the same distance in a day against what we did running over the mountains and camping early.

We reached Fort McDowell close by the bosque of the Río Verde in two days. A big muscular sergeant with a scar on one side of his face and a no-nonsense attitude showed us where to pitch our tents before we went to eat a hot meal prepared for us by our packers. We were all hungry and ate more than we should to stay in top running condition. Since this was my second signing and I knew army rules and the way to do things, I showed the first-time recruits how to organize their tents, keep their things inside in a way the army wanted, and answered many questions ranging from where the privies were to how often and where they could practice with their rifles and pistols.

Later that evening, I sat by my little fire as the frogs and tree peepers made their songs, bats swooped and circled snatching flying insects, and off in the hills, coyotes yipped and the stars looked as though they lay floating on a soft, black blanket. I was watching the yellow-and-orange flames at the bottom of my fire pit and thinking about when I should take Chita as my woman. She was beautiful and I wanted her as any man wants a woman, but she was also a hard worker and a fine helper. Our children would make us proud—if girls, they would bring us worthy men, and if sons, I would teach them to hunt, fight, and grow big crops. I wouldn't need to do any more army enlistments but farm instead.

I was just starting to doze off to sleep when light footsteps breaking dead winter grass sounded behind me. I cocked my rifle and decided which way I should jump to avoid a pistol shot or a long blade. A boy a year or two before novitiate age said, *"Señor* Keed?"

I puffed my cheeks and breathed a sigh of relief. "Hmmph. Speak. I listen."

"Mister Sieber say for you come to his tent pronto. He say it's in about the same place near scout tents as during your last enlistment."

"Hmmph. I hear. I come."

"Gracias. I tell him."

I nodded. *"Enjuh."*

That boy's work might keep me safe from going in the wrong tent.

I pulled on my moccasins, carried my rifle in the crook of my left arm, and headed for Sieber's big sidewall tent.

I WALKED FOR a little while and noticed all the oil lantern lights scattered across a big field of small white tents. There seemed to be more scouts here than during my first recruitment at Camp Verde. Nearing Sieber's tent, I saw the glow of a lantern inside and stood at the entrance flap to announce I was there by clearing my throat.

Sieber leaned out from his stool and looked past the tent flap. I knew he could at least see my legs. He called, "Hey, come on in, Kid. We need to talk."

I entered the soft yellow light from the lantern on his worktable filling the tent and made the peace sign, waving my palm parallel to the ground. Sieber, sitting on a field stool, was making tracks on papers with an army brand at the top of the sheet. He signed back. "Sit down and take a load off, Kid. I need to make you a first sergeant this enlistment as I told you earlier. At that rank, you'll make two times the money you make now as a private, but the responsibilities will be greater. You ready to touch the pen for that rank?"

I grinned and nodded. I hadn't realized a first sergeant made that much more money for his service, and the men including other sergeants already seemed to see me as their leader. *Ussen gives me Power and Chita her womanhood, I marry sooner than I thought.* "Where little black-water spear? I touch."

He grinned and held out the shaft of the little spear he used to make black-water marks on paper for me to touch. After I touched what he called the "pen," he made tracks on the paper and signed my name as "Kid." He made me a copy and, after folding it, handed it to me and said, "Keep this with your other medicine pieces if any officer asks to see it."

I took it and slid it into my vest pocket and sat down on another camp stool like the one Sieber used.

Sieber made a cigarette and we smoked to the four directions.

Standing, Sieber stepped out of the tent to throw the cigarette remains to flare up in his little fire and then came back to sit down on his stool with a grunt.

Leaning forward with his left hand on his knee, and his right hand rubbing his chin, he said, "So here's the deal, Kid. Some of the Indians who got Noch-ay-del-klinne killed are still running wild." I frowned. "You know? The Dreamer."

I nodded. "I know Dreamer. Thought all those Apache, including the scouts who got him killed, were either hung or in the house with bars."

Sieber shook his head. "Unfortunately, not. They've been hiding for a year. Now they've got some idjit named Na-ti-o-tish leading 'em. My spies tell me that he thinks if he hits the White Eyes and Blue Coats hard, a lot of the Apache on the reservation would take the warpath to support them that's in hiding.

"You remember Albert Stirling, San Carlos chief of police that the Chiricahua killed when they left with Loco?" I nodded. "Well, Na-ti-o-tish and his boys ambushed his replacement, Cibecue Charley Colvig, and three of his policemen. For a while, they got the whole country stirred up believing all the White Eyes at San Carlos were murdered. It took a handful of suns to calm everybody down, but the White Eye settlers are mucho angry and Na-ti-o-tish has fifty-four fighting men, which for Apache is a good-sized fightin' force. The army wants to corner and wipe those boys out before they can do more damage."

I crossed my arms, leaned back on the stool, and said, "How we do this, Sieber? Na-ti-o-tish has big country for hiding."

Sieber nodded. "I'm sure he's somewhere in the Tonto Basin. There're five army camps around the basin. We're here at Fort McDowell. Then there're Camp Verde, Fort Whipple, Camp Thomas, and Fort Apache. There're soldier and scout columns leaving all these camps to join up in the basin to hunt and catch Na-ti-o-tish and his boys. I'm leavin' with my scouts first thing in the morning, after we eat. We're supposed to meet Cap'n Chaffee and a lieutenant named Morgan with scout companies from Verde and Whipple at Wild Rye Creek tomorrow evening. Think your boys can cover forty miles up the mountains and over the western rim of the basin tomorrow?"

"Hmmph. We ready. Easy run. Already do two days like that to get here. I have men ready to leave *mañana* after they eat."

Sieber grinned. "Then get to it, First Sergeant Kid. I'll see you in the morning. Your sergeant's jacket is there on the edge of the bed. I think it'll fit you."

I grinned and gave him the Blue Coat salute, tried on the jacket—it fit good— and left his tent. I ran back across the field to my scout tents, called a meeting, and told them the plan and that they should make ready to leave on the run when Sieber wanted to leave. They all said they would be ready, and they were.

WE PUSHED HARD across the mountains past old Camp Reno to Rye Creek. We were still running up the creek as the shadows filled the creek's canyon and darkness filled the land and stars the sky. But we soon found the camp of Captain Chaffee and *Teniente* Morgan with their scouts from Verde and Whipple. We made camp and were cooking a deer one of my scouts had brought down for supper. After that early start and long run, we were all very hungry.

We were in the middle of our meal when a man wounded in the shoulder staggered up to the fire holding his arm. The scouts set aside their meals and, shooting glances into the dark bosque on the burbling creek, grabbed their rifles and laid low scanning the darkness. We helped the wounded man while he told us his story, and soon the scouts went back to their suppers. The man said his name was Sigsbee and that Apache had attacked his brother and him at their horse ranch on the headwaters of Tonto Creek. The Apache cut off his brother and a workman when they tried to save some stallions in a log corral. They killed men and cut them up.

Lieutenant Morgan shook his head. "Why do those bastards do such god-awful things?" The scouts and I said nothing but knew they disfigured the bodies so they'd be ugly and unwanted at the Happy Place. Sigsbee told us he held off the attackers until it was good dark, and then he slipped away to come here. *How did he know we were here?*

Sieber, who was now in charge of all the scouts, had us finish our supper and made sure we had plenty of cartridges. He and Chaffee started us running for Sigsbee's ranch with them following. Although we ran in the dark and the trail along the creek side was rough and rocky, a big half-moon high above the mountains gave us plenty of light to avoid tripping over rocks and tree roots. Frogs stopped croaking and night birds were still as we rushed by, but the tree peepers kept up their songs.

We reached the ranch, found the mangled bodies, and put them in a decent grave under a tree near the cabin where the wounded man lived with his brother. Sieber, Chaffee, Morgan, and I were glad we had beaten all the other troops expecting to join us here. We knew if we could stay ahead, we would have first chance to fight the enemy.

Sieber called me aside and asked, "What do you think Na-ti-o-tish and his men will do? They're headed north up the creek."

"Hmmph. Na-ti-o-tish go where he sure we come and then ambush. He wait at good place for watering our animals." I crossed my arms and thought for a little time before deciding what I'd do if I were him. "He go General Springs, put men on cliffs and in trees up the pass to rim top near springs and ambush soldiers as trail climbs up to wagon road."

Sieber nodded. "Yeah, that's about what I was thinkin'. Okay, that's where we're headed. I'll tell Chaffee and we'll go."

Colonel Evans from Fort Apache, who had been fighting Apache for many harvests, was in charge of all the groups who were gathering to fight Na-ti-o-tish, but we were well ahead of him and his men, and if we could stay ahead, we would fight the hostiles first. Evans's scouts cut our trail as we ran up the creek. Evans sent an officer's patrol after us. It guided Chaffee and Sieber to a war council with Evans after both groups of scouts and soldiers made camps to eat and rest. Sieber told me about the council after he returned.

Sieber said Evans told Chaffee and him that he—Evans—had trouble with his scouts who apparently had no stomach for a fight with Na-ti-o-tish and his men. His scouts convinced Evans that his troops were too far behind to ever catch up with the Apache. Chaffee and Sieber convinced the colonel that Na-ti-o-tish and his men were close and would, as I told him, stop at General Springs to fight. There're steep cliffs where the trail climbs out of the basin onto the Crook Road that runs by General Springs, and that trail leading up from the basin would be a good place for an ambush.

Sieber told me later that Lieutenant Morgan, in charge of Evans's scouts, couldn't get them to move and ask him to take over. I knew Sieber would look each of them in the eye, they'd know quick he wouldn't put up with their reluctance to fight, and all he had to do was nod in the direction he wanted to go and say "Let's go, boys," and they were on their feet ready to go. He brought the scouts back to our camp with him and told us his plan to head for the canyon pass up to General Springs, but he would climb to the top of the rim with the scouts up a canyon well before we got to the canyon pass and then move along the rim until we found where the ambush was laid on the other side.

We left camp about the time of no shadows, following the trail toward the pass. We kept scouts out on the wings of most of our group in case Na-ti-o-tish planned to ambush us before the pass, but nothing happened. Three hands off the horizon later, Sieber had swung north and led us up a steep canyon to the top of the rim and through the tall pines where the other side couldn't see us. Leaving most of the scouts hidden, we found good cover on the edge of the rim and, using holes in the brush around us, scanned the far wall of the canyon using our soldier glasses to look for Na-ti-o-tish's men waiting in ambush. It didn't take us long to find them hiding in the trees directly on the other side of the canyon about seven hundred yards away. We moved so they were in sight and directly across from us and waited for Chaffee and the other troops to arrive.

Chaffee soon found us and used many White Eye and Blue Coat swear words when he saw the warriors we had found. Colonel Evans was not long coming down the trail. Chaffee met him and, saluting, prepared to turn over his soldiers to Evans to command, but Evans told him it was Chaffee's fight and his to command. A smiling Chaffee began deploying his soldiers along the rim while Sieber and his sergeants watched Na-ti-o-tish's men on the other side. Chaffee motioned Sieber to him. They talked for a short time before one of the soldiers shot before ordered to and the battle began early. The Apache down on the other side of the canyon I watched didn't move and waited to shoot until they had a good target. Most of the fire in our direction came from the top side of the ridge behind the cliffs where the warriors hid. It was wasted ammunition. The range was too far as the ricocheting bullets whizzed and whined off canyon boulders below us.

Sieber motioned me to him. I scrambled through the brush, weaving as I ran. Low branches slapped me in the face, but I didn't care as long as it wasn't a bullet. When I reached Sieber, he pointed to the rim on the far side well behind where Na-ti-o-tish's men were and said, "I want to take you and your best scouts with Captain Kramer and Lieutenant West with Troop E of the Sixth with Chaffee's Troop I on a big circle around from the east to get behind Na-ti-o-tish's boys and, when we're close enough, attack them from the rear. We're likely to find their horses, so we'll take those to keep Na-ti-o-tish's men from runnin'."

Sieber rarely misjudged a fight situation, and he was right about this one too.

We found the pony herd. The men guarding them were paying more attention to the sound of gunfire and trying to understand what was happening than they were to the horse herd, and it was easy for Sieber and the scouts to stay in the tree shadows and wipe the guards out. Most never knew they were being attacked until they were shot.

Some scouts took the horses and led them away back to the canyon road and over to General Springs while Sieber and I led the troopers toward the back of the Apache firing into and across the deep canyon trail. They were beginning to retreat back away from the canyon when they ran into us.

One of our scouts saw his father and brother with Na-ti-o-tish's men. He threw down his rifle and ran toward them, yelling their names. Sieber saw what was happening and shot him in the head. He was dead before he hit the ground and the only scout we lost.

We were cutting Na-ti-o-tish's men down like a sharp knife swung through green grass when dark clouds that had been gathering all afternoon opened and poured a river of freezing-cold water down on us and then hit us with great hailstones, some the size of a fist. We took shelter where we could find it, close to tree trunks or rock overhangs, but no one could see more than four or five long rifle lengths in front of us. The rain and hail lasted about half a hand, and we were all so cold we were shaking and standing in ground-covering hail a hand width deep. Na-ti-o-tish's men slipped away and disappeared.

The next day, most of the troops returned to their stations. Sieber and the scouts followed Colonel Evans in search of the escaping Apache. We learned that a little over half the band returned to the reservation, but the rest didn't survive. The bodies of Na-ti-o-tish and two of the scouts who joined the band lay where they fell. Blue Coat casualties were two soldiers killed, nine wounded. One scout, the one Sieber had shot deserting to the other side, rode the ghost pony.

THIRTY

NANT'AN LPAH RETURNS

MOST OF THE scouts under Sieber's command rode horses we captured from the Na-ti-o-tish band. Sieber directed four scouts to return the horses to Fort McDowell, make ready to return to action if needed, and to rest and refresh themselves. The scouts riding with Sieber and me and Colonel Evans and his troopers trailed the Apache who had escaped.

Corydon Cooley sometimes worked for the army as an interpreter. At his ranch, we learned that what was left of Na-ti-o-tish's men had stopped there for rest and food. They were headed back to Fort Apache and their families and told him that over twenty warriors had died in the fighting.

When we learned this, Colonel Evans and his men decided to return to Fort Apache, and Sieber, our scouts, and I headed there with him to await further orders. At Fort Apache, Sieber worked on making black-water tracks for his after-action report. I led the scouts drilling and worked with them on the firing range. Even though the Chiricahua had disappeared into the land of the *Nakai-yes*, we worked and drilled the scouts to be ready for action as soon as they raided north of the border. Nothing much happened for three or four moons until a sun in the Season of Large Fruit (August/September) was disappearing behind the mountains. It was one of those lazy, slow days that don't come often enough. I stopped by Sieber's tent to swap gossip and learn plans and a possible schedule. This tent was where he worked and slept, and during the fiery sun in the Season of Large Leaves both sides and entry flaps were usually up to let any breeze pass through the shade it gave. Sieber was stretched out on his bed with his hat lying over his eyes and drawing deep, close-to-snoring breaths.

As soon as I started to back out of the tent, not wanting to disturb him, he said without moving his hat, "Had some good news today, *amigo.*" I started back into the tent and took one of his folding stools as a seat.

"Speak. I listen."

His muffled voice from under the hat said, "General Crook will be back here tomorrow and wants to meet with me and talk to the Apache chiefs who ain't happy with the agents who've been in charge. It means the Apache won't starve in the Ghost Face because of crooked agents stealing their rations, and they won't be on the edge of war as they have been for a long time.

"He's also planning to council with the chiefs of the bands and his soldier chiefs to get their opinion about what should be done to ensure the Apache don't break out of the reservations like Geronimo and Juh did last year and then came back for Loco, who didn't want to leave in the first place. I'm supposed to meet with him here after the chiefs and he and the council talk. He'll talk to his officers. I suspect that's gonna be sometime in December. I figure he must be tryin' to develop a plan to bring the Chiricahua in Mexico back here come the Season of Many Leaves."

Sieber pulled his hat off his eyes and sat up, throwing his legs off the side of his cot. He leaned over to grab and pull on his boots and made a thunderclap noise, passing some bad-smelling air. White Eyes have no manners, although he knew I didn't care. Most Apache wouldn't do that in front of anyone. He grinned and said, "Big meal of beans at the time of no shadows."

I nodded, ignoring his comment about the thunderclap noise. "Ummmph. You think he goes into land of *Nakai-yes?* If he go there, much blood flows in the Blue Mountains."

Sieber shrugged and said, "I know that, and you know that, and it's likely *Nant'an Lpah* knows that, but one way or the other, he's gonna make damn sure them Chiricahua ain't stayin' in Mexico so they can raid north of the border anytime they feel like it."

I said, "I'm not so sure I want to go. The *Nakai-yes* don't want the Blue Coats south of the border, and I'm guessing from what I saw at Sierra Enmedio the troopers and scouts would be outnumbered two or three to one. One trooper against one Apache, that trooper loses more often than not. One trooper facing three or four Apache won't have a chance."

Sieber nodded. "It's too close to Ghost Face to do an expedition into those mountains. He'll wait until the Season of Many Leaves next harvest to go. I tell you, Kid, if it was me, I wouldn't reenlist when your time is up at the beginning of the next Ghost Face. I'm chief of scouts. I'll have to go, but you won't if you don't reenlist. Think about it."

I nodded. "I think."

AFTER *NANT'AN LPAH* heard Apache complaints at Fort Apache, he left with Sieber, Captain Bourke, and Corydon Cooley as an interpreter for a council to hear more complaints from all the band chiefs on a wooded bench deep in a canyon on the Río Black near where it meets the Río White to form the Río Salt. Sieber told me later that *Nant'an Lpah* listened to the complaints of more than a hundred leaders who were there. It was always the same story—the People, robbed of half their rations, stayed hungry when they couldn't gather food from the wilds around the reservation. Fortunately, Tiffany had let the Chiricahua get as much from the land as they could, or breakouts and blood would have flowed then.

Nant'an Lpah finished his talks with the Apache about the middle of the moon the White Eyes call "November" in the time we Apache call the Season of Earth Is Reddish Brown. He chose dependable officers to help him manage the reservations. These officers included Captain Crawford, whom I knew from my early days at San Carlos. He always tried to do the just and right thing for the People. *Teniente* Gatewood was in charge of all the White Mountain Apache at Fort Apache and was admired and respected by his men. *Teniente* Davis, whom I didn't know, was a new chief and in charge of Apache scouts at San Carlos. Sieber was *Nant'an Lpah's* chief of scouts and would have his tent at San Carlos. McIntosh and Bowman were his helpers. My friend Mickey Free, enlisted as a scout, was the interpreter for Davis and ranked like me, a first sergeant.

DURING THE SEASONS of Large Leaves, Large Fruit, and Earth Is Reddish Brown, I continued to drill the scouts at San Carlos with *Teniente* West and they practiced often with their rifles and pistols at the firing range. To measure how well their rifle accuracy was improving, I counted the number of times they hit the inside circle of their painted targets the army gave them to use. They shot at their targets once a week, and the record I had showed the number of shots in the inside circle grew at a good gallop. I told Sieber what was happening, and he was very happy. He said my idea to use number of hits in the inside circle as a measure of shooting progress was brilliant and I ought to be a professional soldier with the Blue Coats, but that was something I never wanted. Our scouts became much better in drills too. Sieber said he would match them against regular soldiers doing the same drills anytime.

SIEBER RETURNED FROM looking over scouts at the forts and camps in Arizona. He watched *Teniente* West and me drill the scouts at San Carlos, nodded his approval, and said, "You and the *teniente* have done a good job with these men. I need to talk to the *teniente* for a while before supper, and then you and I need to talk after supper at my tent."

I saluted and said, "I come moonrise."

He nodded and saluted back.

AS THE MOON floated up over the eastern mountains, I found Sieber smoking his pipe and sitting on his blanket by his fire. As I drifted out of the night and into the firelight, he grinned and made a motion for me to sit down on the far end of his blanket and I did. The night was growing cold, the coyotes yipping and night birds still squawking. Ghost Face would come cold and angry in about a moon.

Sieber crossed his legs and held his hands out to the fire, glancing over at me. He saw I had a blanket over my shoulders and was warming my hands. He said, "Gettin' kind of chilly, ain't it?"

I nodded. "Always gets cold quick this close to Ghost Face. You have words for me, Sieber? Speak. I listen."

"Yes, sir, I have words for you. First, you're doing a very fine job as first sergeant. Your men are all becoming good marksmen and know exactly what to do on drill commands. They're in good physical shape, and *Teniente* West says good things about your leadership. All that'll save lives when fights come."

"Hmmph. Your words make me feel good, Sieber. What is bad news?"

"You're gettin' wise in your old age, Kid. This time, there's no bad news. But you need to choose."

I frowned, not understanding what he meant. *What you talk about, Sieber?*

"Remember, when you touched the pen for this enlistment, I told you that you might not want to touch it for the next enlistment. Now that choice needs to be made."

I frowned again. "Speak straight, Sieber. Still another moon until my enlistment ends."

"Here's the deal. *Nant'an Lpah* is planning to go after the Chiricahua in Mexico the Season of Many Leaves. I'd guess by White Eye time, that would be in early May. Right now, he's sellin' his big chief back east on his visitin' and talkin' to the Mexican government and their military so he can cross the border to go after the Chiricahua and not have to fight the Mexicans too. He's gonna travel by train to talk to el presidente, Díaz, and then he'll talk to governors in the states of Sonora and Chihuahua before he comes back to start organizing his expedition to get them Chiricahua."

"What he do, Sieber?"

"Well, the nant'an plans to use about two hundred scouts led by me, Cap'n Crawford, and *Teniente* Gatewood, and about forty mounted troopers led by Cap'n Chaffee. They're mainly goin' to protect the packtrain with seventy-six packers with about two hundred and fifty mules that's gonna carry about a hundred sixty rounds of ammunition for each scout and trooper who will be carrying forty rounds in their bandoliers, plus the usual tents and blankets, sixty days of food supplies and cookin' hardware. He's gonna set his main camp up in Willcox, where the train stops, and have all that material including resupply in Willcox. He's gonna recruit the most physically fit scouts. When it's all collected and organized at Willcox, he's gonna move all that's goin' across the border to the San Bernardino Ranch that County Sheriff Slaughter owns. When put in its final form around the first of May, we'll cross the border and head for the Río Bavispe and the mountains beyond where the Chiricahua are supposed to be hidin' out. There's just one problem."

"What problem, Sieber? Plan sound good. *Nant'an Lpah* has much light behind his eyes."

"The problem is, we don't have any idee where the Apache camps are in those mountains. Right now, all he can do is make a wild guess and get very lucky. We could hunt for those camps for years and never find 'em. Unless he can find a truthful man who knows where the camps are, we won't have a snowball's chance in a July desert of bein' successful. But he's gonna try. So are you goin' with the scouts or not?"

I thought for a short time, grinned, and said, "I go."

Sieber nodded. "I hoped you would say that, but I don't want you to go as a scout."

"Why not?"

"If you go as a scout, you'll be busy with your first-sergeant duties. I need you to go as my assistant again so you can be my eyes and ears up and down the trail. You know what I mean, sniff out trouble before it finds us. Would you be willin' to do that? Just not reenlist for six moons. I can get you paid. How about it?"

I crossed my arms and stared at my friend while I thought it over. "I should go as scout. But you need me free? I go as assistant."

Sieber puffed his cheeks and blew. "Thanks, my friend. I'll owe you one."

"One what?"

Sieber grinned and shook his head.

THIRTY-ONE

COURTING CHITA

THE SERGEANT WHO did the paperwork when I left the army as a scout said it was only three days before the White Eye god's birthday that they called "Christmas." I touched the pen for Captain Crawford, whom I knew well from earlier suns. He said he hoped I would return to the scouts quick. I gave the sergeant most of the equipment and supplies I had been given as a scout but kept the bandoliers, the soldier glasses, and the nice revolver and paid for them with my last pay as a scout. Crawford gave me a pass so I could visit my family in Aravaipa Canyon and my future woman at Hashke Bahnzin's lodge on the Río San Pedro about a hand's ride from my mother's *wickiup.*

As I rode the twisting ridge and canyon trails on the south side of the Río Gila past Mount Turnbull to Aravaipa Canyon, I thought about the harvest I had finished as an army scout. I had learned much about the way the Blue Coat army thought and fought. Some of their ways were good—others, only chiefs with no sense would use. Sieber had taught me much. His biggest lesson was, if you hesitate to act in battle, you lose. I had seen that lesson played out several times and knew it was true. I was glad Sieber wanted me to ride into Mexico after the Chiricahua with him and General Crook. I knew this ride would teach me much about "expeditions."

Thoughts of Chita floated through my mind like bright white puffy clouds in a blue sky. I saw the glow of her quick smile, her head modestly bowed with her shining black hair falling over her shoulders, her eyes searching mine, and the warmth of her hand in mine. I wondered when we could marry after her

Haheh. Her woman time hid from us, deliberately teasing us, making us yearn for each other, wanting us to come together before we were married. I want her, but I refuse to shame her father and mother or her for the pleasure we might share. Most girls her age already had a child, some even two. What should I do if she can't have children? I would still want her but would need another woman or more to give us children. How many wives should I have? What was the number of wives *Capitan* Chiquito had? Six? I don't want that many. Two including Chita, but no more than three. *I haven't seen her in six moons. I wonder if she still wants me.*

The sun was beginning to hide behind the mountains when I rode up to my family's lodge among those of *Capitan* Chiquito's band in Aravaipa Canyon. The wind had appeared earlier in the afternoon, cutting and burning every piece of exposed skin. I was very glad I was at last out of most of it, going down the trail between the protective walls of the canyon. My mother's lodge was against the southside canyon wall in a spot Wind left alone. She was wrapped in a blanket and squatted by her fire as she roasted meat on sticks, steamed baked mescal, baked bread of some kind in a covered iron pot sitting to one side in the coals, and stirred a couple of pots of some stew, its smell making my stomach roar with hunger. My father competed for her when he was a young man and she was a beautiful young woman. They laughed often when they told the story around the night fire about how she had chosen Father over a man named Rip, who was angry she didn't choose him and swore to get even. I didn't understand that. Men shouldn't fight over women. I believed that if you lose one, go find another.

Mother was still pleasing to men's eyes. When she looked up from her cooking fire and saw me, a big smile filled her face and she pulled back the *wickiup* door blanket and spoke to those inside. My brothers and sisters came running out yelling, "Ohyessonna! Ohyessonna!" My father followed them and lifted his arms like wings as he walked toward me saying, "Ho, my son comes home. A good time is here."

I greeted each one. It was good to be with my family and take some rest. I sat outside with my mother and father while she finished making our supper. They asked me about life in the scouts while my brothers and sisters crowded together behind Father and me to hear us talk. I told some good stories, but nothing they could not have already heard on ration day that was usually filled with gossip at San Carlos. Still, my brothers and sisters listened with close attention, sometimes nodding to what I said like they had heard it before but mostly stayed still, taking in all I had to say.

Finally, my mother ran them off to bed, and she and my father sat out to talk and watch the flames die down to coals. My father wanted to know if I planned to rejoin the scouts and seemed surprised when I shook my head and said not for another six moons.

He frowned and said, "Why not?"

"Sieber wants me to ride with him and help manage the scouts when General Crook goes after the Chiricahua. There are things I can't do if I'm in the army in the land of the *Nakai-yes*. Sieber has done much for me. I won't and can't turn him down."

Father stared into the fire a short time and then looked at me. "So, Crook goes after the Chiricahua in the land of *Nakai-yes*. Hmmph. I thought he might do that. You must be very careful down there. If the Chiricahua don't get you, the *Nakai-yes* will. They're like the White Eyes. They can't tell one Apache from the other and will shoot you thinking you're a Chiricahua."

I nodded and smiled. "I hear you, Father—and you know how good my ears are."

"Your test of that was many harvests ago, my son. But yes, I know how good your ears are."

My mother said, "When will you go to Hashke Bahnzin's lodge? You know he no longer lives in a *wickiup*?"

I shook my head. "No, I haven't visited him since my last enlistment and he lived in a big *wickiup* on the río. What is it? A big *tipi*?"

Mother laughed, clapped her hands, and said, "You'll see. I know Chita is eager to see you. Still, she has not had her *Haheh*, when many girls her age already have children. I grow anxious for my first grandchild. I pray every day that *Ussen* soon blesses her with becoming a woman. Do you still want her?"

I gave her half a smile and nodded. "I go to Hashke Bahnzin's lodge tomorrow. I doubt I'll be here for one of your good suppers. Chita and her mother always seem anxious to cook for me. I'm eager to see her too. I'm eager to take her as my woman so we can make you many grandchildren, but everything in its season. *Ussen* will decide when she's ready to be a wife and mother. I'm patient, like a good hunter waiting for deer to come. She's worth the wait, and Hashke Bahnzin thinks I am too. He runs off other suitors who say they wait on her. This I know."

Mother crossed her arms and leaned back looking me in the eyes. "The baby I birthed as my first child has become a very wise man who is tall and handsome. Patience is rewarded."

I SLEPT LIKE I had been knocked in the head between my brothers and sisters in my mother's *wickiup*. At the morning meal, sitting by her fire talking and laughing with my brothers and sisters, I ate until I was packed full of her acorn bread and venison stew left from the night before. When the sun was halfway to the time of no shadows, I went to a place of privacy on the creek, washed, and put on my White Eye suit clothes. I left my dirty clothes with my mother and then saddled my pony and headed for Hashke Bahnzin's lodge.

MY PONY JOGGED south along the wagon road on the east side of the Río San Pedro while I enjoyed the cool air, the birds singing in the brush and the sun warming the left side of my face. To the southeast, the Galiuro Mountains grew rough and dark where *Capitan* Chiquito's and Hashke Bahnzin's People often hid during the times when the White Eyes made war on us.

After riding for about a hand above the horizon, I came to a trail that led off the main trail to large, cleared fields that had been fenced and crisscrossed with ditches to carry water for the planted fields. Other fields held grazing horses and cattle. An adobe house stood in the back of the fields, and I could see several others in the trees out behind the fields. Women sat against the side of the adobe house in the warm sun working on baskets or sorting seeds for planting in the Season of Little Eagles.

I reined my pony to a stop in a place where it was hard to see and used my soldier glasses to study the women. It didn't take long to find Chita sitting in the adobe-house doorway speaking with her mother. Both women worked on large flat baskets with black-and-red geometric designs. Ah, Chita, you are a very talented woman. I also saw men working in a field behind the adobe house. It looked like they were building some kind of shed.

I lightly spurred my horse to jog down the hard caliche wagon trail toward the house. All the women looked up when they heard my pony's hooves on the hard earth growing louder as it approached them. I saw Chita look up from her basket work and stare at me for a short breath before she stood with a smile filling her face and, tossing her partially finished basket aside, ran toward me yelling, "Ohyessonna comes! Ohyessonna comes!" Her mother covered her mouth as she and the other women stood laughing to see Chita running for me.

Showing affection in public was bad manners, but I didn't care and neither did the women.

I kept my pony moving, and as she approached me, I leaned over my saddle and lowered my forearm for her to grab on to. She took a tight hold on my helping arm and swung up behind me as easily as pitching a blanket on a mount before a saddle. She threw her arms around my middle and squeezed. "I thank *Ussen* that at last you come. My heart has wings." We galloped toward the porch and its shade.

We stopped in front of her mother. Chita slid off the saddle, yelling, "Mother, Ohyessonna comes. I must run and wash and put on a clean dress. Don't let him run away before I get back."

Her mother and I smiled at each other as Chita ran through the doorway into the cool darkness. Her mother said, "It is good to see you, my son. Our daughter speaks of you every day. How has life been in the scouts?" The other women drew close to listen to us. They didn't care that it was bad manners. It was not like we were strangers. I told them a little about my last enlistment, about battling Na-ti-o-tish and how General Crook returned to make things right at the reservation and planned to bring the Chiricahua back from the land of the *Nakai-yes*. The expressions on their faces told me they didn't like that idea. Chiricahua were often enemies of the western tribes.

I started to explain, but Chita ran out the door in a fine, new-looking outfit, asking me and the women how she looked. They all said she looked very nice and I should be proud of her. I said, "I am proud, very proud of the girl soon my woman."

Her mother smiled and said, "You two, sit on the other side of the doorway and talk all you want. I'll sit here. Hashke Bahnzin will come from the fields with the men soon. He will be happy to see you again with Chita. I think, soon she is a woman. Then you marry? You see me again no more."

Her mother was right. At the time of no shadows, the men came from what they were building in the field to eat. Hashke Bahnzin gave us a big tooth-filled smile. He walked up and made the all-is-well sign. I made the same sign and stood. He took me by my shoulders and said, "You come. *Enjuh*. Soon Chita has her *Haheh*. Then you marry. We talk after a meal. You tell me what you do with scouts. I tell me my plans for this place. Someday it will belong to Chita and you. Come. Let us eat."

We talked a long time after the meal. I was impressed with all he had done with his *rancheria* since I had last been there. I was very impressed with Chita.

Every time I returned, she was more beautiful and mature. She understood many things most women didn't know, and she knew how to make good meals that filled me up. Every day that I rode back home and then returned the next day, I wanted her for my wife more than ever.

During those days, we walked where her mother could see us and talked of everything on our minds. She turned pale when I told her I was going after the Chiricahua in the land of *Nakai-yes* with General Crook. I promised her I would be brave, but not foolish, and come back alive. She said if I didn't, she'd kill me. We both laughed.

The Ghost Face arrived with a cold fury blowing too hard to travel, and we had to stay apart for ten suns while Wind swept the earth clean before it warmed back up. After the wind stopped, I rode to see my future woman. Time was fast approaching when I had to head for Willcox and meet Sieber and his scouts. When I told Chita, she made a sad face, but she knew it was what I needed to do. I spoke with Hashke Bahnzin a long time about his farm and how I could help him when I returned. His words stirred my spirit, and I wanted to farm with him after I took Chita for my woman. Now all our plans depended on when her womanhood came.

THIRTY-TWO

GENERAL CROOK'S CHIRICAHUA EXPEDITION

I LEFT MY family and Chita to follow the Río San Pedro south about a day's ride before turning east and finding a place to camp in a small, secluded deep rock overhang in some cliffs on my way to Willcox. The black soot on the overhang ceiling and a fire pit, its stones scattered and charcoal-black embers many moons old in the loose floor dirt, said this was a resting place for Apache on the trail. I roasted some meat my mother had given me and ate it with a round of mesquite bread she had included. It was a cold night, but my pony and I were well out of the wind and rested easily listening to the coyotes yip off in the distance and the small animals scrambling in the brush that overhung the recess opening.

The next morning before sunrise, I mounted and pushed on toward Willcox. I followed an *arroyo* to the top of a low range of hills and then down across the llano to more hills, until my pony topped one where I saw the great white playa, an iron road running southwest past it, and in the distance a building where iron wagons stopped. Beyond the place where iron wagons stopped, a little farther east, stood short lines of white-wall tents. I guessed the tents belonged to the army, and that's where I needed to go.

A hand later, I had crossed the iron road and was close enough to the white tents to see Blue Coat chiefs passing in and out of them. They were too far to recognize their faces, but I knew I would find Sieber among them.

As I came to the first tent, a red-haired sergeant passed out its flaps and recognized me. "Ho, Kid! It's been a while. If ye're a lookin' for Mister Sieber, his tent is the last one in line here. They're all officers' tents. Cap'n Crawford and Lieutenant Gatewood are due in the next day or two with their scouts. Cap'n Chaffee won't be in with his soldiers and packers for another couple o' weeks. The general's office is in that rail car parked on them tracks toward the back."

I made the all-is-well sign, smiled, and nodded at him when he gave me the Blue Coat salute, and I saluted back before I jogged my pony down the tent line to Sieber's tent. He heard me dismounting and stepped to the flaps of his tent. Holding on to them to keep the wind from shaking and rolling them, he stuck his head out and saw me, and his face filled with a smile. "Welcome, Kid. Glad you're here."

"Ho, Sieber. You say come, I come."

"Come on in this tent out of the breeze. I'll get one of the sergeants to set you up a tent next to mine. The horse corral is a little farther down the line and ought to be pretty crowded when them packers and soldiers come in, but we'll manage. We'll be eatin' at the general's mess. I think they may already be cookin' it. He's gettin' ready to head for Mexico in a couple of weeks. You have a good visit with your folks?"

"Hmmph. Good visit. Visit with my family and future woman's family."

"That's good. I spent most of my time in bars and at card tables in Prescott this Christmas. Made a little money, too, enough to keep you paid, and me playin' for a while. We've got to figure out how to find them Chiricahua camps down in Mexico before we leave. If we don't, this here little march is gonna be a waste of time. If you had to look for those camps by yourself, how would you do it?"

I stared at the tent wall thinking while Sieber sat behind his table moving his writing stick he held between the fingers of one hand up and down its length.

I shook my head. "Find Chiricahua camp, first ask Chiricahua at San Carlos where they camp in Mexico when close to first waters of Río Bavispe. I hear Chiricahua scouts say they know where Geronimo and Juh camp in mountains? I use 'em. Make 'em show me. They lie, I leave 'em there. They lie no more."

Sieber grinned. "When did you get so bloodthirsty, Kid? I had the same thought but hadn't pitched it to the general yet. Come on, let's find the sergeant managing the tents and get you one set up close to mine."

The wind was beginning to die, but it still wasn't comfortable, especially to my eyes, with the dust it was carrying. Sieber found the sergeant he wanted and asked that he have a tent set up close to his. Then he motioned to me and practically yelled against the wind, "Come on, let's get some beans."

The packers who were to manage the mule trains also did the cooking for the officers and *Nant'an Lpah*. While we ate their beans and meat, Sieber introduced me to a White Eye packer who was about my size and age.

Sieber said, "Tom Horn, this here is my assistant, Apache Kid. Kid, this here is Tom Horn, packer, but wantin' to be a chief of scouts."

Horn grinned and stuck out his hand. I gave it two good pumps, and we nodded acknowledgment of each other, but I was not smiling. This White Eye didn't know my People. He'd be worse than some of the no-account agents we had to deal with. He saluted and said, "I'm happy to have a job of any kind with you boys. This here work gits my blood a rushin'. See ya later. Got to get some packin' work done and train some more mules with these new frames."

As Tom Horn walked away, Sieber mumbled to me, "That boy is all hole and no post."

"What means that, Sieber?"

"It means he's learning and knows how to talk a good line, but he ain't got the wood to make it happen—yet."

WITHIN HALF A moon of suns before the nant'an's trip to visit the big chiefs in Mexico, powerful medicine happened. *Teniente* Davis, commander of the scouts at San Carlos, captured a White Mountain man named Tzoe. His skin was so smooth and peach colored, the soldiers called him "Peaches." He had married two Chihenne sisters. When Geronimo's warriors came for his People, they forced him to go south with his wives and a young daughter. After crossing the border, the Blue Coats that Sieber and I rode with disobeyed their big chiefs and attacked Loco's People. The next day, *Nakai-yi* soldiers ambushed them early in the morning and fought with them from *arroyos* all that sun. In that fight, the *Nakai-yes* killed both his wives and his little daughter and badly wounded him. Now, a harvest later, he was ready for war.

In the Season of Little Eagles, Tzoe and his best friend Beneactiney went with Chato and Bonito on a fast raid north across the border looking for weapons, ammunition, and supplies. When they raided a charcoal camp near the mining village of Tombstone, a White Eye hiding behind a tent killed Beneactiney. Two or three days later, in a night camp high on a mountain overlooking San Carlos,

Tzoe stared at the distant twinkling of home fires and listened to the night birds. He decided that his medicine told him he should return to San Carlos to look after his People. Chato, Bonito, and the other warriors agreed. Who were they to argue with *Ussen?*

At San Carlos early two or three mornings later, Tzoe put up no resistance when Davis's scouts, who had seen him creeping into a White Mountain reservation camp, took him. After talking to Tzoe, *Teniente* Davis sent him to *Nant'an Lpah* for more questions. I saw Tzoe step off the iron wagon from Bowie Station smiling even in chains as his guards marched him over to talk with the nant'an in his iron wagon. After a couple of hands, he came out the nant'an's door in a first sergeant's uniform. Sieber learned his name and that he had agreed to lead the nant'an to Chiricahua camps near the first waters of the Río Bavispe. The nant'an asked Sieber to talk to Tzoe and then tell him what he thought. Sieber did this while I listened. We were both convinced Tzoe spoke true and knew where the camps were—a place he called "Bugatseka," and the maps showed as Mesa Tres Ríos. Nant'an made Tzoe a first sergeant so it wouldn't raise suspicions when he was at the head of the column leading the way.

When Sieber told the nant'an he thought Tzoe told the truth, but that it would be wise to question other Chiricahua scouts, the nant'an said, "Get it done." We questioned all the Chiricahua with us separately about where they thought the camps of the Chiricahua close to the source of the Río Bavispe were, and two gave us consistent answers. They agreed with Tzoe on camp locations. We told the nant'an we thought he could use them. He spoke to each one separately and said to Sieber, "If Tzoe fails us, we'll use these scouts to locate the camps."

Nant'an Lpah returned from the land of the *Nakai-yes* six or seven suns after Tzoe came. He looked satisfied and told his chiefs that the Mexicans would leave us alone after we crossed the border if we minded our own business.

AFTER ALL THE scouts came in with their commanders, Nant'an moved his resupply camp and scouts to the border and made a camp on fine grazing grass near the springs feeding the little Río San Bernardino beginning at the Slaughter Ranch.

The scouts all running, left the Willcox camp first. The wind was blowing hard and filled with dust off the playa. *Teniente* Gatewood had all the scouts line up and rode down the line looking each man in the eye. At the end of the line, he turned his pony to face the direction we were running and pulled his long knife—the Blue Coats call it a "saber"—dangling from a sheath at his side.

He raised the knife high into the wind and pointed it toward the sky. He yelled, "Ugash (Go)!" The scouts took off like a flock of birds, each running at a pace and direction comfortable for him. We could have been at the border in a day, but it took us two because the wagons carrying backup supplies were much slower than we were crossing the caliche and sand.

Our last days at the border passed in a rush, but the mule train and the scouts were ready. I thought our chances of finding the Chiricahua were good, but I wondered what would happen when the shooting started. According to Sieber, we left the first day of the moon the White Eyes call "May 1883." I was happy to run with the scouts. I was slow because I hadn't run much distance since becoming Sieber's assistant.

Our days of running carried us up the east branch of the Río Bavispe past ranchos and small villages that had withered and died from too many Chiricahua raids. We passed Bavispe and along the río that had survived the Apache and ran on south to the village of Huachinera before Tzoe turned east into the mountains and followed narrow trails on high ridges. We soon found signs of cattle and lost bounty taken in raids. Far below the narrow trails on ridges and cliffs, it was easy to see and smell the animals that had fallen off the trail to crash on the boulders below.

The packtrain and troopers protecting them were slowing the scouts down. We stopped for a couple of suns on top of a ridge with good water high on a mountain where the Chiricahua had left some weak cattle. We slaughtered the cattle for our meals and baked bread to carry with us. To cover more ground faster, most of the scouts left with packtrains that supported them. Sieber and the Blue Coat chiefs planned to send back for the rest moving at their normal pace to hurry forward when a Chiricahua camp was found.

Three suns later, as I looked across a canyon lighted by a golden, flaring sun pouring out its last light, we saw a camp. Watching it with my soldier glasses, I saw there weren't many warriors helping the women and children make jerky from slaughtered cattle. We learned later that the place was the camp of Chato, Bonito, Naiche, and Chihuahua.

Using my soldier glasses, I saw thirty *wickiups* in two groups and every bush in or near the camp covered with drying meat. There were big baskets filled with big juicy juniper berries and other baskets filled with nuts or dried vegetables. In a grassy area below the *rancheria* was a herd of about fifty horses and mules, and the cattle that had not been slaughtered were grazing nearby. Sieber worked out an attack plan that divided the scouts into groups to capture the horses and mules, and attack the camp to take prisoners, which were mostly women and children and old men. Once the prisoners were gathered, the scouts could claim anything they wanted to keep before destroying the camp and the food supplies there.

The attack was successful, but many of the women and children disappeared into the brush. I was with Sieber, watching the attack with my soldier glasses. Those taking the horse and mule herd also caught two or three young boys and a girl riding near the herd. I saw an old woman, who had been working at preparing baskets of food, stand with her hands up and say something to two White Mountain scouts who approached her. The scouts said something back. She answered and smiled. A scout pulled his big army revolver and, grinning like a coyote ready to pounce on a rabbit, cocked the revolver and shot her in the heart. She was still smiling when she fell backward. It made me angry when I saw the old woman killed. Someday, scout, when you face me, I'll put a bullet in your heart for that old woman. Blood for blood is the Apache way.

IN THE DAYS that followed, Crook changed his initial camp location and met with Chihuahua, who was angry that his old aunt had been killed by scouts but told Crook he would bring his People in. Geronimo and thirty of his best warriors had been in eastern Chihuahua looking for people to kidnap. They wanted to trade them for Chiricahua—including his and Chato's wives—the *Nakai-yes* had caught and sold as slaves. Somehow Geronimo learned that Blue Coats had taken their camp—I was told later he had a vision—and rushed back in disbelief with the warriors and four women and a baby they had taken captive.

Geronimo and the warriors and leaders were astonished the Blue Coats had come into the land of the *Nakai-yes* and found their camp. Geronimo was convinced Crook was a god to have done it. After General Crook spoke to the leaders as a group and in private several times with each one, they realized there was no place else to hide and if men with red headbands, the scouts, helped the Blue Coats, the Chiricahua would always be found. They had to either fight to the death or surrender and live life on a reservation under White Eye supervision. General Crook promised that their reservation would be managed as it should be and that they would have their own piece of the reservation where they wouldn't have to deal with other bands. They chose life and returned to live on a reservation.

THIRTY-THREE

RETURN TO SAN CARLOS

MOST CHIRICAHUA LEADERS, including Naiche, Geronimo, Chihuahua, and Chato, didn't want to leave Mexico and Bugatseka for San Carlos until they found all the People in their band. Many in the bands saw the smoke signals to come in but thought they were from the scouts trying to trick them and stayed away from the scouts and Blue Coats. Crook left the leaders to collect their People but warned that, if they didn't meet him at the border, settlers thinking the Apache were out raiding might attack them on the way to San Carlos. The leaders acknowledged they understood and promised to stay in the mountains unseen until they reached San Carlos.

Crook returned to the border via the eastern side of the Sierra Madre rather than the western side from where Tzoe had led him to Bugatseka. He hoped to avoid villages, believing that seeing so many Apache—well over five hundred counting the scouts—might cause unnecessary panic and shooting and start another war. After a couple of suns, Sieber and I left to return to San Carlos. Crook wanted Sieber to see the agent and plan for where the Chiricahua could live until they found a piece of the reservation they wanted to claim as theirs.

Although I wasn't in the army anymore, Sieber asked me to ride to bands scattered over the reservation and look for trouble spots—resistance to the Chiricahua coming to San Carlos—and for places where the Chiricahua might want to live. I traveled the reservation and spoke to men from the different bands who enlisted with me in the scouts. I knew they would speak straight. I learned that no one wanted to fight with the Chiricahua, but they wouldn't tolerate the Chiricahua trying to always get what they wanted even if it meant shedding blood.

I looked over the land both at San Carlos and at Fort Apache and decided the best places for Chiricahua farms were at Fort Apache along Turkey Creek or near the agency along the east fork of the White River. I told this to Sieber, who later told *Nant'an Lpah*. He took it all in, thanked Sieber for the information, and said no more. The next year, when the Chiricahua moved to their part of the reservation under the command of *Teniente* Davis, they settled along Turkey Creek and later some had farms along the east fork of the White River. I don't believe it was from anything I told Sieber. More likely, it was a natural fit for them after Geronimo wanted the reservation boundary removed so the Chiricahua could live and farm on Eagle Creek in the Natanes Mountains, but *Nant'an Lpah* said no, that the reservation boundaries, by treaty, didn't move. By law, the great chiefs far to the east couldn't force settlers on their ranches to move. I remembered the San Carlos agent moving the reservation boundary in from Globe. The same law the White Eyes have about reservation boundaries doesn't apply to Apache.

WHILE *NANT'AN LPAH* waited for the Chiricahua leaders to come in with their People, I visited my People and Chita with her People. I told them what it was like to find the Chiricahua in the land of the *Nakai-yes* and how clever *Nant'an Lpah* had been in convincing their chiefs to return to San Carlos. Chita seemed even more beautiful than she was the last time I saw her, but still she was not ready for her womanhood ceremony. I wanted her more than ever, and she me, but I would not dishonor the lodge of Hashke Bahnzin or risk having him come after me because I had crawled in the brush with his favorite daughter, shamed her, and made her less valuable to her family.

After fighting my desire for her suns and nights, I decided I'd return to San Carlos and serve another six months with Sieber. By then Chita should have had her womanhood ceremony. If not, then maybe another six months in the scouts, saving my pay and waiting for her. When I spoke of this with Chita, her eyes were close to losing water, but she nodded she understood. She told me in a strong, mature woman's voice to come to her father's lodge anytime I could, and I promised I would.

I spoke with Hashke Bahnzin before I left. He praised me for my patience and promised Chita was mine after her womanhood ceremony. I told him I planned to reenlist in the scouts and would return for a visit when I could. He grinned and said, "You come. One day you stay."

I FOUND CAPTAIN Crawford in the place he called "office" at the San Carlos Agency house. He sat at his worktable scattered with papers of many brands and black-water tracks. A Blue Coat sergeant sitting at a table guarded the office doorway every day while people waiting to see Captain Crawford sat in chairs lining the room. The sergeant's duty was to turn away people who had no real business with the agent and to ask Crawford if he would see people wanting to see him. The day I went to reenlist, the door to his office was open and no one waited in the room where the sergeant sat. I knew the sergeant, and he remembered me from the Big Dry Wash fight.

He said, "Howdy, Kid. Long time no see. What can I do you out of?"

I frowned in confusion and pointed toward Captain Crawford's office. He held out the palm of his hand for me to wait and stood and stepped into the office. I heard him mumble something to Crawford who said, "Of course! Send him in."

The sergeant motioned me through the door and closed it. Captain Crawford stood with a big grin as I came in and held out his hand saying, "First Sergeant Kid. I'm glad to see you. I hope all is well with you and your family."

"Hmmph. All well."

"What can I do for you on this fine day?"

"Six-month scout reenlistment. First sergeant before. Now same again? Sieber commander?"

"Glad you want to reenlist. The army can always use men like you. Hold on for a bit while I find your papers."

He looked in a drawer and pulled out a thick set of papers grouped in something he called a "folder." He opened the folder and started flipping pages until he found mine about halfway through the set. He held it up and read it. Then he grinned and nodded.

"Well, First Sergeant Kid, your record here says you're a good sergeant, very dependable, and you look after the men for whom you're responsible. I'm happy to sign you up. I understand Al Sieber is going to be out and about often as chief of scouts, but his duty post will be here. I need you here to help *Teniente* Davis, who will command the scouts who'll help him get the Chiricahua settled and move whatever they own to Fort Apache. My guess? I think the Chiricahua will want to go to Turkey Creek or the east fork of the White River. They're not all here yet."

There was a sound of running feet and children's whoops just outside his window. Crawford smiled and we waited until he was sure they were gone before we talked again.

"The band leaders are still rounding them up. Who knows when they'll show. I'll check with Davis to be sure he needs you. He and his scouts will be making trips to the border to escort the Chiricahua here as they come in. That sounds like what a man of your talents can do. How about supporting Davis this enlistment? I think he'll have most of the action."

I crossed my arms and thought while I stared at the wall to one side of Crawford's table. I can't stay with Sieber all the time. Davis is good commander for the Chiricahua. I see good action when all return.

I said, "Davis good commander. I serve. I touch pen."

Captain Crawford smiled and nodded. "I think that's a wise decision. Let me put these papers back and fill out a form for you. You said a six-month reenlistment, right?"

I nodded. "I say that."

"*Enjuh.* I know you'll enjoy working for *Teniente* Davis."

NANT'AN LPAH SENT *Teniente* Davis to the border in the Season of Earth Is Reddish Brown. His orders were to watch for returning Chiricahua and to prevent White Eyes wanting revenge for past raids from attacking them as they returned to San Carlos. Davis had a packtrain of supplies and a company of twenty scouts made up mainly from Chiricahua who had returned with Crook in the Season of Large Leaves. I served as first sergeant for Davis's company of scouts on the trip to the border where we waited for the returning Chiricahua.

We put up our tents on the Slaughter Ranch at the border. I planned watch rotations, and we ate with the packers from the packtrain. Half a moon passed, but we saw no one—*Nakai-yi* or White Eye.

I got up one morning just before sunrise, intending to wash in the Río San Bernardino. It was getting cooler every morning, but the birds still stirred in the brush and the sun made the mountains look like they were flowing with *pesh klitso.* The packers who cooked the morning meal weren't up yet, but there was enough light to see. When I crawled out of my tent, my jaw dropped. Standing in front of *Teniente* Davis's big tent were eight Chiricahua men, three women, and two children patiently waiting for the *teniente* to come out. I recognized none of them. I walked over to them, made the all-is-well sign, and asked when they had come. One man said it was just before first light. They stood close to the *teniente's* tent not wanting to risk an ambush like those killed at Aliso Creek.

Teniente Davis stepped out of his tent, grinned, and made the all-is-well sign and asked that I find Bowman, who was his interpreter, so he could talk with these people and then to awake the packers so the People could eat soon. I found Bowman washing at the río. He had not seen the Chiricahua at the front of *teniente's* tent. He smoothed his wet hair back with his hands, whipped them dry on his shirt, and headed for the *teniente's* tent. The packers were already up starting a cooking fire. When I told them that we had thirteen more mouths to feed, they were surprised. They hadn't seen the Apache at *Teniente's* tent, but no matter, they had plenty and knew the things Apache liked to eat. They made a nice morning meal for all of us.

TENIENTE DAVIS SENT me and five scouts with enough supplies to get us back to San Carlos with the newly arrived Chiricahua. He told me to turn them over to Captain Crawford, who would look after them until the missing chiefs returned with their People, and to return to his camp as soon as I could.

Late in the moon the White Eyes call "October 1883," Naiche and Gil-lee appeared with about nine warriors and twice as many women and children. Half a moon later, Chihuahua and Mangas came in with about ninety of their People. It seemed that, every few suns, more Chiricahua trickled into *Teniente's* camp on the Slaughter Ranch. We escorted some back to San Carlos. Some we didn't escort, and they risked settlers attacking them, but they made it to San Carlos without any fighting. The human flow stopped for a while in the middle suns of Ghost Face.

My six-month enlistment ended the last day of the moon the White Eyes called "January 1884." Very curious to learn if Chato and Geronimo would return across the border or stay in the land of the *Nakai-yes,* I wondered if Crook would have to return to Bugatseka and get them. Since I had heard nothing from Chita, I reenlisted with Captain Crawford the next day. I also wanted to learn how the Chiricahua would do if they went to one of the places on the reservation I had recommended to Sieber.

Chiricahua reappeared again at the camp of *Teniente* Davis. This time it was Chato's band of nineteen and it drove a big herd of horses and mules they planned to keep. Chato was very cooperative. He told *Teniente* Davis that he knew how to get through the mountains to San Carlos without settlers seeing them. I liked him and thought he was a major warrior who could teach me a thing or two. *Teniente* Davis let him go on by himself but warned him not to let settlers see his People. They might be attacked and his herd of horses and mules stolen.

Late in the same moon after Chato arrived, Geronimo with twenty-five warriors and seventy women and children came driving a herd of three hundred fifty prime cattle—cows and calves—he had stolen from ranches along the border and in raids deep into Chihuahua. He wanted the Chiricahua to have their own big herd at San Carlos, and he didn't want to hurry them along to avoid them losing weight, but *Teniente* Davis told him they had to move fast or settlers and ranchers who had lost the cattle in the first place would come over the border after them or bad White Eyes might steal them. We moved Geronimo's People at a fast pace, but even so, Davis had to trick White Eye lawmen who appeared at Sulfur Springs Ranch, where we stopped to rest. The lawmen had orders from the big chiefs in the East to keep the cattle and arrest Geronimo. Davis outsmarted the lawmen and hid the Apache and cattle until Geronimo reached San Carlos.

Captain Crawford came out to smoke and speak with Geronimo. Crawford told him *Nant'an Lpah* said Geronimo must return the cattle to their owners in Mexico or sell them to the reservation and he would distribute the money to the owners. Geronimo thought taking his stolen cattle was unfair. He argued long and hard that the cattle belonged to him. They were loot taken in war. Crawford didn't budge. Geronimo eventually threw up his hands in frustration. Crawford sold the cattle to San Carlos and surrounding ranchers and distributed the money as *Nant'an Lpah* said he must.

The Chiricahua chiefs and Geronimo, after learning they couldn't have farms and ranches along Eagle Creek, which was outside the reservation, decided Turkey Creek at Fort Apache was the best place for them. Captain Crawford and *Teniente* Davis started planning how they would move the Chiricahua along with all the ration supplies, horses and mules, wagons, farm tools pulled by horses or mules, and things they already owned to Turkey Creek.

THIRTY-FOUR

TURKEY CREEK

HALF A MOON before *Teniente* Davis led the Chiricahua to Turkey Creek, a man from the White Eye village named Willcox brought a wagonload of boxes to San Carlos and asked to speak to Captain Crawford. After they talked, Crawford sent for *Teniente* Davis and the three held council. Davis told me later the man's name was Frank Randall. The boxes in his wagon held equipment for catching images on glass plates smeared with a magic potion. These images the White Eyes called "photographs" or "pictures," and they were much more accurate and detailed than anyone could draw. Davis and Crawford talked to the Chiricahua leaders to convince them that there was no witchcraft involved in Randall's image capture and all who had their images made this way were safe. They said making photographs was like following a woman's directions to make bread.

At first the Chiricahua leaders refused to have photographs made by the image catcher, but Captain Crawford had much light behind his eyes. He asked Tzoe to have his image captured. Tzoe stood in front of a big painting of desert plants and pots with actual plants Randall set up in a room at the agency. With just the painting in the background, Tzoe looked like he was standing in the desert. The Chiricahua leaders all watched with their arms crossed and staring with hard looks at Tzoe while his image was captured with the magic potion-covered glass. They did not like Tzoe and hoped it would kill him. They believed he had betrayed them all. Randall also had Tzoe stand between two seated scouts and again positioned them and adjusted his image catcher before doing his ceremony to make the image capture.

When he said he was ready for another, there was a long silence. None of the Chiricahua leaders moved until Naiche and his wife Haozinne came forward. Randall gave him an old rifle that wouldn't shoot and had Naiche sit on a high stool with Haozinne behind and to the side of his left shoulder. Randall went through the same ceremony capturing their image as he had with Tzoe and the scouts. Chato watched all this with interest and decided he would be next. Randall had him pose with the same old rifle he gave Naiche. He captured Chato's image in two different settings, one with him standing and the other kneeling. Kaytennae, alone, Nana's *segundo*, and Kaytennae with his wife and adopted son followed Chato. It was easy to see Chato and Kaytennae disliked each other from the frowns they made when they faced each other. Others followed Chato and Kaytennae for their image capture. Geronimo was last to have his image captured. He took the old gun and kneeled with it while making a hard face and, like Chato, stood for his second image. After Geronimo, Nana and Chihuahua sat in front of the painting and had their images captured.

A couple of suns later, after Randall had made other photographs and done his ceremony to make the images appear on the glass plates, he laid them out on top of a white cloth spread out on a table. The Chiricahua leaders who had their images captured were astonished that the image looked exactly like them. Geronimo especially like his. He said it made him look fierce all the time.

The image capturing Randall did was not new to me. Three harvests earlier, an image catcher had come to San Carlos. Our images were captured then by a man named Fly. He came from the mining village the White Eyes named Tombstone. I had my image captured several times with my scout friends Massai and Rowdy when I was in my White Eye suit, and later, we stood on a stack of boulders with a couple of our Blue Coat leaders.

ABOUT HALF A moon after Randall left, Davis led the Chiricahua to Turkey Creek on the Fort Apache Reservation. It was an easy trip down the wagon road toward Fort Thomas before Davis turned east and then north up to the llano along the Natanes Mountains and then to the trail up the side of the Natanes Mountains cliffs.

When we reached the Río Black, it was flooded, swirling and roaring out of its banks, and dangerous to cross. Davis decided to wait there on the río's south side for the water to go down, but after it hadn't moved much in a couple of days, he used a trick that he had learned in his younger days hunting ducks by wrapping the wagon beds in canvas so they floated. He had the men pull them across with rope and tackle. The Chiricahua knew how to get the livestock across at a ford they found downstream where the water was slow enough and not too wide for the animals to swim across. Davis had the Chiricahua and their supplies and personal things across the río in two days. He stopped on the far side for three days to let them dry out and rest before going on to Turkey Creek.

Not long after we made camp to dry out and rest, *Nant'an Lpah* and his officers crossed the río and were surprised and happy to see us. He thought it would be another month before we could get across the Río Black. He met with the Chiricahua leaders and commended them for their hard work. Chato and then Geronimo and others asked that *Nant'an Lpah* help them get their People out of slavery in the land of the *Nakai-yes*. *Nant'an Lpah* promised to do all he could to get the Chiricahua women and children out of *Nakai-yi* slavery if their men caused no trouble. When Chato heard this, his face filled with a big happy smile, but Geronimo just crossed his arms and nodded. Chato promised *Nant'an Lpah* that he would do everything he could to support *Nant'an Lpah*'s work and if the nant'an could get his wife and children out of slavery in the land of *Nakai-yes*, then he, Chato, would be grateful. The White Eyes would always have a Chiricahua friend. Little did anyone know that this was the seed that grew into Chato and Geronimo becoming enemies and saved many Apache, *Nakai-yi*, and White Eye lives.

AT TURKEY CREEK, Davis set up his camp in the shade of tall pine trees on a flat place along the creek bank. He had a four-man tent with a wooden floor for his private quarters and a big hospital tent where he kept a month's supply of rations for the Chiricahua, and where he did his army paperwork. It had a small iron stove from which he heated the tent in the cool mists of the morning and made the best-smelling coffee. Mickey Free had his tent close by, as did Sam Bowman, who served as his cook and general camp helper. *Teniente* Davis thought he would get the most cooperation out of the Chiricahua leaders if he had scouts picked from their bands.

He asked me and the scouts under my command to sit with him in the shade by the creek while he told us what he planned to do. He made and lit a cigarette and we smoked to the four directions. High overhead, an eagle screamed. A soft breeze whispered through the tops of the tall pines, shaking the branches and making spots of sunlight dance in the shade where we sat listening to the low gurgle of Turkey Creek.

Teniente Davis said, "Boys, you did a mighty fine job getting the Chiricahua to Turkey Creek. Now I have to figure out how to best manage the People in these little camps up and down the creek. I've decided to create a company of scouts from the Chiricahua bands who accompanied us here. They'll serve as policemen and help maintain the rules *Nant'an Lpah* made that I have to enforce, especially the ones about tizwin making and drinking and wife beating. I expect it'll take me a half a moon to find and recruit the men I want in the bands that moved here. When I have them, I want you to go down to Fort Apache and become members of *Teniente* Gatewood's White Mountain scouts. I've already asked him if he was interested in having you in his scouts, and he'll be happy to get you. Next spring, after the Chiricahua go through a winter at Fort Apache, I expect I'll be askin' you to come back as scouts, but that's gonna depend on circumstances. I just want you to know that I've been proud to serve with you. You all are a credit to your People. Any questions?"

We had no questions. We looked at each other and shrugged and then, at Davis, we shook our heads. No questions. We each shook Davis's hand with two good pumps and wished him good luck. In ten suns, we rode to Fort Apache and found *Teniente* Gatewood, who welcomed us and showed us tents we could use while we were his scouts.

OUR FIRST MAJOR work for *Teniente* Gatewood was to support *Teniente* Davis. *Teniente* Davis sent word one night that the next morning he planned to arrest Kaytennae, who had been planning to ambush him and escape the reservation taking as many Chiricahua as he could back to the land of the *Nakai-yes*. *Teniente* Davis wanted cavalry support in case Kaytennae's arrest led to fighting. Captain Allen Smith led two troops of the Fourth Cavalry and six troops of *Teniente* Gatewood's scouts to Davis's tent on Turkey Creek.

When the request for scouts came in, Gatewood asked if the Aravaipa scouts would accompany Captain Smith. We knew the country, and we knew the individuals who might cause trouble. We were the natural choice to go, but if we had friends there and were slow to defend ourselves in a confrontation with our friends, then we would be at higher risk than his regular White Mountain scouts. Of course, we agreed to accompany Captain Smith. Gatewood had asked, not ordered, us to go because of our knowledge of the new Turkey Creek settlements, but we understood he knew the potential danger and was trying to make the wisest choice of scouts to go.

We arrived at *Teniente* Davis's tent before dawn and stood at ease in the cool pine tree night shadows while *Teniente* Davis explained the situation to Captain Smith. Davis said he didn't expect any trouble, especially when Kaytennae's men realized there were two troops of cavalry and five scout companies ready to back his orders and asked that we stay mounted about two hundred yards behind his tent. Davis returned to his tent.

We soon saw a man heading up the ridge to Kaytennae's camp with a message that *Teniente* Davis wanted to see him pronto. We waited. Davis had also sent his new scouts to ask the Chiricahua leaders to all come to his tent. They knew cavalry were waiting back in the shadows behind the tent and they came armed.

The darkness was fading, but Kaytennae had not appeared. Davis sent the messenger again. Soon Kaytennae and his men appeared on the ridge trail down to the creek. Smith had his troopers and scouts ready to move at the first sign of trouble. Kaytennae and his men stopped in a stand of pine trees about a hundred yards from Davis's tent. Kaytennae said something to his men and then came on toward Davis at a fast walk, stopping three feet in front of him. He snarled something at *Teniente* Davis, who calmly answered him. In the growing light, using my soldier glasses, I saw Kaytennae's face and it showed fear.

He turned and walked back to his men, who strung out in a line with their rifles leveled, walked toward him. Even at the distance we were from Davis's tent, we could hear Kaytennae's men cocking the breech locks on their trapdoor Springfield rifles, and the occasional birdcalls suddenly stopped. It was still, only the creek speaking. When Kaytennae reached his men, he turned and walked with them to within two long rifle lengths of Davis. Davis's scouts Charley and Dutchy stepped to either side of him and cocked their rifles and pointed them at Kaytennae at the center of his line of armed men. Again, Kaytennae stepped closer and he and *Teniente* Davis exchanged words.

Davis did something very brave. He stepped up and unbuckled Kaytennae's cartridge belt mounted with a holstered revolver, took it away, and laid it over his arm. I saw Kaytennae's shoulders sag and he looked at the ground. He waved for his men to back up and they stepped back, looking at each other in confusion and concern. I learned later that Davis had told him he was under arrest and had to go to San Carlos to hear charges from Captain Crawford.

Bonito offered to escort Kaytennae and stand surety for him to surrender to Captain Crawford at San Carlos if *Teniente* Davis would give him back his weapon. Davis nodded and handed the revolver and cartridge belt back to Kaytennae. Scout Charley and Chihuahua volunteered to ride with Bonito and Kaytennae.

Davis walked over to Captain Smith and handed him a note for telegraphing to Captain Crawford that told him everything was under control and the cavalry could return to Fort Apache. The night was long, but *Ussen* was good to us. No blood flowed on either side.

THIRTY-FIVE

MY WOMAN CHITA

CAPTAIN CRAWFORD HELD a trial for Kaytennae. Crawford was the trial judge and prosecutor. Twelve western Apache chiefs were the jury and Hashke Bahnzin the jury leader. Kaytennae made his own defense. When the jury reached a guilty verdict, Crawford sent Kaytennae in shackles to the little land in the western big water the White Eyes named Alcatraz for three harvests. There as punishment, men were kept in cages and worked hard during the day to finish building its unfinished parts. I paid little attention to descriptions of this place but wished I had three harvests later.

As my time remaining on my enlistment drew short, there wasn't much to do at Fort Apache. Tzoe decided he would stay in the scouts, fearing some of the Chiricahua men might try to murder him for showing *Nant'an Lpah* where their camps were. Tzoe's main job at Fort Apache was carrying messages between the commanders of Fort Apache, Turkey Creek, and San Carlos.

One hot day, I sat in the shade of the sutler's store porch smoking a cigarette, thinking about what it would be like to live with Chita, have children, and learn the wisdom of my successful father-in-law. Tzoe came jogging down the wagon road headed for the commander's quarters. He glanced at the sutler store windows, saw me, and began to smile. He reined in his roan pony to where I sat frowning and wondering why he was suddenly interested in the store or me.

Tzoe's little smile turned to a big grin as he slowly and deliberately teased me as he guided his pony up to the watering trough and let him drink while we made the all-is-well sign.

"Ho, Kid. I didn't see you sitting there in the shade until I was close to passing you."

"Ho, Tzoe. You have a message for me? Speak. I listen."

"The Aravaipa and Pinal bands plan a big womanhood ceremony for four of their young women in five suns. Chita is one of them. She say to me, 'You see Ohyessonna, tell him my womanhood ceremony is next full moon. You tell him after that day, he speaks with my father.'"

Tzoe's message made my blood race, and I heard it pounding in my ears as I said, "How many days before next full moon?"

He thought a short time, tapping the end of his thumb with his fingertips as he counted. "Next full moon comes in eight suns."

I nodded. Just as I had thought. "Your message warms me, Tzoe. Soon I have my woman."

He smiled, made the all-is-good sign. "May *Ussen* give you and your woman good Power. I come to the ceremony if my chief says I can go. Once, I had two wives and a child. They kept me satisfied and busy, but they were killed and I was wounded at Aliso Creek. Your coming days will be better than mine. I go."

He pulled away from the water trough and put his pony in a long lope. I soon saw him arrive at the commander's workplace, leaving me standing on the store porch, my arms crossed and mind filling with all the things I needed to do. I went to my tent, gathered all my things in a cloth bag, and put my rifle in its saddle case, and all my army things in a separate bag that fit in the larger one. I tied the big bag on the back of my saddle. It was two suns before my enlistment was up. There was little going on, and I guessed that Captain Crawford would let me out of my enlistment early if I asked, especially if I was going to take a woman. I found a sergeant named Angry and told him I was leaving to see Captain Crawford and didn't expect to return for many moons. He smiled and nodded when I told him that I planned to take a woman and start a family. "*Teniente* Gatewood"—Scout commander at Fort Apache—"is out with some scouts looking for a man who belongs in the calaboose. I'll tell him you've gone to see Crawford. If your enlistment is finished in two days, you should get to San Carlos on the day your enlistment is finished and life will be smooth. May your Power give you an easy ride."

"Angry is a good scout. I owe you. *Adios.*"

I RODE SOUTH until darkness left by the disappearing colors of the setting sun made it too hard to ride at a good lope without expecting me or my horse to be hurt. I made a hidden camp in a deep canyon and brushed down my pony in the deepening darkness while he nibbled at the brush and I ate from a sack of trail food. By first light, we were in an easy lope again on the trail to San Carlos Agency.

Just as clouds to the west were beginning to show all the colors of the setting sun and it was getting cold, I rode up to the San Carlos house the Blue Coat officers used for their work. I found Captain Crawford at his worktable. The table of the man who guarded his door and kept out those he didn't want to see had nothing on it and the man was gone. I stood in Crawford's doorway and cleared my throat. He grinned when he looked up and saw me.

He said, "Ho, Kid. You're a day early." I was surprised that he remembered tomorrow was the day my enlistment came to an end. He was nant'an for over a hundred scouts. "I hope you're planning to reenlist."

I shook my head. "No, Captain. Soon I take a woman, start a family, and work my farm. Woman very beautiful. Her father is Hashke Bahnzin. Much to learn about farming. Hashke Bahnzin offers help. I take, but one sun, I return to scouting for the army."

Crawford stood, reached across the table, and gave my hand a couple of good pumps. "Well congratulations. That's a mighty fine thing, taking a woman, and I wish for you all the luck. Of course, we'll miss your service, but it sounds to me like you've chosen a smooth road. Let me get your paperwork, and payment voucher. Why don't you just keep your equipment and use it when you reenlist?"

"Hmmph. Nant'an has clear eyes and sees far. This I do."

Nant'an Crawford smiled and said, *"Enjuh,"* and then started pulling out my papers with the black tracks that kept a record of my service. Between what I had saved and what I had earned in the past moon, I had enough money to give Hashke Bahnzin a good bride gift for Chita, and something special for her.

I LEFT EARLY the next sun, crossed the Río Gila, and headed for my father's camp with *Capitan* Chiquito on Aravaipa Creek. It was a peaceful sun, bright with birds from clouds of bushtits tweeting to crows calling. I arrived at my father's lodge when the sun was two hands above the horizon. My father sitting on a big rock near his *wickiup* while sharpening my mother's ax flashed a big smile when he saw me dismount. He said, "When I learned it was time for Chita's womanhood ceremony, I knew I see you soon."

I made the all-is-well sign. "Ho, Father. You read my mind too well, and I know you often talk with Hashke Bahnzin. Yes, I come to stay a while, claim my woman, and learn to farm with Hashke Bahnzin. Maybe you have a grandchild by this time next harvest."

He nodded. "That is my hope, my son. Your mother and the band's women are finishing a big mescal bake for the ceremony. She will be very happy to see you and knows why you come so far. What is it, three days' ride from Turkey Creek?"

I poured coffee into the cup he offered me, its dark blue enamel with white speckles hot on my fingers as I shifted the cup between my hands.

"Yes, three long days. The coming days are busy for me and my woman. She must learn what to do during the womanhood ceremonies. I must find a place for us to have our alone time and gather the horses I plan for a bride gift for her mother and father with the blankets and silver bracelets I bring. Is old Santo the lead *di-yen* for the ceremony?"

Father nodded. "Yes, he and three others. There will be feasting for four nights, and Santo will use the big flat field behind Hashke Bahnzin's adobe lodge. Hashke Bahnzin is a man of wealth and is not afraid to show it. All his People and those of *Capitan* Chiquito will attend the ceremony. It is a rare thing for four girls to have the ceremony at the same time. All the women in both bands work together for a big feast. I know Hashke Bahnzin wants you for his son-in-law. He has refused offers from many others."

"Will you represent me to ask him for Chita? I will offer five horses and two Navajo blankets."

"Five horses and two Navajo blankets for a woman, even a chief's daughter, is a very good offer, my son. Chita is a fine girl, soon to be a woman, but I think he would take four or even three horses for her if you ask."

"My father is a wise man, but I want Hashke Bahnzin to know how much I value Chita. If he asks for five horses, offer him six. I have money for another horse and horses for my wife and me."

"*Enjuh.* My son is wise. I do as he asks."

The western sky clouds were ablaze when my mother returned to her lodge carrying a sealed basket of baked mescal on her head. Her laugh was full and her smile big when she, with my brothers and sisters, saw me. I was very happy to see my family and to know that soon Father would ask Hashke Bahnzin to give me Chita if she would accept me.

FATHER, DRESSED IN his best clothes, went to speak with Hashke Bahnzin the next morning. He returned before the time of shortest shadows. He let his pony into the corral where I had been working with my horses and walked over to stand beside me, a solemn look on his face, and crossed his arms.

Seeing his face, I worried something might have gone wrong. "Father, will Hashke Bahnzin give me Chita?"

Smiling, close to laughing, my father said, "I wish you had been there to watch us. I sat with Hashke Bahnzin at the eating table in his adobe lodge. Eating food from high off the floor on a table seems hard to do, but I wander off the trail. We drank coffee across from each other in the low light of the room and talked of farming and crops. All the time, he was smiling. He knew why I had come. I finally told him that you wanted Chita and asked what he would consider a good bride gift for her parents."

Father continued his story. "Hashke Bahnzin rubbed his chin, thinking. 'I have not seen your son in many moons, and neither has my daughter. Is he still a first sergeant in the army scouts?'

'He was until four days ago, when he learned of her womanhood ceremony. He didn't reenlist so he could come here without waiting for army permission and ask you for her if she is ready.'

'What will he do if she is not ready to leave her mother?'

'Wait and farm until she makes up her mind.'

"Hashke Bahnzin scratched his chin again and said, 'Chita now has her womanhood, and her mothers have trained her well. Your son has spent many evenings with us, and we have talked often. You have trained him very well, but he is still a young man and does not have much wealth. Tell him three horses and a Navajo blanket and her mother and I will give Chita to him after her ceremony. Tell him I expect as custom says, that he and my daughter will live nearby and help me farm.'

"My father said, 'Three horses and a Navajo blanket is not what Ohyessonna wants to offer you.' Even as I spoke, Hashke Bahnzin's face grew dark as a storm cloud. He was angry and about to say something I knew we would both regret later. I held up my palm to stop him.

"I said, 'My son wants to offer you two fine Navajo blankets and five horses as a bride gift to you for your beautiful daughter.'

"Hashke Bahnzin laughed out loud and said, 'You use a tease on me older than the grandfathers I have seen used before and I still took the bait. Yes, of course five horses alone with no blankets is a fine bride gift. I happily accept it all. Chita is his after her womanhood ceremony, but remember, I want them to live nearby and farm with me.'

"I smiled and said it will be so and we parted in good spirits."

I laughed. "My father is the best of men." I pointed out to him the horses I planned to give Hashke Bahnzin and the paint pony I planned to give my bride.

Father nodded and said, "You do well, my son. Truly, you have a man's body and mind. Will you find a place up Aravaipa Canyon to have alone time with your woman?"

"Yes, I go up the canyon after I eat a little from my mother's pot on the fire."

THIRTY-SIX

ALONE TIME WITH MY WOMAN

I RODE UP the canyon to the place where it turned and wiggled like a snake crawling east and then in about five miles turned southeast, its water gurgling between benches covered with willows, oaks, and manzanita. I remembered the cat hunt when Jimmie Stevens and I had made up the creek and killed the big cat near the end of the wide place where I was. I had seen much warfare since then, and the thought of the big cat stalking us no longer gave me worry. Besides not fearing it, we had not seen the kind of cat we killed since then. I rode farther up the creek along the trail until the bench widened. There was plenty of wood for fires, a deep pool for swimming and bathing, high and steep stone canyon walls to protect us from marauding bad men, and tall saplings that would make us a nice *wickiup*.

I made the *wickiup* frame, spread a large canvas over it, used a good blanket to cover the door, put two more blankets on the floor, and left a sack of pots and pans inside, and then laid brush on top to hide the canvas and a circle of rocks near the door for our fire. As the canyon walls began filling the canyon with deep black shadows, I finished and left. On my ride back, I tried to imagine Chita and me alone there together for the first time.

It was full darkness when I returned to my mother's lodge, and the family had already eaten. I washed in the creek, ate my mother's good meal of beef, mesquite bread, and beans with peppers, and happily talked with my family until the stars had rotated to the middle of the night.

FOUR SUNS AND nights of ceremony and feasting on the baskets of food the band's women spent days preparing galloped past like a runaway horse. I was ready to leave from the first day but knew we must stay until the four days of ceremony and nights of feasting were complete and Chita had, in her turn with the other girls, blessed the People as *Ussen's* white-painted woman. When the moon was at the top of its arc on the fourth night, flageolet music began and young men danced the circle dance until dawn at the invitation of the People's young women. Chita and I danced all night. I never took my eyes off her, nor she me. Her glittering eyes and laugh made me want her for my woman even more than when I dreamed about us.

With the coming dawn, the young men gave the young women their dance gifts and some announced they were planning to start a new family. Chita, standing with Hashke Bahnzin and his number-one wife, was the last one to receive her gift as I led the black-and-white pony out of where I had hidden her behind Santo's *wickiup*. The mare carried the silver-trimmed saddle my father had won in betting on my race with Gonshayee and had given me after I won. I had enough money from my scout pay for a new leather bridle also trimmed in silver to go with it.

Hashke Bahnzin and his wife grinned and nodded. Chita's jaw dropped and her dark eyes glowed as I handed her the reins and said, "Chita, daughter of the great Chief Hashke Bahnzin, this pony I give to you for dancing with and blessing me, and in the hope you will become my woman. Your father has accepted the bride gift my father offered him for you. Do you accept me as your man?"

Her smile matched the morning sun glowing behind the mountains. "I have waited many suns for this sun. I say yes. I accept you as my man."

Hashke Bahnzin said in a loud voice so all could here, "I am proud my beautiful daughter whose spirit yesterday rode the sky with *Ussen* now accepts Ohyessonna as her man. May they live long and prosper with many children. I am proud to have him in our family."

The People, including my family, walked by smiling and touched us to feel our Power. My father gripped my arm and said, "You have never disappointed us, my son. Work hard and learn much from Hashke Bahnzin." My mother also touched me and, smiling, said, "My son."

When all the People passed us by and went to their lodges, I said to Chita, "I have a place for our alone time when you are ready to ride."

"Let me change my womanhood ceremony gown for riding clothes and get my things to take with us. I won't be long."

"You are my woman. Do as you need to make ready. I'll be here."

She nodded and disappeared into her father's adobe lodge.

CHITA WAS TRUE to her word. I didn't wait long. She wore a shirt, light jacket, and skirt that let her easily mount her new horse. We left Hashke Bahnzin's adobe and rode for Aravaipa Creek. She rode proud and straight beside me as we followed the wagon road on the bluff above the burbling creek and tall treetops swayed gently in the breeze. We said little as we rode side by side, glancing at each other often and smiling.

When we came to the end of Aravaipa Creek at the San Pedro wagon road, I took the lead and went down the side of the creek where I had made our shelter. When we reached where I had built our *wickiup*, I stopped and dismounted. Chita glanced around, her eyes wide. "I... I thought you told me you had made us a shelter, but I don't see one?"

I laughed. "Look through the trees to your right." She stared through the trees and slowly scanned all the bosque. Finally, she stared in the direction of the *wickiup* I had built close to the high canyon wall deep in the bosque. There was a breathless "Ha!" and then a grin as she looked at me. "Our shelter is very well hidden, husband. Your work is very good. Come, show it to me." She dismounted and, leading our horses, weaved past brush and big trees until the *wickiup* suddenly rose in front of us. "You did a fine work making this *wickiup* so hard to see. May I look inside?"

"Of course. This is where we sleep during our time alone."

She handed her reins to me, pulled back the door blanket, and stepped inside. When she came back out, she nodded. "I was right. You've done the *wickiup* very well, husband. We'll be very comfortable here." Her hands came to rest against her sides, and with a twinkle in her eyes, she said, "And what else do you do very well?"

"Only you will know, woman. Let us finish our camp, bathe in the creek, and rest. We've been up all night long dancing, and then riding for three hands to our secret place. Perhaps you'll make us an evening meal after we bathe and rest?"

As she looked up at me, her smile was brilliant. "A woman always takes good care of her man. We'll eat when you're ready. May I bathe first and in private? Soon we'll bathe together after my modesty accepts you."

I made the all-is-well sign. "I wait for your modesty to tell us when it will not shame us when we are together in our nakedness, and *Ussen* blesses us with one mind and body."

She waved as she headed for the deep pool in the creek I had shown her. I leaned back against a large tree and made a cigarette with a new fresh sack of *tobaho*. The smoke relaxed me, and I was drifting into the land of dreams when she returned from the creek. Her long hair lay damp on her shoulders, her cheeks flushed from scrubbing.

"Go bathe, my man, and I will fix our first meal for our alone time."

I staggered to my feet, did a poor imitation of a Blue Coat salute, grabbed my little sack of supplies and, nodding at her, said, "Hmmph. I go."

When I returned, good smells filled my nose from beef on an angled stick roasting over the fire, the fat slowly dripping into the flames making popping noises and flaring. There was also mesquite bread, wild potatoes, steamed yucca tips and, for the end of the meal, juniper berries and prickly pear tuna.

She saw me coming and motioned for me to come sit beside her.

"Your bath was good? Our meal is ready. Your pan and knife are beside you. Hand me your pan and I will fill it, and then mine." We ate in the cool shade of the canyon wall and trees behind us and spoke of the things we had heard and seen in the womanhood ceremony and during the dance.

Chita said, "I'm so happy I had my ceremony. I was very tired waiting on it and often wondered if you waited for me as I have you. But you never wavered, and that has meant much to me."

"Chita, you are a woman worth waiting for, even if we were both gray hairs when you had your ceremony. I think of you often and have yearned to make you mine since our first meeting in the sutler store. This sun, a dream has come true."

I put my pan down and drew her to me. I kissed her for the first time. It was a soft, sweet kiss, but I felt the fire she had for me. We drew apart. Her eyes were shining. "I have never known a man's kiss like that. I've always had cheek kisses from my family. Now I know why. That kiss has made a warm fire for you in my heart. Soon it will burn even hotter."

I could only nod and say, *"Enjuh."*

By the time we had cleaned up around the fire, the clouds were ablaze with oranges, yellows, purples, and reds. We sat shoulder to shoulder talking by the fire, a blanket over our shoulders, as cold night air filled the canyon and Coyote called to his brothers. As the darkness waited for the moon to rise, we kissed again and let our shared passion fan the heat from the fires that were flaming in our hearts. She stood, pulled me up, and led me to the *wickiup* doorway blanket, pulled it back and I went inside with her. Standing in the dark, we kissed for a long time and then she pushed apart from me and told me to be still. I could hear her unbuttoning and pulling off her shirt and skirt and folding them to toss to one side of the *wickiup*. She sat down and I could hear a blanket pulled back and her slide under it and then flip over the blanket corner on my side.

She said, "Now, my man, come to me in the darkness."

The cold air brought prickles to my skin as my shirt, vest, pants, and breechcloth disappeared from my body. I sat down, pulled off my moccasins, and pulled up the blanket to my chin as I felt the warmth and smooth flow of her body. I slid closer and we kissed again. I heard her whisper, "Come to me, my man, and make me your woman."

That night, such joy and pleasure I had never known. If the White Eye legend was true, I had found the other half of me. We rarely left the *wickiup* for the next ten suns except to bathe together in the creek and to eat.

THIRTY-SEVEN

THE BEST OF TIMES

CHITA AND I returned to the lodge of Hashke Bahnzin after eleven days of time alone. Even then, we wanted to stay much longer. But Chita knew we needed to help Hashke Bahnzin prepare for the Seasons of Ghost Face and Little Eagles. We took the canvas off the *wickiup*, loaded the horses with what was left of our supplies, and headed down Aravaipa Creek to Hashke Bahnzin's *rancheria* the way we had come.

Near the time of shortest shadows, we came to Hashke Bahnzin's adobe lodge. His women were making a meal to feed farmers who worked with him and came in at midday to eat for strength at work until the sun was falling into the western mountains. We were surprised to see a new adobe *casa* near Hashke Bahnzin's lodge. Someone already lives there—thin cloth over the windows, a blanket over the door, and a smoke pipe from a fireplace or stove pokes up from the roof. How did they build it so fast, and for whom?

Hashke Bahnzin came out of his adobe, his sleeves rolled up to his elbows, saw us, and spread his arms. "Ho! Chita, you return to your father's house and bring with you a fine young man, your husband." His round face filled with a big mischievous grin. "You must know each other good after eleven days of time alone. How do you like the new house that we build for you?"

Chita's lips made a big O of surprise. She looked at me. I was surprised too. I shrugged to show my ignorance. She turned to her father and said, "My father is very generous. Is it ready for us? After we eat, we'll be ready to work in the fields if there is nothing else we need to do to finish it."

"I know of nothing else to do for your adobe. Take the rest of the day to fix it as you like. We'll begin work together after the morning meal."

I said, "Woman, do with our new lodge as you like. After we eat, I go to the fields with your father."

Chita nodded. *"Ch'ik'eh doleel."*

FROM THE TIME we returned from our alone time until well into the Season of Earth Is Reddish Brown, we worked hard, long days. I felt the muscles in my arms and upper body strengthen from the farm work, and I ran often to keep my wind good and legs strong.

Chita and the other women had much to do. They cut grass with long curved knives for our animals or to sell to San Carlos. They harvested grain and vegetables from their gardens and fields. They went, into the mountains to harvest and bake hearts of mescal in big pits the boys and young men out to impress the girls helped dig and layer the bottom with big rocks. While they waited three days for the mescal to bake, they filled big baskets with acorns, mesquite and paloverde pods, and juniper berries. I helped Hashke Bahnzin and others with their cattle and sheep, training horses, fixing broken tools, using his big yellow wagon to haul crops and supplies for other families, and hunting deer and mountain sheep in the Galiuro Mountains.

Chita and I were in the blankets holding each other close many nights. A moon after we returned from our alone time together, she made a special evening meal for us and no others. As we ate near the warm stove, the smell of fried meat and onions filling the air, she said, "My man, I have news."

I raised my brows in question. "Speak, woman. I will listen."

Her smile was as bright as the sun. "A child grows in my belly."

My jaw dropped in surprise. *"Ussen* has blessed us! Are you sure?"

"One of my mothers and I visited a *di-yen* who has a ceremony for learning such things. There is no doubt a child comes to us in eight moons."

I shook my head. "I don't doubt you, but so soon after you became my woman, you carry our child. This child will be special. Are you free from any sickness?"

She giggled. "Just what women have early as their belly begins to grow. It will pass."

We talked long into the night about the future of our child and what we would do if it were a boy or a girl child. I hoped that if the child were a boy, he would have the opportunities I had to learn White Eye and Blue Coat ways and he could learn farming side by side with his grandfather. If the child were a girl, I hoped she would have as much beauty, light behind her eyes, talent, and insight as her mother. She wouldn't wait long for a good man to court and ask for her.

As we eased under our blankets, I leaned over to kiss Chita, and she put her hand on my chest and said, "My man, the *di-yen* says this must be the last time we do anything under the blankets until we're ready to try making another child."

"*Ch'ik'eh doleel,* woman. I understand." I grinned, shaking my head. "But this way makes me understand why a man needs more than one woman when he starts a family."

Chita smiled and gently punched me in the chest. "Enjoy this time while you can. It will be three or four harvests before we can make another."

Lying beside my woman after we were one for the last time in three or four harvests, I stared at the black ceiling, my hands crossed and resting on my chest. I thought of many things, but like an echo in a deep canyon, the thought kept bouncing in my mind, *three or four harvests is a long time to wait for drawing your woman to you under the blankets. I know we can wait, but such a long time!*

IN THE SEASON of Many Leaves, on a cold night when the moon hid its face from us, Chita asked me to go for her father's women. They came running, bringing lit lanterns, made a fire in the stove, and ran me out of our adobe to sit with Hashke Bahnzin on his porch. He made a cigarette and smoked with me in celebration of a new grandchild coming. He told me some good stories of things that had happened at the birth of his children. Of all his women, he said he wanted Chita's mother most and they were ready to try for another child when the *Tohono O'odham,* Anglos, and *Nakai-yes* attacked our camp near old Camp Grant. He hated to lose that woman, but at least he had saved Chita, who was like her in many ways. I remembered that night all too well but wished I couldn't. Chita was too young to remember much except what Hashke Bahnzin had told her.

The sun was just lighting the dawn, mists were rising off the río, and birds in the brush were beginning their songs when we heard the first cry of life from my daughter. When the sun cleared the horizon, Hashke Bahnzin's oldest wife came to us and said, "My son, your woman has someone for you to hold. Go to your lodge. Soon Hashke Bahnzin will come for visit." We both stood. He grabbed me on the shoulder and said, "All the People are happy for you and Chita, my son, but none more than me."

An old woman, her face covered in deep canyons of wrinkles and long gray hair pulled back in a bun, was boiling bedding in a big iron pot near our door. When she saw me, she waved me to the door, smiling with only three teeth in a gum-filled grin. Nearing the end of her life, she welcomed its new beginning. I entered the cool darkness inside. Chita, her hair still wet from sweat made while pushing our child out of her body, sat up in our bed, resting her back against the wall and holding the baby to her breast. She looked at me with warm eyes as I stood there taking it all in, a memory for a lifetime, and waved me to her side.

"Husband, come see your beautiful new daughter."

"Woman, you and the baby, you are good?" I sat down on the edge of the bed and studied every line of our daughter in her blanket. "Yes, my man, we are fine."

"She is truly beautiful. There will be a long line of men outside our door when she is ready to take a man."

"That is a time and place far away. We will have many harvests to watch her beauty grow and train her to become a desirable woman."

I nodded. "Yes, we will. If she's half as desirable as her mother, many will want her. I'll have to hide you both." We both thought then that our lives would sail into the future with the children and land of our dreams. Little did we know how fast our lives could change.

FIVE SUNS AFTER the birth of our daughter, a Blue Coat sergeant and four privates came galloping up at the head of a plume of dust to Hashke Bahnzin's adobe. Hashke Bahnzin came out to meet them. The sergeant stopped at the hitching post by the door and made the sign of respect Blue Coats use.

He said, "Hashke Bahnzin, the commander at Fort Apache has asked me and others to spread the word that about a hundred and fifty Chiricahua under the leadership of Geronimo, Naiche, Mangas, Chihuahua, and Nana have left the reservation and appear headed east before they break south for the border. Cavalry and scouts under Lieutenant Davis and Chato are trailing them east toward the Black Range in New Mexico territory but have had no engagements yet. We're warning others down Río San Pedro. Old Geronimo is mighty tricky, so keep your eyes open for trouble coming your way."

Hashke Bahnzin made his hand wave of respect. "We keep eyes open, Sergeant. Water horses here? We have food. You want?"

"Thanks for the food offer, Chief. We'll water our horses, but we're in a hurry to warn as many people as fast as we can. *Adios.*"

"*Adios,* Sergeant."

I wondered then why Geronimo and the chiefs decided to leave after all the promises I had heard they made to General Crook about staying peaceful. Half a moon later, Chato, *Teniente* Davis's first sergeant in his company of scouts and a lead Chiricahua scout at Fort Apache, whom I saw often when I did scout work at Fort Apache for Captain Crawford, was recruiting men for scouts to support Captain Crawford. His horse, a roan with a blaze face, jogged down the wagon road as the sun falling in the west was just beginning to shoot long black shadows across the valley. I was putting away the tools we had used that day when I saw him stop at Hashke Bahnzin's, and they started talking. Hashke Bahnzin looked over in my direction and waved for me to come join them where they were sitting under a big tree, drinking coffee.

As I approached, Chato stood and made the Blue Coat salute. "Ho, Kid. We have not seen you since you left the scouts to marry. Hashke Bahnzin tells me you work hard and are a proud father of a new girl child. *Enjuh.*"

I nodded. "Chita, Hashke Bahnzin's daughter and my wife, has given us a beautiful daughter and I learn much about farming from Hashke Bahnzin. We hear that Geronimo and other Chiricahua leaders run for the land of the *Nakai-yes.* Why did they leave?"

Chato made a face of disgust and shook his head as I poured a cup of coffee. "Geronimo was convinced *Nant'an Lpah* was coming to put him and others in the guardhouse for stories and lies told against him and for the rules they broke against *tulapai* making and drinking and wife beating. The day before he left, Geronimo told his brothers, who were in *Teniente* Davis's scout company, to kill Davis and me, take all the scout ammunition in the *teniente's* tent, recruit as many scouts as they could, and join him in the mountains to the east of Fort Apache. *Teniente* Davis gathered his company the evening Geronimo left, but he told all the men to butt their rifles and me, Charley, and Dutchy to shoot anyone who raised his rifle."

Chato's face filled with a big grin and he shook his head.

"Ha! His brothers decided assassination was too risky and slipped away in the dark. *Teniente* joined a new captain at Fort Apache to chase those renegades. We could see their dust in the distance and wanted to go faster to catch them, but even though we begged him, the new captain wouldn't risk an ambush. With his lead over that rough country, we couldn't catch Geronimo, only follow.

"*Teniente* Davis and I left the scouts with the new captain and came back to Fort Apache, where *Teniente* used the talking wire to tell *Nant'an Lpah* what was happening and asked what we should do next. Bonito and I started recruiting scouts from Fort Apache. We need more experienced first sergeants for the men we have. I came to ask you to reenlist, but I understand now is not a good time with the work you have here and a new child in your family. I'll be going into the land of the *Nakai-yes* with *Teniente* Davis and Captain Crawford to find and destroy their camps and drive the Chiricahua back to the reservation. Can you join us later when we return from the land of the *Nakai-yes* to resupply and recruit more men so we rest those who go now?"

I listened to Chato, who I knew spoke true, and saw Hashke Bahnzin slowly shaking his head. This was a bad time and we both knew it. The White Eye settlers would be anxious to avenge Geronimo raids on anyone who was an Apache. Much blood might flow if we weren't very careful.

"*Sí*, Chato, I think on it, but as you say, I cannot leave my People now to help hunt for those you call 'renegades.'"

Hashke Bahnzin said, "Sergeant Chato, I would be happy for you to share my food and get some rest in my lodge before you travel on."

Chato nodded. "You are a great chief, Hashke Bahnzin. I accept your offer. Allow me to put my horse in your stable—I wash my riding dirt off and come to your adobe."

Hashke Bahnzin nodded. "*Enjuh*, Chato. Soon my wife has our meal ready. Join us when you are ready. I know Ohyessonna, the man you call 'Kid,' has a wife waiting for him."

I nodded and gave Chato a salute before I left for my meal with Chita and our daughter.

I WAS PROUD THAT Chato, who would be leading the attack against the renegades in the land of the *Nakai-yes*, had gone out of his way to recruit me. I often thought about the hard trails and attacks against the renegades I would see if I led my men. Stories about Chato and the scouts in fighting and camp raids south of the border filtered back to us and fired my imagination even more.

On their first trip to find and fight the Chiricahua, Chato led Crawford and

his scouts into the land of the *Nakai-yes* through what he called the "back door."
They entered on the eastern side and crossed the Sierra Madre Mountains, the
eastern branch of the Río Bavispe, the *El Tigre* Mountains, and then moved
up the western branch of the Río Bavispe past Oputo. In this way they came
up from the south toward a Chiricahua camp rather from the north as the
Chiricahua expected. Chato and about thirty scouts found and attacked the first
camp, which happened to be Chihuahua's, and took about fifteen women and
children while most of the men escaped. Chato saw how to fight with a clear
eye. He would be a good man to follow and learn from.

Late in the Season of Large Fruit, Chiricahua up from the south, a part of
Chihuahua's band tried to draw the attention of the Blue Coats away from his
brother and *segundo*, Ulzana, who raided Fort Apache and San Carlos. Chihuahua
wanted to take some of Hashke Bahnzin's horses and cattle. The Blue Coats had
warned us this might happen. We posted guards to watch over the horses and
cattle at night and didn't have to wait more than a handful of nights before the
raiders came.

The moon, big and bright but not yet full, cast its soft white light over the
field where the cattle and horses snuffled for the last few green tidbits of grass
and brush in the cold air surrounding us. Guards, me among them, sat on our
horses hidden in the coal-black shadows from the tall trees and brush in the río
bosque. A steady wind pushed the clouds along above us and sighed through the
tops of trees. I heard the splashing of water as horses crossed the Río San Pedro
just behind us. All the men with me cocked their rifles and waited. Soon we saw
men like they were on shadow horses jogging toward the groups of cattle and
horses scattered over the range.

A second smaller group splashed across the río and stopped. A match's little
flame burst into a much larger one at the head of a torch used to light two more
torches. The riders began walking their horses toward the adobe houses where
Hashke Bahnzin and his family lived. Seeing the men with torches in their hands
heading for the house of my wife and daughter, and that of my father-in-law,
lit its own fire of rage in my gut. No! These renegade attacks cannot stand.
They must die. The first group to cross the río was closing in on the livestock
when I cocked my rifle, sighted on the fire carrier two hundred yards away,
and squeezed the trigger. My rifle's thunder knocked the fire carrier out of his
saddle and the other guards turned their fire on the first group headed for our
livestock. At least two of those men slumped forward on their horses' necks
and turned them to run for the río. The men with the one I had shot out of the

saddle dashed in to pick him up, and once one in the saddle had him holding him in front, they raced for the river.

My rage was slow to cool, but we had done well driving those Chiricahua off. I knew what I had to do next. These raids could not continue. The sooner they ended, the better and safer we would all be. Little did I know the dark winds soon to blow over us.

THIRTY-EIGHT

THE DEVIL'S BACKBONE

CHITA AND I spoke often about the renegade threat while we ate our evening meals. I couldn't get it out of my mind that if I wanted my wife and daughter safe from their threat, then I had to help eliminate it. Chita understood why I wanted to find and fight the renegades, but she thought our family was better off if I stayed where we were. What she couldn't understand was how strongly I felt the need for action, the need to take the fight to the enemy. I wasn't ready to farm the rest of my life, and I believed finding and fighting the renegades in the land of the *Nakai-yes* was my last chance for serious battle before the Apache finally stopped forever fighting among themselves. I tried to explain this during our meals, but I didn't think she grasped what I tried to tell her.

We talked for half a moon on these things until one night she made a feast of roast beef, steamed mescal, beans with chiles, prickly pear tuna, mesquite bread, and nuts and juniper berries. The night was cold and the wind was pushing clouds that passed great shadows flying along the ground in the moonlight, but it was nice and warm in our adobe. The food was so good we ate with gusto and had not yet started our evening talk when Chita said, "Husband, I know your heart. You must enlist in the scouts and go with your brothers and Blue Coat chief to the land of the *Nakai-yes*, find the renegades, and bring them back peacefully or force them to surrender. Our daughter and I will stay near my father's adobe when you are gone and be here for you when you return. I have said all I have to say."

I heard the wind moaning through the trees, felt my heart thumping fast as though I were running, and my entire body filled with love for this beautiful, wise woman. My jaw dropped and I stared at her.

"My beautiful woman is wise to know her husband's heart. We must end any danger from the renegades. I want to help do it. You see that. *Enjuh.* I go in two days to touch the pen for my enlistment in the scouts." She smiled and nodded.

We told Hashke Bahnzin what I planned to do. His eyes gleamed as he said, "Soon we will be able to work in peace. Be strong in the battles to come, my son. Your family will be safe with us." We spoke with him long into the night about our families and the days to come.

I STOPPED TO see my father and mother and the rest of their family on my way to San Carlos. I told them I planned to enlist again to help end the renegade raids that might come our way. My father nodded. "I think it is wise to do this, my son." Although she said nothing, my mother was quiet and often glanced at the stars when she swallowed. I could tell she was not happy that I was again leaving my family behind to risk a good life with my beautiful wife fighting desperate Chiricahua.

The ride over the ridges from my father's lodge to San Carlos was long and twisting through deep canyons and over high ridges, but as the sun was painting the clouds many shades of red, orange, and purple, I rode up to the San Carlos Agency building. Dismounting, I asked a soldier just coming out of the agency where I could find the workplace of Captain Pierce. He told me which door to go in and which dark passageway to use. I found the office of Captain Pierce. He was sitting at his worktable covered with papers holding many White Eye black-water tracks. There were even some papers with the talking-wire brand on them. Someday I will learn to read those tracks. Since the sergeant who guarded his office entrance was gone, I stood outside his door and cleared my throat for an invitation to enter. He looked up from his papers, saw me with his eyes widening in surprise and a smile filling his face, and motioned for me to come in and sit in a fine, polished dark-wood chair in front of his table.

"Kid! It's good to see you again. How is that growing family of yours. Chato told me after he went to see you that you had a new baby."

"Hmmph. I like to see Captain Pierce. Family good. Last moon, renegades try steal livestock, burn houses, but we drive 'em off. Now I reenlist. Protect families. Captain Crawford looks for more recruits after four moons in land of

Nakai-yes? Chato say Crawford scouts need first sergeants with experience. I go with Crawford?"

Pierce crossed his arms and sat back in his chair. "Yes, sir. You can do that. Did you bring what you kept your last time in service? What do I need to supply you?"

"Hmmph. Crawford save my things from last enlistment. I use those. I need cartridges for my lever gun and pistola. Heavy blanket and tent."

Captain Pierce made black-water tracks on paper and made his mark at the bottom. Then he pulled a paper from a wooden cabinet behind his worktable holding many such papers and, with a little black-water spear, marked out that I didn't have a woman and child. He repeated what my duties were and said that, after I touched the pen, I would be a first sergeant. Tom Horn was Crawford's chief of scouts, Lieutenant Maus was Crawford's number two, and Lieutenant Shipp was third in command. After I touched the pen, Captain Pierce signed a paper identifying me and sent me to retrieve my old things and to get any new things I needed, and then to find Crawford's scout companies.

Wandering down the line of scout tents, I found Crawford's chief of scouts, Tom Horn, and his Chiricahua first sergeant of scouts, Noche. We talked and I learned that the Apache at Fort Apache and at San Carlos were either up in arms waiting for Ulzana to attack or following Blue Coats who were trying to catch him. Horn avoided this turmoil and believed others would catch Ulzana, who, rumor had it, wanted badly to catch Chato and kill him. Chato had decided not to reenlist. His time in the land of *Nakai-yes* led him to decide he needed to rest and farm. But he still had time in his enlistment and led Chiricahua scouts who wanted to catch Ulzana. Ulzana managed to escape all those after him and disappeared into Sonora, his trail pointing for the Carcay Mountains in Chihuahua.

BEFORE WE LEFT for Sonora, we had one last inspection. Captain Crawford was happy with his four companies of scouts and glad to see me among his scout leaders. He said this to Tom Horn, who looked at me, grinned, and said, "Yes, sir, Mister Sieber picked us both for his scouts and we both done purty good." Crawford grinned at the comment and moved on.

Horn took a detachment of ten scouts, me among them, to follow Ulzana's trail in Sonora. It led toward the Carcay Mountains in Chihuahua. We lost that trail but found the one leading from the Carcay Mountains toward the Río Aros south of Nácori Chico.

On the sun the White Eyes celebrate the birth of their god, Captain Crawford led his men south toward Nácori Chico. Tom Horn with Noche led me and nine other men south to cross the Río Aros. It was easy to cross, but its water felt like melted ice. We scouted both sides of the Aros and on the south side found a trail showing a trail of five Chiricahua who soon merged into a bigger one that included cattle and horses. Horn sent two of the scouts back with tracks on paper telling Captain Crawford what we found. Crawford sent the rider from the advance scouts back to his supply camp where he left packers with their supplies. The rider told them that Captain Crawford wanted them to come forward and follow his trail. Then Crawford led his scouts forward and crossed the Aros into the hard forbidding land between the Ríos Aros and Sátachi.

Horn and Noche took great care to avoid renegades seeing us by moving only at night. We all knew the trail we followed pointed for the *Espinosa del Diablo*—the devil's backbone—some of the roughest, most inaccessible ridges and mountains rising in the Sierra Madre. It was very hard to walk or ride through its maze of canyons. They were deep and shadow filled. We often couldn't see their bottoms when we started down narrow, barely visible, rock-strewn trails on closely packed ridges standing at attention like soldiers in long lines. We knew we were on the right trail after seeing butchered cattle carcasses as we drew closer to the last ridge separating us from the canyons and ridges of *Espinosa del Diablo*.

We climbed to the top of the last ridge and saw the Chiricahua camp on a big bench on the side of the next ridge on the Río Aros. We sat down among the boulders and junipers on our ridge and used our soldier glasses to study the camp. Confident no one could find their camp, they posted no sentries to watch the opposing ridges.

Horn and Noche motioned to Juan Segotset and me to come over to them. We crabbed and crawled over to Horn, Noche, and Fatty, who were sitting together by a big boulder. While Fatty kept his glasses on the camp below, Horn said to Juan and me, "I'm keeping the boys here with me while you two make it back to Cap'n Crawford and tell him we've found the renegade camp. He'll be happy to hear that. Maybe this is his chance to bring Geronimo and his followers to heel and take 'em back to San Carlos. Tell him we'll meet him here if he comes. You lead him back the fastest way you can. If he wants to just follow Geronimo, come back and tell us and we'll follow and stay in contact with him. Make it fast, boys. I suspect ol' Geronimo is gonna wanna move in two or three days." Juan and I saluted and took off.

I WAS GLAD I had kept my wind and strength after I married. The trails back to where Juan had delivered dispatches to Captain Crawford made my legs ache running downhill and made me feel like a boy on his first long run climbing mountain trails. Crawford had come forward and was making camp as long black shadows were reaching across the canyons and clouds carried brilliant reds and purples.

Juan and I found his tent in the falling light. He squinted at us and, recognizing us as part of Horn's advance scout, stepped forward to meet us.

"Scouts! You look like you've been running hard a long time. What news?"

I spoke better English than Juan and, working to speak and catch my breath at the same time, said, "Tom Horn say... find Captain Crawford. Say... we find Geronimo camp. Camp on high ridge in *Espinosa del Diablo*. Ask what we do?"

Captain Crawford's teeth snapped together like a trap closing and, grinning, he shook his fist. "How far? How far is this camp?"

"Hard trail crosses many canyons and high ridges. We run half a day before find you."

"So, if we started now, we could be there before daylight?"

"That is so, Captain."

He yelled, "Sergeant! Get the men fed and ready for a hard night's march." He turned to us. "Like you, the scouts have marched half a day, but I know they can do an overnighter. If we can pull this off, we can end this war and all go home. You men think you can find your way back in the dark?"

I glanced at Juan and he was already nodding. "We find way, Captain."

"That's my scouts. Eat hardy with the men. There's just a fingernail moon tonight, so not much light. This won't be easy. I'll leave behind those who won't have the strength to keep up with us for this march and take only one mule to pack ammunition. All right, let's get to it."

THIRTY-NINE

GERONIMO'S CAMP ATTACKED

THERE WAS LITTLE moonlight that night as we ran back across ridges and canyons to reach Tom Horn and his advance scouts. Every time we started for a canyon's floor from a high ridge, it was impossible to see the bottom and I felt the muscles in my legs quiver as I thought, *What a good place to hide, even from Apache scouts, but one slip now and it's the end.* The Blue Coats had put on moccasins to keep down the noise of their passing and left their boots with the packers who would follow later. I was surprised that only one or two men fell and were hurt. *Ussen* blessed us with good running Power in that cold black air.

Juan, who led the way, was approaching the big boulder where Tom Horn and scouts were when we left. There was a dull gray behind the mountains to the east. Dawn was coming. Tom Horn stepped from behind the boulder. In the dim light, I saw him give a hand wave for the all-is-good sign. Crawford motioned for the men behind him to stop as he came forward to talk with Horn and Noche.

Horn said, "Howdy, Cap'n, glad you could drop in this mornin'. We been watching the Chiricahua since Kid and Juan left to tell you we'd found the camp. They're so confident nobody'll find 'em here that they ain't got a single sentry on watch. We're here up above 'em, but it's still a long range to shoot. What you want to do?"

Crawford crossed his arms as he walked around thinking before he returned to Horn. "I want to surround the camp. I know the range for rifles is long. It's likely we won't hit many in dawn light. But it's near the middle of Ghost Face, so they'll have most of their food supplies with them. If we can run 'em off and destroy their food supplies, they'll surrender or starve. What do you think about that plan, boys?"

Noche made the all-is-well sign. "Cap'n make good plan. Chiricahua hungry for a little while, but few die in fight. *Enjuh.*"

Tom nodded. "How you want to spread out the troops, Cap'n?"

He looked first at the stars and then where Horn pointed toward the camp. "We're northeast of their camp. Harrison and I will get in as close as we can on the north side so we can take the horse herd. Horn, you, Maus, and Shipp cover the other three directions. Listen for a shot from my men with the horses before you start shooting. Let's end this war today. It's past time those Chiricahua go back to Turkey Creek. Good luck!" Horn, in the lead, went to the east side, which was near enough for his shots to do some damage and would have the sun in the faces of those who shot back. *Teniente* Maus took the south, and *Teniente* Shipp took the west.

We were approaching our positions, and dawn was fast driving away the darkness. The movement of our men sent small rocks rattling off the path they followed through the brush to get in place. I was afraid the mules and burros would hear the noise, and they did. They started braying and some Chiricahua crawled from under their blankets to check on the horse herd near the river.

Too soon, shots at the men headed for the mules, burros, and horses exploded in the dawn light. I didn't doubt they came from White Mountain scouts looking for revenge against the Chiricahua for Ulzana's raid that had killed relatives living near Fort Apache. I didn't blame them, but they should have waited. I watched the camp and was impressed at the discipline its leaders—Geronimo, Naiche, Chihuahua, and Nana—showed. Geronimo climbed up on a rock and started yelling for the women and children to drop everything and run toward the southwest for the river, splitting the positions of Shipp and Horn's men. I tried to knock him off that rock with my rifle, but the range was too long, the bullets raising puffs of dust below the rock. Other Chiricahua leaders spread their men into more protected positions that split the four directions and returned fire. Most shot toward the fire coming down on them from Horn's position, but the light was so bad and the range so long neither side hit anyone. Soon the Chiricahua men disappeared into the brush toward the río and slipped away toward the southwest, leaving everything, including their horses and mules, but not their rifles, pistols, and bullets. The scouts crept into the village and, finding no one, set up their victory howl and did a little dance while some of our scouts followed the Chiricahua across the river but never got close enough to bring down or catch anyone.

A couple of scouts did get within yelling distance of Naiche and called for him to surrender. He said no, not this day, but he would talk to Crawford. When the scouts who followed the Chiricahua across the Aros returned to the camp, we lit cooking fires. As the men cooked and ate, they ransacked all the Chiricahua belongings looking for treasures left behind. I found and kept a nice carved doll I knew my little daughter would like and a fine necklace of silver and turquoise that, when spread out, made what the White Eyes sometimes called a "squash blossom necklace" for Chita. As the sun sailed past the time of no shadows and gave its warmth to our backs, we began to gather all the food stores we couldn't use and the Chiricahua's clothes and blankets into a pile for burning. Two hands passed as the sun fell toward the horizon. A woman from the renegades up on a bluff watching their old camp being destroyed waded across the Aros and approached a scout watching her with his rifle in the crook of his arm. In the tongue of the *Nakai-yes*, she asked to speak to Captain Crawford. The scouts, grinning like coyotes with a cornered rabbit, although she showed no fear, took her to Crawford, who sat on a blanket among the boulders about a hundred yards from the south edge of the camp. He stood to face her as she approached.

She said, "You are the chief of the scouts and Blue Coats who destroys the Chiricahua winter camp, so we starve in this time of Ghost Face and suffer the cold night?"

Crawford crossed his arms and slowly nodded. "I am the chief of these men. Your People have made war on White Eyes and Mexicans. Stop your war and return to San Carlos. You will have food and blankets. What happens to your men after murdering and burning the homes of many settlers and ranchers, only my chief can say."

The woman stared at him a moment and then said, "Naiche wishes talk with you. Will you do this and when?"

I saw the satisfaction in Crawford's face, and the woman did too. "I've sent for my supplies, a White Eye *di-yen*, and my interpreter, Concepcion, whom I believe your chiefs trust to use good words when he speaks for you or me. He comes late today or early *mañana*. I want to use him so there is no misunderstanding in what we discuss. Tell Naiche I will smoke and talk with him and his leaders *mañana*, two hands before the time of no shadows. We'll meet on this side of the river, next to the horse herd."

"This I tell Naiche."

She turned to go, but Crawford stopped her. "Wait. Wait a little while as we load a mule with food for you to take to your People and then you go."

She nodded and smiled. "I wait."

The scouts got busy, found a large mule—knowing the Chiricahua would eat the mule too—and loaded it down with big carry baskets of food they had found. They made a rope halter for the mule, led it to where Crawford and the woman talked, and handed the lead rope to Crawford, who handed it to the woman. She nodded and turned to wade back across the río. The scouts, all of them again grinning like coyotes, watched her lead the mule up the ridge. They knew she was Lozen, a powerful warrior, sister of Victorio.

As the sun began hiding behind the mountains, casting long shadows, the fires that had burned food and other camp supplies were slowly dying out, sending pillars of smoke high into the sky before they bent over and went their own way. Cooking fires burned, and good food saved from the fire of destruction being gobbled down by the hungry scouts sent a mouth-watering smell across the camp.

Captain Crawford told us we could build big fires for warmth in the cold night air and sleep for as long as we wanted, since most scouts and troopers had not slept in two days. Crawford spread his blankets with his officers and Tom Horn in the first boulders near the south edge of the camp. The scouts were all weary, and I and the other sergeants needed to rest too. With the sun gone and the big fires roaring, it was a bright cold night. I lay down and watched the stars. Soon the darkness of the night, the warmth of the good *Nakai-yi* blankets, the fire, and the blanket of stars covered me in sleep.

I OPENED MY eyes to see dawn's lifting darkness and clouds of mist off the río drifting through the camp. A scout sergeant—I believe it was Harvey Nashkin, who had helped run Victorio down before the *Nakai-yes* got him—crawled out of his blankets to make a fire. It wasn't long before an old fire-blackened coffeepot began to burble. I crawled out of my blankets to find a privacy bush.

As the dawn came and an orange glow formed behind the mountains to the east, I sat by Nashkin's fire with other scouts drinking coffee and talking about the meaning of yesterday's events. We heard some scouts yell, "Mexicans are coming." We all thought they were Captain Wirt Davis's men, sent to bring a packtrain of supplies and ammunition and an interpreter, Concepcion, to support Crawford in his talks with the Chiricahua. The scouts who saw them yelled greetings in Apache.

We waited a couple of breaths in the cold, crisp air to hear the visitors' reply. We didn't expect their answer. The roar of long-range rifles from positions in the white boulders about two hundred yards above us filled the camp air with the whine of angry bullets. They hit a couple of scouts still sleeping and a man by the fire.

Surprised and shaken, Nashkin and I grabbed our guns and, with the scouts, crabbed to cover behind boulders near *Capitan* Crawford's sleeping place. We told the scouts not to return fire, believing those firing didn't know who we were. There were a few scouts high on the ridge east of the camp who didn't hear the order and kept blazing away at the shooters below them.

Captain Crawford was on his feet and ordering his officers and Tom Horn to learn what had happened. Following the line of boulders providing cover, they headed toward Nashkin and me behind a big boulder. Crawford took a white cloth from a nearby soldier, a *di-yen* (a medic), who had followed the officers. Tom Horn and the officers crawled up to us and asked, "Why are we being fired on?" We could only shrug our shoulders and stay out of the line of fire. Still under cover, they moved as close to the middle of the camp as they could and many times yelled in the tongue of *Nakai-yes*, "We are American Army officers! The shooting must stop!"

After a short time, the shooting stopped. Crawford, Maus, and Horn came out from behind their boulders unarmed to meet ten armed *Nakai-yi* officers led by a tall muscular major. Horn was about thirty paces in front of Maus and Crawford, who was waving the white cloth he took from his soldier *di-yen*. Horn stuck out his hand to shake the hands of the *Nakai-yi* officers and said words welcoming them to our camp. Their leader and four or five others ignored him and walked up to Crawford and Maus. When they were about two paces apart, Maus said in the *Nakai-yi* tongue, "Don't you see we're American soldiers? Look at my uniform. Look at my captain's uniform."

I saw the *Nakai-yi* leader frown and, looking over the camp, appear confused. He started to explain that they assumed the scouts were renegades, and he seemed sorry this had all happened. As they talked, for some reason I could tell he lied.

I turned to a couple of scouts nearby and motioned them to me. I said, "Go to the supplies. Get a case of ammunition. Take it around to the men. Tell them to reload their bandoliers." They had nearly emptied them the sun before. "Tell

them I said to be ready for a fight but not to shoot until I tell them to fire. I
don't trust the *Nakai-yes.*" The scouts grinned, saluted, and crabbed through the
boulders to get the ammunition.

While they passed out ammunition and the scouts and troopers refilled
their bandoliers, I used my soldier glasses to study the *Nakai-yi* heads above
protecting boulders on the north side of the camp who were watching what
was going on. Then I studied the men who waited on their officers while they
talked to Crawford, Maus, and Shipp. I shook my head in disbelief. Every man I
saw looked like a Tarahumara and were enemies long hated by the Chiricahua.

There was a stillness hanging ominously in the cold bright air as the sun
slowly rose above the jagged mountain outline above us. Nashkin, the scouts, and
I heard a laughing *Nakai-yi* sergeant yell to his men, "Scout hair is good and long
and the best thing to make hair ropes, so kill them all and we'll get their hair."

The scouts yelled back, "Don't run away if you are men. You're going to meet
up with men today, not women and children like you kill before."

The Tarahumara yelled back, "We're the ones who cleaned out Victorio's
bunch. We killed Victorio and we'll kill you too."

Fatty, a lead Chiricahua scout who had been with Horn and Noche in the
advanced group of scouts, yelled, "All right, get ready. We're going to fire on
you right now." The sharp snaps as the scouts slid the long .45-70 cartridges into
their trapdoor rifles, closed the door over the cartridge, and pulled the hammer
on the breach back to full cock could be heard all over the camp. The big *Nakai-yi* major, who saw the heads and barrels of more than fifty scouts not thirty
paces behind our officers, began backing up toward Tom Horn.

I heard Crawford say to Maus, "For God's sake, don't let them fire."

The big Mexican major, who I learned later was the great hero in Sonora
and Chihuahua, Mauricio Corredor, claimed to have shot and killed Victorio
and now looked the color of a White Eye as he waved his hands palms out,
saying, "No tiros, no tiros (Don't shoot, don't shoot)."

Maus turned toward the rocks where the scouts were lining up their targets
and, holding his hands up palms out and waving them a little, yelled, "Don't
shoot, don't shoot!" I told my scouts to hold their fire. Crawford climbed up on
a boulder as tall as a man and waved his white cloth back and forth to show we
wanted only peace.

One of the men, who had come with Corredor, took cover behind a small
tree about twenty-five paces from Crawford's rock. I saw him raise his rifle and
point it at Crawford, and I whipped my rifle up to shoot him, but I saw him

too late. He fired the first shot and it hit Captain Crawford in the forehead. A roar of gunfire from both sides filled the morning. Dutchy, who was Crawford's striker—an orderly—and I fired at the same time and hit Crawford's shooter an inch or two apart in his chest.

All the officers immediately became targets as bullets whined past them and slapped against the boulders, but the only one hit was Captain Crawford, who slumped down and slowly rolled off his rock. Corredor turned to Horn, who had no gun, smiled, and snapped off a shot that hit him in the arm, and then ran for the high hill to the east. He couldn't have known three scouts were in hiding there, and the Chiricahua, Binday, slowly rose, took careful aim, and ended Corredor's suns with a shot to the heart.

In less than three long breaths, the scouts had killed nine of the ten *Nakai-yi* officers who had come to talk, but more obviously to try to learn how many men we had. I thought all along they planned to say pleasing things to the officers and then try to kill us all.

After a while, the Tarahumara retreated to some hills to the west of the officers and shot toward us for a while but never hit anyone before giving up and retreating to their camp. They had lost all their leaders and weren't sure what they should do. We had given them a good whipping but lost our chief. Fortunately, *Teniente* Maus was next in command after Crawford. I had been around Maus long enough to know that he knew how to lead and was a good chief who could be depended on to look after his men.

All the scouts, me included, felt the darkness of grief and despair fall over us when we learned that Captain Crawford was still breathing with that wound in his head and blood and brains splattered on his face. The *di-yen* with us, whom the Blue Coats called "surgeon" arrived late in the afternoon, coming in with ten pack mules hauling supplies and ammunition from Captain Wirt Davis. Surgeon looked under the red cloth Dutchy had wrapped around Crawford's head, shook his head and, through clenched teeth, said there was nothing he could do.

The next sun, *Teniente* Maus with Concepcion and Tom Horn took six mules we had captured back to the Tarahumara who claimed we had no right to be in the land of *Nakai-yes*. *Teniente* Maus produced a paper that said our presence there was all legal. Surgeon did what he could for their wounded, and then the Tarahumara packed up their mules and headed up the trail to the east, starting their long walk back home.

Around the fire that night, *Teniente* Maus told us we would be leaving the next sun and to be ready at dawn. Captain Crawford still lived. It was a rough trail filled with stones we had to follow back. As we sat wondering how we could march with the captain still living, the *teniente* seemed to read our thoughts and said, "I know what you're thinking. We'll take turns carrying him on our backs until he dies. Then we'll let a horse carry him. It's the best we can do. You boys, see if you can't come up with a pack and harness that we can use to carry him."

FORTY

CAPTAIN CRAWFORD DIES

THE SCOUTS MADE a pack rig that looked like a man-sized *tsach* for the men to take turns carrying Captain Crawford on their backs. We wrapped him up in a blanket and tied him to the board, which also had a rainbow of bent sticks over his head to protect it as much as we could to keep him out of any additional pain. The foot piece on a baby's *tsach* was where he sat, and his legs dangled free. Because it was raining, we covered him and the *tsach* with a small piece of canvas saved from fires that destroyed the Chiricahua camp. The man who carried him used straps from the frame, and we rigged up a head band he could use to balance the giant cradleboard and put his neck muscles to work effectively lifting and leaning into the load.

Teniente Maus wanted to go west for a while to put as much distance between us and the Tarahumara as possible to get the renegades wanting to meet once more in a surrender council. Noche led us out of the Río Aros canyon in a steady rain that soon soaked all we wore. Walking was miserable and extra hard carrying the heavy load of a grown White Eye on our backs. But, no one complained, even the soldiers who often cursed, calling on their god. We hiked up a canyon that led west out of the río canyon and led across a low pass with little streams of water rolling down the trail making the trail and its rocks slippery and movement slow.

Teniente Shipp carried Captain Crawford first. He trudged along, as we all did, wiping the rain from his face, wanting to be sure he didn't slip or fall with the man we all respected. Shipp surprised me at how strong he was. He made it halfway to the low pass before exhaustion made him ready to pass his burden on to the next man. *Teniente* Maus took the next turn. He went farther than did *Teniente* Shipp, but not much. Tom Horn carried Crawford over the pass and down the other side, a distance twice that of the officers. We all had a turn carrying Captain Crawford and a scout who had been wounded but not as bad or in the same place as the captain. When I put Captain Crawford down for the next man to carry, the muscles in my legs quivered and my feet felt like I wore heavy iron moccasins.

By the time Noche reached a little creek rolling with water and a bosque on both sides, the rain had stopped. He found a good place to camp as the sun was nearing its hiding place behind the western mountains. I guessed we had come about four miles as the army counts distance. We were all too tired from having covered such a short distance.

We cooked dried meat and vegetables saved from the Chiricahua camp. The firewood was damp and cast a cloud of smoke over the camp, but we ignored the smoke and damp cold, eating as fast as we could to stuff the hot food in our bellies. Steam from the wet ground seemed to rise and push the smoke up. Stars began to show as the clouds moved east.

We finished our meal and were rolling cigarettes when a Chiricahua woman wrapped in a blanket appeared walking through the ground mists toward the fire of *Teniente* Maus. All the men paused, staring at her, wondering if she was a ghost or real. When Maus saw her, he stood, held up his hands palms out, meaning for the men to be still, and went with Concepcion and Tom Horn to meet her. I realized it was the same woman who had crossed the Aros to ask for a meeting three days earlier. I was close enough this time to hear her clearly.

She said, again in the *Nakai-yi* tongue, "My chiefs see how the *Nakai-yes* betray your captain. He goes to the Happy Land?"

Teniente Maus understood her Spanish and nodded. "Captain Crawford is a strong warrior, but soon he goes to the Happy Land. Now, I speak for our chief."

She glanced around the fire, her eyes black and shining like the obsidian arrowheads the grandfathers used. "My chiefs want words with you at sunrise on other side of this hill where spring flows. Bring who you want with you, but no guns, on any who come."

Teniente Maus crossed his arms, paused for a long breath, and then nodded. "We'll see you at the spring on the other side of this hill when the sun rises."

She stared at Maus and then said, "Let it be so."

Maus nodded and turned to look for any disagreements among the men behind him. He saw no frowns or shaking of heads and turned back to her, but she had already disappeared in the smoke and mists.

THE NEXT MORNING, *Teniente* Maus led Tom Horn, Noche, Concepcion, me, and three other scouts to the meeting place the woman had described at springs down the hill from where we camped. It was very cold and we all wore blankets. The sun was still below the outline of the eastern mountains but rising fast. Just as the sun cleared the mountaintops, two horsemen rode out of the shadows. As they approached, I recognized them as warriors who had been with Geronimo when the Chiricahua ran for the land of the *Nakai-yes*. They were Natculbaye and Atelnietze, both experienced and powerful.

Concepcion looked at them and frowned. He said, "Where are your chiefs and leaders?"

Natculbaye stayed on his horse but made the all-is-well hand wave. He said in Apache, "They come here tomorrow at this time. They had to be sure you planned no tricks. If you try to trick us, we will fight to the last Chiricahua. Unwrap your blankets and let us see that you have no hidden rifles or pistols on you."

Teniente Maus unwrapped his blanket to show no weapons. When we saw what was happening, we all took off our blankets and let the Apache take a close look. We had no weapons with us, and we were glad they found none.

After a short time of close looks, the Apache made the all-is-well hand wave and said again that the chiefs would meet us here at sunrise the next sun. Maus nodded and said, *"Ch'ik'eh doleel."* Squaring his shoulders, he led us back up the hill to our fires, breakfast, and a day to dry out.

THE NEXT MORNING, as the orange-and-yellow glow behind the eastern mountains grew brighter, we worked our way down the hill to the place where we had spoken the day before. At the spring was a large flat place with no rocks or brush, and near the center of it in the growing light sat Geronimo facing the way we would come. Behind him were Naiche, Nana, and Chihuahua and fourteen men encircled Geronimo. Each man sat with his rifle upright, held by the barrel like a sheep staff, every bandolier filled with ammunition. Geronimo motioned us toward him with a wave of his hand as the men opened the space in their circle to let us through. *Teniente* Maus walked up and sat down about two carbine rifle lengths away from Geronimo, and the scouts formed a semicircle and sat down behind him. Tom Horn and Concepcion sat directly behind him to assist with interpretation.

The air was cold in this little low place, little clouds rose off the spring water as it bubbled from the rocks, and our breath made us look like little White Eye iron wagons rolling down the steel road. My heart was pounding as I wondered if I would see my wife and child again. We sat and stared at each other in silence for ten or fifteen breaths as Geronimo and Maus stared at each other.

Looking *Teniente* Maus in the eye, Geronimo said in excellent Spanish, "Why did you come down here?"

Teniente Maus stuck out his chin and said, "I came to capture or destroy you and your band."

A smile wiggled on Geronimo's face as he stood and stepped over to shake *Teniente* Maus's hand. "Your answer is a good one. You speak true no matter the threat. That means I can trust you to give an accurate report of this meeting to *Nant'an Lpah.*" He walked back to his original seat in the council and sat down with a grunt and said, "Now I tell you why I left Turkey Creek."

He told a long story about how *Teniente* Davis, Chato, and Mickey Free plotted to get rid of him.

I didn't believe half of what he told.

When Geronimo finished his personal tale of woe, he said, "Now we talk terms for peace. We wanted to stay here in the land of the *Nakai-yes.* We thought you would never find us, but your scouts, our People, did and the *Nakai-yi* Indios, the *Rarámuri,* found us and wanted to take our hair for *Nakai-yi* gold. We have not seen our families since they were taken from us in your scout raids the last Season of Big Leaves. We would talk with *Nant'an Lpah* about these things and maybe agree to return to Turkey Creek when we get our families back. We still want to discuss what we do among ourselves. In two moons, we will meet with *Nant'an Lpah* near the border at San Bernardino to talk about what we do. I leave you nine of my People to guarantee we will come to talk and claim them back. Do you agree to this, *Teniente* Maus?"

Teniente Maus, keeping his eyes fixed on Geronimo, slowly nodded. "This I tell *Nant'an Lpah.* He will want to hear the words and desires of the Chiricahua who left the reservation and tell you what he thinks. We will wait for your People in our camp."

Geronimo also nodded and said, *"Ch'ik'eh doleel."*

THE NEXT SUN, about the time of no shadows, nine people, *Teniente* Maus called them "hostages," walked into our camp as though appearing out of the air—good Apache. Two of them were warriors—old Nana and a warrior I didn't know—and seven women and children. One of the women was the young Mescalero wife of Geronimo. She was obviously three or four months pregnant—I expected as much. Another was a little girl looking sickly who soon died and the oldest wife of Naiche and her son I heard the White Eyes at the place called "school" named Paul. Nana's wife, Geronimo's sister, came with Nana. There was also the woman who brought us messages from Naiche and Geronimo and a young boy I did not know. They all looked underfed and were happy to eat meals we offered them.

We left our camp and headed for Nácori Chico the sun after the hostages came in. We were still carrying Captain Crawford on our backs, for he still breathed. Near the middle of the day, Captain Crawford opened his eyes and we could tell he recognized us. *Teniente* Maus put his arm around him and said he would arrange his affairs. In a very short time, Captain Crawford again lost consciousness and the next day, at about the same time, rode the ghost pony for the Happy Land.

We were all sorry to see him leave us. He had been fair in all his dealings with us. The need to carry Captain Crawford on our backs was no more. We wrapped him in canvas and tied him over a horse. By then, the wounded scout was strong enough to ride, and our pace increased. We found our supply packtrain two or three suns from Nácori Chico. It was a good thing we found it when we did. With nine new mouths to feed, we were starting to run low on supplies. I kept a close eye on Geronimo's Mescalero woman. She looked good, even if pregnant as I suspected. Too bad she took an old man like Geronimo. I decided that if they ever divorced, I might take her and their child to make my family larger. She was a brave woman, and I liked to look at her.

WE REACHED NÁCORI Chico four days after Captain Crawford rode the ghost pony. *Teniente* Maus found four boards and nailed them together to form a box for the body of Captain Crawford in burial until *Nant'an Lpah* could send a detail and wagon for the body and a respectful burial north of the border. We were lucky. It was the Ghost Face season, and cold kept Crawford's body from stinking and helped preserve it until soldiers from Fort Bowie reclaimed it.

Teniente Maus wrote a report he sent to Fort Bowie for *Nant'an Lpah* describing what had happened to Captain Crawford and the agreement we made with the Chiricahua. We left Nácori Chico the same day we buried Captain Crawford. The suns were cold and the mountains high as we marched for the border. In ten days, we had marched through the Sierra Madre, destroyed Geronimo's camp and convinced him he couldn't hide in the land of the *Nakai-yes*, and put up with Mexican military who killed our commander and wanted to attack us but were afraid of the ferocity of our People, the scouts. Crossing the border, we made it to Lang's Ranch, a supply point for the packtrains in the land of *Nakai-yes*. We rested a day while *Teniente* Maus tried to telegraph *Nant'an Lpah* but could not reach him. The next day, he sent *Teniente* Shipp and some scouts to escort the prisoners to Fort Bowie.

Teniente Maus at last reached *Nant'an Lpah* on the talking wire. For the next four suns he answered *Nant'an Lpah's* questions about why the *Nakai-yes* hadn't been "whipped" worse than they were after Crawford was killed. Maus began to think the nant'an blamed him for Crawford's death. Of course, Maus was not responsible for Crawford's murder, but he worried just the same. On the fifth sun after we made camp at Lang's Ranch, *Nant'an Lpah* sent orders to *Teniente* Maus to make a camp near the border on the Río San Bernardino, wait for the Chiricahua to come, notify him when they came, and keep them there until he arrived.

The next sun, we moved our scout camp twenty-five miles west to San Bernardino and then about seven miles south down the Río San Bernardino and made a camp as the sun was disappearing in orange and red clouds. I expected Geronimo to appear when he said he would, which meant we had over a moon to wait. I decided we should take my company of scouts and keep them busy learning the land in case the Chiricahua ran and we had to chase and catch them. Important times were coming.

FORTY-ONE

SURRENDER AND BREAKAWAY

FOR THE NEXT moon and a half, when we weren't exploring the country, my company of scouts and I watched for the Chiricahua from a mountain the *Nakai-yes* called "Pitaicache" a little north of where Río Bavispe makes its big turn from flowing north to south. Our watching site offered our horses and mules water and grass and gave us a good view of most of the San Bernardino Valley. I liked using soldier glasses to look up the valley and see the yucca in bloom and the different greens from gourd vines with pods ready to bloom, thick groves of dark creosote bushes, and the light greens of mesquite and prickly pear.

I also took two or three men with me to scout the valley llano and mountains west of the little Río San Bernardino for canyons where the Chiricahua might hide or come out to spring ambushes. We found canyons and *arroyo*s where it would be easy to hide many warriors, and I made memory of those places thinking if the council with *Nant'an Lpah* didn't go well, then those canyons were where scouts should look first if the renegades left the council. *Teniente* Maus made his camp along the Río San Bernadino about a hand's ride from the border so he could send couriers in a hurry to Fort Bowie.

When two moons had passed since our meeting with the Chiricahua in the land of the *Nakai-yes*, just as Geronimo had told *Teniente* Maus, a smoke column showed on a high mountain to the west. We answered with our own smoke and *Teniente* Maus and Concepcion, who Maus often used for talk interpretations, came down to our place on Pitaicache to watch with us for the Chiricahua. Soon

Geronimo and Naiche appeared at our watching-place tent as if out of the wind, saying, "We come. Ready to talk. Where *Nant'an Lpah?*"

Maus said, "Where are your People?"

Geronimo shrugged his shoulders and said, "They are nearby. They come when we signal."

"When you decide where you want to camp, I'll let *Nant'an Lpah* know you're here and he'll choose a day for your council."

Geronimo frowned and looked at Naiche, who raised an eyebrow in question. "We camp near here. When Nant'an come?"

Teniente crossed his arms and, giving his head a little shake, looked at both men. "You won't camp north of the border?"

Geronimo made half a smile and slowly shook his head. "Until we talk with *Nant'an Lpah*, we stay in the land of the *Nakai-yes.*"

Maus frowned and began filling his pipe. "If you're not willing to camp across the border, then I'd suggest you move up much closer than here. If Mexican soldiers find you're camped near the río, they might attack you and your families, and there's nothing we can do about it. The closer you are to the border, the better chance you'll have to get away and the better we can protect you."

Geronimo walked outside with Naiche and they talked privately in council. A cool breeze filled with the scent of yucca flowers blew down the little río and made their hair whip around their faces as they spoke and gestured with their hands. Geronimo finally nodded he agreed, and Naiche and he returned to *Teniente* Maus standing under a piece of canvas used for a sunshade in front of his tent.

Geronimo, motioning toward Naiche, said, "Naiche and I agree. We move camp up to Canyon de los Embudos, but no closer till *Nant'an Lpah* come."

Teniente Maus blew a stream of smoke into the breeze. *"Enjuh.* When you establish your camp, I'll move mine within sight of yours. I'll send a courier with a message to *Nant'an Lpah* that you've come and are camped in the *Canyon de los Embudos.*"

Geronimo sent smoke high in the air telling the Chiricahua to come forward. As the sun was turning the clouds in the west many colors of red, yellow, and orange, the Chiricahua were making rough *wickiups* in an easily defensible, deep black rock depression with high sides on the edge of the Canyon de los Embudos. Across an *arroyo* from the Chiricahua, *Teniente* Maus set up his camp with the scout tents set in orderly rows near his tent.

After the camps were in place, *Teniente* Maus called the scouts together in front of his tent by a big fire to keep back the coming darkness and, with Concepcion sitting on a stool nearby providing the interpretation, said, "Scouts, you have worked long and hard chasing the Chiricahua in the land of the *Nakaiyes*, and the trails you've walked and battles we fought with the Chiricahua and Tarahumaras are near to finishing this war.

"*Nant'an Lpah* comes. He'll be here next sun or the one after. You know the Chiricahua are in a bad mood from drinking mescal and whiskey the Tribolet brothers sell them, and they've been waiting a long time for the nant'an to come. The nant'an has good reasons for doing things the way he does. It's not our job to question his ways. I want you to avoid any contact with the Chiricahua so they have no excuse for running or fighting.

"After their council with *Nant'an Lpah*, they'll be our prisoners. We'll move them to Fort Bowie. From Fort Bowie, I believe a train will take them to Florida. This we learn after the council and the nant'an talks with his chief on the talking wire.

"Again I say, leave the Chiricahua alone unless you have no other choice. Do you understand my words?"

We all said, "*Ch'ik'eh doleel* (all right)." The council ended and we returned to our cooking fires, where the fine smell of fat from meat dripping in the fires made us even hungrier than when we began cooking.

THE NEXT SUN, *Nant'an Lpah* and those riding with him came into the canyon. He stopped to eat and talk with the packers who had brought supplies to feed the camp people. *Teniente* Maus sent his soldiers to help the travelers with their things and show them which tent they could use and where they could eat. I was surprised to see Kaytennae, the young war chief *Teniente* Davis had disarmed at Turkey Creek and Captain Crawford had sent to the little land in the big water to the west for three harvests. He was there less than two harvests and now he walked free? If he was free, I knew it was because *Nant'an Lpah* wanted it so.

Nant'an Lpah finished his time-of-no-shadows meal, told the packers *adios*, and found a shady place where he could sit on a ledge near the little creek running down the canyon. His men gathered around him, and the Chiricahua who had been drifting into our camp from theirs found a place where they could watch and hear what went on. Finally, Naiche and Geronimo came and sat on the ground near the nant'an, who had chosen to sit above them.

Geronimo had much to say, most of which I had already heard when he met with *Teniente* Maus in the mountains of the *Espinosa del Diablo*. Nant'an listened while he lightly tapped the ground with a yucca stalk. When Geronimo finished, the nant'an said, "Your mouth talks too many ways." Geronimo said something I didn't hear and began to stand to leave with the warriors who were already backing away, but Naiche waved a hand for them to be still, and no one moved.

Chihuahua and his brother Ulzana suddenly appeared riding up with a small herd of horses they had found. Chihuahua and the nant'an shook hands, and then Chihuahua and Ulzana edged into the back of the group surrounding the council to listen.

Nant'an had his say and told them they must surrender and live in a faraway place called "Florida" for two harvests. This was for their own good to prevent White Eye settlers from taking revenge for the past raids and killings the Chiricahua had done. He also said that if they didn't surrender, then he would find and kill them all if it took fifty years. I believed him, and the Chiricahua did too. He told them to return to their camp, talk it over, and give him their answer in two suns.

There were talks around the Chiricahua fires long into the night with people like Kaytennae and the White Mountain chief Alchesay the nant'an had brought with him. The next morning, the same man from Tombstone who had captured my image and that of other scouts six or seven harvests before now captured Chiricahua images. He finished after the time of shortest shadows, and soon the Chiricahua were in councils that again lasted far into the night.

Lying on my blanket, I stared at the stars and was glad I was not a Chiricahua who would have to live in this place the army chiefs called Florida far to the East, even if it was for only two harvests. The White Eyes seemed to have a special talent for breaking a man's spirit. I promised myself that I'd never let them do that to me.

THE NEXT DAY, about the time of shortest shadows, Chihuahua surrendered to *Nant'an Lpah*. Geronimo and Naiche soon followed. There was much shaking of hands and good words between the nant'an and the chiefs. The scouts still kept their distance from the Chiricahua so a newly born treaty wouldn't die an untimely death. Unfortunately, it did for some. The Tribolet brothers sold Geronimo enough whiskey and mescal to make all the Chiricahua drunk two or three times. After Geronimo shared the whiskey and mescal with all the Chiricahua, many warriors were very drunk and even shooting toward scouts and soldiers. But their bullets were way off their target and no one was hurt. I wanted to take the whiskey and mescal away from them, but *Teniente* Maus said no. Let them be hungover the next morning.

It was hard to get the Chiricahua moving the next day. They staggered north about four miles and stopped to camp. Maus wanted to keep moving, but Geronimo told him that the Chiricahua were all hungover and needed to rest and that they were in an ugly mood and might hurt anyone who interfered with them. It was best to stay away from them, which we did. They didn't sober up but had another night of drinking. There were two camps, the one led by Geronimo and Naiche and the second, which drank little, led by Chihuahua. But the next day, they moved on without complaint until they stopped about two miles from the border. Geronimo told Maus they needed to rest and didn't feel well. This time, Chihuahua's Chiricahua camped farther from the Naiche-Geronimo camp than the night before. I knew they were planning something. They weren't going to cross the border.

Sometime late in the night, Geronimo and Naiche and sixteen of their men and twenty-two women and children disappeared. All the Chiricahua camping with Chihuahua stayed. The next morning, *Teniente* Maus's face looked like he had eaten bad meat as he told sixty scouts to try to find Geronimo's trail and sent *Teniente* Shipp and twenty scouts on to Fort Bowie with Chihuahua and his People.

The scouts thought, at first, Geronimo and Naiche would head south and climb into the mountains where they often camped and would be hard to find and even harder to bring back. Instead of heading south or east, they ran west farther into Sonora while taking only two or three horses and a mule.

We were short of supplies when we started trailing the renegades, and by the time we approached Fronteras, they had split into many different trails, making it impossible to follow them all. Our supplies were fast running out. *Teniente* Maus called a halt to the chase and headed to Fort Bowie.

GERONIMO FAILED TO keep his promise of surrender to *Nant'an Lpah* after the nant'an trusted him. *Nant'an Lpah* knew he looked like a fool to his chief and asked for a different command. His chief sent him to lead the army on the northern plains and sent Nant'an Miles to take his place. Miles believed the scouts had helped Geronimo and Naiche and couldn't be trusted. He stopped using the scouts in the chase for the Naiche-Geronimo band. When I heard this, I thought my days as a scout were over, but Captain Pierce used us tribal policeman and I was happy to stay close to San Carlos and near my family. I never dreamed that disaster would fall on me like it did and turn my good life upside down.

FORTY-TWO

A DARK WIND

A MOON AFTER the Naiche-Geronimo People were put on a train headed for the place the White Eyes called Florida, my six-month enlistment ended. Despite missing my family, I had no doubt I wanted to stay in the scouts and, the next day, reenlisted with Captain Lee, First Infantry at San Carlos. With the Chiricahua all gone east, there were fewer tribal confrontations at San Carlos and most of the tribal police work was on individual crimes like *tulapai* making and drinking, or theft or fights where knives came out over arguments, usually over who won or lost while gambling.

Most of the scouts and I liked a good drink of *tulapai*, but not enough to make us drunk, so we didn't pay much attention to rumors that a big drink was planned by a band camped about ten miles north of the agency. My father sent word by one of his friends that he planned to attend a *tulapai* drink with friends about two hands' ride north of the agency at San Carlos. He asked that I come and visit with him and the family for a while since he and my mothers and brothers and sisters would be much closer than if they were in Aravaipa Canyon. I sent word back to my father by courier heading down the Río San Pedro that I would try to visit if San Carlos was quiet and Sieber didn't have me working.

IT WAS NEAR the end of The Earth Is Reddish Brown season and the suns were warmer than usual and the nights comfortable. The *tulapai* drinking north of San Carlos Agency had been going on for two suns, and I still had not visited with my father and his family. I was sitting with Sieber having a smoke and drinking his coffee as we watched the evening sky colors change to black, fill with stars, and softly spread a blanket of darkness over the banks of the Ríos Gila and San Carlos like a mother covering her sleeping baby. The warmth of the day was fast disappearing and the horizon light disappearing into darkness when we saw the outline of a rider in a big hurry coming down the trail from Globe. Even in the falling light, we could see the dust his charging horse was kicking into the big plume he left behind. I heard Sieber mutter, "Oh, hell. Mark my words, Kid, here comes trouble."

The rider was one of the scouts in my company. He reined in his horse, lathered and nostrils flaring as it sucked in all the air it could. I stood and said, "Ho, Corporal, what news? You ride dangerously fast in the falling darkness."

He threw one leg over his saddle and slid off his horse. He took a couple of steps toward us, stopped, stood straight, and made the hand wave of respect the Blue Coats used. He said, "Chief Sieber and First Sergeant Kid, I ride like the wind, but a dark wind, to get here with news you will want to know."

"What dark wind do you blame for your hard ride?"

Dust covered the scout's clothes and sweat rivulets ran down his cheeks, leaving streaks of mud while he puffed to get his breath.

"Sergeant Kid, your father has been killed at a *tulapai* drink. Gon-zizzie shot him in the back. I know he meant to do it. They were all drinking but not drunk yet. Rip was talking to Gon-zizzie from the time they started drinking. Even as the smoke cleared from Gon-zizzie's rifle, Rip shouted, 'So, Toga-de-chuz, you die after taking the woman I want and telling me I was not good enough for her. Soon the great warrior Gon-zizzie also takes the life of Ohyessonna, who came from her body. I will be satisfied.'"

I felt I was hit in the middle of my chest by a hard-thrown rock as a roaring fury grew in my guts and roared in my ears and the news that my father was gone tore at my heart. I had to kill Gon-zizzie and his brother Rip before the sun rose again.

The corporal said, "I see the fury in your face, Sergeant. Wait, there is more. Gon-zizzie saw Toga-de-chuz's friends pulling their knives to come after him. He threw down his rifle, his eyes big, and ran for the horses. He was about to jump on one still saddled when a *reata* loop flew over his head and pulled tight around his throat to throw him to the ground.

"Toga-de-chuz's friends were on him with their knives raised, but the man with the *reata* threw up his arms and yelled, *'Nt'ah!'* He ran to the horse Gon-zizzie had tried to take, jumped on him, and just as Gon-zizzie was getting to his knees and pulling the *reata* off his neck, the rider jerked the *reata* tight, wrapped quick loops around the saddle horn, kicked the horse in the ribs and let out a loud 'Yeh ha!' The horse took off out into the llano dragging Gon-zizzie behind him. He dragged Gon-zizzie through patches of prickly pear, over gravel, and through deep dust and stands of mesquite and ocotillo.

"When the rider returned, you couldn't tell the piece of meat on the end of the *reata* had been Gon-zizzie. They looked for Rip, but he was gone. What was left of Gon-zizzie, they burned in a big fire. That is all I have to say."

Sieber sat listening with his arms crossed, his cigarette hanging from the corner of his mouth and its coal edging closer to his lips. I sat listening with bowed head. The rider stood patiently waiting for orders. Off in the distance, we heard coyotes yip, and nearby we heard the burbling of the rivers and, in a tree, an owl calling. There was no doubt in my mind then that Toga-de-chuz had ridden the ghost pony. Finally, Sieber tossed the cigarette on the ground and, grinding it out with his heal, said in a soft, firm voice, "Kid, you go on with this man to collect your father and his family. Rip may have pushed Gon-zizzie into killing your father, but let it be. Now we must live under White Eye rules. Unless Rip had a direct hand in the killing, there is no White Eye rule that says he's responsible. Take as much time off with your family for the burial of your father as you need. Now go. I don't want a war started among the Aravaipa."

I saluted Sieber to let him know I understood his order. I grabbed my saddle, bridle, and rifle before I walked over to the corral to claim my horse.

WE BURIED MY father in the cliffs far up Aravaipa Creek and sent songs and prayers asking that *Ussen* welcome him as the great man he was and that his ghost pony make a fast journey to the Happy Land. Sieber told me not to avenge my father by killing Rip because that was not the White Eye way. I always tried to do what Sieber said I should do as a scout.

My mother as my father's number-one wife insisted on staying at the *wickiup* place they had shared, and his number-two wife agreed with her. They burned the old *wickiup* after his burial. No one wanted his ghost to return. Mother and number-two wife raked the ashes and charred wood from the old *wickiup* spot into a pile on one side and, within a day, had constructed a new *wickiup* and covered it with new canvas for their children and themselves.

I knew over the growing seasons and into the Season of Earth Is Reddish Brown, Toga-de-chuz's women and my brothers and sisters had worked hard growing food in their gardens, baking hearts of mescal, and gathering mesquite pods out on the llano, acorns from the oaks along the creek, and juniper berries. I still had half brothers with them who were good hunters. My father's family would be well cared for in the Ghost Face.

For the next moon, Sieber let me visit my family several times and check on my mother. I stopped at her *wickiup*, on the way to spend two or three days with Chita and our child, and had a cup of coffee with my mothers and brothers and sisters. We were still filled with sorrow over the loss of my father, and my mother always had one question. "When will you kill Rip and make the world smooth again?" I tried to explain, each time she asked, that my scout chief told me to leave Rip alone. The White Eyes demanded proof and not hearsay to punish anyone accused of murder. Rip only talked to Gon-zizzie about revenge, and his hands had nothing to do with killing Toga-de-chuz. She listened and nodded she understood, but the next time I came, she asked the same question and I gave the same answer. I also had to explain myself to my wife and father-in-law for why I wasn't taking blood revenge against Rip. Unlike my mother, they only asked me once, but I could see the same question again and again in their eyes. On the long rides between San Carlos and Aravaipa Canyon, I asked myself the same question and finally decided the answer depended on another question—did I want to live as an Apache or deny my People and live as a White Eye? I knew many of my People were asking themselves the same thing.

ON ONE OF my trips back to visit my family, I stopped as usual at my mother's *wickiup*. Three elders in my father's band came to stand at her *wickiup* blanket door, and one cleared his throat for entrance. They asked for a council with me when she invited them in. I agreed to speak with them but wondered what they wanted to talk about. It was windy and cold in the canyon that sun, but my mother said the rest of her family would visit friends while she stayed and served us. That was good for the elders, and I nodded my appreciation for her generosity.

After the family left, I built up the fire. One of the elders, who everyone called "Old Juan," wore his gray-and-black hair in a long braid down his back and had a long angry scar on his face, spoke first. He said, "Ohyessonna, my brothers here said I should speak for them and will accurately report what we say here to the council of our band. Is this good for you?"

"Yes, it is good for me. Speak, Juan. I will listen."

Outside, the wind's fury seemed to slow. My mother filled our cups from her old black coffeepot and then moved to sit down behind the blanket with Navajo designs that served as a wall for her sleeping place. We could see her feet and legs there, and she heard every word said.

Old Juan blew the steam off his cup and took a good swallow of the fiery brew. He smacked his lips and said, "Hmmph, good coffee…. Ohyessonna, your father, our band's chief, was a good man. We all knew him and what he stood for. He raised a fine son who band elders and all the White Eye chiefs respect. He draws men to him like bees to honey, and when he gives an order, his men obey without question. This is very good."

The other two elders who sat on either side of Old Juan were nodding their agreement. "We need a new chief to replace your father and his good judgment. All the elders have spoken with each other, and we have only one name we think is best for our band." I'll never forget firelight dancing in Old Juan's eyes when he said, "That man is you, Ohyessonna. We ask you to be our chief. That is all I have to say."

One of life's circles completed for me. When I was a boy, I said I wanted to be chief when my time came, and my father had said one day that I would be chief. I remembered the race I had with Gonshayee. His growth stopped soon after we raced. In a harvest or two, even though he was older than most of my friends, he was in height close to or a little shorter than everyone else. Except for me or one of my brothers, Gonshayee was about the best warrior in the band my father once headed. It was often hard to get a straight answer out of Gonshayee about anything of importance, and for that, I didn't care for him.

The elders sat staring at me as I thought about their offer. I wanted to be a leader of scouts, and I wanted to be chief, but I preferred the scouts. If the band had a good warrior leading them, they would be safe under the leadership of *Capitan* Chiquito and Hashke Bahnzin.

I said to the elders, "Your offer honors me, and I'm proud to hear your words about me. But there is a challenge to my family honor I must resolve. I cannot be your chief when this question hangs over my head, and I still lead scouts. I say choose a great warrior to be your chief. I ask you to think of making Gonshayee our chief."

I heard a groan of disappointment from the other side of my mother's blanket.

From the looks on their faces and slow nods of their heads, I knew they had already discussed him when considering the men for chief. Old Juan said, "You wear your honesty well, Ohyessonna. We talk over your thinking."

I said, "*Enjuh*. Let us speak of other things that worry you about the band. Can I pour you more coffee?"

We emptied the pot and talked for another hand. The elders seemed disappointed and at the same time relieved that I had chosen not to be chief.

THE MOONS OF the Ghost Face Season and then Little Eagles passed and still I had no answers to how I should deal with Rip, but I could tell the People knew I wanted to live like a White Eye. Sieber could tell I was still trying to decide what I should do. Near the beginning of the Season of Many Leaves, he said to me, "Your enlistment is up in two or three suns. You gonna reenlist again? You're the best scout I have at San Carlos. I'd like to see you stay."

I enjoyed the scouting life too much and the friendship and guidance from Sieber to leave the scouts and said, "Scouts good work, Sieber. I reenlist."

He grinned and said, "That's good news for me, Kid. Let's smoke on it." I nodded and he pulled his papers and sack of *tobaho* from his shirt pocket. His quick fingers rolled a smoke that we shared to the four directions. This was serious business. I felt good smoking with Sieber.

Three days later, I went to Captain Pierce to close my current enlistment and planned to reenlist the next day. Pierce did my paperwork and asked if I planned to reenlist. I nodded, and he grinned and said, "*Enjuh*. I have business I have to take care of tomorrow, but Captain Lee will be here to take care of your papers when you come to reenlist." We shook hands like we were both White Eyes, and I wondered then what I was doing.

A MOON PASSED, and on that same sun, the earth shook like some demon animal below was trying to get free and destroy us all. Boulders bounced down canyon walls, big trees fell, water in the rivers rolled and waved like they were being shaken in a big bowl, and all people and animals had trouble standing. It was the worst of omens that something very bad was about to happen to the

People. *Di-yens* all over the reservation performed their medicine to keep the roaring animal under us calm and in its cage. Sieber learned from Captain Pierce that the worst earth shaking was south in Sonora and that it killed fifty-one *Nakai-yes*. No one at San Carlos was badly hurt. We had better *di-yens* than the *Nakai-yes*. For the next ten days, we felt the earth tremble but less each sun but again no one was hurt.

About ten suns after the first big rumble, I had just finished a sun of training with scouts who had enlisted for the first time when Sieber motioned me over to his tent. When I walked up, he held up the coffeepot as if to ask if I wanted a cup. I shook my head, and he motioned me to a chair by his writing table.

He said, "Howdy, Kid. How's scout trainin' goin'?"

"Hmmph. Trainin' goes good. New men learn fast."

"That's good. I wanted you to know Captain Pierce and I are goin' to look over scouts and facilities at forts and subagencies."

"When you go? Who in charge while you at Fort Apache? Who I report to?"

Sieber grinned again. "We'll leave in about seven suns. While we're gone, you'll report to yourself."

I frowned. I didn't understand what he meant.

He laughed and slapped the table. "Sorry to confuse you with my little joke, Kid. I want you to oversee the guardhouse and all the scouts here at San Carlos."

My jaw dropped and Sieber laughed again.

"Well, what do you say, Kid? You want my job while I'm gone?"

"You say you want me for this job, then I do. How long you and Captain Pierce go away?"

"Pierce and I will be gone about half a moon. Glad to know you agreed to lead as chief of scouts while I'm gone. I know I can always depend on you to get the job done, whatever it is."

"I do my best, Sieber."

He nodded. "I'm sure you will, Kid. In a day or two, we'll go over all things you'll need to keep an eye on while I'm gone."

"Ch'ik'eh doleel."

A dark wind was coming to blow my life away. I couldn't hear or see it, but in the back of my mind, for reasons I didn't understand, I sensed the darkness coming despite the honor Sieber was showing me. Perhaps the demon in the earth was angry with me.

FORTY-THREE

THE *TULAPAI* DRINK

IT WAS FIVE suns after Al Sieber and Captain Pierce had left me in charge. As the rising sun poured light across the reservation, I learned from a scout who had a little drink during the night while on duty that a *tulapai* drink was going on in a camp on the way to Globe. I scratched my chin as I often saw Sieber do deciding his next move. These were hard times. I knew I ought to stop the drink and make an arrest or two. But the People feared the great beast under the earth sometimes shaking its cage. It didn't seem right to stop it even though one of those drinks had gotten my father killed six or seven moons earlier. I thought about what to do all that sun and decided that not only would I let the drink go on, but I'd also ease into the camp and have a cup or two. After wrestling for moons with the question of whether I should defend my family's honor by killing Rip or not, I needed a good drink.

I had two half-brothers at San Carlos enlisted in the scouts and decided I'd take As-ki-say-la-ha, the youngest one, with me and give him a little guidance about drinking *tulapai*. He would have some wisdom for me about what to do about Rip.

WHEN I SUGGESTED we disappear that night for a while to get a little *tulapai*, As-ki-say-la-ha didn't stop grinning the rest of the day. After the evening meal, we took our saddles and bridles to the corral and saddled our best horses and acted as though we were leaving for the evening on normal scout business.

The dust-filled road to the *tulapai* camp was easy to follow. In less than a hand, we rode into a camp where there were no little children and everyone had a cup of some kind in their hands. We had our eating hardware with a cup on our saddles. When some of the older men saw me, they said in loud slurred words, "Look! The favored scout and his youngest brother come to take us, some even his own People, to the calaboose for drinking *tulapai*! He should not be allowed to do this to anyone, much less his own People."

Two or three rocks flew out of the crowd starting to surround us. One rock hit my horse, who reared at the unexpected strike and wanted to run, but I held him in place. Two more rocks missed me and one hit As-ki-say-la-ha on the side of his arm. He pulled his revolver and pointed it toward the stars. The sound of him cocking it quieted the crowd around us. I had to grin. Little brother learned fast. I said in my loud drill voice, "Hold, brothers! We intend no harm. We come only to sample your *tulapai*. We mean you no punishment for breaking the rules. Keep the stones in your hands before someone is shot!"

There was a collective "Hmmph" from the men with the rocks. No more rocks flew as the crowd thinned out. As-ki-say-la-ha holstered his revolver, and we rode over to the rope corral and tied our horses to a post where they could reach a big pot of water and loosened our saddle cinches. Men continued to watch us with suspicion but minded their own business. There was a feeling in the air like a black wind filled with thunder arrows before a storm.

We found the *tulapai* pot, big and black, watched over by an old gray-headed woman. I said, "Grandmother, can we sample your good *tulapai*?" With a big happy smile, she held out a wrinkled, bony hand and took our cups by the handles. She poured a dipper full into each cup and handed them back to us. We nodded our thanks and drank our *tulapai* sitting back-to-back on a big boulder growing out of the sand.

After a couple of swallows, I said, "This *tulapai* has a good taste. I don't remember any I've had before tasting like it. What do you think?"

As-ki-say-la-ha snorted, "It's not bad, but I had better before Father was killed."

I knew As-ki-say-la-ha was trying to sound like an experienced man. I didn't say anything as we drank and listened to the insects in the brush, the swoop of bats through the air, an occasional puff of breeze winding through the creosote and mesquite and Wolf calling to a brother in the distance as the moon rose slowly from behind the northeastern mountains. The moon was up and brighter than it had been the day before. We finished our cups of *tulapai*. As-ki-say-la-ha took my cup and went to ask the old woman for a refill.

He soon returned as I watched men stagger around the camp or sit down in the grass on their blankets and pass out. As-ki-say-la-ha, after taking a swallow of *tulapai*, said, "Ho, brother. Have you decided what to do about Rip?"

I looked down at the gray water in the cup. The more *tulapai* I drank, the more I thought about what to do. My brother's warm back comfortably pressed against mine in the cold night air, and the *tulapai* stirred thoughts in my head that had been floating around since our father was murdered.

I said, "If I had my way, I kill that son on a coyote's tit. Sieber says if Rip had a direct hand in Toga-de-chuz's killing, then I could go after him, that the White Eyes wouldn't bother me. But, since he had no direct hand in killing Father, I must leave him alone if I want to stay a scout."

"Can't we sneak in on him, take care of business, and disappear back to the reservation like we'd never left?"

"I thought about that but decided too many things could go wrong and leave us in the calaboose when the tribal police came."

As-ki-say-la-ha said, "You're a great shot with that Winchester. Why don't you just shoot him at long range and return to San Carlos plenty quick?"

"I've thought of that too. The scouts have some fine trackers who could follow me all the way back to my tent here. But you know just sitting here talking about it with you is helping me clarify my mind. If you were going to kill Rip, how would you do it?"

As-ki-say-la-ha was quiet thinking about my question for so long that I began to think he hadn't heard me, but he finally said, "I'd just shoot him with a scout rifle at long range. Father told me one time that those big army bullets could kill a buffalo at a thousand paces. Think what one of those bullets would do to a man? I wouldn't want to be hit with one anyplace on my body."

"Hmmph. You make sense, little brother. One more cup of *tulapai* and we return to camp."

He was grinning, proud I had listened to him, when he handed me his cup for our last refill.

The old woman smiled again when she saw me coming. "You men seem to want to get drunk in a hurry."

"Not drunk, Grandmother, just in need of a little comfort is all."

She cackled as she filled the cups and said, "You're a nice-looking man. Come on over to my *wickiup*, and I'll give you all the comfort you can stand. I've been a widow too long."

I smiled and shook my head as she handed me the refilled cups. "Not tonight,

Grandmother." We were both teasing and she knew it, cackling that raucous laugh of hers, as I said, "Some other time I try your comfort, Grandmother."

WHEN I RETURNED to our boulder, I was surprised to see Gonshayee standing there with his arms crossed and swaying a little from side to side, drunk, and waiting for me. He said, "So, First Sergeant Ohyessonna, when do you plan to go to the canyon and take care of Rip? Don't you want to face the man who killed your father?"

So Chief Gonshayee had learned that I had recommended him for the job and that I had been first choice by the elders. He infuriated me and he knew it. "I kill Rip, but not before I find a chief and run him to death for insulting words."

Gonshayee made the Blue Coat hand wave of respect and then stumbled off into the darkness looking for someone else to insult.

The men who had wanted to throw rocks at us had gotten a lot more friendly and were talking to my brother when I returned with the last refill of *tulapai*. Most wanted to know how we liked their women's *tulapai*, and they asked when Sieber and Pierce would return.

I said, "I believe in the next ten suns or so. Just depends on what they might have to straighten out at Fort Apache and the subagency after the ground shook us all. Just to stay safe, you men ought to close this drink in two or three suns. Sooner rather than later."

They looked at each other with solemn faces and made little nods. One of them said, "That's what we plan to do, Sergeant."

I said, *"Ch'ik'eh doleel."*

They started moving away from our boulder seat as a cold wind came up. As-ki-say-la-ha and I finished our *tulapai* and went to saddle our horses. Even though it was cold that night and a good breeze blew, the *tulapai* had us sweating and the breeze felt good.

ON THE RIDE back to the San Carlos Agency, I thought more about killing Rip. I knew I had to kill him and leave San Carlos without telling any Blue Coat officers. Killing Rip was my personal family business. Leaving my post without permission was strictly against the army's rules of conduct. I expected Sieber would be angry that I broke his trust for my family's honor. He might want to put me in the calaboose for a while. I decided that was a risk I had to take.

We rode to the scout *wickiups* at San Carlos and went to the *wickiup* of our half-brother, Margey, snoring wrapped in his heavy blanket. I opened the blanket door and tapped his foot with the barrel of my rifle. His snoring stopped in an instant. We knew I had awakened him when we heard the clicks to full cock of his pistol.

He said in a low voice, "What you want? Who are you?"

"Take it easy, brother. It's your brothers, Ohyessonna and As-ki-say-la-ha. We go to find Rip and avenge our father tonight. You want to ride with us?"

We heard the hammer easing down on his revolver. "I ride with you. Bachoandoth and Nahconquisay are in tents on either side of me. We speak of this before we sleep. They will want to go with us. Ask them?"

I thought about what could happen at Rip's camp in Aravaipa. Five men after him was better rather than two or three. I answered, "They are good men. They do what I say. Brave. I ask 'em."

I tapped the feet of Bachoandoth and Nahconquisay and they, too, rose from their blankets with pistols drawn as had Margey. They even suggested there were others who would want to ride with us, but I said no. If the group was bigger than five, and that was too large, the army might start thinking breakout and come after us like we were Geronimo escaping Turkey Creek three harvests ago.

While the scouts going with me made ready for three or four days on the trail and loading their bandoliers, I went to my tent and made ready myself. The desert night was cold. I shivered, but I suspect it was more from the excitement of knowing that, one way or the other, I'd get rid of this load on my shoulders that got heavier every day. I hated to disappoint Sieber, but I had to do it. I might even have to spend a month in the guardhouse and be reduced in rank, but I didn't care. This business had to end.

FORTY-FOUR

A DEBT PAID

I LED MY little band of brothers into the night across the cold Río Gila and followed the west-side trail around Turnbull Mountain. The steady rhythm of our horses' hooves on the caliche trail reminded me of the steady drumbeat at a dance and, for me, filled the darkness with calm. We rode while the fingernail moon arced over into the southwest a little south of the main trail, and we came to a spring leaking out of a jumble of boulders into a small natural tank. We watered our horses and enjoyed handfuls of the good cold water. I decided to rest there until sunrise.

We unsaddled and hobbled our mounts, ate from our scout rations, and wrapped in our blankets to sleep in the tall grass near the tank until dawn told us it was time to go. After watching a brilliant sunrise casting gold and orange on high clouds and eating a little more, we fearlessly rode into the growing light as if we were old-time Apache on a war raid.

Two hands past the time of shortest shadows, we approached Aravaipa Canyon where the hills sloped down to the canyon walls carrying the creek to the Río San Pedro. I took the trail through the bosque along the creek that led from old Camp Grant into the canyon where, about six miles from the Río San Pedro, *Capitan* Chiquito had his *rancheria*. Springs fed good water to the creek there to keep the water level near constant, even in dry moons. The availability of the water all harvest made it easy to irrigate the land with *acequias* (irrigation trenches). Rip had his little group and access to land he farmed on the upstream edge of the *rancheria*.

Three hands after the time of shortest shadows, the light was bright and hot. We didn't know if we were easy to see on the trail through the bosque until we came within sight of the *rancheria* and stopped still undiscovered. There were no people moving about in the village. It seemed the villagers were either taking a siesta or working in the fields where we couldn't see. My heart began to beat faster, and my mouth was suddenly dry. Cocking my carbine, which shot a single .45-70 cartridge before reloading, I looked for Rip but didn't see him. I dismounted, gave the reins to Margey and told the scouts to wait for me out of sight in the bosque while I walked ahead in plain sight to those in the *rancheria*. As I approached Rip's side of the *rancheria*, a young woman left a *wickiup*. Seeing me, her eyes grew wide and her mouth formed a big circle but no sound came from her. She turned, hiked up her long skirt, showing some good-looking thigh, and sprinted for the creek behind the *wickiups*. I knew one of Rip's wives was running to warn him I was in the village with a long gun. She ran a hundred yards down a long dirt row filled on each side with bright green growing vegetables and, at the edge of the rows, a new acequia not yet finished, leading to the creek. I walked fast to stay two hundred yards behind her.

As she neared the creek, she found her voice between gasps for air began screaming, "Rip! Rip! Ohyessonna comes! He comes!"

Rip, up to his knees in the creek water while digging the creek entrance to the new acequia, stood up with a frown on his face that said, "You stupid woman!" He looked to both sides of the creek and behind him in quick turns and, guessing I had men with me on the other side of the creek and knowing that I could easily outrun him, didn't try to run. I knew he saw me striding after her with a carbine in my hands. He stood his ground and bent over to wash his hands in the brown, dirt-filled water swirling around him as I came nearer.

Rip shook the water off his hands and stood up straight with his arms raised at his elbows and his palms up flat toward me as little streams ran down his arms and dripped off his elbows in a steady beat that, like a White Eye clock, ticked away his life drop by drop. The canyon became very still. The cacophony of birds was no more. I stopped within a hundred yards of him and yelled, "Ho, Rip! You know why I come. You were the voice behind the murder of my father. You must die even if it means the end of me."

He yelled back, "Shoot, fool, if you think you can kill me from there. I'll be gone if you miss."

He looked behind him, I know thinking that he might yet run and survive. But I was too quick for him. The carbine came to my shoulder, the middle of his chest filled my sights, and I fired just as he turned again to face me. The big lead bullet hit him in the heart, flew out his back in a spray of blood and flesh, and glanced whining off a tree trunk behind him. Rip pitched backward, as though kicked by a mule, to sprawl dead in the creek bank dirt. His woman ran to his body screaming, "Rip! No! Rip! Rip! Murderers! Rip!" but Rip was already on the ghost pony headed for the Happy Land. At last it's over. The weight is gone from my shoulders. I've done my duty to my family.

I walked back to my horse, striding purposefully upright with my rifle in the crook of my arm, daring anyone to oppose me. My men and I rode back down the bosque trail to the San Carlos trail.

WE FOLLOWED THE trail across ridges and through canyons until the sun was falling behind clouds painted in deep colors of red, black, purple, and orange fast bringing the night. I thought about riding on to San Carlos in the dark but decided to camp near a tank that rain had filled. As-ki-say-la-ha made a small fire among the boulders that would be hard to see beyond the tank. Margey killed a deer on the trail not far from where we camped. We cooked the venison skewered on sticks angled over the fire and ate it with a little hardtack from our rations. After we finished eating, we sat among the boulders and smoked cigarettes.

Margey took a draw and blew it in a long stream toward the stars halfway up from the horizon. He said, "Ho, brother, we left to kill Rip without scout chief saying we can go. Will we serve time in that stinking guardhouse because he didn't say we can go? What do you think?"

I shrugged and took a puff on my cigarette. "The White Eyes don't care if we kill each other. But being absent without permission is big medicine, a question of a chief's power. You men shouldn't get guardhouse time because I asked you to come with me and I was in charge. How much time I'll get depends on what mood Sieber is in when he hears the news we've left. Tomorrow we'll have been gone five days. Not a long time, but if Sieber is mad about it, I could be kept in the guardhouse a moon or two and have no rank when I get out. Only Sieber knows."

A blanket of quiet settled over us as my brothers and friends thought over what I told them.

As-ki-say-la-ha said, "It may be costly in terms of days in the guardhouse, but we've settled the debt we owed Rip, and our family will be satisfied even if the White Eyes don't care about us."

I finished my cigarette and ground out the coal with my bootheel. "Yes, the business with Rip is done. Now we pay the singers for this dance we do."

We wrapped in our blankets and slept in the cold air as the coals in the fire turned to black powder. The next morning, we ate more of the venison, washed dirt from faces and arms, and headed down the trail toward San Carlos. I wondered how much time we would have before Sieber and Pierce returned.

WE RODE STEADILY all day, stopping at the spring where we had camped before to eat some rations, and rest and water our horses. In the middle of the downward fall of the sun, we rounded the west-side trail around Mount Turnbull. We were near where two trails joined and led to the ford across the Río Gila when we saw a figure sitting his horse near the trail, watching us come, and waiting to see us. Even at a long distance, I could see with my soldier glasses that he was an Apache, and soon recognized him as Gonshayee.

We rode up to Gonshayee as the sun was coloring the horizon and long shafts of sunlight were shooting through the clouds. I stopped when we reached where Gonshayee waited. I said, "Ho, Gonshayee. You have something to tell us? Speak. We listen."

Gonshayee said. "Ho, First Sergeant Kid. I learn you leave without permission to kill Rip. I talk to Captain Pierce. I say I know you and that you want to come in. He say, 'Tell Kid to come when he wants. The sooner the better it is for him and his scouts.' I have spoken."

I made the hand wave for "all is good" and said, "Gonshayee is a good chief. We follow him to Captain Pierce."

Gonshayee, with a solemn face, turned his horse toward the Gila and San Carlos. We followed him across the Gila as the Indians in the agency and army areas stared at us and walked up to watch us pass by. There were warriors on their horses in the crowd who were armed, their rifles pointed high, their butts held against their thighs. Others walked behind us, but they were also armed. My guts were in turmoil, wondering what Sieber would do to my men and me.

Gonshayee led us to Sieber's tent, where a long table stood near the front flaps. As we approached the table, we saw Sieber, Captain Pierce, and the *Nakai-yi* interpreter Antonio Diaz, following behind them, striding toward us. We dismounted and stood in a line in front of Sieber's table as Pierce and Sieber walked up. Sieber's face was a mask, cold and hard, set in unmoving, unforgiving lines. His jaws clamped in anger, he said, "Hello, Kid." I looked in his eyes without looking away and said, "Hello, Sieber."

Pierce asked Sieber, "Where are the five scouts who have been absent?"

Sieber curled his fingers for us to come forward.

We all stepped forward and stayed in a straight line.

With Diaz beside him to interpret, Pierce said, "Kid, give me your rifle."

I opened the breech on my rifle and unloaded it as he and Sieber watched my every move. I laid the rifle on the table with the breech open.

"Kid, give me your bandolier and revolver."

I took off my holstered revolver, pulled my sheathed knife off it because it was mine, and folded the bullet-filled belt around it. Then I took off my bandolier and laid it on the table next to my rifle. I hated this separation from my weapons and even more the separation from my leaders. My guts felt like a hot stone was sinking through them. After I finished, I saluted and stepped back from the table.

Then Pierce went down the line with Diaz translating the same thing to each scout and took their weapons and cartridge belts and laid them on the table as he had mine.

When we were all disarmed, Pierce pointed toward the guardhouse and said, "Calaboose." Diaz explained in Apache to us all, although I understood perfectly well what Pierce wanted us to do.

As Pierce disarmed us, a crowd gathered behind us. The People were curious what the army would do to their best scout just for leaving without permission, and their angry, mumbled comments sounded like bees beginning to swarm. This was bad, very bad, but there was nothing I could do.

Captain Pierce had brought Diaz to translate his orders to us so there was no misunderstanding on our part. There was bad blood over money between a scout and Diaz. He grinned and gave the order while showing a sign with his forefinger making a circle on his palm. The sign meant "island" as he said in Apache, "They send you to Alcatraz or even Florida where Chiricahua go."

The angry murmur from the crowd grew louder. I turned toward the guardhouse, and the scouts followed. I hadn't taken more than three or four steps when I heard the distinctive clicks of the hammers on rifles in the crowd pulled back to full cock. Captain Pierce yelled, "My god, Sieber, they're going to fire!"

The last scout in our line tried to grab a rifle, but Sieber kicked it out of his hands. The scout ducked and ran toward the rest of us. We were already starting to run. Sieber dove into his tent just as a hail of bullets filled his tent with holes. After the first round of fire from the People, most of those who had fired from their horses and on foot ran after us.

I headed down the trail along the Río San Carlos with the rest of the scouts, and those on horses led by Gonshayee were behind me trying to follow. I was the fastest runner at San Carlos, and even those on horses were racing to keep up with me. As I raced out of the agency, I saw Lieutenant Elliott with two troops of cavalry saddled and ready to go on a scout. I guessed he would soon be after us.

I learned later that Sieber, diving in his tent, grabbed his rifle and charged up to the flaps of his tent firing at the shooters who were already beginning to scatter. Miguel, a Yaqui Indian who lived with the Aravaipa, jumped in a hole made for digging clay to use in the making of pots and took a shot at Sieber. His bullet, a .45-70, hit Sieber in the ankle and made him a cripple for the rest of his life. I clenched my teeth. I hated to hear that.

I ran until the night began to cover us and knew the cavalry, no doubt chasing us, had stopped for the night. I stopped to rest. Twelve of those who fancied themselves warriors and wanted the excitement of being wild and free followed us. As I ran, I thought about what to do.

It didn't take me long to decide that we had gone from punishment for five days absent without permission to something the army called "mutiny," where it appeared that we as scouts had fired weapons at our own soldiers and run away. Mutiny was a crime punishable by a firing squad death. The other scouts and I had no guns and couldn't fire at anyone, but we were Apache. I knew there were officers who would, because we were Apache, insist that mutiny be the charge. I decided the safest thing to do was go to the land of the *Nakai-yes*. We could join the band or bands of Atelnietze and Natculbaye, who had not surrendered with Geronimo and were raiding mostly south of the border. The idea left a bitter taste in my mouth. We were not outlaws or renegades. We needed clearheaded officers who knew how to make things right, and time for Sieber to calm down and talk sense to the army about what happened.

I told the men that I had decided to double back to Aravaipa Canyon and then consider going south to join a band across the border. They all agreed crossing the border was the best thing to do. When the moon was high, we headed south, circling around the cavalry camp—where men who didn't have horses, including me, stole one from the corral. We crossed the San Carlos llano and Gila and rode again on the trail west of Mount Turnbull. We rode hard all night, stopping only to rest the horses for a while. When we reached old Camp Grant, my brothers led the men to a trail into the Galiuro Mountains while I continued downriver to tell my father-in-law and wife what had happened and to see my child.

FORTY-FIVE

ESCAPE

THROUGH THE COLD darkness, I saw a faint glow behind the Galiuro Mountains as I rode up the wagon road to my house behind my father-in-law's house. Dawn was coming, but the birds were not yet singing. I kept my horse in the grass beside the caliche road to avoid the noise of rocks clicking together and dismounted to tie him to a fence post fifty yards from the houses. I moved in silence up to the blanket-covered doorway of the adobe where my family slept. As I stood in the shadows about to pull the blanket back and go in, I felt the cold round end of a revolver barrel pressed against my neck at the bottom of my left ear and heard double clicks of a hammer being cocked. Hashke Bahnzin said in his rumbling whisper, "Keep your hands where I can see them. Move away from the house door and stand in the light over by the wall of the next house. I want to see your face."

Keeping my back to him, we moved to a wall near a corner of his house. He said, "Keep your hands up and turn slow to face me." I turned and, in the dim light, saw a big smile filling his face as he let the hammer down on his ancient Walker Colt. "Why didn't you say you were my son-in-law? We've been sleepless with worry since you killed Rip. What happened to you after you killed him?"

I shook my head. "Something bad has happened to us since I killed Rip. Captain Pierce sent word by Gonshayee to come in before things got worse. We rode in late in the last sun. Pierce disarmed us and pointed toward the calaboose. There was a big crowd of the People watching what the army would do to its best scouts. The fool interpreter, Diaz, gave the land-surrounded-by-water sign and said that's where we go for leaving without permission. Some in the crowd started shooting. The scouts and I ran. Twelve or thirteen with guns out in the crowd ran with us. I think they wanted the crowd to see them as mighty warriors. I ran up the Río San Carlos and then doubled back here. Lieutenant Elliott, with two troops of cavalry, is hot on our trail. I wanted to tell you and Chita what happened before I disappeared until Pierce and Sieber get things straightened out."

Hashke Bahnzin raised his brows and slowly shook his head. "Things won't get straightened out in your favor, my son. A rider was by here headed for Tucson as the last sun was falling into the west. He stopped for water and said Sieber had been shot in the lower part of his left leg, maybe even in the ankle, and he was blaming you and the other scouts who left without permission, and not some trigger-happy fool for getting him shot."

I clenched my teeth and blew to keep from throwing up. If Sieber refused to help me, it was the end of my life as I knew it. If my brothers and I wanted to live, then we must disappear into the land of *Nakai-yes* and join an Apache band hiding there. Unless Sieber spoke up for us, the army would want to try us for mutiny and desertion, not just being absent without permission. I knew the penalty for such crimes was death by firing squad.

"I must talk with Chita before I leave and tell her to be strong and that in my heart she will always be my woman. Will you look after her while I'm gone?"

"This I have done and will do. You must leave soon. There are many riders on this road who will know to report you here. Return to us when you can."

"I do this, Father."

"*Enjuh.*"

I turned toward my adobe as Hashke Bahnzin disappeared into the night shadows. Chita was standing there in front of the blanket-covered door, her arms crossed and a frown of puzzled concern on her face, her nightshirt falling off a shoulder. I took her in my arms, and she laid her head against my chest as I felt her warmth and smelled her long shiny hair falling over her shoulders. Her nearness and warm night smell stirred me as she whispered, "I've missed my man. Your daughter misses her father. The rider who came just before dark last sun said the army and scouts hunt you. He said they want to kill you or put you in a calaboose for a long time. Will you and the others go to the land of the *Nakai-yes* to avoid this evil thing come upon us?"

"I think on it."

She led me inside to sit by the warm iron stove while I told her about everything that had happened in killing Rip and what had happened at San Carlos when we returned. Her eyes never left my face, and she nodded often at things she had already learned as we sipped cups of coffee she had just made. I told her I had thought about, but not yet decided on, joining a Chiricahua camp in the land of *Nakai-yes*. I was reluctant to go there. By doing so, we were admitting we were outlaws and renegades, not just scouts who had left without permission. Living in the land of the *Nakai-yes* was very hard, especially for the women and children. There had to be a better way. Perhaps letting anger cool about wounding Sieber and then taking the punishment given to us was what we should do.

We grew quiet as I thought on this until Chita stood, took my hand, and said, "The children always sleep late if I let them. I want you under the blankets with me. It could be our last time for a long time together, and my body cries for wanting you. Come." I didn't hesitate to join her under her heavy *Nakai-yi* wool blanket as we heard the birds start to call the morning light.

Two hands later, I kissed my woman goodbye, brushed the tears from her eyes, and rode off for the gray Galiuro Mountains to join my men.

THE SUN WAS near to the time of no shadows. I reached Oak Grove Canyon entrance on Turkey Creek on the northeastern edge of the Galiuro Mountains where the men, my scouts, and I planned to meet. The men hid back in shadows of the high canyon walls in the trees that lined a washout of the canyon. Gonshayee rode out of the edge of the shadows across the canyon. A good breeze rippled through the grass in the bosque along the wash. We heard the "Jeet! Jeet!" from a canyon wren angry that we had invaded his territory. *Don't worry, little brother. I know how you feel. We won't stay long.*

Gonshayee's face, its lines unmoving, had a solemn, distant look like that of a man who knew he had made a mistake but didn't know how to fix it. He said, "Ho, Ohyessonna, our eyes are glad to see you. A lookout returned two hands ago. He said a troop of cavalry from San Carlos met a troop from the direction of Fort Thomas. Both troops had scouts with them to help find us. They move up the Aravaipa Canyon slowly looking for our sign. I think soon we must move. We need supplies. We can raid a little."

"Keep a lookout to watch the trail into Turkey Creek from the big canyon. If he has soldier glasses, tell him to use them. He sees any scouts or soldiers, we ride south. Any man who has a bow with him, send him out to bring us meat. If we're lucky, we rest tonight, ride next sun. You and me we smoke. Then we decide what we do."

Gonshayee nodded and swung his forearm parallel to the ground to show all was well. "We do as you say." He turned his horse back into the trees and loped over to where the men rested. I could hear the mumble from their talk. Soon two men mounted their horses and rode toward the canyon entrance. One had a bow and arrows in a cougar case slung over his back. The other had a case used to carry soldier glasses. I hoped the hunter had luck finding us a deer. I was hungry.

I rode up into the trees where the men had waited and found a small tank filled with water from leaks down the wash that kept it filled. I gave my horse a drink before I cupped my hands and drank handfuls of the cool good water.

Gonshayee came and drank before pulling out his *tobaho* and papers to roll us a cigarette. He lit it with a flaming twig from a small fire, blew puffs each representing one of the four directions into the light breeze creeping across the treetops down the canyon, and then handed it to me. I, too, smoked to the four directions and handed the cigarette back to him. He took another puff and then tossed the remains into the little fire while spitting a piece of *tobaho* off his lower lip.

Gonshayee said, "I am chief of our band. The People want it so. But you know our enemy, the White Eye Blue Coats, better than any warrior at San Carlos. You take the lead and I will follow. We need food, bullets, and horses. Most of the men don't have a horse. What we do, Ohyessonna?"

I stared off toward the opening of our canyon and thought about what to do. Gonshayee was nervously eyeing every move I made, every breath, every blink. I wondered what made him so nervous. Does he know more than what he was telling me?

I said, "We need to break into two groups, which ought to help create a little delay to get out of here until the scouts figure out what we've done. You take eight men and I'll take seven." I took a yucca stalk and sketched a map in the sand.

"I'll go down the eastern side of Galiuro Mountains, then swing southwest across the northwestern edge of the Sulphur Springs Valley—big ranchos there with lots of cattle—to Crittenden, rest in the Patagonia Mountains, and then head back here with what our raids give us. You start out crossing the Río San Pedro at Mammoth—there ought to be several places including White Eye trading posts where you can get supplies and, if you're lucky, a horse or two. Then you go down the eastern side of the Santa Catalina Mountains but west of the Río San Pedro. At the end of the Santa Catalinas, swing west on the southern side of the Rincon Mountains. Then go through the valley between the end of the Rincon Mountains and the end of the Santa Rita Mountains. You'll be close to Tucson, but the mountains will give you cover. There ought to be White Eye traders on the wagon roads to Tucson that have horses you can take. Rest in the mountains when your men need it. Go back toward the Galiuro Mountains and up their west side on the Río San Pedro. Come back here and we'll meet in about ten days. What you think?"

Gonshayee wiggled his nose like a rabbit smelling something good and, smiling, said, "Good plan. I like it. When do we leave?"

"If the soldiers have the officers that I think they do, they'll search Aravaipa Canyon for signs of us first. Before dark, scouts will ride Turkey Creek and find this canyon. We need to leave soon. They won't travel at night, but I think we should. We'll get ahead of them and stay ahead that way."

Gonshayee nodded. "Then we go now."

We called the men together, divided them as we planned, and told them what we planned to do. More than half the men were on foot. They could physically handle running, but riding a fast horse was more to their liking.

We were ready to leave when one of the lookouts appeared and told us scouts had left the canyon and headed up Turkey Creek. I was surprised they were that close. It was time to leave. Gonshayee led his men down to the Río San Pedro and I headed for the eastern side of the Galiuro Mountains.

OUR TWO RAIDING parties were, as Sieber would say, "on fool's errands." The scouts and Blue Coats stayed hot on our trails all the time. We were constantly running from them. There was no time to take supplies from the ranchos we crossed, which meant we had to live off the land, and without women to help us, it was very hard.

During our raids, two White Eyes died. The Yaqui named Miguel shot them. If I had thought more, I would have killed Miguel for making us all look bad. Some of the men told me that Miguel had shot Sieber too. He got to shoot, but we got all the blame.

Each raiding party was one step away from the Blue Coats catching us. Gonshayee made camp in the Rincon Mountains, intending to let his men rest a day or two and take something to eat from White Eyes on trails headed for

Tucson. But in less than a day, soldiers came charging through the camp making the warriors drop everything they had, except rifles and pistols, to escape. When Gonshayee left our meeting place, four of his men didn't have horses. When they found our new camping place, all were on foot and expecting the Blue Coats to attack them at any time.

It was clear that we would never get away unless we went to the land of the *Nakai-yes*, and even across the border, it would be very dangerous unless we could find the hidden camps of Atelnietze or Natculbaye or some powerful warrior we didn't know. I didn't want to be an outlaw or renegade.

FORTY-SIX

THE LONG RUN

IT WAS HARD for me to understand why the army and Sieber were so angry with me and the others for leaving without permission when we had not mutinied. We were only gone five days, and the army and Sieber didn't care if I settled a private debt by killing Rip over my father's murder, and they weren't concerned about "warlike" Apache. They left one, me, in charge of all scouts and the guardhouse while they looked over other scout camps. I was certain that if I talked to Sieber and explained what had happened, he'd cool down and we could get back his company of scouts running, as it should, on the army road.

My men and I returned from Crittenden and camped in a hidden canyon on a low, flattop mountain closer to Aravaipa Creek than where we camped before in Oak Grove Canyon. I sent a man out to find Gonshayee and his men and to tell them where we were. This mountain had a long winding canyon inside the canyon's western side that led toward its top and a big tank of spring-fed water where we camped. There was plenty of firewood and grass for our horses, and plenty of venison roamed the mountain. It was a better place to hide and camp than Oak Grove.

I needed to talk with Sieber but knew the cavalry blocked our way or would kill us before we could reach San Carlos. I called José, who had a fine, fast horse, to come join me by the fire as its flame-painted shadows began to grow on the canyon walls around us.

I motioned for José to sit beside me and said, "José, I need a fast message carrier. With that fine horse of yours, will you do this?"

His eyes were wide as he answered, "I do this, First Sergeant. What is message, and where does it go?"

I nodded. "You're a good man, José. Someday you'll be a scout sergeant. I send this message to Captain Pierce, the agent at San Carlos. Wait until he gives you an answer before you return. If you don't return in four suns, I'll know you ride the ghost pony from Blue Coat bullets or they have locked you in shackles. You still ride knowing these risks?"

He nodded. "I go. What is message?"

"Say to Captain Pierce only, 'The scouts, the other men who ran with us, and I, First Sergeant Kid, are tired of running. Cavalry troops and scouts stay hard on our trail. Tell the troopers to stand at ease and let us pass to San Carlos. We'll come to you. I give my word that this will happen. I give my messenger two suns to wait for your answer. I know you must ask your big chief and send word to your officers hunting us.'

"That is my message. If you leave tonight and ride hard, you can be at the agency in the morning."

"Hmmph. I go now, First Sergeant."

I gave him my salute of respect. He grinned and saluted back, took his saddle to his pony, and rode down the canyon.

A SUN, NEAR nightfall, after José left, Gonshayee led a line of seven weary men into camp. While the men satisfied their thirst and began roasting venison on sticks tilted over the fire, he told us how they had lost everything, including their horses, at a camp in the Rincon Mountains. It took over half a sun for them to all gather at their backup place. Most wanted to head south for the land of the *Nakai-yes*, but Gonshayee talked them into returning to our camp. I was sorry that my band also had little to show for our efforts. I told Gonshayee and his men that I had sent José to tell Captain Pierce that if the troopers left us alone, then we would surrender. Gonshayee made a face and shook his head but said he was ready to return. He knew that, with the scouts and me blamed for the shooting, he and his men would go free. I also knew that because there was shooting and Sieber as chief of scouts was wounded, even if my scouts and I were not part of it, we'd be punished and spend time in the calaboose. My scouts and I were tough. We could survive a handful of months in the calaboose. The Blue Coats would take my rank, but I'd earn it back again. I just needed Sieber to understand what had happened, and I knew he would.

Late in the sun of José's third day, our lookout flashed with his mirror, "Rider comes." I was on my feet and ran up to the outlook's place. He pointed down the canyon, and in the falling light, I made out a little dust plume from a single rider. I strained to see him with my soldier glasses, puffed my cheeks, and blew. The rider was José.

I walked back to our little fire and waited, feeling the chill of the night air facing away from the fire and hearing its snapping and popping and the little animals scrambling in the brush around the spring. I owed José much for taking the risk to carry a message to Captain Pierce. I was anxious to hear what he had to say.

José's horse, lathered up from a hard run, snorted at the few horses we had hobbled under the trees as José dismounted. He led him to drink at the spring, looked around, and grinned at all of us. He hobbled him and uncinched his saddle and pulled it and the bridle before letting him graze on the green grass that grew tall from the tank's water overspill. José took a couple of handfuls of grass and wiped his horse down. I thought as I watched him, That man will be a first sergeant someday.

When he finished caring for his horse, he walked out of the shadows with seventeen pairs of eyes on him. He came to me, saluted, and said, "First Sergeant Kid, Captain Pierce says, 'Tell Kid and others to come. Come in two suns. No soldiers stop you.' He say he talk to big chief Miles on talking wire. Miles say, 'Are you man who keeps word?' Captain Pierce say, 'Yes.' Miles say, 'Tell First Sergeant Kid and his scouts to come in. No soldiers stop 'em.'" As if with one voice, the men said, *"Enjuh!"* and raised their hands to the stars.

THE NEXT DAY, I sent Gonshayee and his eight men to Captain Pierce with a message that I return two days later with my men. Those in my group lent Gonshayee's group their horses to ride. I lent Gonshayee my horse. I planned to run from Aravaipa Canyon to Captain Pierce's workplace at San Carlos.

That evening, my men and I went to my mother's *wickiup*. She was fearful the soldiers had already killed me and was happy to see us all. She fed us, and then the men and scouts with me rolled in their blankets to sleep in the bosque along the creek while my brothers and I spoke with our mothers. We told them that it was possible we would be held in the calaboose for months but comforted them with the idea that it wouldn't be longer than a harvest—after all, we hadn't done any shooting and we had only been gone without permission five days. I said to them, "The Blue Coats will be reasonable in their punishment of us for breaking their rules."

I wanted to see Chita and my daughter before I left. My mother let me use her horse to ride to visit in our adobe at Hashke Bahnzin's rancho. After all the riding on the run from the cavalry, it seemed a short ride to visit my family. As I approached the adobe, a lantern still lighted the window of our house. I hobbled my mother's horse and pulled its saddle where it could graze behind our adobe house while I visited Chita and the children. I stood by the door blanket and cleared my throat to announce I stood there.

Chita said, "Come to me, husband. The children are with my father this night."

I lifted the blanket and stepped inside to see her sitting with a lantern just behind her shoulder giving her hair a golden glow while she sewed on a shift for our daughter.

"How did you know it was me?"

She laughed. "How could I *not* know it was you, husband? Stories travel fast in this country."

I laughed and gathered her in my arms. I told her I was running to San Carlos the next sun and might be kept there in the calaboose for moons but I'd be back. She bowed her head and said, "Just stay alive and come back to us, husband." She looked up with a big smile. "Now come to my blankets while I don't have to sit and worry waiting for you."

That night, *Ussen* blessed us with great pleasures that I would remember often in the moons to come and carried me through hard times. I left my wife wrapped in our blanket against the cold air to watch me go in the glow driving away the stars in the eastern sky. I saluted her with the White Eye sign of respect before turning to ride away, fearful that if I looked back at her, I would never return to the Blue Coats at San Carlos.

MY MOTHER HAD an early morning meal of mesquite fry bread, steak, steamed hearts of baked and dried mescal, and coffee waiting for my men and me. She sat by the fire to watch my brothers, scouts, and men with us eat. There was little said, but the looks she gave me said everything that needed to be said.

When we finished eating, the men caught and saddled their horses. My mother gave me a pair of new moccasins to wear on my run to San Carlos. They fit perfectly and, after wearing my heavy cavalry boots, felt like I had nothing at all on my feet. She said, "I remember well the race you won as a man-child and your father gave you that rifle. May your race today be as rewarding."

I said, "My mother warms my heart. I return as soon as the Blue Coats free us."

She smiled and nodded as she wrapped her blanket about her as long bright shafts of sunlight burst down the canyon.

My men waited for me to lead them up the trail. I made the sign that all was well to my mother and brothers and sisters who, from the door of our mother's *wickiup*, watched us go. I ran up the creek wagon trail, the men on their horses strung out behind me in a gentle jog. The birds began a loud chorus welcoming the sun and saluting us as I ran by. I remembered that, twelve harvests ago, I had run the other way down the trail racing a bigger boy who thought he was faster than me because he was taller, but I won that race even when he tried to beat me with low tricks like trying to knock me down a canyon wall while he ran on.

I stopped to drink at the end of the wagon trail and told the men when they watered their horses that I would beat them going across the canyons and ridges and if I got too far ahead, I would wait for them on the trail to the west of Turnbull Mountain. They smiled and nodded, some not believing I could get that far ahead of them.

Running across the rough country was exhilarating. Out on the flats of the mesas, I felt like a deer running in the warming morning air, running past junipers and yuccas, running free and easy, and knowing nothing would stop me. As I ran, I thought about what I would do when I got out of the calaboose and decided I would not scout for the army but spend time working on my farm with Hashke Bahnzin. It might not be an exciting life, but at least I would stay out of the trouble I was running toward.

A wind came up from the west and helped push me along. I reached Turnbull Mountain two hands before those who followed me. Water at a nearby tank filled by a spring was good and refreshing. I sat on a boulder in the shade of a juniper on a hill where I had a clear line of sight to the Río Gila. While I waited, I used my soldier glasses to study the San Carlos buildings. I noticed there were six troopers with their horses at Captain Pierce's place. They sat around as if waiting for something or someone.

It was two hands after the time of shortest shadows before I saw the scouts with the other men come down the trail and head for the spring I had used. They watered their horses and themselves and were resting in the shade of junipers when I approached them.

I said, "Ho, brothers. You don't ride as fast as I run." There were smiles and nods. "I have studied San Carlos across the Río Gila and seen troopers I think are waiting for us. When they come to take us to the guardhouse, don't resist them. I don't doubt that they'll let our friends who rode with us go. I know my four scouts and I will be held until the soldier chiefs decide what punishment we will have for leaving without permission or even mutiny since we ran to safety when shooting started. If they decide it was mutiny, even though it was not, we may spend several moons in the guardhouse, but when we get out, we'll be forever free."

They all said, *"Ch'ik'eh doleel."*

I said, *"Enjuh.* Mount your ponies and follow me across the Río Gila. Let us put this dark wind that blows no good behind us."

The trail down to the Río Gila was used often and filled with dust. It was easy to see our trailing cloud as we came to the ford across the río. I saw the Blue Coats mounting their horses, but they stayed in a two-by-two formation. A crowd gathered on both sides of us all the way to the agency door except where the Blue Coats sat their horses.

I stopped in front of the agency and waited while my breathing returned to normal and the men on their horses stopped in a line behind me. Captain Pierce came out the door and closed it behind him. He was dressed in his full uniform and wearing a white hat. His facial expression showed no emotion. We stared at each other, neither of us looking away, before he said, "As I expected, you kept your word, First Sergeant Kid. General Miles has already appointed officers for your court-martial. Lieutenant Baldwin will speak for you. He'll meet with you about your defense sometime in the next two days."

Pierce motioned toward the troopers waiting on their horses. "These soldiers are here to escort you and the scouts who rode with you to the calaboose where I directed you to go three weeks ago, but you ran. The other men with you live on the reservation. No evidence exists against any of them for the raids we have endured for the last three weeks. They are free to go, but if the tribal police have to come get them for any bad behavior, it will go especially hard on them.

"First Sergeant, do you or your men carry any weapons?"

I shook my head, as did the four scouts.

"Very well. Any questions?"

"I want to speak with Mister Sieber."

"No. He is expected to be a witness against you at the court-martial."

My guts felt like I had eaten bad meat, very bad meat. We were headed for the guardhouse for many moons if Sieber didn't convince the Blue Coats we meant no harm.

"Any more questions?"

We stood there in silence, barely breathing, as he motioned the soldiers over to escort us to the guardhouse. I saluted Captain Pierce and then walked with my four scouts to the guardhouse. We were walking into darkness and facing a hard wind in the days to come.

ADDITIONAL READING

Ball, Eve, Lynda A. Sánchez, and Nora Henn, *Indeh: An Apache Odyssey,* University of Oklahoma Press, Norman, OK, 1988.

Ball, Eve, *In the Days of Victorio, Recollections of a Warm Springs Apache,* The University of Arizona Press, Tucson, AZ, 1970

Barrett, S. M., *Geronimo, His Own Story, The Autobiography of a Great Patriot Warrior,* Meridian, Penguin Books USA, New York, New York, 1996

Bourke, John G., *An Apache Campaign in the Sierra Madre,* University of Nebraska Press, Lincoln, NE, 1987. Reprinted from the 1886 edition published by Charles Scribner and Sons.

Bourke, John G., *On the Border with Crook,* Charles Scribner's Sons, New York, New York, 1891.

Capitan Chiquito: a personal history of an Apache Chief, 1821—1919, Texas A&M University Press, College Station, TX, 2022.

Carmony, Neil B, Editor, *Apache Days & Tombstone Nights, John Clum's Autobiography, 1877—1887,* High-Lonesome Books, Silver City, NM, 1997

Cozzens, Peter, *The Earth Is Weeping,* Alfred A. Knopf, New York, 2016.

de la Garza, Phyllis, *The Apache Kid,* Westernlore Press, Tucson, AZ, 1995.

Debo, Angie, *Geronimo, The Man, His Time, His Place,* University of Oklahoma Press, Norman, OK, 1976

Goodwin, Grenville, *The Social Organization of the Western Apache,* Original Edition Copyright 1942 by the Department of Anthropology, University of Chicago, Century Collection edition by the University of Arizona Press, Tucson, AZ, 2016

Haley, James L., *Apache: A History and Culture Portrait,* University of Oklahoma Press, Norman, OK, 1981.

Hutton, Paul Andrew, *The Apache Wars*, Crown Publishing Group, New York, New York, 2016.

Ingstad, Helge (Translated by Janine K. Stenehjem), *The Apache Indians, In Search of the Missing Tribe*, University of Nebraska Press, Lincoln, NE, 2004.

Kühn, Berndt *Chronicles of War, Apache and Yavapai Resistance in the Southwestern United States and Northern Mexico, 1821–1937*, The Arizona Historical Society, Tucson, AZ 2014.

Mails, Thomas E., *The People Called Apache*, BDD Illustrated Books, New York, NY, 1993.

McKanna, Clare V, *The Court-Martial of Apache Kid*, Texas Tech University Press, Lubbock, TX, 2009.

Opler, Morris Edward, *An Apache Life-Way, The Economic, Social, and Religious Institutions of the Chiricahua Indians*, University of Nebraska Press, Lincoln, NE, 1996.

Opler, Morris, *Apache Odyssey, A Journey Between Two Worlds*, University of Nebraska Press, Lincoln, NE, 2002.

Robinson, Sherry, *Apache Voices: Their Stories of Survival as Told to Eve Ball*, University of New Mexico Press, Albuquerque, NM, 2003.

Sweeney, Edwin, *From Cochise to Geronimo, The Chiricahua Apache, 1874–1886*, University of Oklahoma Press, Norman, OK, 2010.

Thrapp, Dan L., *Al Sieber: Chief of Scouts*, University of Oklahoma Press, Norman, OK, 1964.

Thrapp, Dan L., *The Conquest of Apacheria*, University of Oklahoma Press, Norman, OK, 1967.

Wilson, Britt W., Soldiers vs Apache: One Last Time at Guadalupe Canyon, *Wild West Magazine*, October 2001.

Worchester, Donald E., *The Apache: Eagles of the Southwest*, University of Oklahoma Press, Norman, OK, 1992.

"The Apache Kid, Red Renegade of the West," *Arizona Highways*, May 1939.

W. MICHAEL FARMER combines fifteen-plus years of research into nineteenth-century Apache history and culture with Southwest-living experience to fill his stories with a genuine sense of time and place. A retired PhD physicist, his scientific research has included measurement of atmospheric aerosols with laser-based instruments. He has published a two-volume reference book on atmospheric effects on remote sensing as well as fiction in anthologies and award-winning essays. His novels have won numerous awards, including three Will Rogers Gold and five Silver Medallions, New Mexico-Arizona Book Awards for Literary, Adventure, Historical Fiction, a Non-Fiction New Mexico Book of the Year, and a Spur Finalist Award for Best First Novel. His book series includes The Life and Times of Yellow Boy, Mescalero Apache, and Legends of the Desert. His nonfiction books include *Apacheria, True Stories of Apache Culture 1860-1920,* and *Geronimo, Prisoner of Lies. Among his most recent books are the award-winning novels The Odyssey of Geronimo: Twenty-Three years a Prisoner of War, The Iliad of Geronimo: A Song of Blood and Fire, Trini! Come! Geronimo's Captivity of Trinidad Verdin, Chato: Desperate Warrior, and it's sequel, Chato: Proud Outcast.*

www.ingramcontent.com/pod-product-compliance
Lightning Source LLC
Chambersburg PA
CBHW031336020726

47499CB00005B/1288